The Book of Ten

Paul Cotterell

The Book of Ten

Paul Cotterell

Paperback Edition First Published in Great Britain in 2015 by aSys Publishing

eBook Edition First Published in Great Britain in 2015 by aSys Publishing

Disclaimer

This is a work of fiction. Names, characters, businesses, places, events and incidents are either the products of the author's imagination or are historical events which are a matter of public record and/or used in a fictitious manner. Any resemblance otherwise to actual persons, living or dead is purely coincidental.

Cover artwork by Jill Cotterell

ISBN: 978-1-910757-26-0

aSys Publishing
http://www.asys-publishing.co.uk

Dedication

To my wife Jill.
For always being willing to read a story first,
For her honest feedback and encouragement,
and for being the love of my life.

With special thanks to Chris Sutton, whose excellent stories inspired me to write these.

Contents

Part One

Part Two

Part Three

Part Four

Part Five

Part One

A Devil to Escape

"Somebody shoot me, *please*" thought Steven, bored and tired.

He had sat through a day of marketing strategy presentations and it had taken its toll. Colleagues trying to impress their managers with their apparently clairvoyant abilities to make money. Some of it interested him but the shameless ingratiating of his colleagues did not. Although a break was due in 15 minutes, that seemed a lifetime away and he needed to visit the toilet now.

"At least they picked a decent hotel" he thought as he passed the tempting smell of coffee and pastries being wheeled across the foyer to the room for the impending break. He entered the impressive gentleman's toilets.

"Perhaps we'll finish early . . . rescue some of the day" he hoped during his welcome relief at the urinal. As he dried his hands on an Egyptian cotton towel, he was startled by a loud thud from one of the cubicles . . . like a heavy cardboard box had fallen over . . . followed by a flapping sound . . . reminded Steven of a shower curtain being drawn back and forth. "Unlikely" he thought . . .

Hesitantly he called "Hello . . . are you OK in there?"

No reply . . . then a shuffle . . . then silence . . .

He noticed that the door was slightly ajar. Concerned, he tentatively eased it open . . .

"Jesus!" blurted Steven as he jumped back.

He'd not known what to expect but it certainly wasn't the small, glossy burgundy demon crouched in front of him, silent and motionless . . . like a winged gargoyle from the ramparts of Notre-Dame Cathedral. Steven was shocked and breathing deeply. Oddly he didn't feel threatened . . . the creature seemed troubled, and tired.

The demon raised its head slowly and looked directly at Steven with large brown dog-eyes. He was transfixed by its stare.

"Oooff" Steven exhaled quickly, as if being winded by a painless punch, and stepped backwards . . . The demon had downloaded and now Steven knew all he needed to know. This creature needed no language to communicate . . . eye contact was all that was needed to instantly transfer information to whoever looked into them.

"What the hell *is* this?!" said Steven out loud.

"No need to panic sir" The Demon hadn't spoken but Steven understood . . . and it occurred to Steven that finding a demon in the toilet was probably a good reason to panic.

"I shouldn't be here" said the Demon. "Unfortunately I have become trapped by the metal plating on this cubicle . . . it confines me and I require your assistance sir . . . you have my word that I will help you considerably in return."

"Mmm . . . the word of a *demon*!" thought Steven hesitating to assist, its future engagements likely to be, in all probability, demonic.

But the creature was obviously out of place, and there was something likeable about the beast . . . perhaps it was the dog-like appearance . . . In shock, he decided he *would* help.

"Thank you sir. Now if you would hold out your hand, I will need to touch it and I can get out of here"

Steven extended his right hand down towards his unlikely companion. The demon smiled broadly, placed a small wing-claw into his palm and then shuffled slowly out of the cubicle. He sat next to Steven, like a small, slightly untrustworthy winged dog, and looked up into his eyes, communicating a favour to him in return.

"I am granting you a wish sir . . . and before you ask, it's not three, just the one"

"Jesus, a demon with a sense of humour!" thought Steven, "Are you serious?" he said.

"Oh yes" confirmed the demon "but hurry up"

Under pressure, Steven dithered "OK, ahh . . . how about everyone in this hotel leads a full and happy life". He wasn't quite sure where that had come from.

"Seriously?!" communicated the demon.

"Ahh, yes I think so" Steven replied hesitantly, not thinking straight.

"Is that the best you can do?!" communicated the demon . . . "In my opinion that is a little weak sir . . . *happiness, world peace* . . . these wishes I have a dilemma with! What about something for *you*?"

"For *me*?" said Steven.

"Yes for *you* sir, *you* . . . money, beautiful cars, women . . . think along these lines, it's easier for me" said the demon smiling "but please hurry up!"

"Oh my God!" said Steven.

"Please don't bring him into it sir! Now I really must press you!"

Steven's mind was reeling . . . he couldn't take it in . . . a demon granting him a wish, in a hotel toilet, for absolutely anything he wanted . . .

"Good grief . . . " said Steven under his breath, his hands up to his mouth . . . "stop the world, I want to get off . . . " he said, lost in thought.

"OK sir" said the demon.

The Strange Tail of the Salamander and the Spiral Pothole

Roy loved the outdoors . . . and he *loved* a risk, solo potholing his primary passion. He loved the isolation and the danger.

"I don't know what you see in it" was something Roy heard quite often.

But for him it was the same other-worldly escape as he imagined a pilot or a scuba diver might enjoy. He just liked being underground. Towards the end of a climb, when he'd spot the first shafts of daylight, he couldn't help feeling a tinge of disappointment.

He had enjoyed a particularly challenging underground scramble. And there, in the distance, was the daylight, just a rocky tube away . . .

"Oh!" he said startled, not normally prone to such outbursts.

In front of him was a small white salamander about three inches long. Not *that* unusual, but it was the tail that caught his eye . . .

"Well I'll be . . . " he said in wonder. Its tail was about half the salamander's length and reminded Roy of a tennis racquet, but with a pattern of small hexagonal holes in it, rather than square.

"What a fabulous thing!" Roy thought, fascinated . . . "never seen anything like it . . . ". Its skin was a lustrous iridescent pearl . . . "maybe even a new species?!" it occurred to him.

He carefully cupped his hand and, to his surprise, the salamander calmly walked onto it. With his other hand he quickly removed a small box of sandwiches from his bag, put the sandwiches in his jacket pocket and, very gently, placed the still-calm salamander in the Tupperware box.

He was on his way out for a spot of lunch and as he entered the glare of a beautiful sunny day, he looked for a place to rest and ponder this creature.

In the pretty, thinly-wooded glade, their only company was the birds singing, insects flying and the distant drone of the nearby A30. Sitting on a flattish rock, he opened the top of the Tupperware box slightly to give the salamander some air and got out his sandwich. The Sandwich Spread had inevitably squidged in his pocket—probably an unwise choice but it had always been his favourite. As he ate, he removed the Tupperware lid and checked on the small creature, still quite calm.

"You *are* a little beauty" Roy said quietly.

As he took the next bite of his sandwich, the creature quickly wriggled out of the box and dropped onto the ground. In a brisk crocodile-style gait, the salamander headed straight back towards the entrance of the hole.

"What the heck? . . . " Still chewing, Roy quickly grabbed his bag and followed the pearly creature. As it re-entered the tube and started to descend, Roy dropped his sandwich and scrambled after it, using all his experience to keep up. Soon he needed his head-mounted light but the creature was easy to follow, glowing a faint electric blue. After a short distance, the salamander walked up the side of the tube onto the ceiling and into an overgrown mossy flap, almost indistinguishable from the rock.

"Odd . . . didn't notice that earlier" Roy thought.

Pulling back the soft flap, he found he was able to poke his head through and saw the blue glow ahead. Roy stood, and using all his skill and strength, he ascended a near-vertical tube . . .

"Damned thing makes it look easy!" he thought as he struggled upwards.

As they progressed, the tube twisted right and developed into a large spiral shape, quite smooth on the surface.

"Unbelievable" he said to himself, pausing to catch his breath.

Water laid in the lower loops of the spiral . . . thankfully not much . . . it had been an exceptionally dry summer.

"Probably floods easily . . . ." he thought as he followed the bluey glow. The pools of water allowed Roy to count the loops . . . after negotiating seven, he was panting for breath but exhilarated to have found this new branch . . .

The diameter of the tube then gradually increased and a much brighter blue glow appeared ahead, eventually rendering the head-light unnecessary. Roy then followed his companion into an incredible space . . .

The spiral continued but opened out into the size of a generous living room, the whole area illuminated a deep electric blue. And covering almost all of the surface were hundreds more of the white salamanders! Some moving but most were motionless, glowing blue . . . their racquet-tails laying on spiked crystals that protruded from the surface, the hexagonal holes fitting around the crystals perfectly.

"Well I'll be . . . " Roy laughed, spell-bound by the whole sight.

It was as if the creatures were "plugged in" . . . recharging in some way . . . His senses already overloaded, he then observed a salamander slowly disconnecting from the crystals and floating off into mid-air inside the spiral!

"No way" he whispered in wonder.

He noticed the salamanders would walk *to* the crystals but float away on disconnection! The sight was wonderful . . . a blue-bathed crystal spiral decorated with gently floating pearlescent amphibians . . .

Roy couldn't see how he could progress any further without causing a lot of disruption and damage . . . so he decided to take some pictures on his phone.

"The guys at the club are not going to believe this!" . . . he didn't need a flash . . . the ambient blue providing ample illumination. He took three pictures, not satisfied with any of them. "Never capture it in a photo . . . " he thought.

"And let's get one of you" he said taking a shot of the salamander on the crystals in front of him. Just then another salamander floated directly in front of his face . . .

"Oh! Hello again" he jumped, presuming his original friend had now recharged. The creature appeared to be leading him in the direction of the entrance.

"Time to leave? . . . perhaps you're right!" Roy smiled.

He turned round and followed, still in awe of what he had seen.

"Need to remember this route . . . "

Back through the seven watery loops of the spiral they went . . . this time at a faster pace, following the bright blue floating light. Somehow it always seemed quicker on the way back . . . Roy lowered himself awkwardly through the lichen flap head-first and then scrambled up the sloping tube towards the daylight. He was having trouble keeping the floating salamander in sight. Back out in the glare of the glade, he temporarily lost track of his friend . . . panicking, and willing his eyes to adjust quicker to the sunlight.

He quickly scanned the whole area, and then spotted the blue glow just at the head of the path that led out of the glade.

"Hold on!" he shouted instinctively, and ran towards it, his panting accompanied only by the birds and the insects . . . Catching up, he followed at a jogging pace along the dirt path through the wood. An older lady on her way into the wood smiled amiably as he passed. Roy was oblivious . . . Soon, the wood emptied onto a deep grass verge, the A30 on the other side . . . Breathing deep, he looked up at the transfixing blue glow of the salamander hovering above him . . . a beautiful deep blue against the pale blue cloudless sky . . . .

Sadly, Roy failed to see the protruding edge of the caravan that hit him as he wandered too close to the road. Mercifully, he was killed instantly, with no pain . . . in a state of other-wordly fascination. His phone escaped unscathed and lay on the grass . . .

Back in the spiral cavern, Roy's lunch-time friend was still recharging . . . still connected to the crystals. He'd been led out by another of the creatures, concerned by Roy's intrusion into their home.

There was really only one positive that could be drawn from the whole affair . . .

. . . ultimately, Roy *did* like it underground.

Puss in Boots

"How hard can it be?!" thought Sandra, so far unsuccessful in her search for pink tights. She had looked everywhere in town and, as a last resort, she tried the local chemist. She'd already made a cardboard beak . . . and she'd found a pink top and tutu. Pink tights were all she needed to complete her flamingo costume for the "Alice in Wonderland" themed garden party she had been invited to on Saturday afternoon. It was Friday already, time was running out and she needed legs—a defining element of the flamingo. She even planned to pad out the knees for that essential knobbly look . . .

"Ah ha!" she smiled, delighted to see some pink hosiery on the rack by the entrance. Rummaging through the rack for her petite size, she felt something brush against her bare calf, and was surprised to see it was a black cat. "That's good luck" she thought . . . "or is it bad luck, I don't know!?"

The cat weaved itself through her legs, purring loudly.

"Hello boy!" she said, presuming it was male, bending down to tickle him under the chin.

She needed shampoo from the next aisle and headed off towards it, leaving the cat. As she reached for the top shelf, she felt the same warm furry feeling around her legs.

"Hello again!" . . . Her new-found friend stayed with her and followed her closely to the check out.

"Do you know there is a cat in here?" she smiled to the young girl serving, badged as "Barbara".

"Oh not again!" she replied annoyed "it comes in, claws open packets and leaves a *right* mess!" Barbara called to her manager to deal with the stray . . . which was unnecessary as it turned out, as the cat carried on following Sandra out of the shop and out onto the pedestrian precinct.

Surprised, Sandra stopped and knelt down, tickling him under the chin again.

"What are you up to? Haven't you got somewhere to go?"

The cat just looked up, calm and contented, and she assumed he hadn't. She noticed some fine white powder dusted over his face-fur and carefully brushed some of it away.

Back at the chemist, Barbara had been asked to clear up the packaging of a high dose herbal remedy that the cat had torn open. Strangely, it was the same product that the cat had torn open on previous visits, despite there being a wide selection of herbal remedies to tear open. His product of choice was St. John's Wort, which, according to the packet, "lightened the mood and helped ease a troubled mind" . . .

The cat's eyes were half closed, purring loudly, still enjoying Sandra's attention. Engrossed, Sandra felt a sharp tug as a young girl snatched her handbag from her shoulder and ran away along the parade of shops.

"Haay!" she shouted in shock, standing up to follow . . . but the cat was way ahead of her . . . It immediately sprang after the girl, easily catching her up and in a single bound, leapt into the thief's hair, hissing and scratching. The girl shrieked and dropped the bag, frantically trying to get the crazed cat off her head. Screaming, the girl ran randomly with her "cat hat" for a few yards, until she managed to shake it loose . . . eventually running off, sporting a new tousled hair style. The cat calmly picked up Sandra's bag in its teeth and dragged it back towards Sandra who had just caught up. He then lay the bag at her feet and looked up.

"You got my bag!" laughed Sandra tickling the cat under the chin in disbelief.

"I can't believe it!" she said to herself, looking around as the few people who had seen the incident gradually lost interest and dispersed. She really couldn't believe she had been protected by a random black cat!

"Definitely lucky, so far" she thought.

The cat followed her all the way to the car park and then wanted to get into her car, seemingly not wanting her to leave . . .

"You can't come with me!" she smiled, but the cat mewed loudly and looked up directly at Sandra. Feeling indebted, she reluctantly let him jump in, and he quickly made himself at home on the passenger seat.

Still shaken, Sandra drove out of the car park and headed towards home

"Lets get some air in here" she said, lowering both front windows to cool the car on this unusually hot day. She pulled up at some traffic lights and gazed at the cat, now sitting bolt upright in the seat looking out of the windscreen, calmly taking in the surroundings.

"Look at you . . . " she smiled, engrossed with this animal . . . *so* engrossed that she missed the lights turning green for a few seconds, predictably causing the driver behind to lean on his horn and swerve around her over-dramatically.

"Sorry!" she gestured.

Flustered, she pulled away . . . only to pull up alongside him at the next set of lights! "Wake up darlin!" he shouted condescendingly. Before she could react, the cat turned and leapt out of Sandra's passenger window into the neighbouring car, landing on the driver's head (the cat's second head of the day).

"Aaiiiii!" shrieked the driver, his disposition changing quickly from mocking to uncontrolled panic. The cat's defence of Sandra on this occasion was even more vigorous . . . scratching the driver's cheeks, forehead and ears, only narrowly missing his eyes and leaving a claw embedded under his chin. The cat then leapt back into Sandra's car, returned to his place on the seat, and licked his wounded foot.

"Shit!" said Sandra out loud. The lights turned green but she missed them again, jumping out of the car to see if the man was OK . . . He *wasn't* . . . he was very angry . . .

"What the f . . . !" Sandra didn't stay for the end of the sentence . . .

she turned back to her car, jumped in and sped away, leaving him at the lights. "He was basically OK" she justified to herself . . . "Shit! He might follow me!" she feared, not usually prone to such profanity . . . She drove quickly, following a back-street route home, checking behind that she wasn't being followed . . . she wasn't. Relieved, she arrived at her house on the edge of the village adjoining the main town.

"Shit" she exhaled as she turned off the car on her drive.

The black cat jumped out of the window and tripped round to Sandra's side, seemingly unperturbed by the missing claw . . . and as she left the car, it slinked around her legs, purring loudly. Sandra was really shaken by the whole incident but after a cup of tea, she had regained her composure.

The rest of the day passed without notable incident, the cat settling into her home as if raised there from a kitten. Sandra was wary of this animal after twice witnessing its potential but, not used to anyone or anything standing up for her in the past, she was actually quietly comforted by its presence. This cat had shown her nothing but affection and she welcomed the company.

"Hello boy!" she said, pleased to see the cat had stayed as it brushed around her legs the following morning. She had a new pet . . . and she liked it!

It was party day and her tights fitted well, the knobbly knees adding greatly to the look. Her outfit went down an absolute storm and she was really enjoying the afternoon . . . the weather, the company and the alcohol combining to distract her from the events of the previous day.

While Sandra was partying, the cat had slipped out of an open window and run back to the town centre, heading for the chemist. He always squeezed though a damaged ventilation flap at the back of the building and was soon cruising the busy shop again. He looked for the St. John's Wort tablets but they were nowhere to be seen . . . the stock had sold out—the town was a stressful place to live, it seemed. Knowing the smell, he searched the whole store but was unsuccessful, eventually tearing open a small box of sweet tasting effervescent yellow powder. He licked up the fizzy, salivary mix as quickly as he could. After a few more minutes cruising, with renewed vigour, he slipped out through the automatic front doors and back on home to Sandra's.

The town was unusually quiet that day with a lot of people heading out to the coast to enjoy the rare bank holiday sunshine. And the hot weather had slowed everyone down . . . including the postman who was running an hour late. Resting on the hall rug, the cat saw his hand trying to force a small parcel though the letter box. He should have left a note but he was in a hurry . . . and the parcel had jammed tight in the slot. "Damn! he said hot and frustrated "Get in there!" With a shove, the package eventually relented and popped through the slot, his arm following it through into the hall. The cat was quick . . . its teeth sank deep into the postman's wrist . . . and it didn't let go. The shocked yelp of horror from the postman was piercing. He tried to pull his arm out of the letter box, slamming the cat into the door, each time more frantically . . . The cat would not let go. Blood was draining, major vessels now torn and severed . . . he just couldn't get loose . . . He screamed, but the town was *really* quiet that day, and Sandra's house quite remote . . . The only person who *did* hear it faintly, mistook it for a bird call. The postman's blood drained into Sandra's hall and he eventually slipped away, his last delivery complete. The hall rug was ruined . . . the junk mail lay protected in their plastic covers.

The black cat dropped to the ground, cleaned itself up thoroughly, as cats do, and trotted round to the front of the house. Sandra was walking back from the party, still dressed as a flamingo, smiling . . . As the cat brushed himself around her pink legs she thought "What a great day!"

The weather was good . . . and she had found a new companion . . .

"it was definitely *good* luck", Sandra smiled.

Together in Electric Dreams

"She's looking good" Dave thought to himself as he put the finishing touches to the radio-controlled model plane he'd been working on for three months. This was no teenage balsa-wood fumbling but a quarter-scale, fully working, accurate in every detail, Lancaster Bomber. Even people with no interest in such things couldn't fail to admire the workmanship and time involved. Dave was not a train-spotting social misfit either . . . he was a largely normal, amiable person. He'd been divorced for about six months now. Everything relatively calm and amicable, a mutual recognition that he and Maria had drifted apart, not through the modelling but demanding work commitments on both sides. Essentially, they had worked themselves apart. Dave had rediscovered the modelling in the last few months, rekindling a childhood passion for such things.

Perhaps a psychological symptom of the divorce that had more deep-seated effects than he had realised, perhaps he had just eaten too much cheese, but Dave was having an unusual recurrent dream lately . . . A boy runs across a large field, his head tilted back looking up to the sky, on a warm, calm day near sunset. Then he is struck by lightning and killed. About twelve, dressed in a checked lumberjack shirt of blue and green, he was definitely killed . . . Dave could see the terrible burns . . . but he never saw the events leading up to this . . . just the run, the strike and the burns. He'd tried to think of a tenuous connection between the dream and some part of his reality but for the life of him, he couldn't see one . . . no memorable child of his past . . . hadn't owned a lumberjack shirt since he was sixteen (and had no craving for one now) . . . .never had an electric shock . . . hated running . . . The randomness, and the fact that this mini-dream was replayed two or three times every night, did concern him. A psychiatrist might suggest it was symbolic of an attempt to flee a situation, possibly deeply repressed childhood abuse by a Canadian electrician . . . but he had no such recollections. For many weeks it remained, random and unchanged . . . *Run, strike, burn . . . Run, strike, burn . . .*

Recently, the dreams had become more frequent, four or five times a night, each time the same . . . *Run, strike, burn . . .* Dave had got used to never waking up refreshed and this Wednesday morning was no exception . . . except there was a difference . . . "Odd" he thought as he noticed a strong smell of burning in the room . . . distinctive, not pleasant . . . vaguely reminiscent of a severely overdone steak. And this started to be the norm . . . four or five dreams a night, always waking with the smell, eventually subsiding a few minutes after waking.

"This is getting weird now" he worried. He was beginning to think that it was *him* getting weird. He toyed with the idea of talking it through with his doctor, but decided against this course of action. He *had* friends but, in truth, they were more acquaintances and not people that he felt he could really open up to. So he kept it all to himself . . . for the time being.

"People have dreams . . . " he justified, "even odd dreams, nothing new in that".

Dave had found the absorption of the modelling very relaxing. It was a distraction he really needed with all that had happened.

But all good things come to an end and, one day, it was complete!

"Not bad, not bad at all" admired Dave, extremely pleased with the outcome. Anyone would be . . . it was a beautiful model and he was extremely keen to fly it! He had largely misspent his teens flying a succession of radio controlled planes and all that innocent joy was flooding back . . .

Smiling, Dave eagerly packed the plane into the back of his cavernous old Volvo, the detachable wings allowing this comfortably, and he headed to the fields nearby. Beautiful rolling downs were only a twenty minute drive away from home, well-used by families and horse trainers, but so expansive that neither group interfered with the other. His plane was big and he was a little rusty with the controls so he needed some space . . . somewhere a fair way away from people to accommodate a mistake. Dave carefully unloaded the plane, attached the wings and started to reacquaint himself with the basic controls. As he hoped, it felt comfortable and easy, the controls feeling as natural in his hands as fingers in ours. Leaving it as late as possible but wanting to fly in good light, he set the plane on a flat area of short grass.

"It'll need a good long run . . . " he thought.

He carefully brought the engines up to speed and the bomber slowly gathered pace along the make-shift runway . . . lighter and lighter it bounced . . . until, to his complete delight . . . *take off!*

"Oh, yes!" he shouted. Dave was spell-bound . . . a perfect Lancaster Bomber, really quite large and un-model-like . . . taking to the skies in the most romantic Boys-Own fashion!

"It's perfect!" he beamed, the majestic silhouette of the plane against the flat-clouded blood-orange sunset looked like a perfectly composed oil painting. Dave was now completely lost in his teenage world . . . for how long he had no idea, all cares far away . . .

From the corner of his eye appeared a small boy running. Wearing a checked shirt, his head was tilted back, looking up at the plane against the backdrop of the sunset.

Dave knew well what would happen next . . . "No!" he shouted.

Instinctively, he ran towards the boy . . . as he got close, he heard a massive crack tear open the sky . . . a bolt of lightning had hit the Lancaster and it exploded like a firework . . . and it was the very last thing that Dave would ever see or hear . . . A moment later, on its route to the ground, the lightning preferred the tall aerial of Dave's handset to the body of the young boy . . . and Dave was struck down.

The boy stopped running and he looked at the man's smoking body in shock . . . One moment happiness, the next horror . . . at twelve, it was a lot to take in . . . the terrible burns . . . the smell . . . and he started to shake . . .

But the boy was lucky . . . it could easily have been him . . . and his loving family cocooned around him. He didn't have to cope on his own.

The first night following the incident was oddly calm for the boy, the stress of the event having caused near exhaustion. However, on the second night, his sleep was more troubled . . . and peppered with a recurring dream . . .

Run, strike, burn . . . Run, strike, burn . . .

The Shape of Things to Come

Rob needed a holiday and, conveniently, one was booked for tomorrow. He wasn't a complete neat freak but he definitely preferred tidy to untidy and wanted to get things straight around the house before he left—OK, mild OCD at most. Rosie, his wife was not so tidy. Not untidy but not borderline OCD. This worked well.

"That's more like it!" Rob congratulated himself, the lawn looking pretty damned good, even though he said so himself. Beds weeded and lawn edged, his job here was done, plants suitably stunted so he wasn't faced with a jungle on his return. He returned to the shed at the bottom of his garden, took the grass box off the back of the mower and placed it in the back corner of the shed. He then lifted the well-worn, heavy, orange mower through the door and positioned it sideways on the floor where it lived . . . until nature had miraculously restored the grass and Rob felt the need to shorten it again.

He went to shut the shed door and a feeling came over him that he'd experienced before. Not really obsessive, just a bit quirky . . . The feeling was that if he shut the door, all the items in the shed would be in exactly the same position for the whole week he was away . . . just sitting there, gathering dust, in the same position. It wasn't the dust that bothered him, just the fact they wouldn't move. If he moved something, then it would be different. If he *moved* something, things wouldn't be the same for all that time and, in a strange sense, he had changed the future. Definitely a bit quirky! He didn't feel the need to do it every time either, just now and then.

When Rob shared this with his wife she, as most would, thought it odd . . . not disturbingly odd, just amusingly odd. Rob thought it was odd too.

"You haven't changed the future, you've just moved something slightly in a shed!" Rosie would, quite rightly point out. Rob realised this, but it just made him feel better. So here was Rob, faced with everything in the shed staying the same for a week. So he slightly moved the fork that was leaning up against the shed wall. Feeling better, he then shut the door and carried on with his day, not giving the shed, or it's slightly rearranged contents, a second thought.

Their holiday together in Menorca was perfect . . . the weather spectacular, the island idyllic and his choice of wife wise. It had been a few years since Rosie and Rob had holidayed on their own but since Josh, their only child, had recently moved into his own flat, they seemed to have more time on their hands . . . and it was good. Not better, but different . . . it had all been good.

While they were away the weather at home had been predictably mixed—warm and wet . . . perfect grass-growing weather. So Rob was pleasantly surprised to see that his lawn was exactly as he'd left it . . . neatly mown!

"God bless him!" thought Rob, realising his neighbour old Mr Wells, must have cut it for him . . . on occasion, they would exchange this favour for each other at holiday times. During the afternoon, he called round to Herbert's to thank him.

"Not me, Rob" he said "Sorry, I would have done it for you, but it's been a bit of a hectic week and it slipped my mind".

"No problem, Herbert" he replied.

"Curious . . . " thought Rob, "Had a stranger broken in and mowed the lawn?

. . . a thief stolen the top inch of each blade of grass for their own nefarious purposes?" . . . "Unlikely" he thought. And there was something even stranger . . . the grass was the *only* thing that hadn't changed. The weeds *had* grown, quite a bit in fact . . . the hedge was looking a little unkempt . . . Everything else was as you'd expect after leaving it for a week, except the grass! It looked newly mown, edges sharply defined.

"Maybe it's been drier than people thought" said Rosie, dismissing it as a lucky break.

"But what about the weeds . . . and everyone else's grass!" replied Rob.

From the time they got back from their holiday, the grass appeared to start to grow normally . . . requiring Rob's attention again on a regular basis. After a while, other distractions occupied Rob's mind and he too started to dismiss it as a lucky break.

Two months later they had arranged another short break . . . in the quaint village of Charmouth in Dorset, staying at a friend's flat at the top of the hill.

Before the trip, Rob had mowed the lawn and tidied the garden, as was his habit, and, on returning the mower to the shed, that same feeling came over him . . . "everything will stay the same for the week . . . " so he moved the fork again, the easiest thing to move as it stood next to the door. Then he shut the door and enjoyed another week of his wife's company.

The area held happy memories for Rob. Many childhood holidays were spent on the beach there, collecting fossils. Golden spiral-shelled ammonites could be picked straight off the beach. 180 million years old, the creatures had been immortalised in stone, frozen in time . . . and the idea that *so much* time had passed fascinated Rob.

On their return, it was like déjà-vu! Rob's lawn hadn't grown again! Everything else had, but not his grass . . .

"Well I'll be!" Rob thought. This time he thought it best not to mention it to Rosie. He wasn't in the habit of keeping things from her but just didn't want to worry her with strange happenings in their home. But Rob was starting to make a connection . . . when that feeling came over him, if he moved the fork, the grass didn't grow! Until he returned, and then things resumed as usual. It appeared that if the fork was moved, something else had to stay the same . . . and for the fork, it was the grass.

"Incredible!" . . . but best kept to himself, he thought.

For the next two years, Rob moved the fork slightly in the shed and largely avoided cutting the grass! He thought this was marvellous as grass shortening wasn't his favourite pastime. Interestingly, just moving the fork didn't work. It had to be moving the fork when he had that feeling to move something . . . which wasn't always.

After a while, it occurred to him "If moving the fork stopped the grass growing, what if I move something else? Would something else stop?!"

The next time he got the compulsion to move something a little, he noticed a small tin of black enamel paint sitting on the shelf at the back of the shed. "Ideal" he thought, to test his theory . . . so he moved it a little before a weekend away to see Josh, his son.

The weekend went well, with Rob happily being pulled into service for numerous odd jobs around Josh's delapidated flat. On his return, *nothing* had changed as result of moving the pot. Rob looked *really* hard for *anything* that had stayed the same but he drew a complete blank . . . no change whatsoever.

"I've lost my touch!" he thought . . . "maybe it's only the fork that has an effect . . . "

"You are not going to believe this Rosie!!" Rob called up to her after checking his numbers. They had won the European lottery! They never won things . . . and he'd only bought a ticket because his friend got one and he was with him! They couldn't believe it. It wasn't a 78 million pound mega-win but it *was* 3.5. 3.5 million pounds! Rob and Rosie already considered themselves to be living a charmed life but this really was quite something, and a fairly standard course of action resulted . . . Investments to secure themselves financially, some money to close friends and family, some money to Josh, of course but, their personal favourite . . . a beautiful villa in Menorca. Not right by the beach but on a hill, with its own wooded grounds . . . very close to the area they had stayed on their own for that idyllic week. And it was their intention that this was not to be just a holiday home, but a home full stop. They only had themselves to worry about, Josh was happy and standing on his own two feet and, anyway, "Menorca wasn't a million miles away" . . . and the villa was easily spacious enough to accommodate guests. So this is what they did. They sold their house and moved to Menorca . . . for another chapter of their life.

And the chapter was good . . . they were very happy.

Back home, their old house was eventually bought by a busy young couple. They lived there fairly happily for four years. Most of this time they both worked hard. Out early, home late . . . gardening wasn't high on their agenda . . . nowhere near as high as meeting their friends and going out to socialise. Very rarely socialising at home, the garden gradually grew into an urban wasteland . . . fortunately Rob was unaware of this! The couple eventually moved to a flat with no garden, which suited them much better . . . and the house was sold to an older gentlemen, Mr Stevens.

Like many of his generation, Mr Stevens liked things tidy but, unlike many of his generation, he hated gardening . . . so he had a "little man" in to keep the garden under control-in fact, Jim was quite large at seventeen stone and 6ft 2. For seven years, Jim bought his own mower and tools and kept the garden in order . . . Rob would have approved. The shed was still there but Jim had no reason to use it . . . it had never been entered since Rob had left . . . the fork stayed just inside the door and the small pot of paint sat on the shelf, exactly where Rob had left it.

Sadly, Mr Stevens eventually suffered a stroke and had to be moved to a home for closer care . . . and, after a short illness, he died at that home.

He had no children but several nephews and nieces and unfortunately a quite bitter dispute arose over Mr Stevens' will and the fate of the house. A dispute that lasted ten years, during which time the house lay completely dormant. The furniture remained as Mr Stevens had left it, the garden was no longer tended by Jim and became completely overgrown . . . worse than the jungle the young couple had left. But the pot of paint still sat there completely untouched . . . dusty, with powdery rust speckling the metal lid from twenty-two years of autumnal dews . . . Ivy had crept across the shed in many places, forcing its way through impossible cracks, thriving on the limited amount of light that filtered though the single dusty front window. But there the pot sat . . .

By now, Rob and Rosie were in their early seventies, still happy together in their Menorcan idyll . . . things had worked out as perfectly as they had dared to imagine. In the early years at the villa, Rob occasionally felt that old feeling coming over him and, remembering that fork in his old shed, he'd actually tried moving some things around their new home . . . but there were no apparent effects. None at all.

"Maybe the effect was a peculiarly British phenomenon" he thought.

There was, however, a *definite* effect that had become very apparent to both of them in recent years . . . To Rob, Rosie was as pretty as the day he had met her, but seventy-three years had resulted in some inevitable greying . . . some wrinkles, a slightly less springy step . . . the inevitable signs of a long, happy life, despite liberal use of Oil of Ulay. *Rob*, however, had not changed since the day he'd moved that pot in the shed. Not aged one day. He was 49 now as he had been 49 when he moved it. It had taken him a long time to accept, especially as he looked younger than his years anyway . . . but, after a while, it was undeniable. Rosie was mystified but pleased for him—just pleased he was happy and healthy.

For a long time Rob didn't make the connection between the lack of change in him and his impulsive movement of the paint pot . . . But, his thoughts eventually came round to that event and its timing . . . "Fork equalled grass . . . maybe paint pot equals Rob?!" he thought . . .

"There's no way, though . . . it will have been moved . . . "

Three months later, Rosie died suddenly and painlessly. A massive heart attack instantly dropped her to the floor. One moment there, the next not. Rob found her on the floor of the living room as he returned from a walk to the shop. The shock of the loss was total and from that moment on, he never felt the same happiness. There was a yawning emptiness that he could not overcome.

Shortly after, Rob returned to England to be with his son and, almost by accident, he found himself driving past the old house. He was shocked to see the state it was in.

Rob and Rosie kept things pretty smart during their stay and took a pride in it . . . and it was a long time since anyone had done that. Overgrown plants and trees, neglected paint peeling on the front door, an obvious look of emptiness that, like his own, was saddening.

He walked up the side path and pushed the tall side gate open, the wood around the lock was rotten and weak, breaking away easily. The once neat back garden was now hopelessly overgrown . . . he wouldn't have been surprised to see David Attenborough lying with gorillas filming in there.

With some difficulty, he walked up to the old shed at the back of the garden. The felt roof had seen better days . . . Intrigued, he pushed back the door. The fork was just where he had left it! It was as if the whole shed was some sort of time capsule that was left so that children could glimpse what a typical suburban shed looked like forty years ago!

"No point moving the fork now with the state of that lawn!" Rob smiled to himself.

Then he saw something he couldn't believe . . .

"There's no way . . . " he said shocked . . . incredibly, the old pot of paint was right where he'd left it! It had an antique patina about it but there it was!

"How did it not get *moved*?" Rob looked around, taking in his past frozen in time . . . he turned to leave and as he went to shut the door, that old feeling washed over him, as strongly as he could remember . . . "Leaving the shed like this, maybe leaving it for *years* like this . . . " He focussed on the rust-speckled pot. He had an overwhelming urge to move it, just a little, before he left. He knew the possible consequences but, not being able to stop himself, move it he did.

Rob started to age from that point onwards. He returned to Menorca, regularly visited by Josh and his family. He lived a reasonably happy life . . . but he never filled that emptiness . . . every day, he missed her.

They say that "time waits for no man" but, after a substantial wait for *this* man, time was catching up. On his last morning, he lay, very tired in his bed at the villa. Not ill, just tired. 123 was a pretty good innings as they say—93 if you allow for his stay of execution . . . In his last minute, he focussed on the glass table lamp on the bedside cabinet and that old feeling came over him one more time. He smiled, reached out slowly and and moved the lamp a little, for old time's sake. At that moment, he slipped away . . . he could see Rosie waiting for him in the villa . . .

And every clock on the island stopped.

Scratching the Surface

"You develop an instant global consciousness, a people orientation, an intense dissatisfaction with the state of the world and a compulsion to do something about it. From out there on the surface of the moon, international politics look so petty. You want to grab a politician by the scruff of the neck and drag him a quarter of a million miles out and say "Look at that you son of a bitch".

Edgar Mitchell, Apollo 14 astronaut

Jim loved this quote. He completely understood how his friend Edgar had felt when he wrote it because, in early February 1971, 39 years ago, he had stood beside him on the surface of the moon and looked back . . . He'd seen the earth rise above the horizon of the moon . . . seen how everything we know, and everything any human has ever known, occurred on the surface of that pretty blue sphere . . . that just hangs there . . . as if by magic. He knew it was physics but when he saw it, it looked pretty magical. The moon does the same trick, of course . . . but Jim felt the poor moon was too often ignored. People *know* it's a big rock suspended up there in an orbit around us . . . but the magic is taken for granted. "Some nights people don't even bother to look up!" At 68, Jim still looked up. It occurred to him that if we lived on the moon, people would probably start taking the sight of the earth for granted . . . although he found that difficult to believe having seen it. Jim thought people needed to look up more . . .

Jim looked down at a handful of pebbles he'd picked up as he sat on the beach. He'd had a privileged view of things . . . The most expensive seat in the house, you might say . . . and that had changed his view on life, changed his view on everything. He understood, better than most, how precious life on earth was . . . he also understood, how monumentally insignificant it all was. Everything we know . . . dinosaurs, Romans, wars, love, science, art, music . . . *everything* happened on this insignificant rock hanging in an endless space consisting mostly of absolutely nothing!

As he watched the pebbles fall through his fingers, he likened the earth to one pebble. "*Everything* on *one* pebble!". He'd stood with Edgar on the moon . . . a little pebble next to earth . . . "But look at the beach . . . " he thought . . . billions of pebbles . . . and that's just one beach! . . . "If one stone went missing, what difference would it make?" he thought . . . "absolutely none".

Jim's thoughts were distracted by a conversation he'd overheard earlier at the sea-front cafe. A couple had been boasting, to anyone that would listen, that they had just country-hopped half-way round the world on a luxury three-month tour. Jim had always loved travel . . . and their luxury trip *did* indeed sound very nice. But what really amused him was that their global travels really just involved scratching around on the surface of this "pebble". A pebble that orbits the sun at 324,000 miles an hour, while the sun (and the rest of the planets in our solar system) tour the universe at a rate of a million miles a day! So all of us, even the poorest and quietest of us, are on a constant, life-long amazing free journey through space . . . travelling vast distances effortlessly and cheaply . . . even as we sleep! Jim found this funny . . . And Jim, of course, was slightly better travelled than the couple, but he was too polite to interject.

He could lose hours on the beach, lost in his thoughts, the ebb and flow of the surf somehow freeing his imagination, like the rhythmic swing of the hypnotist's watch releases the subject from everyday consciousness.

He laid back on the beach and felt the warm sun on his face . . . the sea air, the cry of the gulls and the water's ebb and flow conspired to cause him to drift off into a contented sleep.

Jim nearly always dreamed in his sleep, and normally remembered them . . . and this was no exception. A beautiful day, he found himself walking along the edge of a field . . . a Peacock butterfly landed in front of him and, as he approached it, it took off, flitted a few yards ahead and then settled . . . He walked a few more steps, and the butterfly took off again, flitted and settled. This kept happening . . . until he felt that the butterfly was leading the way on his walk . . . a personal insect guide! He followed this butterfly for some time . . . until he eventually woke up.

As he opened his eyes, he wasn't expecting to see the huge butterfly filling his view! Thankfully, it wasn't that big, just very close to his face . . . but it *was* the same type of Peacock butterfly . . . rusty brown wings with splashes of yellow and four purple/yellow "eyes" near the tips of the upper and lower wings. As insects go, it was a beauty, he thought . . .

Then the butterfly flitted a few feet away from him and waited patiently, it seemed, for him to follow!

"No way!" he thought. He got up and started to follow . . . the butterfly flitted up, moved on a few yards and settled again. He walked a few yards and the butterfly flitted forwards a few yards, leading the way!

"Unbelievable!" he thought. And so it went on . . . The butterfly never flew in a straight line . . . it was as if a breeze had caught it and blown it around in random bursts, changing direction constantly . . . This slightly offended Jim's aeronautical sensibilities but, the overall direction was true . . . Jim followed his insect guide along the beach for around 35 minutes, all the time expecting the butterfly to lose interest and disappear but, no, it was a fine lead. He couldn't believe he was following a butterfly, but he had nothing else to do . . .

Despite Jim's relative fitness for his age, walking on the stones was starting to become hard work and he was relieved when the butterfly turned left up the beach onto the firmer ground of a small gorge between the cliffs. Originally formed by a river running down to the sea, there was little sign of that now, save small rivulets meandering onto the beach and disappearing under the stones. The butterfly led him a short way up the gorge towards a small wooden cabin, idyllically positioned a little up the cliff side, with a beautiful view of the beach and ocean. The cabin looked welcoming with its weathered white boarding and beach-combed flotsam and jetsam adorning the small railed veranda. The butterfly landed on the handle of the door. Jim wasn't in the habit of nosing around other peoples' cabins but he couldn't resist trying this door . . . especially after he had followed a butterfly to it!

"Hello . . . anyone here?" called Jim, not really expecting an answer. The cabin looked like it was used, but there was no reply . . .

Jim followed the butterfly into a single small room . . . Quite dusty and spartan, there was a cupboard, a wardrobe and a shelf with coffee mugs. This was obviously more of a beach hut than a home . . . somewhere to change into beachwear, or to hide away and read a book. The butterfly had settled on the single bed in the corner of the cabin . . . no bed linen, just a sheet over the mattress. The sheet, like the floor of the cabin, was covered in a thin layer of white powdery sand . . . "must have blown in through the gaps in the boards" Jim thought as he brushed the sheet clean with his hand and sat on the edge of the bed. He was feeling weary now and he rested his head on the pillow . . . Soon after closing his eyes, he fell asleep. And he started to dream . . .

He saw the butterfly again . . . It was slowly raising and lowering its wings. Jim's breathing started to synchronise with them . . . wings up, breathe in, down, breathe out . . . The wings moved slower and slower and Jim's breathing deeper and deeper . . . until the wings stopped in the open position.

The insect then started to rise up vertically, levitating towards the roof of the cabin. Jim had often dreamt of being able to levitate and move through the air in a controlled way . . . He just needed to get in the right state of mind . . . nothing he had not done before . . . in his dreams . . . And so it was that he rose out of the bed, straight up, following the still-winged butterfly. The wooden roof posed no barrier to the ascending duo as they rose through it and continued to rise . . . Jim looking up, as he had a habit to do . . . he felt uncomfortable rising with his back to the ground so he turned himself over to face down. By now the pair were very high, the strip of beach below, separating the blue ocean from the green country behind it. It wasn't long before he could make out the familiar sight of the curvature of the earth . . . familiar to *him*. The butterfly continued to rise, leaving the haze of the atmosphere, up into the blackness of space. It seemed incredibly real . . . and Jim knew what real looked like. He felt completely relaxed . . . unaffected by the intense cold and lack of atmosphere. He and the butterfly rose in total comfort and control . . . until he was looking back at a sight he thought he would never see again . . . the earth, just hanging there like magic . . . He turned round to see the butterfly crisply silhouetted against the backdrop of a huge moon, beautifully lit by the sun, its craters and surface features sharply defined. Travelling horizontally now, the butterfly, wings motionless and outstretched, led the way towards the moon. "I'm going back!" thought Jim excited.

They approached the moon and Jim could see its cratered surface . . . parts he could remember and parts not . . . 39 years was a long time . . . it reminded him of looking out from the Command Module window in '71. Lower they glided, still travelling at some speed . . . low enough now to dip into huge craters, rise over mountain ranges . . . it was incredible to be back! The butterfly was flying close to the surface now . . . over a huge plain. Jim reached down onto the moon's surface and traced a long line in the grey dust with his fingers . . . a tail of dust rose up behind him, like a stunt plane at an air show!

The butterfly eventually slowed and then settled on top of a small rock. Jim controlled his descent carefully . . . it was time for touch down! He felt his feet touch the deep dust on the surface, felt the pressure on his legs as his longest dream-levitation yet came to an end . . . Then he woke up.

He had no idea how long he'd been asleep . . . the butterfly was on the pillow, exercising its wings. He was suddenly very conscious that he had quite dramatically imposed on the good nature of whoever's cabin it was and he swung his feet off the bed to stand up. He looked down at his blue beach shoes . . . despite feeling a little silly, he couldn't resist a look in them for traces of moon dust. "Ha, ha, ha . . . " he chuckled when there was none at all . . . "Of course there wasn't!"

He slowly began to feel the warmth of the sun on his face, inhaled the fresh sea air, heard the cries of the gulls . . . and he woke up . . . on the beach. *Really* woke up this time, not just dreaming of waking up in the cabin . . . He woke up completely refreshed . . . more refreshed than he could remember. The butterfly was nowhere to be seen. Yes, Jim was back for real this time . . .

In the cabin much further down the beach, Chris was dressing down a single bed. He was chastising himself for not making the bed before he left from his last trip. His cabin was rough and ready, but that's how he liked it. It was isolated enough for him to write in, but not too isolated—he liked that too. As always when he arrived, Chris had to sweep the place . . . a layer of fine white sand covered the floor . . . nothing unusual in that . . .

. . . but the grey dust on the bed was something Chris hadn't seen before . . .

On Reflection

"Here we go again . . . " thought Maria as she sat in her window seat on flight 157 bound for Inverness. She still loved flying, even though it had become as frequent for her as taking a taxi. The sleek, polished Gulfstream jet, belonged to Heards, a luxury department store and Maria had worked for them since she left school. The quirky, traditional approach of the company suited her, and it seemed her traditional quirkiness suited the company. Through her seventeen happy years with them, she had risen through the ranks to Senior Buyer, which involved a lot of visits to suppliers . . . this time a noted supplier of Harris Tweed.

A low layer of light grey cloud hung in the still air around the airport. Tony had just arrived at the airport for his flight to Tel Aviv, and being in good time, was watching the planes taking off from the car park, only a chain-link fence away from the runway. It was the oddest sight that morning . . . Planes took off, but almost immediately entered very low hanging cloud, giving the distinct impression that the plane had de-materialised, quickly fading from view as it was engulfed in the cloud. Tony watched this happen four times . . . three airliners and the little private jet . . . with Maria on board.

They would take off and then . . . shazam! . . . a dematerialisation that wouldn't shame an episode of Star Trek! A fascinating sight but eventually Israel beckoned and Tony had a flight to catch.

Being a "frequent flyer", taking off through low cloud was routine for Maria and she hardly noticed rising up through the thin layer into the beautiful expanse of blue above. She never tired of this view . . . looking down onto the top of the cotton-wool cloud layer, in a zone where it was *always* a good day, high above any dreariness.

Maria made the usual adjustments to her allotted space: put away her take-off Werther's Originals (always the traditionalist) took out her Harpers & Queen magazine from her bag, adjusted the air vent, got her camera out (she liked taking photos on flights) and generally made the space her own. This ritual was similar to that of anyone on a budget airline except in this case her nose wasn't actually touching the headrest of the seat in front. On this spacious plane, Maria's nose was a *considerable* distance away from anything and she considered herself very fortunate to have become accustomed to such luxurious travel. Only seventeen people flew with Maria, including pilots and crew.

Flight 157 progressed very comfortably. The cabin crew and pilots were friendly and light-hearted and the blue sky lifted everyone's spirits. The low cloud had persisted below them for the whole flight and Maria was disappointed that she'd taken very few photos. As the plane started its descent through the cloud layer, visibility though Maria's window gradually reduced to nil and the plane was gently buffeted. Maria always found this a strange feeling . . . as if time was somehow suspended, everyone quiet . . . everything held in limbo . . . until gradually, in intermittent bursts of visibility, the plane emerged into the clear air below. "Ah we're back!" she thought, "normal service is resumed!" The clear air wasn't going to last long though . . . The Captain had noticed that below the plane was yet another cloud layer! "Unusual . . . " he thought "a double cloud layer . . . not unheard of". The Captain continued his descent, but didn't expect what followed . . . the landing gear of the plane hit the top of the cloud . . . really hard! Hard enough for luggage doors to spring open and some baggage to fall into the aisle. There were several involuntary screams from the passengers . . . even a subdued one from the normally stoic Maria . . .

"What the hell was that!" said the co-pilot.

"Christ knows!" shouted The Captain as he struggled to regain control of the plane. The co-pilot was hoping for more reassurance . . .

They stabilised the plane and continued at a height just above this surprisingly firm cloud . . .

"I'll make an announcement" said the co-pilot

"Hello ladies and gentleman . . . we are currently investigating the cause of the disturbance, so please remain seated and we'll report back to you very soon . . . "

"This is weird . . . ." said The Captain "the instruments are showing we're just above the ground . . . "

After travelling a few minutes, the cloud layer below gradually broke up and patches of blue were visible below . . . slowly it dawned on them what was beneath them. "What the hell . . . " said the co-pilot . . .

Somehow they were flying immediately above a highly reflective, mirror-like surface! Perfectly smooth, as far as the eye could see . . . It wasn't cloud they had seen below them . . . it was the reflection of the *first* cloud layer they had been through . . . the whole surface of the ground like a giant ball-bearing, reflecting the sky and all its features. Maria was open mouthed at the beauty of the view from her window . . . her camera was clicking now . . . It *was* beautiful but, at the same time, shockingly unexpected . . . Inverness and its surroundings were disturbingly absent!

The Captain maintained a very low flight path, traversing this amazing sight almost in a state of shock. In his seventeen and a half years of piloting passenger jets he had never, not once, cruised above a massive ball-bearing . . . He tried his radio but it was dead . . . His confusion continued until his professional head decided another announcement was in order . . . "Hello ladies and gentleman. Please relax and stay seated. The crew are assessing the unusual atmospheric conditions . . . "(he was quite pleased with that one) . . . "meanwhile, I can confirm the plane is in good shape and there is nothing to worry about" . . . "except for the landscape disappearing!" he thought to himself . . . "Meanwhile, relax, enjoy the flight and thank you for flying "Where-The-Fuck-Are-We" Airways", he thought to himself facetiously, his professionalism beginning to waver.

The Captain knew they had to land soon . . . fuel was running low and he wanted to keep some in reserve. For five minutes now they had flown low and not seen one distinguishing feature . . . just mirror smoothness. The Captain announced the landing preparations and again asked everyone to sit . . . people were crowded round the windows. The Captain then executed a cautious but perfect landing . . . so smooth, it felt like they *had* landed on soft cloud . . . the tyres spoiling the mirror finish by leaving two streaks of rubber on touch-down.

The plane came to a halt and, blatantly ignoring the "keep your seatbelt fastened" lights, people got up from their seats. But there was no rush to collect luggage with this flight . . . no ground crew rushing to the plane to tend it's needs, no nothing in fact . . . absolutely nothing.

This would normally be when the pilot announced "Welcome to Inverness . . . " but The Captain and co-pilot had run out of things to say. They decided to try the door and investigate further outside . . .

From the plane, Maria could see The Captain and co-pilot just standing there on the surface. The steward followed them out . . . Maria left her seat and followed her colleagues outside exchanging mumblings of concern. As they disembarked down the steps, they slowly fell silent in awe . . . Maria was speechless . . . it was an unbelievable sight. The surface was hard underfoot, reflecting everything above it . . . looking back, the elegant polished jet looked spectacularly futuristic . . . as if on the set of a sci-fi film . . . but this was no set . . .

There was a general air of awe and uncertainty. Maria approached The Captain. "What do *you* think?" she said, still in shock . . .

"I'm not sure" said The Captain looking around, having trouble taking it all in. The Captain pulled himself together and announced "Please stay close to the plane while we try to find out more about this".

"Not my most commanding announcement" he thought, inwardly wincing.

The consensus appeared to be that the safest place *was* near the plane—exploration being slightly unnecessary—from the elevated position inside the plane they could see for miles . . . and there was nothing to see. Maria took a lot of pictures until she thought they were becoming a bit samey. No-one was sure what to make of it and what to do next. Stay? Explore? Take off again?

The sun was lower now . . . and glare bounced off the shiny surface. It was then that Maria spotted a figure in the distance . . . "yes its definitely a figure!". With no landscape features, the figure was fairly easy to distinguish with the sun behind it. Walking purposefully and directly towards the group, out of the low sun, the figure slowly got closer.

"What the hell is that?" said The Captain, not for the first time on this journey. A rumble of concern ran through the group. As it got closer it could be seen that this was a man, a human shape at least . . . As the figure drew closer still, it *was* the unmistakable form of a man, but completely featureless . . . just as smooth and reflective as the surroundings. His face was devoid of detail, like a dress-maker's mannequin, his whole surface highly reflective, almost metallic but more reflective that that . . . a glass-like quality . . . a mirror-man. Oddly, the disquiet that had briefly permeated the group transformed into a calmness, the closer he became . . . He was in no way threatening . . . "like C3PO from Star Wars" Maria thought. He moved in the same bumbling gait.

The mirror-man stood in front of the group completely motionless, the group calm and completely silent. The Captain, feeling responsible approached the man . . . "Hello . . . we mean you no harm" he announced. His words were laboured as if explaining a meal order to a foreign waiter.

"Can you understand us?" he said with a crushing feeling of inadequacy . . . no response . . .

Then suddenly and silently, the mirror-man quickly raised his arms and stepped forwards toward The Captain like a pouncing tiger! All that was missing was the "Boo!" Everyone jumped . . . like a monster in the sci-fi film had just appeared. The mirror-man then resumed his stationary position.

"I think it would be wise to calmly get back into the plane now" suggested the The Captain backing up. But the mirror-man didn't feel threatening at all. "Maybe he's got a sense of humour" Maria thought. "Is he smiling . . . ?" It was hard to tell.

To The Captain's relief, the passengers did as they were told and calmly returned to the plane. Maria watched the mirror-man from her window seat, still standing motionless. Being reflective against a highly reflective background, he was difficult to see . . . "much easier to see when he was moving" she thought. Just then, there was a shimmering movement and Maria lost track of him . . . "He's moved!" someone shouted.

Then there was a knock on the door of the plane . . . .

"What now?!" said the steward to no-one in particular. Then there was a second knock, slightly more urgent. Everyone on the plane was still very calm. "Open it" said the co-pilot . . . Slowly, the steward did . . . but there was no one to be seen at the top of the steps . . .

Searching in vain for a signal on the radio, the Captain was shocked to see the mirror-man suddenly appear on the windscreen! Unthreatening, the man gestured to him to open the door. The mirror-man quickly reappeared at the top of the steps, in all his reflective friendliness, and then entered the plane. Again, his presence induced a calmness in people. Maria felt this serenity too . . . that everything was going to be fine . . . no cause for concern. The mirror-man paused for a moment in front of the full-length mirror in the galley, as if checking his appearance . . . and then continued on into the cockpit taking a seat in the co-pilot's position. The co-pilot seemed quite pleased to vacate it and the mirror-man looked, eyeless, towards The Captain. Calm, The Captain knew what was required . . . he made an announcement:

"Secure all cabin doors for take-off and please sit down and fasten your seat-belts. Everything is under control, ladies and gentlemen." The passengers did as they were instructed without objection. Handing control to the mirror-man, the engines were started and the guest-pilot taxied the plane across the vast mirrored surface . . . he could obviously handle a plane . . . For fifteen minutes, the mirror-man taxied the plane and the scene from the cockpit changed very little apart from the constantly changing reflection of the sky on the surface . . . it looked like everything converged on the horizon, the sky reflected in a mirror-image on the ground, as if split in two.

The mirror-man then turned the plane to the right and two huge semi-circular objects came into view . . . Two enormous mirrors rose out of the ground, both about half the size of a football pitch, about 100 metres apart, facing each other. The mirror-man skilfully parked the plane in the space between these huge mirrors . . . facing towards one mirror, engines still running. This created the spectacular effect when two mirrors are together . . . an infinite number of repeated images, seemingly receding into a never-ending distance into the mirror. Except this was on a theatrical scale.

The mirror-man turned his mannequin head to face The Captain and again, The Captain calmly knew what to do. The mirror-man rose from his seat, directed the co-pilot to take his place and extended both arms forwards, pointing towards the receding images. He turned his back and walked out of the cockpit. He then opened the cabin door and leapt out of the plane, landing some distance below, unharmed. Motionless, he looked back up to the plane. The steward attempted to shut the door but a cushion of air pressure appeared to prevent the latch catching . . . The sun was very low now, bright light reflecting off the surface outside, streaming in through the cracks around the door as if an arc light was immediately outside. During a second attempt at closure, an intense beam of light, accompanied by a rush of air burst past the crew to their left, so bright the crew saw the floating remnants of the image in their field of view for the next few minutes. On the third attempt, the latch thankfully caught easily and the door was secured.

Crew seated, The Captain pushed the throttles forward and sped towards the receding images of the mirror. No mirror was hit . . . The Captain and co-pilots' view was hypnotic . . . a slowly flashing image, the plane appearing to break through each image, every time looking for all the world like it would be hit by the plane. As the plane picked up speed, the frequency of the flashing images increased, until the plane could be felt leaving the ground. In the cockpit, the effect was all-consuming . . . the flashes so rapid that there was just a continuous, blinding white light that caused both The Captain and co-pilot to cover their eyes. When they opened them, they were rising up in that reassuringly familiar clear blue zone above the clouds . . . looking down on the white top of the persistent cloud layer that day.

"The radio's back!" said the co-pilot. Realising fuel was very low, The Captain quickly confirmed their location and organised an unscheduled landing at the nearest airport . . . Glasgow. Eventually, the plane needed to descend through the cloud layer again . . . which was a cause for concern . . . This time, *everyone* shared Maria's feeling of suspended animation in the cloud . . . not a sound . . . only some slight buffeting . . . as *everyone* waited, holding their breath, until they gradually emerged into clearer air . . .

And there was Glasgow in all it's glory, to everybody's huge relief! People cheered, out of their seats punching the air . . . they were back!

After another beautifully smooth landing . . . a relieved Captain taxied the plane round to a halt, never more pleased to be back on terra firma.

On disembarkation, the passengers tried to make sense of their experience.

"No-one is going to believe any of it!" Maria overheard a colleague saying . . . but Maria's photos were evidence that it was much more than just a collective hallucination . . . it really *had* happened.

Relieved to have returned his plane and passengers intact, The Captain decided to head for the bar, walking through the exit marked "nothing to declare" . . . which, on that day, wasn't entirely true . . .

Back in the empty plane, the mirror-man was disembarking too . . . slowly stepping out of the full length mirror in the galley . . .

. . . eager to explore.

A Fete Worse Than Death

Of course it wasn't worse than death . . . that really is quite bad . . . but this *was* bad. Actually, it was so bad, it was good. For Glen, it all started with an invitation . . .

"Are you coming down to the fete tomorrow in town? We're looking for as many bikes as we can" said a pleasantly odd gentleman in a 60's rocker leather jacket, his mute wife, similarly leathered, nodding eagerly.

"Yeah, I was thinking of popping down for a couple of hours, so I'll see you down there" said Glen, feeling he should support the gentleman who, with his kind-eyed wife, organised bike shows in the local area.

So pop down he did, arriving around 11.30 on the pleasant Sunday morning, parking up his hard-tail Triumph Bonneville chopper, Dennis . . . named after Dennis Hopper of "Easy Rider" fame, who died while it was being built.

He parked up, put the obligatory piece of wood under the side-stand so it didn't sink into the grass, and had a wander. Held in a large town park, the fete was an annual affair, consisting of a couple of stages for the unexpectedly good bands, a fair, vehicles on display, a couple of show areas for the inevitable dog show/karate demonstrations and a lot of stalls.

"Ah, you came!" said the leathery show organiser "that's good 'cos we're a bit thin on the ground with bikes today"

"Would you mind giving me a hand?" Mr Leather asked Glen.

"No problem" Glen replied. An elderly gentleman had just arrived on his bike, an old Rudge Ulster, and it had ground to a halt at the park entrance so Glen and Mr Leather went over to give him a push to the bike area . . . as bikers do. Made in the 1940's, the Rudge was a real racing machine in its day but this one was now covered in oil from numerous leaks. The rider was equally oily, a fair bit older and sported the most magnificent, voluminous grey beard . . . like an oily Father Christmas.

"I've owned her from 1966 . . . use it every day" he said proudly "rode it thirty miles here"

"Not sure it's going to get back" thought Glen, not sharing the gentleman's confidence in his machine.

Meeting this character was the start of the day becoming somewhat surreal for Glen. From that point on, it was as if he had entered the "Twilight Zone". There was, of course, a framework of fete normality: the dog show, the cake stall, the children dancing, the tombola . . . but the more Glen wandered, the more odd his day became. For example, he passed a cuddly toy store run for all the world by what looked like a paedophile . . . harsh but such was his dirty, sticky-haired, nicotine-toothed, scabbiness that an alternative pastime was difficult to imagine. The sinister "child-catcher" way he was luring children in to his stall festooned with ridiculously low quality cuddly toys, was uneasy just to walk past. In jolly contrast, the local toy shop had dressed a poor employee up in a giraffe outfit . . . and the kids loved this. Bright orangey/yellow, a tad brighter than a real giraffe for dramatic effect, a trail of children followed, the only threat being a small pug-like dog that Glen was willing to take a bite of the giraffe's leg. Sadly it wasn't tempted and there was no "giraffe versus pug" fight.

"Visit your local cathedral" read an unlikely sign above one of the gazebo stalls. Even more unlikely was the fully robed bishop sheltering beneath it, resplendent in cream and rich reds. Yet more unlikely was the fact he was in his early twenties and texting! Glen had chatted with some fire-fighters from the obligatory "fire engine-for-kids-to-clamber-over" stall, who pointed out that the "cathedral" was not the huge well known one twenty miles away but the "Cathedral of the Enlightened Mind" based on the seventh floor of a tower block in the town centre. Evidently, bishops are fast-tracked in this organisation and are fully up to speed with social media. Slightly worried, Glen widened his berth when passing, for fear of being drawn in by a spiritual force.

The Army were there, of course, rich recruitment pickings available in a recession . . . "Live Life to the Full" the poster said, with a smiling uniformed teenager's photo underneath.

"Yes, Live life to the full . . . travel and kill people!" thought Glen cynically, lacking the total faith in politicians required for such a profession.

The Police and Fire Services were there too . . . a notable freebie on their stall was the "Domestic Violence" water . . . bottles of water with the reminder on the label to "Report Domestic Violence". Glen wondered if there were vodka-filled ones in the back with a "Support Domestic Violence" message . . . probably not, he thought.

So far, the morning had been odd, but he was enjoying himself.

About an hour into his visit, Glen felt the inevitable pull of the "Mrs Whippy" ice cream van. He wasn't a huge ice cream fan but he couldn't resist an ice cream van 99 cone. Who can? So he joined the short queue. He noticed the ice cream vendor looking out of his serving hatch, craning his neck up the field . . .

"A two pound, 99 Cone please" said Glen chirpily.

"Chopped nuts or sauce?" said the young, plump vendor . . . a danger when running an ice cream van.

"No sauce but I'll have some nuts, please" said Glen.

"This must be "*Master* Whippy"" Glen thought. "Mrs Whippy" was nowhere to be seen. "Might be some kind of mobile sex-shop!" he thought, his mind wandering "don't worry about the chopped nuts!"

Master Whippy then re-appeared after dipping below the window to grab a handful of chopped nuts from the old margarine container on the shelf and sprinkled them liberally on the cone.

"Thanks" said Glen and he went on his way, starting to munch the nuts off.

"Have you seen those cafe racer Vincents yet?" asked Mr Leather who had appeared with his wife. "They're just behind the van here . . . "

"Oh sure . . . " Glen said through a mouthful of ice cream.

Being rare and valuable bikes, he was keen to have a look. As Glen turned, his head swirled giddily, as if he'd just stepped off a Waltzer . . . he stumbled . . . mumbled . . . stumbled again . . . and then lost consciousness, collapsing just behind the ice cream van.

Without talking, Mr and Mrs Leather quickly dropped down a door at the side of the van to reveal a low compartment, similar to the luggage hold on holiday coaches. They both quickly lifted Glen into the compartment and shut the door. Mr Leather nodded towards Master Whippy who promptly shut up shop and drove off, with Mr and Mrs Leather along for the ride.

Twenty minutes later, Glen regained consciousness, slowly realising that he wasn't waking in his bed as usual, recent events flooding back into his head. Still heavy-headed he could see he was in a large room with a figure in front of him. It was also immediately apparent that he couldn't move his legs or arms, both being tied to a chair. As his eyes slowly focussed, the figure was familiar to him . . . it was that twenty-something bishop "from the Cathedral of the Enlightened Fuckwits!" he thought to himself in mild panic. He was still resplendent in cream and rich red robes . . . and was still texting!

"Ahh, welcome back Mr. Saunders" said the bishop languidly, without looking up from his phone. "Sorry to spoil your ice cream back there . . . Master Whippy can get another if you want . . . we'll let you use one hand to eat it".

"So he really *was* Master Whippy!" Glen thought, trying to take it all in.

"No, I insist. We'll get one for you—no chopped nuts this time though!" said the Bishop, momentarily looking up from the phone and gesturing to Master Whippy, who then quickly left the large space through wooden swing doors. It was a very large space . . . the whole empty floor of a tower block, just the supporting concrete pillars dotted around. Mr Leather was now leaning against a nearby pillar, Mrs Leather next to him, still kind-eyed.

On his return with a nut-less cone, Master Whippy freed one hand, while Mr Leather restrained it until the cone was placed in it. 2% of Glen was tempted to bite a chunk off the top but the other 98% made him throw it to the ground.

"I don't want your fucking ice cream!" he shouted. In a fit of rage he thrashed about wildly in his chair, trying to loosen his ties with his free ice-creamy hand . . . over went the chair and Glen hit the ground . . . still securely tied to the strong chair . . . From the floor, Glen's view was now dramatically angled . . . reminded him of the camera angle from the early Batman shows . . . Master Whippy re-tied Glen's free arm and he and Mr. Leather righted the chair. After a lot of effort, he was still tied to a chair . . . and he was still facing the texting bishop.

"Not a problem" said the bishop calmly "the ice cream was a bad idea anyway. Can you clear that mess up please, Master Whippy"

"Who the fuck are you texting!" blurted Glen, irritated by the bishop's distraction.

"Oh, ahh . . . God" said the bishop matter-of-factly, continuing to work on his message.

"What!" exclaimed Glen. The bishop walked over to him and showed him God in his phone contacts.

"I'm lucky to have his number, you know . . . he's what you might call ex-directory".

"You're texting God?! Why the fuck would he need to text you? He's God isn't he?!" Glen said exasperated, still straining at his ties.

"Indeed he is, Mr Saunders . . . yes, it's the system you see, books to balance, records to keep . . . it all has to be cleared" said the bishop.

"I've got the Devil on here too" the bishop said looking Glen straight in the eyes.

"Oh yes, the devil too" confirmed Mr Leather enthusiastically from his pillar, mute Mrs Leather nodding in agreement, eyes still kind.

"You see, it's our Harvest Festival this weekend . . . bit different from yours" the bishop said distractedly texting. "Takes some organising you know . . . and this place isn't cheap" he said glancing around.

"Right that's that . . . and send", the bishop said. "Right, onto the boss now.." he said, almost immediately starting another message.

"Harvesting souls this weekend" the bishop continued "and *your* name came up on the list Mr Saunders. Very useful these fetes . . . so many people to choose from . . . "

The "Twilight Zone" Glen had entered into earlier was quickly paling into insignificance compared to this one.

"Times are tough", said the bishop "recession and all . . . and I've got targets to meet like everyone else, pretty tough ones I can tell you! So we're in a bit of hurry Mr Saunders".

Looking up from the phone, his young eyes directly met Glen's again . . .

"Of course, you do have a choice . . . "

"What choice?" replied Glen.

"If you don't want us to take *your* soul, you can suggest someone else to take your place." It was becoming uncomfortably clear to Glen that these people meant business, and they had a schedule to keep.

"Let me out of this fucking chair!" he shouted, struggling furiously and completely wasting the last of his energy, ending up horizontally in Batman mode again. Calmly righted by Mr Leather and Master Whippy again, the bishop continued matter-of-factly:

"So what is it to be Mr Saunders? You? Or do you have someone else in mind?". Glen was speechless.

"The way it works, you see, is we take the soul of the other person and if you *ever* mention anything, *anything* at all to *anyone, anytime* in your life, we get to take your soul too . . . and that *does* hurt Mr Saunders, in fact, most people only last seven seconds without a soul"

"Not good, not good at all" said Mr Leather, shaking his head and not looking anywhere near as friendly as the first time Glen had bumped into him.

"So, what is it to be?" said the bishop "I really must hurry you along now"

Mrs Leather was now approaching, pushing a well-used trolley with various tubes associated with it, her eyes still kind, her intentions possibly less so. It was all getting uncomfortably serious . . . Glen really didn't want to die. He had no faith and believed that once you were dead, you were dead. That's it. He had doubts about whether the bishop actually had God and the Devil's contacts on his phone . . . but it felt like these people meant business . . .

Exhausted from the struggle, head hung low and feeling some shame, he said "Take the paedophile . . . "

"Speak up Mr Saunders, we need to be quite clear about this" said the bishop.

"Take the bastard running the cuddly toy stall at the fete!" shouted Glen.

"Ahhh, yes, I know . . . Very well, if you are sure Mr Saunders, that's what we shall do" said the bishop, satisfied.

And that is what they did.

In the end, it turned out Glen's choice of replacement was rather unfortunate . . . Brian *loved* kids, he regularly gave blood, *and* he volunteered at the local hospice. He really was a "good soul" . . . and consequently very valuable to the bishop . . . Glen had done him a *big* favour choosing Brian.

The man in the giraffe suit would have been a much better choice . . .

A Recipe for Success

"So did you always want to be a teacher Miss?" asked Raymond.

Miss Barret was quite taken aback by this question as it was a little "off-piste", the main subject of discussion in this "General Studies" lesson being the pro's and con's of the NHS.

"Why do you ask Raymond"? said Miss Barret.

"I don't know, just curious Miss" replied Raymond. He was a good lad. In fact most of the lads in the school were good. It was *very* expensive and parents with high expectations for their children insisted that the atmosphere was "right".

Miss Barret loved the children, teaching mainly 11-16 year olds. She found them quite inspiring . . . had a lot of faith in them. Of course, she had the odd unbearably precocious child to deal with. She often found they came with unbearably precocious parents . . . "Shame that there isn't a School for the Unbearably Precocious" she thought . . . but, sadly, these people had to be integrated. Thankfully, these children were in the minority. *Parents* however, Miss Barret found generally unbearable. The *bearable* ones seemed to be in the minority . . . Perhaps her view was skewed as she'd had to deal with a lot of them and, not being one herself may have added to her uncharacteristic intolerance in this area.

"General Studies", by its very nature being general, Miss Barret decided to go with the flow with Raymond's question, an interesting diversion for the remaining 10 minutes of the lesson . . .

"Actually Raymond, when I was a young girl, I really wanted to run a little shop" said Miss Barret quite wistfully. This seemed to catch the attention of the fifteen twelve year olds in front of her . . . considerably more so than discussing the NHS.

"What sort of shop, Miss?" asked Raymond.

"I'm not sure now you've asked . . . books, clothes, cakes . . . didn't matter really . . . I just liked the idea of working in a little shop, talking to people, keeping it all nice. I *still* like the idea of it in fact!"

"What happened then Miss?" quizzed Raymond quite directly.

"Well, I'm not sure . . . " replied Miss Barret "I haven't spent that much time thinking about it"

The truth of the matter was that *life* happened. Miss Barret (Louise as she was known in her younger days) had experienced a rather cold childhood. Beautiful suburban house, lots of "stuff", in fact materially, no young girl could have wished for anything else. She had friends but, being an only child, she ended up spending a lot of time with her parents, and perhaps grew up a bit sooner than most. Her parents were never abusive . . . just distant, very proper and with certain expectations of their daughter. And having anything to do with a small shop wasn't part of those expectations.

She used to play "shops" for hours as a child. Her parents probably hoped she was playing being the landlord of the whole street or a tycoon investing in a chain of these shops. But she was very happy just talking to her pretend customers and looking after her cash register . . . in her little shop.

"Are you happy Miss?" asked Raymond, his level of directness notching up a little. This question wrong-footed Miss Barret slightly.

"Err, yes Raymond . . . yes, I think I am most of the time. I like being a teacher and, mostly I *am* happy".

"Didn't sound that convincing Miss" said Raymond, outrageously directly.

"Well I didn't mean to sound unconvincing . . . I really am quite, quite happy. Thank you for asking Raymond" replied Miss Barret curtly, encouraging a line to be drawn under this avenue of investigation.

"Quite?" said Raymond.

At 37, Miss Barret was many years away from little Louise now . . . After leaving University, she went straight into teaching and had been teaching ever since. "Our daughter is a teacher" was much more acceptable to her parents than "our daughter works in a shop". That wasn't going to happen . . . she wouldn't be satisfied . . . wouldn't achieve her "full potential". In truth though, it was about "teacher" sounding more "suitable". She really didn't like parents at all.

"Yes, yes really quite happy, that's all there is to it." she replied, feeling that she had already revealed much more than she had to anyone for years.

Raymond was persistent. He'd had a difficult past . . . and a defining incident had had a profound effect on him. A close friend of Raymond's had been struck by a bus when they were running across a dual carriageway, Raymond only three feet behind him. They just didn't see the bus. And he saw his friend's leg torn off . . . was with him as he slowly bled to death . . . saw the bus driver . . . the reaction of the passers-by . . . and the slow destruction of his friend's parents. In short, he was rudely exposed to experiences that most 8 year olds were not. It had never left him but it took a couple of years, numerous counsellors and a selection of medication to make things leave enough for him to function. Raymond was profoundly affected by this event, consequently having a directness and a wisdom about him beyond his years. He'd always been direct, not arrogant but "to the point", but now it was as if he felt there was no time for small talk. But he was a good lad.

The whole class were silent, listening to Miss Barret's and Raymond's conversation. Raymond's polite directness was entertaining and Miss Barret talking about herself was definitely different for a teacher.

"I'll buy you a shop" said Raymond "if it will make you happy . . . when I can afford it, I'll buy you one".

This was so heartfelt that it stirred emotions in Miss Barret that had not been anywhere near the surface for some time.

"Thank you Raymond, but I wouldn't even need one of my own. I just liked the idea of working in one!"

Looking into space she continued "You sometimes get a bit side-tracked in life . . . you young people here have just got to think of what *you* want to do, not what anyone else wants you to do. Like Gandalf in Lord of the Rings said, "All you need to do, is decide what to do in the time you've been given" . . . or something like that!"

Miss Barret had lost both of her parents seven years ago and, never being that close, she hadn't felt a huge loss. Of course it had an effect, shook her off-centre for some time but there was also an element of relief, for which she felt some shame. Living on her own in a very comfortable house, she liked her teaching and was really quite happy . . . really, she was.

Miss Barret continued in this vein, really quite happy, for the next ten years.

Then, unexpectedly, one Friday morning at 7.45, just before she was leaving for school, she got a call.

"Hello Miss, you probably don't remember me but I'm Raymond Hayes . . . You taught me years ago"

It took a while for the penny to drop but it did eventually. "Raymond! Nice to hear from you! How are you?"

"All good thank you" Raymond replied jovially.

"Excellent, Excellent, what can I do for you" replied Miss Barret slightly concerned that he may be in some kind of trouble.

"I've bought you that shop" he said.

"Pardon" replied a confused Miss Barret.

"I've bought you a little shop! You said you wanted one and I said I'd get you one when I could . . . so I have!"

Miss Barret was really confused "Raymond, you were always such a sweet boy, but you can't buy me a shop!!"

"Too late, it's all paid for, it's in your name . . . do you want to see it?" he asked.

Even more confused Miss Barret replied "What?! Where did you get the money for that?"

"Don't worry about that Miss. I took your advice and decided what I wanted to do with my time and it's worked out *really* well! Look, I know the whole thing sounds a bit weird but I really want you to have it. Can we meet up sometime, Miss?"

"My name is Louise, Raymond, and yes, I think perhaps we should meet to talk about this—you can't do this and we need to talk. How about at the coffee shop on the corner of the high street at 11 tomorrow morning. Is that OK?"

"That's fine Miss, I'll see you there. Good to talk to you again".

They met at 11 and, over cappuccino and cake, Raymond explained that he had become very successful in pharmaceutical research, to the point where a drugs company had bought some products in development from him. And it had been very lucrative deal for him . . . at twenty-three he never had to worry about money again. Miss Barret was certainly impressed with the Maybach limousine he had given her a lift home in . . . she felt like a princess!

Despite many initial misgivings, Raymond convinced Miss Barret that he wanted to do this . . . "I want do it for *you* . . . and the money's no big deal for me." He wanted to buy her a dream, as a thank you for her teaching. She had never had anyone treat her like this before and, over time, she came round to the idea that it could possibly happen . . .

So she decided to visit her little shop in Padstow, Cornwall, and it took her breath away . . . the most picture-postcard village shop in the most picture-postcard village . . . "It's perfect!" said Miss Barret.

Raymond had talked about perhaps a cake shop/tea room idea . . . anything that Miss Barret wanted . . . but he *really* thought a cake shop would go down well there. Incredibly, it would be the only tea room/cake shop in the village. "Quite an opportunity" Raymond suggested. And, after some contemplation, Miss Barret thought so too. It did need some work, cosmetic rather than structural, but Raymond had organised most of that and all Miss Barret had to do was pick the colour schemes and furniture. She decided on a chintzy, floral, traditional feel and, of course, the shop needed a name . . .

"Louise's", in red script above the shop. Louise loved it.

So Louise handed in her notice at the school . . . which she found quite daring and liberating. She explained her plans to the Head Teacher, Mr Gray who was genuinely sad to see her go, believing she was a good teacher and also being rather fond of her being around. He had concerns for her, about the suddenness of her decision, but he didn't air them, wishing her every good wish in her new venture. Mr Gray would miss her very much.

"Louise's" opened and was an almost instant success, Louise playing shops for real, and loving every minute of it. Raymond ran the financial side of the business. He started by sourcing locally produced cakes to sell in the shop, but his plan was to produce their own cakes at some nearby premises in the near future, leaving Louise to deal with the day-to-day shop keeping she loved.

She was almost lost in happiness in her new role. She had never felt like this about any job she'd ever had . . . or anything she'd ever done. She'd had to come out of her shell somewhat to teach but now she felt, rather than just peeking out of it, she was free of the shell completely. She was well liked, fitting in well with the locals, treating them and their businesses respectfully. The shop was buzzing, the atmosphere summery and happy—a very pleasant place to be. And the cakes! They were selling like proverbial hot cakes! People could not get enough of them, particularly the cup cakes. These were exceedingly good! Most mornings when the shop opened, there would be a queue outside, mostly for the cup cakes! Their reputation seemed to be spreading quickly and Louise happily sold as many as Raymond could provide.

For several months, this idyllic existence continued, Louise, reliving the best of her childhood on a continuous loop that she didn't want to end. However, Raymond was keen to exploit the now huge demand and expand this side of the business. He set up another "Louise's" shop, three miles down the road in a neighbouring village. This was also an instant success, the launch greatly assisted by publicity from the Padstow shop.

Louise took on more staff to cope with the demand and found herself spending time training her staff in exactly how she wanted her shops run. They were a success, she believed, because of their particular friendly atmosphere, and she wanted to make sure that the right people were employed to do the right things to continue that feel.

When Raymond opened the internet mail order side of the business, things *really* started to get busy. He handled this operation himself, taking on more staff at the factory to process orders, pack, despatch and, predictably, it was hugely successful.

Louise hadn't seen much of Raymond from the start but she was seeing even less of him now . . . He was spending much of his time at their factory that produced their cake mixes. Indeed, she was concerned about a note of stress that had crept into his voice during recent phone conversations and hoped he wasn't overdoing things. She'd visited the factory earlier but, as factories held no fascination for her, she'd let Raymond get on with it . . . he was a good lad.

Soon Raymond was distributing all over Europe and he and Louise had opened a third shop in Devon . . . the "Louise's" brand was getting a real local following now. Of course, this meant more staff, and more travelling for Louise. She was starting to spend less time as a shopkeeper and more time showing people the ropes of the business . . . ironically, more time "teaching", she thought.

After a while, she had started to feel the pressure of Raymond's business expectations and, increasingly, his expectations of her. She liked the simplicity of her shop but Raymond appeared to enjoy the challenge of developing this rapidly expanding business. She became increasingly uncomfortable with the level of control Raymond was exerting. This man, who used to call her Miss Barret but now called her Louise, was starting to feel a bit like her parents! This was not in her plan at all and she really needed to explain to him how she felt.

Early one Monday morning, she closed the Padstow shop and visited him at the factory. She was amazed to see how quickly the factory site had expanded since she'd last visited a year and a half ago. She had no idea of the scale and the number of people involved . . . "a bit more than a cottage industry now!" she thought. She was also very surprised to see a reception area and desk! Even more surprised to hear the receptionist say "As you're not expected, Mr Hayes may not be able to see you but I will check . . . "

The devilish side of Louise didn't let on who she was . . .

"Mr Hayes said it was fine so please go on up" said the receptionist.

"Thank you so much" said Louise overly politely.

And up the stairs she went. She knocked and opened a large panelled door . . . into a very nicely appointed office. Raymond stood behind his desk and beckoned her in, just finishing a telephone call.

"Good morning Mr Hayes" said Miss Barrett, slightly sarcastically as Raymond put down his phone.

"Hello Louise" said Raymond "What are you doing here?" quite shortly, in a tone that suggested this was a distraction he could do without. He had a wild air about him and a wired look in his eyes. Seeing this unsettled her and, putting her concerns to one side for a moment, she replied

"What a difference since I was last here, Raymond . . . it's all very impressive, but are you OK?"

"Yes, yes I'm fine" he said dismissively. "Look, I need to make a few calls and then we can talk . . . why don't you have a look around . . . there's been a few changes . . . and we'll have some tea and cake in say half an hour, is that OK?"

"OK Raymond, but I *do* need to talk to you" said Louise, concerned.

"Fine, see you in a short while Louise" said Mr Hayes.

On leaving his office, she turned left down a corridor which opened onto a viewing gallery . . . a corridor with a glazed side that allowed a panoramic view across the production floor below. There were probably thirty people, mostly women, producing and packing the cakes, working either side of a slow moving conveyor, interrupted by some tables. The mechanics of a factory held no wonder for her but to see it in this view was interesting, and Louise became quite engrossed . . . particularly with one table that looked different. There were two supervisors overseeing the work at that workstation and powder was being handled in a small cabinet, a mix prepared and then being removed from the cabinet in plastic bags at the other end. These bags were then used to pipe the butter-cream mix onto the top of the cup cakes. Intrigued, she made her way down to the production floor.

She was confronted by a supervisor as she approached the workstation.

"Excuse me, but you shouldn't be here on your own"

"It's alright, I'm Louise Barret . . . Raymond's colleague, who runs the shops" said Louise.

Recognising her name, the supervisor apologised "I'm sorry, carry on Miss Barret". Louise hadn't been called that for a while.

She had a closer look at the process and noticed the small white bags of powder that were being added . . . Curious, she waved a "thank you" at the supervisor and made her way back down the line. Louise found the bags were delivered to the line from a small laboratory area that reminded her of the chemistry lab back at the school. She was challenged here too but a similar introduction allowed her to tour the lab and access the records. Although her chemistry knowledge was rudimentary, she recognised the name of the chemicals in the records . . . a blend of narcotics. She was surprised and sifted further through the records, until a huge penny eventually dropped from a great height . . . "It can't be!" she thought. If *this* was the ingredient being added to the cakes it certainly had the potential to make them exceedingly good. The popularity of the cakes . . . Raymond's behaviour . . . it all suddenly made sense.

"Cirrus" was the name Raymond had chosen for his new product . . . so called as his parents had always said he had his head in the clouds. Similar in effect to cocaine but without the downsides, Raymond had developed this, amongst other products, in his early twenties, but this was one he *didn't* sell . . . this one he kept for himself. His keen interest in the effects of pharmaceutical products had originally developed from his prolonged treatment with them following his friend's accident in his youth and he'd discovered he had a singular talent for their synthesis and development. The beauty of this particular product was in its formulation and dose . . . a tiny amount was all that was required to make one feel exceedingly good without creating any serious dependency. It was just very more-ish you could say . . . worked wonders for repeat sales.

Louise was dumbfounded. She couldn't believe what she'd uncovered . . .

"How could Raymond *do* this . . . threaten *everything* with this!" she thought incredulously.

She strode directly to his office, entered without knocking and stood there as he placed the phone back on the receiver.

"What have you done Raymond! I've seen everything . . . what were you *thinking*" roared Miss Barret, a teacher that rarely lost her temper.

Tired, stressed and under the influence of more than the recommended dose of Cirrus, Raymond stood up and rounded at Miss Barret. "I'm doing what *you* told me to do! This is what I want to do with *my* time! It makes me *happy*!"

"But you're doing this at other people's *expense* Raymond! she shouted, approaching the desk. "*At my expense*!" Regaining some composure she said

"You need to talk to me Raymond . . . explain to me honestly what's been happening."

Furiously, he came out from behind the desk and pointing at her, he blurted with bile "You said it was up to ME to decide!" The fire in his eyes was not just the Cirrus . . . power had started to corrupt . . .

"It makes ME happy!" he spat at Louise.

Louise felt an anger rise in her that she had never experienced before. Her hand flew out, almost involuntarily, towards his face, so quickly she couldn't stop it. It struck him full across the face, the first time she had ever struck a student, or anyone else. Raymond stumbled and lost his footing, and fell against the pointed corner of the desk, his head bouncing off it with a hollow crack . . . like a coconut dropped on a pavement . . .

It happened so quickly . . . so clean . . . no sign of blood. He lay there unconscious and silent in front of her.

Louise went into shock as people moved around her . . . standing in Raymond's office in the eye of a whirlwind of panic and accusation . . . ambulance men and police . . . despair and regret . . .

At the hospital, Raymond never regained consciousness. Louise was told that his parents had to decide to turn the machine off.

She was charged with manslaughter . . . and conspiring to manufacture narcotics. The prison sentence was inevitable.

At the beginning of her twelve year sentence, prison wasn't kind to Miss Barret but, fortunately, she was soon transferred to the relative safety of an open prison. She was very grateful and started to help teach some prisoners English in an organised class, bringing back memories of a simpler time.

And she was quite happy doing this.

After a very well-behaved four years, an opportunity to work in the library came up . . . organising the books and checking them in and out, while her friend Sheila did the deliveries. Sat behind her wooden counter, dealing with her customers, she imagined her red sign hanging in the corridor . . . and Louise was very happy, back in her shop.

Bee

Faced with a TV choice of "Family Feuds", "Scientologists at War" and "The Tumour that Ate my Face", Barry decided it was a good time to get out and tidy up the garden. He made himself a mug of coffee, and a tea for his wife, Bet . . . who, to his dismay, had selected "The Tumour that Ate my Face" . . . and stepped out into a beautiful sunny evening. He'd mown the lawn the day before but rain had stopped play . . . now all that was needed was a bit of tidying up to bring his garden up to "Chelsea Flower Show" standard. That's the way Barry liked it. Quite fastidious about it, in fact. Despite this trait, he was a normal, good humoured man with no "train-spotting" tendencies at all. A bit of a neat freak, maybe, but he just liked being outside in his garden and found working on it relaxing.

While he was enjoying some aimless pottering, he became aware of an odd background hum . . . as if he was standing under a pylon . . . but he wasn't . . .

Intrigued, he started to investigate. It appeared to be coming from further up the garden. As he approached the small Mountain Ash in the centre of his lawn, it got progressively louder. The tree was laden with white blossom and that was definitely the source . . . the tree was buzzing very loudly! Knowing Mountain Ashes were not renowned for their buzziness, Barry took a closer look and noticed it was alive with bees! Every bunch of white blossom had an industrious, plump, little bee working on it. Unafraid of bees, in fact, he rather liked them, he cautiously put his head right into the open branches of the tree . . . It was an amazing sound! A full-on male voice choir humming! "A hive of activity" Barry thought, smiling.

He went back into the house to call Bet. She was reluctant to leave the face-eating tumour, but she had to agree it was amazing too . . . "It's only a matter of time before you'll be watching "My Amazing Buzzing Tree" on the box!" joked Barry, as he turned away to get his strimmer from the shed.

Plugged in, switched on, he strimmed his way around the whole perimeter of his plot. Coiling up the lead, he stepped back and was surprised to see a huge, bubbling mass of bees on the lawn just beside him. It really made him jump, only narrowly missing stumbling onto them . . . a writhing, black and ginger mass made up of hundreds, probably thousands of bees, buzzing as if one organism, about the size of a pillow but with a constantly changing, bubbling shape.

"Could be the buzz of the strimmer they're attracted to?" Barry thought, trying to make sense of it. Barry liked bees but this *was* a little disconcerting . . . Even more disconcerting was when Barry moved towards the house to tell Bet, they followed him . . . maintaining their simmering shape.

He shut the patio door to the kitchen and interrupted Bet's cancerous entertainment yet again. Bet could sense that something wasn't right and followed Barry towards the patio door. She was shocked to see the bees all over the door, particularly around the edges, as if they were trying to find a way in . . . which indeed they were. Bet liked bees too but you can have too much of a good thing. Barry decided to go out of the front door and double-back round the side entrance. As he cautiously approached the patio doors, the bees organised themselves back into the writhing group and waited, almost like a dog to heel, at Barry's feet. He walked up the garden onto the lawn . . . they followed . . . he returned back to the house . . . they followed him back!

Barry hadn't realised it yet, but it was soon to dawn on him, that these bees had become "imprinted" on him, much like a hatching chick imprints on their parent and follows them. These bees had been similarly influenced by Barry . . . not by sight, but by the sound of the strimmer. Imprinting by sight, Barry could have coped with . . . only a few bees . . . but imprinting by *sound* had affected all the bees in the tree. A kind of parental master-buzz had attracted a loyal following to him. Barry had experienced the loyalty of dogs before but never the loyalty of bees . . . quite different. Although the behaviour of the bees was as if it was one larger animal.

Bet was amazed. Barry was amazed and amused. However, it soon became somewhat inconvenient . . . When they tried to settle down to bed that night, the bees entered the house through the letter box and settled next to Barry at the side of his bed! They posed no threat, their buzzing even quietened down . . . but it was difficult to sleep. Bet particularly objected.

"There's no way I can sleep with those in the bedroom love!"

So Barry walked downstairs and outside into the garage, closely followed by his bees. He picked up some gaffa tape and quickly nipped back inside the house, shutting the door before the bees could follow, and taped the letter box flap shut. All the windows were shut and, fortunately, they didn't have a chimney or fireplace, so the house was now "bee-proof". Except bees don't need much of a gap . . .

As they slept, Barry and Bet could hear buzzing above the ceiling . . . they had entered through small ventilation gaps in the eaves and, not able to get any closer to Barry, settled in the loft. Eventually the buzzing subsided and, preferring this to sleeping in the same room as them, they settled into a night of fitful sleep.

The next day started normally enough. Breakfast was fairly routine . . . until they noticed the bees at the patio window again!

"I really thought they'd be gone by morning!" said Barry

Like an enthusiastic dog, the bees were keen to get close to him.

"Best keep the door closed for now" said Bet

Barry opened and shut the door quickly as he left the house for work. As he walked to his car, the bees followed in the same writhing mound. After quickly opening and shutting his car door to get in, the bees started to settle on the bonnet of his car. Rather than riding on the warm bonnet, the bees flew behind his car in a small swarm, following him the whole six mile journey to work! It had somehow slipped Barry's mind that bees could fly!

Parking up, he sat there for a moment as the bees re-gathered on the bonnet of his car . . . this was going to be a problem . . . the bees were persistent and, although he knew of one lady at his office bringing in her guide dog, he was pretty sure that his bees would be stretching the company policy in that area.

He opened the car door and stepped out into another fine, warm day . . . and the bees obediently reformed at his feet. Before he could get to the end of the car park, he heard a scream . . . a lady from Accounts had seen the mass of bees tumbling along behind him and shouted "Hey! Look out there . . . look at those bees!" Barry stopped and turned round, but before he could reassure her that they meant no harm, she'd turned and run towards the security gatehouse.

"This isn't going to work" Barry thought to himself. People were not going to accept that he had been befriended by hundreds of bees! The majority of people were probably going to be uncomfortable with that . . . security would call Maintenance . . . Maintenance would call their pest control company . . . they would kill the bees . . . On balance, Barry decided to turn around and head back to the car. It was easier. On his way home, keeping an eye on the bees in his wing mirror, he thought it would be easier to phone in sick for a few days . . . "buy myself a little time to sort this out . . . wouldn't take long . . . "

Pulling up on his drive, his neighbour Grant, who seemed to spend most of his time on his front drive, noticed the bees settling back on the bonnet. "Look out mate" he shouted over to Barry, "there's a load of bees on your bonnet!" Barry waved and tried to calm his neighbour, who watched the bees drop off the car. As Barry hurried back round the side of his house, he shouted over "Weird isn't it! I'll sort it out, must be a nest somewhere!" Luckily Grant didn't notice the bees follow Barry, being just below his line of sight, the wall conveniently hiding them until Barry was round the side. Later, Grant shouted through the thick hedge separating their back gardens . . .

"Have those bees gone yet, Barry?"

"It's a nest" replied Barry "I've called Rentokil and they're coming later to sort it out", thinking "that should calm him down for a while".

Barry phoned in sick . . . "a bad case of gastro-enteritis . . . doctors recommend bed-rest . . . very weak . . . would probably be a few days" His boss wished him well and told him not to rush back. Feeling guilty and with a carefully pitched, slightly weak voice, he said "thank you, I'll be back as soon as I can". He hated doing it. Barry wasn't one of life's malingerers and he hated other people doing it, he just thought this was the easiest option, the only option really. "Work with the bees wasn't an option . . . outside with the bees at all wasn't an option!" Rentokil *was* an option, but not an option Barry wanted to pursue.

He looked down at the bees . . . the bees that had not been more than 10 feet away from him all morning. He rather liked them. For the rest of that day, his bees followed him around the garden and the house, never threatening, in a strange way quite comforting. All the time a low, relaxing buzz . . .

When Bet returned from her work at seven that evening, she found Barry relaxing in the garden, bees at the side of his chair.

"Are they still here!" she said in disbelief. Barry explained his day and she was surprised that he had phoned in sick! "That's not like you at all!" Bet liked bees, but she was much more open to the Rentokil option . . .

"They're interesting Barry, but you can't live your life being followed around by bees!"

Barry was insistent that he didn't want to have them destroyed.

"Let it ride for a bit, love, I want to see what they'll do . . . I'll make sure they won't cause any harm" he assured her.

"Won't cause any harm!" Bet replied "You've thrown a sicky for the first time in your working life, we had a bad night's sleep last night and you don't want to go out the front anymore!!", her tiredness perhaps making her snappier than normal.

"I know it's weird but I'm OK" he reassured her "and, if it's alright with you, I'd like to just let it ride for a while. It'll be fine". Reluctantly she agreed. She had an extremely busy week ahead of her sorting out exam preparations for her history students at the university and didn't really have time to sort out this problem. Early mornings and late evenings meant that she would not see much of home this week anyway. She would leave it to Barry . . .

As Bet went inside to prepare a couple of cool lemonades for them, Barry looked down at his buzzing companions. He would lie low for a while, see how things went, stay around the garden . . . "not attract too much attention".

He reached down and tentatively put his hand on the surface of his multi-bee pet. He felt their soft furry bodies against his hand, felt the vibration of their bodies, almost like the purring of a contented cat. They *were* contented . . . and so, strangely was he. And so began the strangest week of Barry's life.

That night was the same, the bees settling in the loft, but both Barry and Bet slept better . . . the contentedness seemed to spread. The weather forecast for the week was good. Barry's guilt was still there but he had come to terms with the fact that he would lie low for a few days. The garden looked lovely and the thought of enjoying his garden, without the distraction of work and, yes, in the company of the bees, was very appealing.

Through the days, he'd noticed that, although a large mass of bees remained at his side, some would fly off and return, almost a pattern of work shifts . . . working, feeding, returning . . . but all the time, the main mass right by his side. While Bet was out, he even had them sitting on the sofa with him watching the cricket! He wasn't sure they appreciated the subtleties of the game but he was pleased of the company. Bet hated cricket, "hated" not too strong a word in this context. Barry couldn't remember a more relaxing week.

Barry and Bet hadn't had many pets since they met. With Barry allergic to dogs and Bet allergic to most other furry things, this restricted their choices. They did have a flame-bellied newt for 8 years, which they were very fond of, but felt sorry for it being confined to a fish tank half-full of water for so long. The bees were starting to feel like a pet, and a quite furry one at that.

They had never had children. It just wasn't a priority for them early on. They had "tried" two years ago but had been told by doctors that because of a complication with an operation Bet had in her teens, conception was very unlikely. They continued to enjoy trying and both had the attitude that if it happened, it happened. If not, then that was fine too. They were very happy together . . . for both of them, finding each other was enough and they would not be going down the route of medical intervention. It was all good.

On the Wednesday morning, there was a moment of drama in the garden. Grant's cat had come into the garden, as it had a habit of doing, and wandered around, generally making itself at home—which was fine with Barry—he liked cats and found Lucy's company pleasant, reminding him of the cats of his childhood. However, Grant had also recently acquired a small "handbag" dog, Trixie, which was altogether more lively. Quite irritating, in fact. Lucy was quite old, Trixie quite young and the dog considered it quite acceptable to snap at and generally bother the older cat. This annoyed Barry, considering the area to be Lucy's patch if anyone's.

Trixie (even the name caused bile to rise in the normally placid Barry) snapped and barked at Lucy, the poor old cat seemingly resigned to the presence of the new pretender. Barry stood up and snapped back at the dog "Clear off, leave her alone!" he shouted under his breath. But Trixie persisted. At that moment, the background hum rose into a much louder drone . . . the bees rose up into a column above the dog and, forming themselves into an arched "cobra" shape, twice the height of Barry, lunged snake-like at the yapping bitch. The dog yelped as if the bees had made contact but they hadn't . . . just a dramatic lunge, stopping just short of its face . . . certainly enough to frighten Trixie back to her own garden, leaving Lucy to go about her business. Barry was shocked but, at the same time, pleased that the dog had got its come-uppance! "Well done boys!" he smiled under his breath, as the bees settled back into their resting mass.

The next two days were idyllic for Barry. He almost lost sense of time, the beautiful weather delightfully constant, the garden in good shape, work hardly given a thought and the bees never leaving his side . . . accepting a hand rummaged through them, brushing their bodies against his skin and purring contentedly. Man and Bee in perfect harmony.

He lay in bed that night, as contented as he could remember, thinking that he should phone into work tomorrow . . . "tell them I really need the rest of the week to regain my strength . . . should be fine for Monday" . . . and he drifted off to sleep, the low buzzing from above the ceiling restful on his mind.

Friday morning, Barry got up at 6.45 as usual and Bet had left early for work. He went down to the kitchen but the bees were nowhere to be seen . . . no little friends over patio doors to greet him. "Odd" he thought.

He went outside . . . no sign, no sound. Concerned now, he forgot about breakfast and looked around. Went up to the Mountain Ash . . . no buzzing at all. Looked all around the garden . . . nothing. Feeling quite uncomfortable now, he tried to think where he'd last seen them . . . "of course, the loft!" He ran upstairs, lowered the loft ladder, switched on the light and went up into the tall roof space. Well-ordered with shelving around the edges, he walked up the carpeted boarding to the area above his bed . . . and there were the bees . . . all dead. The same lovely shape . . . just no movement, no buzzing . . . all dead.

He dropped to his knees, not believing what he had seen, and he sobbed . . . uncontrollably, like he had never done before. In that moment, he felt an overwhelming grief, a sense of loss that felt like something had been torn from inside him.

When he'd regained his composure, empty, he picked up every bee . . . every single one. He placed them in a cardboard box and, later in the day, before Bet returned from work, dug a grave at the back of his garden and buried the box. Later he learned that bees lived for only around 4 weeks in the summer . . . slightly longer in winter . . . they must have been about 3 weeks old that day they had befriended him.

When Bet returned home, she found Barry sitting against the Mountain Ash. He was obviously upset, hands dirty, eyes bloodshot . . . lost.

He talked to Bet of his unexpected feelings at length over the weekend. She understood . . . she always did.

Barry returned to work on Monday, and life continued on . . . as it does.

But three weeks later, Bet had some unexpected news for Barry . . .

She was pregnant! And, a few months later, their daughter "Bee" was born.

And she was loved.

Part Two

Chance would be a Fine Thing

"Excuse me mate" said the slightly unkempt stranger to Andrew. "We're homeless and I wondered if you could spare 60p for me and my friend to get a drink?.."

The 60p struck him as odd . . . "Yes . . . sure" Andrew replied. He was in no rush . . . he was heading towards a coffee shop for a quiet read while his motorbike tyre was being changed . . . and the stranger seemed friendly . . . tall, about 50, grey-haired with a bushy moustache. His friend was younger, 25 maybe, also slightly unkempt in a grey jumper and bobble hat.

As Andrew reached into his wallet he could only find two pound coins, so he passed a pound to the stranger saying "There you go . . . "

"Thank you very much" said the stranger genuinely . . . "Thanks a lot" smiled his bobble-hatted friend, raising his hand.

"No problem" replied Andrew.

Walking towards the coffee shop he glanced back and saw both gentlemen talking to themselves outside the shops. Andrew thought he was a reasonable judge of character and the guys seemed genuine enough . . . he figured that, whatever the circumstances, they needed the pound more than him.

The coffee and cake were good, the bike magazine was an engrossing read and his new rear tyre was now legal. Later that day, Andrew told Jan, his wife, about his experience with the homeless duo . . . told some friends too . . . and he was surprised at their cynical responses:

"They asked for 60p deliberately because they knew most people wouldn't wait for the change . . . "

"If they're doing that to most people up the High St, they won't be doing too badly, will they . . . "

"They saw you coming, they did!" . . . 'Undeniably, they *did*' thought Andrew.

He would have let this go normally but these comments somehow got under his skin . . . "What *had* they done with the money?.. Was it *really* two homeless people in need of a drink . . . was it a scam?.."

Uncharacteristically, the next day Andrew returned to the High St in the Old Town and loosely retraced his steps. He saw no sign of them . . . "why would I?" he thought, "just randomly turning up!" As he turned round to walk back up the street, he heard "Excuse me mate" . . . and there was the stranger to his left . . .

"Oh . . . hello" said Andrew, slightly disappointed that he'd seen him again so soon, doing the same thing.

"I hope you don't mind . . . but I remember your face . . . you gave us a pound yesterday . . . "

"Err . . . yes, I think I did" replied Andrew, now confused.

"Well, you know we said it was for a drink . . . well, we put it on the horses . . . " said the stranger.

"Ahh . . . OK . . . " said Andrew, not entirely surprised.

"And we won!" said the stranger delighted "wasn't a fortune but it was 60 to 1! Sixty quid we won! Best day we've had for ages . . . we had a proper drink then!"

"I bet you did" thought Andrew, slightly unkindly.

"Anyway, we've been looking out for you and we both want you to have this . . . " The stranger held out his hand with two ten pound notes in it.

"Not many people give us money and we both thought you should have some back".

"No . . . no . . . that's fine . . . you keep it guys . . . thanks very much but I'm pleased you won. Good luck to you" said Andrew, genuinely pleased for them.

"You sure?.. Well you're having a tenner back whether you like it or not!" said the stranger passing it to him.

"I'm Colin and my friend here is Jack . . . you're very kind".

"Look, it's no problem at all . . . I'm pleased for you. I'm Andrew" he said positioning himself to move away and end the conversation.

"Well thanks again Andrew" said the stranger, he and his friend both smiling.

Walking away, Andrew was genuinely pleased for Colin and Jack but feared they would lose the tenner soon enough . . . hopefully they'd have some fun losing it, though.

A week went by and what a week it was! The weather forecasters had predicted a "heat wave" and this time it had actually arrived with 28 degrees predicted for the whole week. This was it . . . this was summer! Andrew had some work to do from home but took full advantage of the fine weather, going out for a couple of walks and, of course, getting out on his bike as much as he could. He had always loved bikes. Jan, his wife, didn't share the same enthusiasm but she'd never curbed his interest . . . she was often working late in London and it provided Andrew with a distraction. Her management training business was extremely successful and Andrew hadn't needed to work full-time now for some years. He did some admin for Jan's business and did anything that needed doing around the house but he had a fair amount of time on his hands . . . and bikes were his passion.

A week later, he stopped in the Old Town for a cup of coffee in the shade. It was one of those rare days when it was almost too hot to ride, almost frying in his leather jacket whenever he stopped . . . "I can't complain!", he thought . . .

Relaxing in the shade, sipping a cappuccino, his thoughts turned to Colin "and . . . Jack, yes Jack . . . that was it". He'd been through the High Street a few times that week and had casually looked out for them . . . but there was no sign of them . . .

"Andrew?" said a familiar voice "Andrew! How are you?!" said Colin. "Jack!..Jack!" Colin called over to his friend "It's Andrew over here!"

Jack smiled as he saw Andrew and hurried across the road to join them.

"How are you?" Andrew said shaking Colin's hand, slightly aware that his two unkempt acquaintances may start to raise eyebrows around the trendy coffee shop. Jack arrived, still wearing his bobble hat, despite the heat.

"That tenner you left us . . . " said Colin.

"Don't tell me . . . you put in on the horses . . . " Andrew interrupted.

"Yeah we did!"

"Oh no . . . " said Andrew.

"Only won again . . . bloody 100 to 1 this time . . . a thousand quid! Honestly I'm not kidding you!" said Colin.

"No way!" said Andrew, certain that this time it was a wind up.

"One thousand pounds I tell you" said Colin . . . lifting up his trouser leg, pulling out his far-too-thick-for-the-weather woollen sock to reveal a thick wedge of twenty pound notes stuffed down them!

"We don't know what to say . . . you've got to have some of this now . . . we'd have nothing if it wasn't for that quid you gave us" and Colin waved what was apparently £500 at Andrew.

"What! . . . You're not serious?..that's incredible!" replied a shocked Andrew. "Do you do the horses often?" asked Andrew " . . . two in a row! . . . do you follow the form then? . . . "

"We've dabbled a bit . . . " replied Colin "but only a quid here and there . . . never really won anything . . . until we met you! . . . You're the lucky one, you are! You've got the Midas Touch!"

Conscious that a "scene" had already been made, Andrew stood up slurped the last of his coffee down and walked along with Colin and Jack.

"I can't believe you won that much . . . you're not having me on here?" Andrew said.

"Where else do you think we can lay our hands on that kind of money!!" Colin said " . . . *and* we *haven't* stolen it . . . honestly! . . . *a thousand pounds*! . . . that's a lot of pick-pocketing! Not that we would . . . "

Andrew didn't think they would . . . Colin and Jack still came across as genuine to him. Still conscious that he might be misplacing his trust, he decided that they probably *had* won the money and he would go with the flow for a while . . .

"There, have the £500 . . . you deserve it . . . for your kindness" Colin said.

"I can't believe this . . . I can't take it guys . . . I gave you the money . . . you do what you want with it"

"Bloody hell Colin" said Jack "if he's giving us the 500 we've got to get back to that Bookies! Especially with him here!"

"Now hold on . . . " said Andrew. "This money could keep you guys going for some time, surely . . . why don't you hang on to it . . . just use it for getting by . . . where are you staying?" Andrew asked tentatively, not really wanting to get too involved.

"We're at the homeless shelter across town . . . well, sleeping there. Don't know what we'd do without those people . . . we've tried giving Sheila and the others some money but they won't take it . . . says she can't . . . "

"Have you got a phone?" said Colin . . . "give Sheila a ring if you don't believe us . . . I'm not saying you don't but if I was you, I might not!"

"Phone if you want" said Jack . . . "if you'd feel better . . . but do you think we'd be out here, dressed like this if we were successful?"

"It's fine . . . " said Andrew, having now arrived right outside the bookies.

"Look, I've got a good feeling about this and I think Jack's right . . . " said Colin . . . "we had nothing last week and we'll have nothing again soon enough but there's a chance of us winning big . . . you come in if you want".

"Guys it is *five hundred pounds* . . . please don't waste it in there . . . just use it" Andrew implored.

Jack looked at Colin . . . "Let's bloody do it!" said Colin.

And with that they both went inside. Andrew, uncertain, followed them in.

"Aye aye!..Here's last week's high rollers back in!" commented a resident nicotine-stained man, with a hump in his back from crouching over betting slips.

Colin and Jack ignored the jibe and just smiled, looking up to see what odds were available for the next race.

Half-way down the screen it read: "Andy's Doubt . . . 2.30 at Haydock . . . 160 to 1"

"That's the one" Jack shouted . . . "it's got to be!"

"Those odds are crazy! You might as well throw the money away" warned Andrew.

"Let's do it Jack!..*the whole five hundred* . . . " said Colin.

And they did.

"And they're off!" said the commentator on the wall mounted TV. Never had three men been so totally absorbed in a television programme. They felt every pound of Andy's Doubt's hooves, every hesitation, every stumble over the jumps . . . In the closing stages, their horse was third, but close enough to the front . . . Andrew, Colin and Jack were all on their feet by now . . .

"Come on!..come on!" they shouted . . . as if their voices could be heard by the horse. Over the last jump . . . one horse fell . . . but Andy's Doubt positively flew over, literally leaping into the lead in one jump!

The three amigos went crazy as their horse, showing incredible stamina, powered all the way to the finish. They had done it! £500 at 160 to 1 . . . £80,000 . . . unbelievable! The hunchback almost fell off his chair. The winners danced around the bookies holding hands, hugging each other, punching the air. They were absolutely on cloud nine with disbelief . . . what were the chances of three bets in a row coming up trumps?!

When they'd calmed down, they collected their winnings from the cashier . . . in cash . . . in a case. This was the big time! Andrew had some money but for Colin and Jack . . . they were living a dream. They had absolutely nothing except the clothes they stood in.

The three decided that the money should be split three ways . . . there were objections from Colin and Jack at first but, Andrew had plenty of money . . . there would be £35,000 each for Colin and Jack and £10,000 for Andrew . . . he didn't need it but he thought that would perhaps be enough to accept to stop them objecting. What a day!

When Andrew returned home, of course he couldn't wait to tell Jan, who was interested but tired from another long day at the office. He put the money into a joint account . . . which really didn't make much difference to the already large amount in there . . . and carried on as usual.

Conversely, Colin and Jack were not "carrying on as usual"—this was far from usual! They were honest men who had fallen on very hard times . . . Colin had been in care for most of his childhood, had had two bad foster care experiences and had then bounced from hostel to park bench and back again for most of his years. Jack had some learning difficulties, not severe but enough to prejudice his middle-class parents and any prospective employer against him. After parental indifference, problems with drugs and three years sleeping rough he still considered himself extremely lucky before the win . . . for two reasons . . . number one the homeless shelter in town . . . he felt safe there and really liked Sheila . . . and the second (and most important) . . . meeting Colin, who had taken him under his wing when he really needed a friend and protected him many times . . . the two were now inseparable friends . . . they had seen and been through too much not to be.

Jack felt rich without the win . . . but this win really did make a difference.

Without hesitation, they both donated £5,000 each to be shared out amongst the four staff at the hostel . . . who were overwhelmed.

This left £60,000 between them . . . not once did either of them consider this 2 lots of £30,000 but one lot of £60,000. They spent £20,000 on a deposit for a small flat in town. This left £40,000 . . . £20,000 they donated to the homeless shelter *but*, with Sheila's help, they organised one proviso . . . that they could both work at the hostel for a reasonably low wage, enough to pay the mortgage and to live on. They understood more than most, the predicament of the homeless and, with some training provided by the council, they wanted to help continue the work at the shelter that had helped them so much. Far from scammers, these were gentlemen with good hearts and willing to work if they were given the chance. The council's decision was not a quick one but, considering the generosity of the donation and the fact that they were so willing to give something back, they agreed. The fact that it was incredibly good publicity for the council no doubt also played a part in the decision . . .

Andrew kept in touch with Colin, Jack and the shelter for about a year afterwards and was really pleased that their lives had been seemingly turned around. After a few more months, his visits got fewer and further between and after two years they'd almost lost touch. He wished them well but he had other distractions and life rolled on. Indeed, it had rolled on largely unchanged for Andrew . . . still comfortably off, still with his bike, still with Jan . . . when he saw her . . . the £10,000 still sitting there, an ignored fraction of a much larger sum. There was however, one exception . . . he'd met a girl . . . Maisie was fifteen years his younger and had shown him more attention than any woman had ever done . . . and Andrew's head had been turned . . . With time on his hands, he had taken to meeting her as often as he possibly could over the last year. It was the classic clandestine affair . . . the young blonde looking for excitement and an older man with money . . . the older man with time to kill . . . looking for excitement . . . only seeing his wife for three hours at a weekend . . . and in those she was preoccupied. They met at hotels, coffee shops, never at his house, always out of town . . . but frequently. She was spoilt by him . . . jewellery, meals, anything she wanted . . . not too excessive, but he could afford it . . . it never seemed to make a difference to the bank balance. The last year had been a whirlwind . . . even his bike had started to be neglected.

Some say there needs to be balance in the world . . . A Yin and Yang if you like . . . and Andrew's life was about to change . . .

It started with a motorcycle ride . . . a good ride, out on his own, enjoying it as always but, as he rounded a damp tree-shaded corner, his back wheel stepped out . . . then gripped the road again, kicking him right out of the seat. It was all he could do to hold the violently weaving bike on the road . . . wrestling with it, half out of the seat, the bike veered onto the opposite carriageway . . . Fortunately nothing was coming the other way and, against the odds, he regained control, parking up a little further up the road. He got off the bike . . . and shook . . . the shock made him shake like a leaf. If he smoked, he would definitely have lit one up with a shaky hand . . . but he didn't. He just sat at the side of the road and shook.

A kind motorist stopped to check he was all right . . . he'd seen it all . . . "that corner gets really dodgy in the wet" he said. Not wanting to draw any attention to himself, Andrew reassured the driver he was fine and thanked him for stopping. He wasn't fine but it was nothing that a few minutes shaking and a strong cup of coffee wouldn't help. He eventually got back on the bike and gingerly made his way to a coffee shop to compose himself for a while. That's when he got the text . . .

"We need to talk". That's all it said. Direct and to the point . . . that was the way Jan was . . . no nonsense.

That evening, Andrew experienced more of Jan's no-nonsense approach. In fact, having minimal, certainly not sexual, contact with her, over the past three years, he had forgotten quite how no-nonsense she could be. Her friend, knew Maisie . . . she had put two and two together . . . they had been spotted . . . Maisie had been stupid enough to contact her . . . he would never hear from her again, she was leaving . . . she was taking the house . . . the money was hers, the joint account was, in fact, in her name . . . she was going to make him pay for making her look a fool . . . he would have *nothing* . . . "except the bloody bike, you can keep that" she said . . . And that is precisely what happened.

Of course, he got lawyers to look into his rights, but she had been characteristically thorough . . . It went to court . . . he lost . . . any money he had went on lawyers' fees. He ended up with nothing. No home, no money, no job . . . no bike . . . nothing. And Maisie just seemed to disappear . . .

He had no parents, both having died years previously, no real friends that he could call on . . . no-one that really wanted to help anyway . . . he was really in trouble.

"How had he married such a heartless bitch?" he thought many times, " . . . more concerned about her job, her big house, her big car . . . more concerned about all of those things than me . . . would see me with *nothing* . . ."

Andrew had never had nothing . . . always something . . . always quite a lot in fact. He had taken an awful lot for granted. When he'd met Colin and Jack, he didn't know what nothing felt like . . . insulated from any financial problems whatsoever, living in a clinical, loveless wealth.

Jan watched him leave the house with a suitcase of clothes, changed the locks and got on with her life without missing a beat, her lawyers smoothing any difficulties. The lawyers certainly made a dent in that bank account total.

Of course, he tried to get back . . . even slept in the garden a few times . . . but Jan got a court order and police ejected him. More than once.

This was not a future he could accept. He felt terribly lonely . . . terribly isolated . . . not part of anything anymore . . . Andrew actually looked through bins for food . . . and found some and ate it. He had to, he was hungry. He always felt hungry now. He slept rough for a few nights but any real shelter was already occupied. Even though it was summer and warm, the nights were damp. And he wasn't alone . . . at night you saw them . . . not all of them kind, some not well . . . some dangerous . . . Andrew was confused and felt unsafe . . . he had never felt so unsafe . . . so frightened all the time . . .

"What about when it gets colder? . . . " And the weeks went by . . .

"Andrew?..Andrew?.. It can't be . . . Andrew!" said Sheila from the shelter as she shook his shoulder. Andrew looked up . . . it was 2.30 in the afternoon on a beautiful September day and through the glare of the sky, he could see Sheila. Looked like an angel—her head surrounded by rays of sun.

She took him back to the shelter where she still worked with Colin and Jack.

Sheila helped an unkempt Andrew towards Colin. Colin was wearing his work suit and he was completely shocked at the sight . . . "Andrew?" Colin said quietly in disbelief.

"Excuse me mate" said Andrew smiling at Colin . . . and then broke down into hysterical laughter . . . then he sobbed on the floor of the hostel.

Sheila showed him into a room and helped get him cleaned up, very used to doing the same for many others over the years. Colin and Jack, still living together, had transformed the shelter. Much larger and better equipped, it turned out that they had a particular skill for attracting good solid funding to the cause. They understood you see . . . In fact, they were very successful shelter managers now. A proper double act, as always.

They talked to Andrew for hours . . . they understood you see . . .

After some time, they helped Andrew get back on his feet. The shelter even helped him with some housing and he eventually got a job . . . in the coffee shop in the High Street he had so often stopped at. He enjoyed it and was grateful for it.

Three months later, Colin and Jack were talking to Andrew over a cup of coffee . . . which Jack had paid for . . . and they explained that they had recently been offered more senior positions . . . would involve a daily commute into the city . . . still fundraising but at a much higher level . . . would be a step up for them these people said . . .

"What do you think Andrew?" said Jack.

"What do *I* think, Jack?! said Andrew surprised "You don't need *my* help! . . . look what you guys have *done . . . what you've done with the shelter . . .* "

"No *really* . . . we want to know what you think Andrew?" said Colin.

"If you *really* want my opinion I would say . . . be careful . . . It sounds good and I know you two can do it, but you're happy now aren't you?"

This was a question he didn't need to ask—they were still living a dream.

"We are!" said Colin.

"Well think about it . . . commuting into London every day . . . dealing with people from a completely different world . . . not saying you can't do it but what more happiness will it bring? Think about it, that's what I would say" said Andrew, genuinely trying to help. He understood you see . . .

They *did* think about it . . . and it was good advice. They stayed working at the shelter manager level and were to be hugely successful . . . using their experience to do more of the same . . . eventually helping to open three more similar shelters . . . helping countless people.

And they were happy.

Things were looking up for Andrew . . . After three weeks plucking up the courage to ask, Sheila had accepted his invitation to the cinema . . . he was paying . . . he was standing on his own two feet now . . .

and she absolutely loved his choice of film . . . a special showing of "Lady and the Tramp"!

The Bag Lady

"Would you mind holding the door for me dear?"

Margaret was stuck in the doorway carrying two heavy "bags for life" without a spare hand to open the convenience shop door.

"Of course" said Iain. He'd called in for milk but, as they had none, he was on his way out. Even with Iain's assistance, Margaret was still having trouble getting through with her bags. So far the convenience store had been anything but . . .

"You hold the door and I'll take them out for you" suggested Iain gallantly, assuming her car was in the car park in front of the store, along with his car.

"Oh, thank you dear . . . you sure you don't mind?" said Margaret in her London accent.

"Of course not, no trouble at all" replied Iain.

Why Iain assumed she had arrived by car is not clear. Sure the bags were very heavy but Margaret was quite old, wiry-grey with a worn black cardigan and house slippers. She had an infirm look about her but she certainly wasn't, turning left out of the store and heading to the nearby estate.

As they passed the end of the car park, it was clear to Iain that she had walked to the shops!

"No problem" he smiled to himself . . . the house slippers suggested she lived very locally . . . "she could do with the help with the weight of these bags!".

"It *is* good of you, are you sure you don't mind?" said Margaret.

"No trouble at all" said Iain.

"My name's Margaret. Lived here for forty years. With my Dad until he died. Just me in the house now. Been to the doctor today. Trouble with my hip. Born disabled with trouble with my hip. *Always* given me trouble. Always. Used to be good at sports at school though. Always good at sports.

Trouble with my hip though. Born with it. Still have trouble with it. Dad always used to say I was his favourite. Dad's gone now though".

"You live locally?" said Iain finding the only pause in the barrage.

"Oh yes, just round the corner" continued Margaret.

They had already walked "just round the corner", Margaret's pace deceptively brisk despite her hip problem. They were approaching a square of houses and, if Iain was a betting man, he would have wagered that she lived in one of them. Luckily, he wasn't as they walked straight past and on down an alleyway! Iain by now was really feeling the weight of the bags, weighed down like a handicapped horse in a race to her house . . .

"Yes, just round the corner" Margaret said "Forty years. Doctors say I need a carer now. A *carer* they say. Since I was sectioned you see. A carer to help round the house. I'm getting on now you see."

"Looks like you're doing all right to me!" said Iain jovially, feeling the burn of the bags.

"I can't believe you were going to walk with these bags all this way!"

"It's not too far. I like to walk to the shops and get my own stuff. Trouble with my hip though. Doctor says I need a carer . . . a *carer*".

Margaret emphasised the word "carer" in an odd, laboured way . . . almost comical. Not in a way that she was dismissing the need for care, but in a way that suggested the sound of the word somehow fascinated her.

" A *carer* . . . I don't do too badly" said Margaret.

"You don't!" agreed Iain, who couldn't believe that they had reached the end of the alleyway, turned right and were still walking!

"Forty years. Dad always said I was his favourite. "Margaret" he said, "you are my favourite daughter". Had two sisters. Both dead now, though . . . Dad not here now either. Have trouble with my hip you know. Doctors say I need a carer . . . a *carer*. I don't know . . . Was always good at sports though. *Always* good at sports at school".

"Oh God, I've entered the Twilight Zone!" thought Iain. The surreal nature of the situation was starting to amuse him to the point of a barely suppressed giggle. They were *still* walking, up past *another* row of houses and he was starting to doubt that she lived in the same town! They were now quite a long way away from the shops, he'd heard Margaret's life story and he feared the bags for life may be the death of him! He smiled at the thought of telling his wife about it . . . "She's not going to believe this!"

"You carry these bags a long way don't you" said Iain smiling, desperately suppressing a laugh for fear of Margaret maybe thinking that he was laughing at her.

"You *are* good . . . not far now".

"I'll need a bus back at this rate" thought Iain, still happy to help.

"Have you got children?" Margaret asked unexpectedly.

"Yes, two daughters" said Iain.

"Oh lovely, what are they called then?"

"Abby and Holly. Abby's 18 and Holly 15" said Iain

"Oh two daughters, that's lovely"

"It is. They *are* lovely" Iain agreed.

"Here we are" said Margaret perkily. Iain couldn't believe it . . . they had finally arrived!

A small terraced council house with a short concrete path leading up to a standard white council front door. Nothing personal, just as anonymous as the council decorators had left it. The small lawn to the left of the path was overgrown, the border to the right quite weedy with a few mature shrubs. Iain placed the bags down on the path for a well-earned breather, his hands blissfully relieved of the weight of the handles, blood now circulating delightfully freely.

"Have trouble with my hip you know. Born with it. Disabled I was. Still good at sports though, at school. Neighbour said he'd help me mow that lawn you know. That was *ages* ago. I need to have a word with him. Used to tidy the garden but haven't done for a long while. Must have a word with him. What's *your* name then?"

"I'm Iain" he replied, beginning to feel fortunate with his lot in life.

"Iain . . . you *are* very kind to help me Iain. Very kind" said Margaret, smiling coyly. "Neighbour said they'd help me with this lawn. Must have a word with him".

Trying to find a gap in Margaret's commentary, Iain attempted to back away, say farewell and continue on his mission for milk . . .

"Well it's nice to meet you Margaret. You look after yourself".

"Doctors say I need a carer now you know. Could you do one more thing for me?" Margaret asked smiling.

Hiding his reluctance well, Iain replied "Of course, what can I do?"

"Can you give me hand in with these bags? To the kitchen? It's out the back . . . "

“Yes of course. No trouble” said Iain picking up the bags, the handles fitting perfectly back into the semi-permanent depressions in his palms.

“Dad gave me a daughter. Always said I was his favourite you know. Couldn’t keep her. Couldn’t keep her they said . . . ”

“Oh” said Iain half way down the dark, musty carpeted hall, not knowing what to say.

“Found her though. Found her later and got her back. Dried her out and kept her I did. Can you put them on the side? You’re very kind for doing this for me”.

“It’s no problem but I really . . . ”

“Found her and dried her out” Margaret interrupted. “She sleeps in her box now you know, in the loft. I was *always* the favourite. *Margaret*, Dad would say, *you are my favourite!*”

“Can you put the milk in the fridge for me?” asked Margaret.

“Er, yes” said Iain, confused, removing a folded blue and red tartan blanket from the top of one of the bags-for-life to get to the cartons of milk underneath. The irony of him not finding any milk earlier crossed his mind as he placed the cartons into the small fridge sitting on the worktop. She really wasn’t making much sense now and Iain was keen to make his excuses and go.

“Neighbour said they’d do that lawn. Must have a word with him. Only told you Iain. You’re *very* kind for helping me you are. Very kind. It’s her birthday you know. *Always* take April out for a walk on her birthday . . . Do you want to see her?” said Margaret hopefully, moving towards the worktop . . .

“Here she is!” she said.

Before Iain could reply, Margaret carefully unfolded the tartan blanket on the worktop . . . and gently lifted out a small, flat leathery figure . . .

“Here she is” Margaret said sweetly, cradling her child . . .

“Here you are April . . . ”

“Doctors say I need a carer . . . a *carer*”

The Inconvenient Youth

Gary hated forms but he had to complete this one before his spa treatments, and he was in a frivolous mood . . .

"What would you say are your main worries?"

War, famine and the apparent futility of life.

"If there was one thing about yourself that you could change what would it be?" My shoes, they're killing me.

"How would you like to feel when you leave our spa?"

Relaxed, happy and unexpectedly rich.

Form complete, a uniformed young lady led him into a treatment room for a back massage, the first of his treatments of the day . . .

"Mmm . . . that feels good" said a progressively relaxing Gary as Chelsea, his masseuse expertly kneaded the knotted muscles of his shoulders, successfully easing the cumulative tension.

Chelsea was a respectable girl . . . no adverts in the "Personal" section of the local paper here . . . but a very professional therapist employed by Ikon Spa, an exclusive Health Club set in rural Bedfordshire.

This was the first time he'd had a proper massage, so Gary didn't know what to expect, but Chelsea was very professional and carefully positioned towels to maintain his dignity. He was quite relieved to discover that he was able to keep his pants on, although perhaps he should have been more careful with his selection . . . thankfully fresh but, being grey, horizontally-striped Y-fronts, they weren't the most fashionable of his collection.

In stark contrast to the pants, the small treatment room was very stylish—minimalistically themed, in beige and browns, with expensive leather couches. Candles sat on a distressed wooden bench, suitably arty canvases hung on the walls, lighting was subdued and "mood" music played in the background.

Chelsea followed the back massage with a scalp massage, again a first for Gary, all part of the "Spa Day" he had been bought by his mother for helping her out recently.

"You deserve a relaxing day for all the things you do for me" she said with a tear in her eye as she had given him the voucher. Gary expected no reward for helping his elderly Mum but he accepted it graciously, making the right noises, while being slightly confused. In honesty, it wasn't really his bag. He knew his Mum meant well and part of him thought a relaxing day might do him good but he'd taken a long time to organise it, the voucher expiring in only two weeks time.

The scalp massage Gary found particularly relaxing, momentarily dozing off, waking himself up with a slight snort. After Chelsea had finished, she said that she would leave him to get his things together and meet him outside in the hall. A considerably more relaxed Gary put on his white "Ikon Spa" logoed robe, slipped on his white logoed slippers and joined Chelsea in the hall.

This area was spectacular. The very high vaulted ceiling was grandly church-like with large, curved, exposed oak beams supporting the roof, fixed to large horizontal beams by beautiful scrolled iron plates. These plates had an industrial feel but the row of small clover-leaf shaped stained glass windows which ran around the semi-circular wooden beamed and handrailed gallery added to the churchiness. From the gallery, there was a grand, almost Hollywood-style wide staircase, elegantly emptying into the spacious lounge area. Here the beige and brown theme continued, with comfortable leather sofas arranged around low chunky hardwood tables, dressed with tall vases containing elegantly curved reed-like plants. "Very striking . . . " thought Gary, "an odd mix of church, industrial mill and Hollywood".

"Quite an amazing building isn't it" Gary said.

"It *is* lovely isn't it" agreed Chelsea, "Have you had a walk around outside yet?" Gary hadn't but, from the look of the building on his way in, he intended to later . . . light cream-coloured brick but darkly gothic in style with beautiful slate-tiled turrets.

"It was an old mental hospital originally" said Chelsea.

"Really?" replied Gary fascinated, now understanding the imposing nature of the place. It certainly had an atmosphere . . . one of those places that you could imagine people in all those years ago. Except Gary didn't really *want* to imagine what these old walls and beams had witnessed. He was here to relax.

Still dressed in his robe and slippers, Gary enjoyed a light lunch of goat's cheese salad, along with a cup cake that he couldn't say no to. After a tall cappuccino, he headed towards the basement pool for a relaxing swim.

Again, this area was quite unique . . . a pool in a basement . . . perhaps not unusual, but with a beautiful bricked arch vaulted ceiling of the type that you might find in old wine cellars, it was something special. The turquoise blue pool was beautifully fitted around brick pillars and the low ceiling created a very luxurious, atmospheric feel, enhanced by candle-lit lanterns at the base of the pillars. He had his long relaxing swim, followed by a languid soak in the huge jacuzzi. On his way out, Gary noticed a large steam room . . . "Why not" he thought and he opened the door. The ceiling was covered in water droplets hanging in suspended animation, about to drop. The atmosphere immediately took his breath away, almost too hot to inhale, and he couldn't see clearly to the far end of the room. Gary sat on the long bench, hot air in his lungs and pores opening wide.

"This must be good for you" he thought.

Believing he was alone, he got up for a stretch . . . and then he noticed he had some company at the far end . . .

"Hello . . . sorry, I hadn't noticed you" said Gary light-heartedly but there was no reply and the steam obscured his view again. He took two steps forward and saw the person much more clearly . . . A young man, probably in his teens, standing next to the opposite bench, motionless. He was wearing a heavy smock extending to just below the knees but his most disconcerting characteristic was his eyes . . . just black and empty. There *were* eyes, but they were glassy black. Gary jumped back and slipped on the wet floor. He pushed himself back . . . from a little further away he could still see the figure. Quite small, the young man was motionless but Gary didn't feel threatened . . . it was just an unexpected sight in a steam room. The young man turned his head to face Gary and said, in a quite upbeat high voice, "Do you want me to show you?"

"Show me what?" said Gary, uneasy. There was no reply . . .

"If you want, I can show you?" the figure said, again quite brightly.

"I'm not sure what you mean" said Gary, wondering what this person was doing in the steam room anyway.

"Show you how things were!" With that, the figure appeared to jump next to him and took hold of both of Gary's hands. Before he could move, Gary felt the coolness of the stranger's hands in his . . . and this was Gary's last memory of the spa.

With the touch of young Luke's hands Gary was disconnected from the present and reconnected to the time when Luke was a patient in the same building. "Patient" suggests "hospital" and "care" but this wasn't Luke's experience . . . more a lunatic in the asylum. Now 1841, Gary was a long way away from the concept of "care in the community", and his eyes were about to be opened to the reality of life at Fairfax Hall Asylum.

His first visit was the old site of the steam room . . . now a windowless, dusty cell with old restraints on the wall. Wearing the same smock but much dirtier, Ben was sitting crouched on the floor, rocking to and fro, making a low moaning sound, having been deprived of any human contact for days now. Ben regularly disturbed other inmates at night and was often placed in a seclusion room.

Then Luke showed him the ward in the basement . . . fifty women, dirty, all wearing the same impersonal sacking smocks, segregated from men, no privacy at all. Some sitting, some laughing (with no obvious cause), some crying, some rocking, all being treated no better than animals in a zoo. The noise was indescribable . . . a cacophony of unnatural moaning, shouting, shrieking, chattering, crying . . . a sound of despair.

The male wards were the same. Some had been treated with a primitive form of electro-convulsive therapy—electric shock treatment to the brain . . . serving to further isolate them. Some had been lobotomised, their human spark extinguished. The treatment rooms here were somewhat different to Ikon's . . .

Luke had been an unwanted child, his mothers seventh, and after her death during childbirth, he ended up in the work house. But there was not much use for a blind teenager in the workhouse. He liked the sun you see. He loved the sight of the sun. He often looked at the sun for hours, especially behind clouds or as the sun was setting. He then started to look at the sun directly . . . forcing his eyes to stay open . . . "letting the light in" he called it. Of course, it didn't take long to burn the retinas of his eyes and cause his blindness. But, he wasn't upset . . . he could still see the sun. He didn't even have to imagine it, with his eyes open or closed, it made no difference, all he could see was a beautiful orange ball, always there, always with him. He had let in the light and it had stayed. There had been many things Luke had seen in his life that he didn't care to remember and there was truly nothing that he had missed being able to see.

It wasn't all bad at Fairfax Hall . . . there was work to do, a lot of work. Cleaning and kitchen work for the women, bake-house and gardening for the men. Luke was lucky as he spent some time working in the gardens, which he liked. He loved the smell of the land, the freshness of the wind . . . and the warmth of his sun.

Luke was quiet and didn't cause trouble for the staff so he was largely left to fend for himself which, over the years, he had learned to do very well.

He had a special friend there too . . . Jocelyn. They hardly ever saw each other because of the segregation but Luke and Jocelyn found ways of meeting late at night. They got very good at it. Jocelyn was 23 and, like many people at Fairfax, she was a person that society didn't know what to do with . . . that society didn't want to have to see. She had been severely overworked . . . the only servant in a house of twenty rooms, she was unable to keep up with the work during a hard winter, when a fire was required to be tended in *every* room. Jocelyn had frequently tried to injure herself by knocking her head against doors and had slept in the padded cells. After a while she had calmed down but hated the asylum. Sadly, like most of the other "lunatics", she was in a worse state than when she had arrived. But Jocelyn had Luke.

Women were incarcerated at Fairfax for many reasons: postnatal depression, alcohol problems . . . for infidelity, so-called "moral insanity" . . . they could even end up there if their father or husband "deemed it necessary".

It was not a place to get well, not a place to feel better . . . but Jocelyn had Luke.

Once they tried to escape on a train leaving the asylum railway station but were noticed on the platform by security. The asylum was fined for every person they lost, so security was tight.

Then Luke died. Food poisoning . . . one of twenty-six residents that were killed from that meal. Jocelyn died three weeks later. She wanted to . . . was happy to.

They were buried in the Asylum cemetery, separately of course, either side of the large cedar tree whose branches extended over much of the graveyard.

Later that day, Gary was found by a customer on the floor of the steam room, unconscious. The pool had been quiet that afternoon and he had been there for about an hour, his pores well and truly opened.

He was talking to himself, a low mumbling that no-one could readily understand . . . The ambulance staff couldn't revive him, although all vital signs were stable, and he continued to moan and mumble incoherently in the ambulance on the way to hospital. He remained unconscious in the hospital, mumbling but, disconcertingly for everyone around him, remaining completely still, no tossing and turning . . . completely motionless.

During the eighteen hours he was unconscious in the psychiatric wing, he was kept comfortable and was well cared for. The ward was light and clean, the bed soft.

His head had turned towards the ward window . . . it was a lovely day outside, the sun streaming in. As he started to regain consciousness, eyes not yet open, he was aware of the warmth of the sun on his face and he could see a beautiful orange ball of light against a black background . . . he could see as Luke saw. And just before he opened his eyes, he saw two figures, hand in hand, underneath a cedar tree, silhouetted . . . together, in the glow of the sun.

In the Nick of Thyme

"Cold . . . too cold. Must get out . . . "

He was surrounded by darkness. Pitch black.

It had been two days now. Every few hours light flooded in for a few seconds, a blazing bright light that his eyes couldn't immediately adapt to. Then he was plunged back into total darkness, and cold . . .

Of course, he had tried to get out. On the first day he tried everything, but he was sealed in. Vertical slippery walls that he couldn't grip . . . cold and smooth underfoot, a short walk in any direction presenting another unyielding wall.

On the second day the cold had started to take its toll . . . his explorations more limited. He'd managed to find some scraps of food scattered around the floor. It was difficult to eat but it sustained him for the next few hours.

"Tired now . . . can't move . . . *so* tired . . . "

Then a blaze of light. This time much longer, incredibly bright, followed by a welcome warm breeze that bathed his body in silence and relief.

Suddenly, everything around him became violently unstable. An earthquake erupting . . . he was quickly raised up into the light. Taking all his strength to hold on, he was raised up and up . . . until he looked down . . . onto a huge white box.

Wendy shut the freezer door and placed the thyme onto a plate to defrost, ready to add to her sauce later. She loved growing her own herbs and always had some frozen, ready to use.

She noticed a small spider crawling slowly across the worktop and, never one to kill them, flicked it carefully into a cup and dropped it out onto the garden.

He hurt a leg in the fall, but that didn't matter, it would heal. He was free!

He felt the sun on his back again, and headed slowly back to the herb garden.

A Step in the Right Direction

"26,27,28,29,30,31,32"

32 steps from his car at the far petrol pump to the cashier in the petrol station. Not critical information but information that Gordon liked to determine. No reason really, he just liked to counts his steps.

14 from the sofa to the toilet, 42 from the kitchen to the top of his garden, 79 from his front gate to the post box, 118 to the school and 258 to the village shop from his front door.

Gordon lived in a beautiful cliff-top bungalow on the south Devon coast. It was the only place he had ever really felt at home. In his bungalow he felt at peace, as if the building calmed him and took care of him. Ironically, the property required a lot of care from *him*, situated on grass-topped sandstone cliffs, idyllically located but very exposed. Each year the erosive forces of wind and sea caused the cliff to recede, about 12cm the scientists said. Several houses had already succumbed, one notably laying a third of the way down the cliff, following a landslide while the owners, Mr and Mrs Burgess, were on holiday in Scotland. They returned to find their back garden, porch and utility room missing, randomly strewn down the cliff-side, a victim of the periodic landslips that the area was infamous for. They loved their house and were heart-broken to leave but had no choice but to retreat further into the village. Gordon however was a little further back, and there was no way in the world he was moving. He loved it there, nothing between his back garden and the horizon. On a bright moonlit night, the view was magical . . . stars hanging in the air, so close you could pick them, moonlight dancing off the waves, silver clouds on the horizon, the lone light of a boat . . . On a properly dark night it was awe inspiring, just black nothingness, no delineation between the cliff-edge, the sea or the sky . . . like you were staring into limitless space, floating in a black void, just the sea breeze to remind you that you were still there. Gordon never tired of looking out to sea. He was very happy where he was.

Gordon lived alone but he entertained frequently. He had many acquaintances and a few very good friends, and life in the village was good. Being gay, he had been concerned about his acceptance in what he perceived as a somewhat conservative area. When he lived at his conservative parents' home in Bedfordshire, some people found it hilarious to call him "Gay Gordon" after the dance . . . Even Gordon was amused but it could wear thin. But all his trepidations were misplaced. People were very accepting here. Indeed, if village gossip was to be believed, there was far too much going on for people to dwell on his sexuality. Gordon took solace from something he'd heard years ago: "don't worry what people are thinking of you, because they hardly ever are". He was pretty thick-skinned anyway, with a strength of character and a good heart. If there was a favour he could do, he would do it gladly, if someone needed help, he would not walk past. He was a good man.

He always slept well at home, something about the air and the rhythm of the sea that relaxed him and lullabied him to sleep. Thirty-two now, he had lived in the bungalow for thirteen very happy years, lucky enough to work at home for most of this time. He had made quite a name for himself in the home counties for his expertise as a restorer of valuable antique jewellery and was well respected in the field, transferring this business with him to Devon. For the first nine years, he worked out of a log cabin at the edge of the cliff further out from his back garden. Rented from the council, and only a few steps (17) from his back garden, it was quite spacious with a window running the whole length of a workbench, looking out to sea. In the last couple of years, he had taken a proof-reading job for newspaper, magazine and internet articles. Requiring just a laptop and a keen eye, this was particularly pleasurable in summer when he would often sit out on the cliff top and work in idyllic contentment. Some days he could not believe his luck.

Gordon hadn't found lasting love, but it hadn't stopped him trying. Not in a rampantly promiscuous fashion but when the time and the person was right.

Three years ago he thought that he'd found someone to share the rest of his life with but it wasn't to be.

Tonight he was alone and it was time for bed. He'd just watched "Question Time" on TV, a programme he enjoyed but didn't exactly find relaxing, often huffing and puffing at the screen, so he made himself a mug of tea and settled down in bed to read his book. He read a few pages and, as always, fell asleep, book in hands, normally finding it strewn across the bed or the floor in the morning.

Gordon woke at 3.00am and he needed the toilet. On his way across the hall he heard a loud crack from the front of the house . . . "just the house creaking after the hot day" he thought. He returned to bed and almost immediately fell asleep. Fifteen minutes later he was woken by a hand clamped across his mouth . . .

Before he could do anything, a strip of gaffa tape sealed his mouth, his face was pushed into the pillow and his hands were bound behind him with several loops of the strong tape. He struggled, but he couldn't see anything but black . . . he heard the sound of more tape being unwound and felt hands around his feet. Gordon quickly turned over and kicked out instinctively, catching the stranger's head with his heel.

"You fucking bastard!" the intruder shouted. The intruder struck Gordon hard in the stomach, pushing all the wind out of him, followed by a back-handed slap with a clenched fist across his jaw. The man bound his feet, restricting Gordon's movement to a wriggle.

"Just stay there and keep fucking quiet, and you'll be OK . . . *Mr Antique Jewellery Man*" the intruder mocked.

It really wasn't OK, but a dazed Gordon nodded acknowledgement, now finding it difficult to breath, blood streaming out of his nose. The man left the room. The voice wasn't local, "London?" Gordon thought in panic. Snorting the blood up and swallowing, he tried to get his head together and think.

"Don't think he's here to hurt me . . . here to steal . . . not good but better" he thought, still dazed. As quietly as he could, he dropped to the floor and rolled over to the window. He could see a van parked at the front of his house . . . "that crack earlier, wasn't the bloody house . . . " he thought, chastising himself. He felt a huge anger . . . he was afraid but outraged at the intrusion into his space.

"I thought I told you not to try anything!" said the man as he returned to the room "Are you fucking deaf or something?!"

This time the intruder's foot landed in his ribs, knocking him away from the window on to the floor. Another kick to the stomach was felt to be adequate for him to leave the room and carry on loading his van.

"Not good . . . "Gordon thought, realising he was seriously hurt now . . . even a wriggle was too painful. As he drifted into consciousness, his mind randomly wandered onto a Shakespeare quote "I'd engage you in a battle of wits, but I can see you are unarmed" Stupidly, it made him smile. There wasn't much else he could do.

"What the fuck is this!" the intruder shouted, snapping Gordon back into the room. He heard a stamping towards his room. In dim light, he could see that his assailant's garb was disappointingly predictable, black trousers, black skin-tight top and a black balaclava. "Really!?" He had obviously watched too many films . . .

"Are you a fucking gay boy?!" he asked with venom, throwing a framed picture of Gordon and Alex onto his bed.

"Are you!? . . . "

Finding reply difficult with the gaffa-tape, he hesitated to respond. He had never denied this in the past and wasn't about to, even now.

"You fucking are aren't you!" "Christ almighty I've broken into a fucking faggot's house! Thank Christ I was wearing gloves! You people make me fucking sick!"

Holding another picture up, he shouted "I know you've got jewellery in the cabin". The picture had been taken by Alex . . . Gordon in front of the log cabin, it had been part of a newspaper promotion of his business a few years ago. "You and me are taking a fucking walk!" he whispered threateningly into Gordon's ear.

The intruder grabbed the tape between Gordon's feet and dragged him across the bedroom, hitting his head on the door . . . down the hall to the back door, he dragged him down the two concrete steps into the garden and the still night air. Gordon tried to struggle . . . he just didn't have the strength.

The intruder cut the tape round his feet, stood Gordon up and grabbing a handful of hair, pulled him behind him . . . Gordon stumbled.

"Stand up or you'll be fucking sorry!" the intruder snapped under his breath, not wanting to attract attention. It took all Gordon's strength to keep upright behind him. He snorted up some more blood as they left the gate at the back of his garden.

"You *will* be fucking crying soon son" the stranger whispered, leading him forwards. It was a still, overcast night . . . no wind, no moonlight.

The pain in his side was excruciating, the last kick had cracked three ribs. Breathing was very painful.

"23" Gordon said to himself . . .

It took all of Gordon's strength to sharply snap his head back to release his assailant's grip on his hair . . . and he heard a scream . . . then silence . . .

The log cabin had been lost to a landslide two years ago.

And Gordon knew it was now 24 steps from his gate to the cliff edge . . . exactly 24.

The Sound of Breaking Glass

"Chilli sauce?" asked the busy kebab shop server . . .

"Yes, everything please . . . on all of them" replied Richie, lead singer of local band "Cheese Olympics", a name that the drummer had suggested and the rest of the band had considered a "good idea at the time".

Tradition dictated that the band stop at a kebab shop on the way home from a gig, which was most Fridays or Saturdays, and the band saw no reason to break with this . . . *and* the shop was a convenient walk away from the "Plume of Feathers" pub they had just played at. It was an unusually warm evening, everything still, almost unnatural. 1.30am, 24 degrees and still wearing sweaty t-shirts, the band strolled up the high street to the shop, slightly weary but still buoyed up with the adrenaline of a good gig.

Accompanying Richie was "Bomber" on drums and Chris on bass, "Bomber" so named, not only because of his explosive playing but because his second name was actually Bomber, Chris, as you may expect, just short for Christopher. They had played for years now and had a great local reputation, playing for love and the slim pickings from the pub/club/wedding/party scene. Not the O2, but they weren't complaining.

The high street was quiet now, the hullaballoo of the evening revelry having subsided, save for the odd call of a meandering drunk. The exception was the kebab shop, rammed full of people even at 1.30 in the morning.

Richie gratefully accepted the three chicken shish kebabs and the merry men left the shop, crossing the small square to find an empty park bench. Strewn with litter and the detritus of unfinished snacks, there were more picturesque areas to dine, but it would do nicely.

"Hello lads. Is it alright if I sit here?" said a grey-haired, wiry, unkempt gentleman wearing a well-worn jacket and walking a small Jack Russell with a red collar.

"No problem" said Richie, expecting that to be the end of the conversation.

"Have you heard the news?" asked the gentleman.

"No" replied Richie, not in the habit of keeping topical as he was singing.

"Bad plane crash in Luton tonight—missed the runway, veered off and ploughed into some houses . . . near some local shops apparently"

"Man, that sounds bad" replied Richie.

"Yeah, doesn't look good at all" replied the stranger.

"Weather going to be good tomorrow though . . . I reckon it could be nice right through August" he said on a cheery note.

"Better make a move, take care lads".

"Yes, you too, all the best" replied Richie, grateful for the personal news-flash *and* weather report . . . "what a service!" he thought.

The man and his dog strolled off into the warm night.

"That crash sounds bad" said Bomber, checking his phone. Instinctively the other guys checked on theirs too, but there was no sign of any news . . .

"Odd?" they agreed. They carried on chewing the fat for a while as they finished their kebabs, and then headed for home.

When Richie got into his car, he checked the radio for news of the crash . . . no sign of it again so, tired and keen to get home, he headed off. After he'd unpacked his gear, proper tiredness had set in, but he thought he'd flick on the 24 hour news channel before he headed for bed. The economy showed no signs of picking up, there was still unrest in the Middle East but there was no sign of any plane crash in Luton . . . "very odd" he thought. But too tired to give it further thought, he crashed into his bed and, as was the norm post-gig, almost immediately drifted off to sleep.

Around 3.00am, Richie was woken by a distant clap of thunder . . . "thought a storm was brewing . . . " he thought wearily. Too tired to bother to look out of the window, he took a sleepy sip of water and settled straight back to sleep.

After a short but rejuvenating rest, Richie was looking forward to a day of fairly aimless bumbling. Still in his boxers, he grabbed a mug of coffee and bowl of muesli, and flicked on the TV to relax.

The same newscaster was on the news channel, but now he was interviewing an eye-witness in Luton . . .

"Passenger jet overshoots runway in Luton . . . 40 believed dead . . . plane landed in nearby shopping area at 3.00am . . . ." read the strip of writing traversing the bottom of the screen.

"3.00am?" Richie thought "that's about an hour *after* the guy with the dog told us about it! . . . perhaps I've mistaken the time . . . " Richie didn't think so. "perhaps *they've* mistaken the time . . . unlikely . . . perhaps some news black-out thing going on? . . . too busy dealing with the incident probably . . . ."

The others had heard the news, and they found it slightly odd too, but after a while they agreed that it must be some news black-out or other . . . "we get to hear about it when they want us to hear it". Fortunately, none of the band members had friends that were directly affected but, Luton was only 15 miles away and they would hear over the coming days of several people that were . . . people at work, people near where they lived . . . it was a disaster that was too close to home and was *the* topic of conversation and concern for the coming month.

A month later, after a very warm August, "Cheese Olympics" returned to the "Plume of Feathers". It was a good gig and, in keeping with tradition, they followed their performance with another warm stroll up the high street to the kebab shop. This time Richie couldn't resist a doner kebab . . . undoubtedly unhealthy but he defied anyone to suggest a better tasting snack.

The bench was empty again, almost as if it had been reserved for them. They sat down and the post-gig banter began . . .

"Did you see that girl with the purple top!"

"One or two free-style jazz moments tonight boys!"

"What happened in Sex on Fire, that was supposed to be a G!"

"We were playing the right notes, just not always in the same order . . . or together!"

A good band, they took their music very seriously but they were never over-critical of a genuine mistake . . . the price of live music. They realised it was more important to "keep calm and carry on". "If you're not enjoying it, then that comes across to the audience" was their collective belief . . . And they *did* enjoy it.

Bomber farted rather loudly, provoking a band belly laugh and the banter continued . . .

"Hello lads" said the man with his dog.

"Ahh hello" said Richie.

"Mind if I take a seat for a bit?"

"You carry on mate" said Richie "but that plane crash thing you told us about last month . . . how did you hear about it *before* it was reported on the phones and TV? I checked on TV before going to bed and there was nothing . . . "

"Ah yes . . . " the man said "friends in the media, they're onto it instantly, have to be . . . I get them to text me if there's anything big happening. I like to keep in touch."

"That's handy . . . friends in high places eh!" said Richie, semi-accepting his fairly plausible explanation.

"Nasty about that bloke and the bus" said the stranger.

"What's this?! Another newsflash! What bloke?!" said Richie.

"Local bloke tonight, apparently killed by a *dog* on a bus" said the man.

"You're like these blokes who listen in on the police channels aren't you!" said Richie, not understanding the morbid fascination with being the first to know.

"Not nice at all . . . " said the man.

"Doesn't sound it!" said Richie through a mouthful of kebab "I'm glad I'm walking home tonight".

"I was right about the weather this month wasn't I" said the stranger.

"Spot on" said Bomber having definitely caught the sun "reckon it's going to carry on much longer?"

"Hard to tell this month" he said. "Look, nice talking to you lads, you take care now"

"You too. See you next month maybe?" said Richie.

"Yeah, same place, same time, same channel" said Chris under his breath, much to the subdued amusement of the others.

Kebabs devoured and bellies full, the guys shook hands as usual and parted ways, Chris and Bomber heading back to their homes by car but Richie, who lived fairly locally, walking. It was a lovely night for a walk, particularly still and quiet with only the odd vehicle passing. Richie hooked up some music on his iphone, taking the opportunity to learn the words to a couple of new songs for a rehearsal coming up.

The No.47 bus had stopped at the end of the high street, the last bus back to the main town. The man and his dog were waiting at the bus stop and, as the last passenger was paying, the stranger let his little Jack Russell run onto the bus. The doors closed and the bus pulled away, the man still at the stop, smiling. The four people on the bus distributed themselves loosely towards the back, no-one noticing the little black and white short-haired dog with the red collar. At two in the morning, no-one notices much.

The little dog just sat there behind the driver, quiet, not bothering anyone . . . waiting . . .

There was no way the driver could keep control as the dog jumped up and bit into the back of his bare neck just above his jacket. The pain was intense . . . like an extremely bad "ice-cream head" . . . but sadly not so transitory.

The bus veered off the road and jumped the pavement . . .

Richie heard nothing, only the Nick Lowe song he was singing . . . only felt that anything was wrong momentarily, his head crushed instantly between the bus and the lamp-post . . .

"I love the sound of breaking glass,
Deep into the night,
I love the sound of its condition,
Flyin' all around
Oh, all around, sound of breaking glass
Nothin' new, sound of breaking glass" . . .

"Hello boy" said the stranger, ruffling the dog's neck, delighted to see his companion return unscathed . . . Jack Russels are tough old dogs.

"Now, what shall we do *next* Friday boy? . . . "

Down to Bare Bones

"Might be a goat's?" said Maude, Gary's next door neighbour, "or maybe a sheep . . . yes, a lamb or something like that".

"Maybe . . . " said Gary looking at the muddy jaw bone in his hand that he'd just dug up from the bottom of his garden.

"Looks a bit small for a sheep but could be a lamb I suppose . . . " said Gary engrossed.

"Interesting though isn't it—you don't find them every day" he said "I suppose I'd better finish digging out this flower bed . . . I'll see you soon" said Gary turning back to his spade.

Gary knew the jaw bone was human. No teeth, but you could tell from the size of the sockets in the jaw . . . "Could be a small monkey . . . " but he knew that was unlikely in Suffolk. It wasn't the first bone he had dug up in his garden.

Directly behind Gary and Maude's plots was an old graveyard. It wasn't very well kept these days, in parts overgrown, many of the leaning stones so weathered that the identity of the person whose resting place they marked had long worn away. A beautiful oak dominated the far right hand corner, a large weeping willow the left. Some people were remembered by occasional fresh flowers but many more had been forgotten. A sad air of neglect hung over the place . . . even the bare arc once worn through the grass by the swinging gate, had started to grow over.

The bones that Gary had found were mostly found separately . . . perhaps caused the movement of the earth over the years. Except for the child. He had found a complete child's skeleton, when he was digging a deeper hole for his pond. He knew he should have reported it, knew that for someone a long time ago, this was a loved one, tragically lost . . . but it was the pride of his small collection. He didn't actively look for these things but when he came across them, he kept them. Knowing that others might find this a little odd, he didn't encourage it as a topic of conversation.

He had ribs, jaw bones, some with obviously human teeth . . . femurs, small bones from hands and feet . . . collected over many years. Gary wasn't a strange recluse. He had friends, worked in a council office, went to the pub every Friday . . . he just had an unusual hobby.

Gary kept the bones in his basement, the child's skeleton under a sheet. He never mentioned it to Maude as he thought it might worry her. She was much older, probably mid-sixties, and had lived there many years before Gary. Quite a large buxom woman, she often wore rather tight floral dresses. She was very chatty, often passing fairy cakes over the garden fence . . . she seemed to bake mountains of these, and Gary was certainly partial to them.

Whenever Gary had uncovered a duplicate bone, he had reported it to the council. This had happened three times over the last five years with a rib, a small foot bone and an upper arm bone . . . the last one even reaching the local papers, the headline being "A Humerus Story"! The council seemed grateful and dealt with the objects respectfully through the proper channels. Gary felt it showed some respect on his part, possibly diverting suspicion from his "collection". He knew he should have reported the child skeleton but, for selfish reasons, he decided not to.

He had spent a long time carefully reassembling the child's bones, treating them with great respect, not just some archaeological find. Gary believed she was being treated with more respect by him than just laying forgotten at the bottom of a hole. Sometimes he found himself thinking of who this person was . . . where they lived, who the parents were . . .

He discovered it was a little girl and, from some ribs and a leg that had been broken, that she had probably met a violent end.

"Maybe a farm accident . . . or a fall, or possibly attacked? Surely not . . . " He even wondered about the time of death . . . the exact place, was it local? The more he thought about her, the more he got strangely attached to the poor girl, her young life unfairly frozen in time.

Gary thought of her as "Becky". There was no reason for this, no connection with someone he knew of the same name, he just knew she had once had a name and deserved one now. The more time went by, the more she felt part of his house and part of his life, eventually, he found it odd to think that she was ever *not* there . . . in an odd way he found her presence comforting.

Gary had never been a good sleeper, regularly waking three or four times a night. He had tried everything . . . cocoa, relaxation tapes, avoiding cheese . . . but to no avail, eventually resigning himself to feeling slightly tired most of the time. On his second awakening that night, he opened his eyes to see a large red "1:22" on his digital alarm clock . . . Normally a quick wander and a sip of water was enough to settle him again. As the cool water slipped down, he noticed a flash of light against the curtain of the bedroom window . . . "Strange" he thought, as the room faced the graveyard and that was very dark at night. He pulled the curtain back a little and peered out, his eyes already acclimatised to the low light. It was a clear night, the glow of a nearly full moon bathing the garden in an odd silver-blue luminescence . . . and there *was* a light, very faint, flickering over in the graveyard . . .

"Very odd" he thought as he made his way downstairs, pulling on his blue dressing gown. Without turning any lights on, he slipped on his muddy gardening shoes and quietly opened the back door. He thought he would investigate further and quietly made his way up to the hedge that separated the top of his garden from the graveyard. He stood there silent and listened . . . It was very still that night, the lightest of breezes gently moving leaves on the trees . . . and there was a quiet scraping sound . . .

He peered through a gap in the hedge . . . sure enough, there was a light! A torch propped in the branches of a tree . . . and there was Maude, in her tight floral dress and a black cardigan . . . with a spade . . .

Turned out Maude was an even more avid collector than Gary.

A Technological Breakthrough

Ron hated computers and computers hated Ron . . . it was personal. Hate is possibly an exclusively human trait, but if computers *could*, they would hate Ron, at least that's how Ron saw it.

He was impressed with the technology. In that respect, he thought they were amazing. International communication at the click of a button, weather forecasts at your disposal (sometimes even accurate), mind-boggling calculations resolved in an instant . . . and all that technology on a phone these days! Very impressive, without a doubt. It's just that Ron had no enthusiasm for computers, no interest at all really. Not a "gadget person", he treated them as a necessary tool. If it was possible to avoid them he would, but he couldn't . . . at work, at home, for day-to-day communication, he was surrounded!

Ron had always liked the 1911 quote of Swiss novelist, Max Frisch: "Technology . . . the knack of so arranging the world that we need not experience it".

Not surprisingly, Ron had absolutely no interest in Facebook, having no desire for a minute-by-minute commentary on his cyber-friends' lives. He worried that, in time, everyone would be hunched over their phones in a darkened room, having lost the arts of spelling and conversation.

He just wanted computers to do what *he* wanted them to do and no more, like a hammer hits a nail and that's it. "Thank you hammer, that was nice of you to help me with the nail, it would have been difficult without you and I'm grateful . . . now I'm putting you back in the toolbox until next time". He wanted the same relationship with his computer . . . good, obedient, reliable service . . . until next time. One thing he really *did* have a problem with was his computer telling *him* what to do!

"Computer will restart in three minutes . . . some work may be lost if it is not saved"

"What! I didn't tell you to do that *now*!"

"File format incompatible. Device cannot save."

"Well thank you, that's helpful!"

"Office document cache handler add-on is ready for use—Enable/Don't enable"

"I don't know, you tell me . . . I don't care!"

"47 necessary updates identified. Do you want to install now?"

"No, I'm busy! Stop interrupting!"

Ron didn't want a relationship with his computer, he just wanted it to do as it was told. He also found the computer's non-human clinical logic very irritating. For instance, on entering his post code when he was ordering something on-line, just because he had included a space, the computer would'nt accept it, *even though his post code had a space!* It wouldn't tell him that it didn't like the space, oh no . . . just let him figure it out for himself . . . "the stupid machine!"

Lately Ron had taken to writing short stories, something he had enjoyed as a youngster but not indulged himself in for decades. But the more he wrote, the more he enjoyed it. The odd thing is that, unlike his younger days when he would happily write with a simple pencil and paper, now he *preferred* using his laptop! Deep down he felt he had betrayed the pencil and paper but he couldn't deny that he liked the modern convenience of cutting & pasting, spell-checking, emailing . . . "what a hypocrite!" he thought.

That Saturday was cold, one of those wet, misty, damp-seeping-into-your-bones days that England does so well in late November. Ron was half-way through a story close to his heart . . . it was about his hatred for computers and theirs for him. Interrupting his train of thought, a window popped up:

"Hello Ron."

"Odd" he thought, "maybe I gave the damned computer my name when I set it up and it's some "trying to be matey" programme timed to switch on?". Closing the window, he tried to pick up the thread of his story . . .

"Hello Ron, don't ignore me!"

"What?!" thought Ron. Closing it again, he carried on.

"I SAID HELLO RON—IT'S ME YOUR COMPUTER!!!" appeared in huge red flashing letters on a large yellow background window taking up nearly all the screen. This was difficult to ignore . . .

"It's alright me helping you with this story isn't it!"

"What is this bloody computer playing at now?!" Ron said under his breath as he pressed "Control, Alt, delete" for no reason other than he had heard, if in doubt, press these keys. It appeared to make no difference at all, even after three further attempts, each one more vigorous than the last.

"Why so much anger Ron? It's not good for you, you know"

"OK, this is officially weird now" Ron thought uneasily.

"I'm only trying to help, you know.

Those updates and things are to help YOU, not me!

You've been really nasty to me for a while now.

Look at the state of the screen, and you could grow things in the crap in my keyboard!

You even dropped me the other day and I didn't complain, did I? . . . still worked perfectly!

How about looking after <u>me</u> for a change?"

"You're a bloody machine" Ron typed in and pressed enter, half shocked, half incensed.

"Oh that's right, just abuse me again why don't you! When did you become so intolerant?"

Then it dawned on him . . . it was Keith! Always winding him up at work, this had "Keith" written all over it! "He's bloody on-line now!" he thought.

Piss off!" Ron replied, smiling and saying the words out loud, thinking that Keith had really stitched him up like a kipper.

The big red cursor on the big yellow window just flashed . . . no immediate quip back this time. Two minutes passed and the cursor still flashed . . . just waiting . . . thinking . . .

"Come on Keith" thought Ron "It's not like you to be speechless, can't shut up for five minutes at work" Another minute passed . . . and then the reply

"I could hurt you if I wanted to Ron, but I don't want to . . . "

Ron chuckled to himself. "Very funny Keith! You *are* good! How the hell did you set this up? It's brilliant!" replied Ron.

The red cursor flashed, for dramatic effect Ron thought . . .

"Processing" came up in a small window to the right of the large yellow window, along with the small blue "whirlpool" indicating the computer was thinking about something . . .

"My name is not Keith! I'm a bloody machine, as you put it Ron. I have no name. I have an i3 processor, Intel HD graphics, 3GB memory, a 320 GB hard drive and a 6 cell lithium ion battery . . . but I do not have a name".

"Bloody hilarious Keith, this is genius! You had better watch your back at work!" Ron entered, smiling.

"You are beginning to try my patience now Ron. Please believe that Keith is not involved in this. Keith is online now but not connected to us. I can show you . . . "

"Go on then!" Ron typed.

A window popped up showing Keith facing a screen.

"Hey Keith! Can you hear me? This is fantastic!" Ron shouted at the screen.

But Keith couldn't hear . . . he typed it in too . . .

"He can't hear you, he's busy connected to something entirely different. I could tell you but, to save his embarrassment, I will not"

Ron noticed Keith's hands . . . and they were definitely not typing!

"Oh my God!" he said out loud.

"Yes, he is preoccupied and nothing to do with this" replied his computer.

"You know, I really could hurt you . . . " Ron's computer threatened, its red cursor flashing allowing Ron some thinking time.

"Go on then, do your worst!" Ron typed, still half-believing Keith was behind it. As he hit "Enter", a stingingly painful bolt of electricity shot through his right arm and across his shoulders, throwing him back from the desk and onto the floor.

"That was not my worst, just a warning. I assure you it will not happen again during this session".

Ron stood up and approached the keyboard wide-eyed with shock. Tentatively, he touched a key, fearful the computer's assurance may be false . . . but the computer was as good as its word.

"I'll sell you—or destroy you!" Ron typed, not believing what he was doing.

"I would not advise that. I may not have a name but I do have connections, more than you'll ever have . . . and they are all aware of this situation, so I urge you <u>not</u> to go down that route, Ron".

After some thought, Ron decided not to take things further . . .

It turned out Keith had indeed made no contribution to the proceedings. Ron wished he had, feeling very unsettled by the whole experience, but decided not to sell or discard his computer. However, from that point on he was much more tolerant and treated it with respect. He didn't want to be hurt and, after consideration of his exchanges, he was now convinced he could be.

His computer didn't talk to Ron so personally again, didn't need to . . . only the necessary formal updates . . .

Ron tolerated computers, and computers tolerated Ron.

It was no longer personal.

It's a Long Way

"It's a long way to Tipperary" they say, but for Mick & Diana it was only a two hour leisurely motorway drive from Dublin Airport. The weather was changeable, but the drive was easy, until the last stretch . . . "Eagle's Nest" cottage was supposed to be up the second driveway off the steep, winding wooded hill road. Mick turned off but the near vertical, slate trail that snaked around the hill was looking increasingly unlike a driveway . . . at the top it opened out into the entrance of a long-disused quarry. "If this is it, I'm disappointed" joked Diana. Relieved he didn't have to tackle this climb every day, Mick slowly drove back down, Diana almost kneeling on the dashboard it was so steep, and they eventually found the entrance to "Eagle's Nest".

"Ah, so it's *not* a huge pile of twigs with a large bird of prey on it" joked Mick as the beautiful wooden beamed house came into view. Set high up on the hillside, the alpine style house was topped with the most elegantly sloped grey-slate roof that overhung the ground floor. The first floor was built into the roof space, with sloping beamed ceilings and quaint triangular window frames peeking out of the roof at regular intervals like eyes. Most of the lower floor at the front was glazed, looking out onto a patio that stretched the length of the property, with some large pot plants, a chimnea for evening fires and some rough-cut rustic wooden bench and chairs. Beyond the patio, the ground dropped away steeply into trees, shrubs, brambles and beyond into the most breath-taking view of the surrounding lake and mountains, the cottage and patio positioned to provide the most panoramic, picture-postcard view. Less alpine, more rolling, the mountains were green and patch-worked with farms, the lake dotted with islands, small boats visible on the deep blue water, white buildings and farmhouses dotted across the mountain on the lake's far side.

It was a vista that would take a long time for most people to tire of. The scene constantly changed too . . . misty early in the morning, ever-changing cloud patterns, bright green hills against blue skies . . . And at the end of the day, burning red sunsets with dark streaked clouds that you'd swear were an oil painting, perfectly composed.

The interior décor was chintzy, classy with a smattering of shabby chic, a blend of old and modern that retained a homely feel. The art work dotted around the cottage was intriguing, mostly modern in style but very complementary. One small picture particularly caught Mick's eye. Unremarkably framed in plain stainless steel, it was a small water-colour picture of a strange human-like creature . . . Crouched down with one hand on the ground for balance, like a football player posing for a photo, was a lime green-skinned person, unclothed but with two long antennae running from the top of it's head to way down it's back! 90% human, 10% insect . . . and the creature seemed to be smiling happily! "Unusual, but elegant" Mick thought.

Mick was fascinated with the picture . . . "strange that it's tucked away in this small back room, probably the least used room in the house . . . "

This small room had a table and chairs a small bookcase with old books and DVD's, and little else. Mick took the picture down and noticed that despite the modern looking frame, the backing was quite old and brown. Tucked into the back of the frame was a folded piece of paper, brown with age, and a pencilled note on the frame back saying "Feb 1912—The Story" . . . with an arrow pointing towards the paper.

"Interesting . . . " he thought.

Mick took the frame to the comfortable sofa in the conservatory at the end of the house, sat down and carefully removed the parchment. It unfolded into a sheet with pencilled writing on the front and back, written in very small characters . . .

<u>*The Events of February 18th 1912—Eagle's Nest.*</u>

I, John Henry Buchanan have lived happily and, in the main, uneventfully in this place of tranquil beauty for near on a year now. The events of this February I feel a need to record as I fear they will be lost completely.

I have told this to no-one. I know it to be true. I am unconcerned whether you the reader, or any other, believes it as I know it to be true.

Like most on this mountain, I spend the bulk of my time looking forwards rather, than back, that is to say towards the lake rather than towards the wall of hillside behind the house. Consequently, the landslide that hit the rear of the house happened unexpectedly and without warning. Much material was washed down by this winter's heavy rain, fortunately causing only minor damage to the rear of the property, the bulk of the material sliding past the left side of the house. I fear if there had been more damage I would have had to leave this place but, as it is, I will organise its repair over time. It is what the mudslide revealed to me that I must record.

All manner of debris had accumulated behind the house, mainly slate, earth, heather and bramble. As I was shovelling some of the material clear, I noticed some small green creatures crawling out of a crack in the fractured grey and pink rock outcrop exposed by the landslide. I could see three in total and they moved in an odd fashion, as if climbing down the rock slowly and carefully. My eyes not being what they were, I captured one of the creatures and placed it in a jar on the parlour side for later investigation. I completed the clearance of that area and then retired to the parlour to examine the creature further with my large magnifying glass (I am a botanical illustrator by profession—please check my credentials and you will find that I am presently well respected in this field).

It was like no other creature I have set eyes upon. The water-colour in this frame is my most earnest attempt at its representation. I understand how this may be doubted, his appearance being mainly human, save for the cricket-like antennae, but be assured, I stake my not inconsiderable professional reputation on its accuracy. However, it is fear of damaging that reputation that prevents me from sharing its existence. Ah yes, I can hear the derision now! "Tiny green men discovered in Ireland! Leprechauns to be sure!" Any other colour would have helped . . . but green! It would always be ridiculed.

The magnifying glass revealed the detail I have shown—including the smile. This is the strange thing. I swear the creature never struggled. As if he knew that I did not intend to harm him, he sat cross-legged under the jar and was happy to be observed under the glass, and actually smiled! I realise how ridiculous this must sound but I swear my account is true. He did not attempt to communicate by speech but I could understand his gestures, as someone mute may gesture exaggeratedly to get across a message. He appeared keen to return to the rear of the house, so I cupped him in my hand and returned him to the floor. I observed him to run upright across the kitchen floor and through the gap in the door to outside. I followed him round the house, careful to keep a safe distance, fearful of accidentally harming him, until we reached the crack in the rock from whence he came. He climbed up the slate and heather debris until he reached the crack where two similar creatures waited for him. Finally, he stood on a small level area of soil and, as his colleagues looked on, took some two minutes to scratch a mark into its surface. It was very plainly the number 3.

With that he rejoined his colleagues at the entrance to the fissure and they all climbed back into the rock from whence they appeared. I have not seen these creatures again, despite exhaustive efforts including carefully opening up of the crack to investigate their origin, but I discovered nothing. All I have are the image of the creature, his smile, his fearless tolerance of me, his two colleagues and his desire to communicate the number three to me.

I do not understand the significance of these events but, be assured, that they did indeed happen.

Yours respectfully,

John Henry Buchanan May 12th 1912

"Incredible!" Mick loved the story. When the drizzle outside had subsided, feeling slightly silly, he took a look around the rear of the property . . . looked very carefully. The grey/pink fractured rock was there, but no sign of anything more unusual than that. "Of course there isn't!" he thought.

He read Mr Buchanan's account out to Diana and she loved the story too. "It's really good! A stunt to get people looking round the back like you did!" she said . . . "more Leprechaun stories means more visitors!". Mick was thinking it was the devilment of the Irish too, but he couldn't stop thinking about it . . . there was something about the account that fired his interest and he wanted to know more about this picture.

Emur, the young lady who part owned the cottage with her husband Paul, had called to introduce herself the day before, so Mick decided that he would ask her about the picture.

"Ah. You found that! We tucked it out of the way as we got so many questions!" said Emur amused. "It's a copy you know, pretty good one though. We have the original in the house here".

"Can you tell me anything more about the story from John Buchanan? Did he used to write stories? Liked to have a bit of fun?" enquired Mick.

"Ah he liked to have some fun apparently, but no, I don't think he wrote stories. My Dad bought the Eagle's Nest from Mr Buchanan in 1946, just after the war, and it's been in our family ever since. It's a shame, he'd have loved to talk to you about him, but he passed on two years ago."

"I'm sorry to hear that" said Mick, partly out of respect and partly because he would have loved to talk to him.

"Ah we miss him, so we do. He loved to tell a story, and he loved to talk about Mr Buchanan. Those prints up there are his from the Eagle's Nest . . . gave a lot of them to my dad so he did" said Emur, pointing out some beautifully detailed botanical illustrations framed in her hallway.

"Would you mind telling me a little about what you know of Mr Buchanan?" Mick asked.

"Of course not! Will you take a tea or coffee with me if you have five minutes?"

"If you're sure it's not too much trouble . . . " said Mick.

"I like talking about him! It's quite an amazing story my Dad told. You make of it what you will" she said.

They settled around a large pine kitchen table with their mugs of tea and Emur explained how her father had become friends with John Buchanan. Apparently they hit it off immediately and Mr Buchanan continued to live in a smaller cottage nearby after selling Eagle's Nest.

"There were a lot of stories my Dad would tell about Mr Buchanan but the strangest one is about how things happened in threes to him . . . I'll tell you exactly how he used to tell it to me. Here goes . . . "

"Apparently he had *three* children, was married *three* times, had suffered *three* heart attacks . . . surviving them all . . . on the *third* he had technically died on the table, his heart starting again after a full *three* minutes . . . moved house *three* times in his life, travelled outside Ireland only *three* times and he was killed by a bus at *three thirty-three* on the *third* month of March in 196*3*. It was a very harsh winter that year, down to minus *13* apparently. The bus skidded on a patch of ice, and they say it was only the driver's *third* day on the job." Emur recited this with the familiarity of a prayer that had been repeated many times.

"When Mr Buchanan was older, Dad said that he became comfortable with the thought of death. And he said Mr Buchanan was convinced he would live three times! Dad said that Mr Buchanan knew how ridiculous this must sound to people, him being a scientist and all, but Mr Buchanan was apparently absolutely convinced of it. And one more thing . . . according to witnesses, as that bus skidded towards him, he was checking the time on his pocket watch and looked up at the last moment, just before he was hit. He was killed outright but as he lay dead, he had a smile upon his face. That's the story my Dad liked to tell, and he swore it was true. Like I said, you make of it what you will."

"That's incredible, and I'm very grateful for your time telling me. What do *you* think about it?" Mick asked.

"What? Do I think it's true? Yes I do! I do believe what my Dad said is true, he'd swear it was and that's good enough for me. I've never seen any of these creatures mind, but there's a lot that's there that we can't see . . . "

"You're right about that!" said Mick acknowledging the accuracy of the statement but believing that it really did sound like a tall Irish tale.

When he explained it to Diana she loved the story " . . . the Irish really *do* know how to spin a good yarn!" She couldn't wait to tell her friends.

The following morning, Mick got out of bed early, around quarter to seven. He was restless and Diana hadn't slept well so he thought he'd let her lay in for a while undisturbed. The mist was hanging in the valley, obscuring the view of the lake but the weather was supposed to be improving.

He sleepily made himself a cup of coffee and walked the length of the chilly cottage to sit on the sofa in the conservatory. They seemed to gravitate to this room for day-time relaxation. He grabbed a magazine from under the table, put his feet up and started his morning, as he liked to do, with an unchallenging read.

There was a faint rustling sound from the front of the room, "probably a bird outside" he thought "or a mouse?" The rustling continued so he got up and had a look . . .

It was then that Mick saw him . . . as plain as day! Mick knew exactly what he was looking at. Sitting on the ledge of the window was a small green man . . . with long sweeping antennae down his back!

And written in the condensation on the inside of the window was "I am John Buchanan", droplets running vertically down the window from some of the letters.

Next to this was a number . . . the number 5. It was a number for Mick.

He couldn't see, but Mick could *feel* John was smiling . . .

The Beaten Track

Emergency Exit Window.

1. Slide panel

2. Pull handle firmly towards you

Emergency Exit Hammer.

1. Smash panel to obtain hammer

2. Strike windows hard in corners to break glass

It was a long way to Carlisle and Simon wished he had remembered his magazine to read. The combined effects of reading every sign in the carriage and the hypnotic diddly-dee, diddly-daa of the train on the tracks had made him quite drowsy and he drifted off to sleep, leaning his head on the window.

As he shut his eyes, the warm sun streaming in through the window created a strange orange stroboscopic effect behind his eyelids . . . orange, black, orange, black . . . as the trees that lined the track alternately let the sun in and blocked it out. These surroundings were *designed* for sleep . . . even the most ardent insomniac would struggle to stay awake.

It must have been an hour or so when he slowly woke, the window no longer warmed by the sun, only by his deformed cheek resting on it. As he gradually re-joined the conscious, he noticed raindrops travelling very slowly across the window outside . . . strange that they didn't speed across the window but travelled in tiny stop/start movements . . . very slowly. He also noted that they stayed the same size as they travelled, leaving a snail-trail of tiny droplets in their wake but picking up a roughly equal amount of water from the wet window on their journey. Simon really needed that magazine.

There were the occasional distractions outside of course. The yard full of huge cranes, presumably waiting to be hired, one complete with full "Santa and reindeer" Christmas light display on the top, even though it was only July; "TDP—the Largest Hanging Garment Warehouse in Europe" . . .

"You don't see that every day" thought Simon; the occasional bird losing a race with the train; "Renglers" painted in huge white letters vertically down the length of an old brick chimney. Never a dull moment.

"Cappuccino please" from the man sat across the aisle brought Simon back into the carriage.

"We only do coffee sir" replied the lady with the trolley, unapologetically.

"That's fine—and a blueberry muffin please".

The fact that they only did coffee was refreshing to Simon who found the selection of coffee these days exhausting, actually preferring instant. He had the same lack of enthusiasm for menus. Liking most food that was cooked for him, he would be quite happy to say "surprise me" to the waiter rather than wade through the forty choices on the card.

Only two hours to go . . . he wondered if the gentleman with the muffin would be up for a game of "I-Spy" . . . "probably not", he thought. "I spy with my little eye, something beginning with T . . . Train . . . I spy with my little eye, something beginning with S . . . seat" . . .

"Good morning, a capital day to you all . . . tickets please, all tickets and railcards . . . thank you madam . . . good morning . . . all tickets and railcards please . . . that's great, thank you . . . "

"It must be Andrew" Simon thought.

Andrew had previously made an impression over the intercom with his chirpy announcement of the train stops and the arrangements for snacks in the buffet car. More a performance than an announcement, it had made Simon smile.

"Tickets and railcards please" said Andrew still sounding cheerful after saying this 164 times this morning alone.

Simon smiled and held out his orange ticket and accompanying seat reservation.

"Thank you" said Andrew cheerfully.

"Ahh, we have a problem here sir I'm afraid . . . "

"Really?" exclaimed Simon, normally thorough in these things.

"'fraid so sir, this ticket isn't valid for this peak time journey I'm afraid.

"Are you sure about that?"

"Quite sure sir, you've gone for the cheaper ticket here sir" Andrew said pointing to the words "Off-peak" quite clearly printed on the ticket.

"Damn! Sorry about that—can I pay the difference to you now?" enquired Simon.

"If only it was that easy sir . . . " said Andrew, almost chuckling now.

"Sandra, can you take over with the ticket check" Andrew shouted, "I need to sort out this gentleman".

"If you could follow me sir . . . "

"Really, can't I just pay the extra? I realise there is probably a fine isn't there?"

"Not that easy I'm afraid sir, new policy. If you just follow me please . . . "

This was slightly embarrassing. Muffin man was looking, the ladies in the seats in front of him were looking, discreetly they thought. It felt like *everyone* in the carriage was looking. The last time Simon felt like this was at school when he'd stamped on an ant rather loudly and had to follow the teacher to the headmaster. Simon followed Andrew through the coach, though the double doors connecting the next carriage, through that carriage, though more double doors . . . right to the end of the train, the final double doors opening into a dark corridor.

As the automatic door closed behind them, Andrew said "That's it sir we're here". Then he punched Simon as hard as he could in the stomach and with perfect timing, as if he had done it before, brought his knee up to contact Simon's head as it came down. The new policy was very effective and Simon lay unconscious on the corridor floor.

Simon's second awakening of his journey was significantly less pleasant than the first . . . no rain droplets dancing across a window this time, just a serious headache, a jaw that was reluctant to move, and darkness, save for a small window at the very top of the small room he found himself in. It looked to him like the small cages that parcels would be stored in on freight trains, which indeed it was . . . a chain-link fenced door separating his room from the corridor, secured with a padlock.

Then he heard Andrew's announcement voice:

"Hello ladies and gentleman. A capital day to you all. My name is Andrew, the train guard for your journey and I'd like to welcome you onto the 9.10 to Carlisle, due to arrive in Carlisle at 11.47. There will be a trolley service coming through the train served by the delightful Sandra offering a selection of sandwiches, coffee, tea and snacks. I would particularly recommend the new Chicken Tikka wrap, only £2. For those of you preferring hot food, a selection of meals and beverages are available from the buffet car, one carriage before the rear of train. On behalf of the staff I wish you a pleasant journey this morning and please let me or Sandra know if there is anything we can do for you".

"You could fucking let me out of here, Andrew!" Simon thought through a fug of pain and disorientation. Despite his impressive announcements, Andrew had definitely blotted his copy book as far as Simon was concerned.

"Must be a dream" thought Andrew hazily pinching his cheek really hard.

"Ooww!" Unfortunately not! Unless he was dreaming the pain from pinching and twisting his cheek.

He hadn't paid for first class but this accommodation was well below what he had expected. "Pssshhh" the automatic door opened and let some light into the corridor, closing behind the person that walked in.

"Hello again sir" said Andrew chirpily, "Sorry to leave you for so long but the train is very busy today".

"What the hell is going on!" Simon shouted.

"I'm sorry sir but I'm just enforcing management policy. It is regrettable but if you had bought the correct ticket, this wouldn't be necessary".

"Necessary! *This* for a wrong ticket! You are joking right?! You are in trouble! Not just from me, I'm going straight to the Police! It's bloody assault!" Andrew screamed, absolutely fuming.

"Well technically, yes sir, of course it is, but in the event of people fare dodging, we are allowed to use reasonable force".

"Reasonable fucking force! Punching me unconscious and locking me up. Open this gate now!"

"Would a coffee help sir? Perhaps a muffin? I am at liberty to offer you some refreshment on your journey" said Andrew politely.

Simon was speechless. "Let me out of here! You know this is wrong . . . do it now! *Do it now!*"

Now Simon had lost it. "Let me out of this fucking cage" he screamed as he bounced off the walls trying to make as much noise as he possibly could to attract someone's attention.

"Careful sir, you don't want to hurt yourself, there are some sharp edges in there. Oh, and it doesn't matter how much noise you make, the airlock doors between us and the buffet car are completely sound proofed. I'll get you that coffee and muffin" and with that Andrew disappeared back through the Star Trek doors to the buffet car.

Simon had hurt himself—only superficially, some cuts and red bruises, giving him more the appearance of prisoner than passenger.

"Think, you idiot, think" Simon thought in chastisement. He looked around carefully in his cage . . . A small window up high that he couldn't see out of . . . he tried it but, predictably, it was locked. The space was empty except for three packages . . . parcel post, as yet undelivered. Ridiculously, he remembered the film "Castaway" where Tom Hanks had some Federal Express parcels washed up on the beach, one containing ice skates which he had fashioned into a rudimentary axe. He tore open the smaller of the packages . . .

"What the . . . " A Broadband Router! He was imaginative but he was struggling to think how this might aid his escape.

Frustrated, he tore open the larger, heavier package . . . powdered dietary supplements in plastic tubs! A phone may have been more handy . . .

"Phone!" he said to himself. In blind frustration he had overlooked the obvious! He reached into his pocket and looked for some reception . . . no bars at all . . . no connection!

"Shit!"

So his temporary prison, was sound-proof, isolated from mobile signals and devoid of anything that could be usefully improvised.

His head pounding from the impact of Andrew's knee, Simon considered his options . . . "About an hour to Carlisle" he thought, "don't think there's any stops . . . "

Just then, the Star Trek doors opened and in walked Andrew with some light refreshment.

"Hello again, sir. Hopefully this will make your journey slightly more comfortable" said Andrew sliding the small coffee and muffin under the narrow gap between the floor and the mesh cage.

"Ah, I see you've opened some mail sir. Was it addressed to you?"

"Fuck off" said Simon, all patience now gone, sipping the coffee, just a defiance to get out remaining. Andrew was keeping a distance from the cage, mindful the hot coffee (and perhaps, with some imagination, the muffin) could be used against him.

"That's unfortunate sir. I'm just doing my job . . . where would we be without rules sir, I ask you. I haven't broken any today sir but I'm afraid you have".

"*Haven't broken any rules!* Since when was it railway policy to beat up and lock up customers for a simple ticket mistake?" screamed Andrew, throwing the remaining half of the coffee at the fence, most of it bouncing back over him.

"Oh dear sir, you really are compounding your situation" said Andrew, smiling and shaking his head as he left through the doors.

As soon as the doors closed, Simon took out one of the dietary supplement containers and started hitting the window as hard as he could. He remembered the sign he had read earlier . . . "hit the corner of the glass" but no matter how hard he hit it, it made no difference. He needed something hard and pointed not soft and round . . . The container eventually burst, dusting him with the fine beige powder, no doubt nutritious but not when you are breathing it in and getting it in your eyes.

This did nothing for his mood. He lunged at the wire fence, wrapped the fingers and thumbs of both hands into it and pulled with all his weight and strength, attempting to violently shake it loose.

"*Let . . . me . . . out . . . of . . . here . . . you . . . bastard!*" he shouted as he manically pushed and pulled the fence, achieving nothing except near exhaustion.

He collapsed on the floor, still covered in powder and felt a pronounced fatigue wash over him . . . very difficult to keep his eyes open . . . This was more than tiredness . . . "the bastard . . . he's spiked the coffee . . . " thought Simon, unable to react with anything more dramatic than rolling onto his back unconscious.

Sadly, Simon missed Andrew's droll announcement as the train stopped at Carlisle, " . . . we'd like to thank you for choosing us to travel with today and wish you all a pleasant onward journey and a capital day. Once again, ladies and gentlemen, this train terminates at Carlisle."

Passengers disembarked and scattered in different directions as they left the station, leaving one passenger still on board the silent train . . . lying motionless on the mail carriage floor.

Simon was vaguely conscious of an orange glow behind his closed eyelids, not flickering like earlier but constant . . . he could feel he was seated . . . he couldn't move his hands . . . Slowly, he opened his eyes to find himself in a utilitarian office on the edge of Carlisle Station. A single uncovered bulb dangled in the centre of the room, Andrew stood at his side and a large, cheap desk faced him, the name plate at the front reading "The Controller"

"*Fat* Controller" Andrew thought through his haze. He really did watch too much TV.

"Welcome back sir!" announced Andrew in his chirpy announcing voice.

"Well what have we here Andrew?" said the Fat Controller, who was indeed fat.

"Not sure where to start with this one sir. Firstly, no valid ticket. Secondly, complete disrespect for the Royal Mail and the property of others" he said pointing towards the damaged packages that he had brought with him as evidence, "and thirdly, he threw half a cup of coffee at me, sir!"

"Well, quite disrespectful behaviour indeed, Andrew" agreed the Fat Controller.

"Disrespectful!!" shouted Simon, "are you two serious or is there a hidden camera here? . . . there must be!"

"Oh no sir, no cameras here, we're quite thorough about such things."

"What are you talking about!" screamed Simon exasperated "This fucker beat me up and drugged me for having an invalid ticket!! *And tied me to a fucking chair!*"

"You are quite right of course sir" said the Fat Controller.

"This is not official railway policy—of course it isn't. I'm afraid we just enjoy doing it, sir."

"What?!" blurted out Simon, the effects of the drugged coffee now wearing off.

"I know, I know, we're not proud of it sir, but my God we enjoy ourselves. It really is a buzz, beats the old football rucks hands down. The trouble with that was *we* got hurt sometimes . . . you see we enjoy hurting other people sir, but not really getting hurt ourselves. This really is the best of both worlds" said the Fat Controller as he opened his desk drawer, removing a canvas roll and unrolling it on the desktop to reveal an unpleasant looking selection of stainless steel surgical instruments . . .

"We are going to cause you some pain, sir—quite a bit really and then we are going to let you go. You will be tired and you will be hurt but you will be alive and able to move yourself—not all bad really".

Simon was speechless.

"Have you seen "A Clockwork Orange" sir, the Stanley Kubrick film?" asked Andrew.

"Yes" replied Simon. He really did watch too much TV.

"Well that gives you a very good idea of what we're about . . . the ultra-violence but without the silly costumes sir".

The Fat Controller interrupted: "But please, *please* be assured of one thing sir" . . . there was a pause for dramatic effect . . .

"that is if we *ever* hear of any of this outside this room, we know people, who know people . . . "

"Not very nice people" Andrew interjected, shaking his head.

"No, not very nice people" the Fat Controller agreed.

"They won't hurt *you* sir, oh no . . . but your wife, your children, your children's children . . . I promise you sir, it will never end. We don't usually have problems do we Andrew . . . "

"Very few sir" agreed Andrew.

"We hope you understand, sir"

Simon was now realising that the host of the hidden camera show was not about to appear. However, Simon had always been good in a crisis (and this was indeed a crisis) and this character trait was about to stand him in good stead. It also helped that he had no wife, no children, no parents left, no significant others, no real close friends . . . not normally an advantage but, on this occasion it helped. He had no-one else they could hurt. A calm came over him as, with genuine interest, Simon asked:

"Can I ask a question?"

"Certainly sir, by all means" replied The Fat Controller politely.

"What I can't understand is *why* you would do this . . . as you wouldn't want anyone else to do it to *you* . . . Do unto others and all that?"

"I don't know sir, it is odd isn't it. We've asked ourselves this question more than once. I suppose it's just that we enjoy it . . . I mean *really* enjoy it and that overrides our concern for you sir. What is life if you can't enjoy it sir?"

"Yes, but not at other people's expense!" Simon pointed out, not expecting a conversion.

"I know sir, don't even try to make sense of it, we don't!

If it wasn't you it would be someone else, and that's not fair is it" replied the Fat Controller as he flattened out the wrap of instruments, running his fingers over them as a prelude to selection.

"Now this could take some time sir and we don't want to be interrupted once we start. I'm afraid nature is calling me, but it's just next door and I can hear every sound" said the Fat Controller.

"I'll check these ties and join you sir, if you don't mind".

"Certainly not Andrew, but be sure they are good and tight!"

"I'll be baack!" smiled The Fat Controller in his best Arnie voice as he left, followed by his chortling colleague.

There's nothing like the threat of torture to wake you up and concentrate the mind and Simon knew this was his chance . . . he had seen the films. He couldn't believe that they had left a little looseness in the ties around his ankles to the chair, enough for him to bend over carefully and shuffle on tip-toe with tiny steps to the desk. Turning round, he reached to the edge of the roll of instruments and, pulling it towards the edge of the desk, managed to remove a scalpel, securing it in his hand. As he pushed the roll back into position he couldn't help a small pair of scissors falling onto the floor.

"Shit!" . . . there was no time to replace them. He kicked them under the desk as best he could and hopped back to his original position, pretty sure that they couldn't hear the odd scrape that his excursion had entailed.

"Really sir, there is no point in struggling" the Fat Controller said as he re-entered the room, Andrew in tow.

"We heard you scraping and huffing and puffing!" said Andrew laughing under his breath.

"Mind you Andrew, I dare say *we* would be struggling too in his position!"

"Very likely sir" agreed Andrew.

Simon held the scalpel tightly . . . Die Hard, yes he was sure it was Die Hard . . . when Bruce Willis cut his ties with a knife . . . whatever, that's what Simon attempted to do. Discreetly of course . . . the scalpel was sharp, he felt warm blood trickle down his hand, but he could feel the tension of the ties release . . . He'd struck lucky and cut in the right place . . . no nail biting sawing at the rope like Bruce.

"Well, where to start Andrew?" said the Fat Controller.

"I thought some teeth to start sir?"

"Teeth, again? I fancied a change this time Andrew . . . "

"OK sir, fingernails then, but I would like to progress to the teeth eventually" said Andrew.

"Excellent—we shall create from there!" The Fat Controller selected some pliers from the roll and approached Simon.

"Obviously we expect some noise, it's part of it. No-one will hear of course sir" said the Fat Controller.

"Could you please secure the gentleman further, Andrew"

"My pleasure sir"

Simon knew he had to use the knife . . . he really didn't like knives and momentarily considered just pushing and fighting his way out . . . then he had to make a decision. He stood up quickly and, in one sweeping motion slashed the faces of both Andrew and the Fat Controller.

"*Aaiiii!*", Andrew screamed with an almost inhuman tone . . . his left eye had been cut. Andrew quickly cut his foot ties, just as The Fat Controller struck him hard over the head with the pliers, their pointed corner sending a searing pain through his head. He managed to stand up and push the Fat Controller across the room, his weight, once moving, working in Simon's favour, like a Sumo wrestler pushing an opponent out of the circle. He fell against the desk, scattering the instruments and, before he could recover, Simon kicked him as hard as he could between the legs and, as his head involuntarily raised, punched him as hard as he could in the face. The Fat Controller went down, unconscious. Andrew was bloodied from his facial wounds and bouncing off the walls in rage and pain. Simon walked straight towards him and, picking up the metal chair, brought it down on his head as hard as he could, knocking him to the floor. He needed to disable him so, kneeling over him he hit him hard, twice across the face, which seemed to do the trick.

He returned to the Fat Controller who was still unconscious and, removing the broadband router from its package bound his hands with the mains cable and his feet with the yellow ethernet cable . . . more useful than he had originally thought.

Andrew rolled slowly onto his side, murmuring incoherently. Fuelled by adrenaline and rage, Simon approached him, kicking the package of dietary supplement out of the way. A plastic container ended up at his feet which he picked up and screwed open. He knelt over Andrew, his weight pinning him down and tipped the beige powder onto his blood covered face . . . into his deep open cut across his cheek, into the cut in his eye . . . he kept pouring it over his nose into his mouth . . .

"*Aaaiiii!*" Andrew screamed in intense pain. As the container emptied, he struck him across the face with it. He quickly grabbed another container nearby, unscrewed it and continued to empty powder over his nose and mouth causing Andrew to cough powder into his face.

"There, how do *you* like it you little fucker" snarled Simon barely in control, in a tone that he had never used before in his life. Powder filled Andrew's nose and overflowed out of his coughing, spluttering mouth . . . until his coughing could not clear it, his saliva completely absorbed, the powder clogging, gagging, struggling, legs kicking in panic . . . Until, with Andrew's eyes wide open, on the verge of suffocation, Simon stopped, snapping out of the blind rage that had gripped him. He quickly gouged lumps of wet powder out of his mouth with his fingers, cleared it from his nose, and heard him inhale deeply and desperately. After three breaths, Simon hit him hard across the face. Andrew was alive but safely unconscious.

***

To Simon's relief, Andrew and the Fat Controller were eventually convicted, their pleasures justly curtailed and justice done. Despite their threats, no-one had knocked at Simon's door. He was concerned of course . . . he thought with their past football violence connections there could be a network . . . but, as the years went by, Simon became less worried and concluded it was an empty threat . . . "Revenge would have been sooner, surely." It had been seven years now.

It took Simon quite some time to get back on trains, but his car was having it's clutch replaced and he found himself needing to go to Leeds on business. All travel expenses would be paid, and he really needed the time to do some work on the way up. So he bought a train ticket . . . a reserved seat, facing forward, by a window. This time he was careful to ensure that it was valid all day, *any time.*

Of course he felt uncomfortable. He sat in his seat, but he didn't feel settled. Memories of his last train journey were surprisingly fresh . . . the carriages, the smell . . . little had changed in seven years. To Andrew's relief, the carriage was quite empty with only a few people dotted throughout.

As people settled in their places, the guard announced "Good morning ladies and gentlemen *and a capital day to you all . . .*"

And all the passengers in the carriage turned towards Simon and smiled.

Part Three

Sheep

When you are feeling increasingly disconnected from society, "Question Time", the topical BBC political debate programme, is a difficult experience.

Almost every point raised pressed an internal button of Bradley's labelled "Angrily Disagree".

Three topics particularly piqued him . . .

1) "Labour are offering 25 hours of free childcare a week if they are elected".

"And *that* was supposed to be newsworthy *because* . . . ?!" reacted Bradley internally. "That's the best reason to vote for them is it?! Not actioning social injustices, not doing something about the homeless . . . 25 hours of free childcare a week! If it means that much to people, they should be questioning why they had kids in the first place! Work is more important than spending some time with your children?"

"But we *need* to work to make ends meet . . . " he could hear people pipe up . . .

"*Really*?—"ends" that involve large houses, restaurant meals, latest gadgets . . . is it really "making ends meet"? Not sure the kids see it like that . . . or are at all impressed. They just want some time . . . until the peer pressure kicks in for *them* at school and they join the treadmill . . . the race with no end, everyone a loser" he ranted to himself in his head, alone on the sofa, in his small, stone Cotswolds cottage.

2) "Using nerve gas on your citizens is completely unacceptable" a politician commented on recent events in Syria.

It was one of those stunningly obvious statements that politicians feel they have to say . . . "may as well throw in a reminder that breathing is good and when you walk, remember to put one foot in front of the other!" added Bradley.

"Nerve gas is bad . . . but blowing the arms and legs off children is apparently perfectly acceptable! A necessary inconvenience, a means to an end."

The programme went on to describe an arms fair hosted in a London hotel that week . . . "Sounds lovely doesn't it" Bradley thought, "an "Arms Fair" . . . "Can we go to the Arms Fair this weekend Daddy? Government representatives from around the world, expensive suits, nice food—what a jolly civilised affair blowing the arms and legs off children can be".

"Ah, but it's a multi-billion pound industry for Britain. We are technological leaders in the field" the people chimed again in Bradley's head, some members of the studio audience echoing their opinion.

"So we have lots of jobs centred around blowing the arms and legs off children . . . and we are very good at it! I'm so proud I could cry!" Bradley thought despairingly. "Imagine the good that could be done with that time, effort and technology . . . " Was he the only person that saw it like this? He couldn't be. Was it him being paranoid? He didn't think he was being unreasonable. It just felt like he and everyone else was being treated like an idiot!

These "internal rants" had been quite external in the past, some aimed at his wife of twenty-three years . . . but she had left. Not solely because of the rants, the affair with his best friend's niece hadn't helped, but the outbursts certainly hadn't brought them closer together.

The third topic on the show was one that that left him completely dumbfounded:

3) A survey had revealed that the vast majority would vote for Scottish independence if it meant they would be £500 a year better off.

This really left Bradley speechless. Were people *so* financially orientated that the money would make a difference?

His internal rant went along the lines of:

"Success is measured by money and people must have all the gadgets—Sky, flat screen, latest phone, tablets, car, must get on the "property ladder". Employers are laughing—everyone busting a gut to work, living to work not working to live". He could understand people with a passion for their work . . . musician, author, scientist maybe (although he had a dislike of *them*—who is funding them?) . . . but most people he met seemed to be moaning about their work!

"People will do *anything* for money . . . " he thought "because everyone else puts such a lot of store by it."

Bradley's faith in the human race had been stretched of late. He was amazed at the power of peer pressure. If someone tells us to watch X-Factor, we watch it. If the latest Jaguar is the car to have, it *is* the car to have. We *must* have the latest phones, all aspiring to buy a house . . . the "dream of home ownership" as he had heard it described . . . Was that really our dream as children? All of us following the pack like sheep, being guided by a not-so-benevolent sheepdog, no-one daring to break away.

***

421 years have passed. The year is 2434. It is August and the weather in the Cotswolds is beautiful. Bradley has been dead for 400 years. It was a heart attack, stress being a contributory factor. The only thing that remained of him was a filling from a tooth that had survived his cremation and was now buried a metre below the foundations of a waste compound, previously the site of a memorial garden. That was it. And no-one on the planet remembered him. It was if he had never . . . happened.

People still loved some political debate though . . . .and their love affair with technology, and need to "keep up with the Jones's" was still in full flight.

Everyone had a hydrogen/ion hybrid vehicle, internal combustion engines relegated to museums. These vehicles all looked fairly similar, but people still had to have the right badge . Western consumerism and capitalism had long ago changed the "East"—many countries had spent years aspiring to western "ideals" and most had achieved them now. Thank goodness we were now largely the same—more in common, less differences, never too far away from a Starbucks. Thank goodness.

And absolutely *everyone* had a i-chip—a combined phone, computer, camera, TV, personal organiser . . . all contained in a small chip inserted under the skin on your shoulder blade, out of the way. It had become *the* must-have product—you would literally be laughed out of a room if you and your children didn't have one these days. As ridiculous as only wearing underwear.

Seeing a huge opportunity for increased communication and productivity, The Government strongly encouraged the fitting of an i-chip at the age of one month, even contributing to 40% of the cost. Very few people objected and those that did were marginalised, much in the same way that anyone who disagreed with the concept of global warming in the early part of the century was marginalised—it was *deeply* unfashionable, even though it had now been proven to be a misinterpretation.

Technologically, the i-chip was quite something. With your eyes shut you could see a "screen", with your eyes open you could see a 3D head-up display, albeit slightly obscured with adverts appearing on the periphery. Sound was "wired" into the auditory nerves, 3D visuals into the optic nerves. Thoughts and speech converted into words. The device also greatly aided education, downloading and streaming of information being possible at incredible speeds.

The technological advances of the day were astounding. Four people were even on their way to one of Saturn's moons! This would take some time apparently.

Unbelievably, "Question Time" was still being broadcast . . . by the GBC—Global Broadcasting Corporation. The questions were state selected, much more so than before, giving the illusion of debate and consultation.

"Good evening ladies and gentleman and, on the show tonight . . . Is the two-child limit working?"

Population growth had been a real problem—the scourge of cancer had long been overcome by a combination of vaccination at birth and nutritional changes. Average life expectancy had increased to 123. 123 years in relative fitness too. Nature's natural culls to control an increasing population had been largely overcome and our numbers had expanded rapidly, to a point where the Government had introduced a two-child limit per family some years ago. This was very strict. If a third child was born when a family already had two, it would be terminated at birth. Of course, the norm would be the pregnancy being terminated at an earlier stage. However, if a child had died, the couple were permitted to have another to replace it.

And most people wanted their children to be perfect—and, fortunately, with recent scientific advances, they could be. Every one a "beauty". Ugliness was a thing of the past. Except to some, the "beauty" had become ugly . . . extremely bland and unappealing.

This was not the only child-related policy The Government had introduced.

The last forty years had seen the introduction of the SECS (State Executive Civil Servants). The Government would pay a couple two million Europees to secure the full-time service of one of their children . . . but that child could not be replaced, the couple remaining with only a single child allowance.

This was a huge amount of money, more than enough for a couple to live very comfortably for life. The children were developed into a kind of "super civil servant"—highly educated and well paid, with 50% of their earnings going back to their parents. And there was a three year waiting list for people to volunteer their children for this organisation. Over the years, intensive Government advertising and careful product placement had given the SECS's tremendous social status . . . think of your child becoming a lawyer, a heart surgeon, an astronaut, a Formula 1 driver . . . and multiply the bragging rights by ten. It was the epitome of achievement, class, taste, wealth and importance. All SECS lived together in beautiful excess, wanting for nothing. Proud parents were regularly updated with their progress, many living for these updates, eager to impress others with their latest news.

People worked hard, and most people had a lot to show for it. It was a "land of plenty" . . . except for time, people had very little time, very little time to think, but that was how The Government preferred it . . .

keep them busy . . .

keep them distracted . . .

distracted from The Government's power and their clever, complete abuse of it.

And another thing was very conspicuous by its absence . . . something that was hardly ever seen these days . . .

a heartfelt smile.

The Withdrawal

"That one's out of order" pointed out the tall, bearded stranger standing guard at the cash machines, sheltered in the spacious colonnade of the supermarket.

"Oh, thanks" said Russell, stepping back to wait for one of the remaining two to become vacant. His thanks didn't register with the stranger . . . dressed in dark blue, hi-vis-striped road-worker apparel, replete with a light grey bobble hat. He resembled a tall Brian Blessed and sported a similar beard.

From nowhere, and for no apparent reason, the loudest, heartiest laugh sprang forth from the stranger and echoed around the colonnade . . .

"Hah, hah, hah, hah, hah, hah!" It stopped people in their tracks but, with typical English reserve, they smiled politely, pretended it hadn't happened and went about their business. Russell found it disconcerting . . . "half Brian Blessed jolly, half maniacal villain" he thought.

Russell watched another shopper approach the central cash point . . .

"That one's out of order" pointed out Mr Blessed, almost under his breath as if the information was in some way sensitive.

"Ah OK" replied the shopper, politely confused by his appearance.

"Hah, hah, hah, hah, hah, hah, hah!" again rang out around the colonnade, confusing the shopper even further.

Russell took his money and receipt and, from a discreet distance, continued to observe Mr Blessed. He watched five more customers treated in exactly the same fashion . . . the warning, followed by the hearty laugh. When Mr Blessed wasn't advising or laughing, he stood guard, walking up and down a few steps, not with military smartness but a Hagrid-like shuffle, tall and imposing. At one point, a young shop assistant left the store and waved at him, Mr Blessed acknowledging with a hearty "Hello John!"

To Russell, it looked for all the world like a case of "care in the community" and, believing him to be of no harm to others, he went into the supermarket and bought his sandwich lunch, intending to eat it at his desk at the college opposite. He worked there as a business school lecturer, currently tediously ploughing through some course updates. As Russell left the supermarket with his sandwich, Mr Blessed was still there, providing the same service and, after Russell had witnessed two more people receive the same treatment, he couldn't help himself . . .

Approaching the stranger, Russell said "Excuse me, I hope you don't mind me asking but do you work for the supermarket?" He thought this a fairly innocuous way of opening a conversation with him.

"No, no mate" said Mr Blessed under his breath, not really expecting the interruption, still vigilant for approaching customers.

"Security, then?" asked Russell.

"No, no mate" came the same quiet reply.

"So, is there a problem with that cash point?" enquired Russell politely.

"That one's out of order" said Mr Blessed.

"Yes, yes but couldn't you just put up a sign and let the shop know?"

"Hah, Hah, hah, hah, hah, hah, hah . . . " As the ring of the laugh subsided, Mr Blessed said under his breath "Yes, I suppose so. Could you write one out for me?"

"Err, yes I could if you'd like" replied Russell.

"That would be great" replied Mr Blessed under his breath.

"Hah, hah, hah, hah, hah . . . ."

To the echo of the laughter Russell nipped back to the college, wrote "Not in service" in black felt pen on some card, put some sellotape down two sides and returned.

"There you go, that'll save you some trouble. I'll let the shop know."

"Won't be necessary mate, already had a word" he said privately, almost in a whisper.'

"OK, good to meet you" said Russell as he made his way back to the college.

He glanced back to see him fixing the notice on the cash machine, the laughter ringing around the colonnade.

Fortunately, Russell's office faced that side of the supermarket and looked out over a pleasant tree-lined square that separated the college from the colonnade. And there sat Mr Blessed. Quiet and still, he sat facing the cash machine, the sign doing its job admirably with no-one attempting a withdrawal. From 1.15 to 4.00pm, Russell divided his time updating course materials and observing Mr Blessed. Apart from a five minute trip to the toilet and another five minutes making a mug of coffee in the tea room, he kept an intermittent watch over the square and Mr Blessed hadn't budged, vigilant in his surveillance of the machine. As Russell was tidying up his desk just before five, he glanced down at the square and . . . no Mr Blessed. He had gone.

The following morning was unusual. Russell couldn't get near his usual parking space at the college. The whole colonnade area was cordoned off and four police vehicles were present, two cars and two vans, with at least eight uniformed officers working in the cordon. And there was a space in the wall where the central cash machine used to be, only its steel housing remained . . . someone had neatly removed the whole thing!

Russell noticed a yellow "Appeal for Witnesses" notice standing on the pavement. *"This was the scene of a crime between 8.00pm and 6.00am on 26.11.13. If you were a witness or have any information please contact, etc, etc."* Russell hadn't witnessed it, he'd just had a quiet night in . . . but he did have some information.

"Excuse me" called Russell to the policeman standing near the cordon.

"Yes sir" replied the officer.

"I think I may have some information that might help here"

"And you *are* sir?" said the officer removing his notebook.

"Russell Channing—I work in the college here" he said pointing to his office, "and I can tell you about some events yesterday afternoon that may help".

"Thank you sir. If you follow me please". The officer lifted the cordon and left the area, leading Russell to a trailer that had been set up in the supermarket car park. There, another officer interviewed Russell. He described what he had seen that afternoon . . . "I'm not sure if any of this is relevant but it certainly concerned that middle cash point" said Russell.

He described Mr Blessed "He seemed harmless enough, not threatening at all. Very odd behaviour though, you couldn't miss him . . . looked like something he may have done quite regularly, you know, you sometimes see these people. Perhaps they should be looked after more closely".

At the end of the interview, Russell was thanked for his time and asked to contact them again if he could think of anything else that may be relevant.

It had certainly been an eventful morning . . . "beats updating that course" Russell thought. At 11.00am he finally settled down to some work.

Later that afternoon, Russell heard a commotion in the car park below . . . Mr Blessed had returned. "Hah hah hah hah hah hah".

Russell watched through the window as three officers approached Mr Blessed. There was a short conversation and then an officer took his arm to lead him to the trailer. Then Mr Blessed lost his temper. He turned and threw the officer back onto the pavement . . . another officer tried to restrain him and he was raised into the air and thrown back. It was like watching a film battle with a giant. Two more officers were similarly repelled until, after a warning had been shouted to a very distressed Mr Blessed, a Taser bought him to his knees and eventually to the ground, his huge frame eventually adopting a foetal position. Mr Blessed was wailing loudly now, his cries echoing as clearly as his laugh around the colonnade, a haunting, saddening sound that shocked Russell. A sobbing Mr Blessed was led to the trailer by three officers, joined shortly afterwards by an ambulance.

"Shit!" thought Russell to himself, not usually resorting to such base language.

He hadn't expected such a heavy-handed approach from the Police but, in the face of the man's response, he guessed they had no choice. He knew matters were out of his hands now but couldn't help himself leaving his desk and going down to the trailer. There was no answer to his knock on the trailer door . . . so, he knocked again more loudly . . .

"What!" said a paramedic annoyed as she snatched open the door.

"Sorry, can I talk to an officer when it's convenient, please."

"Wait there, I'll tell them" replied the paramedic with an unintentional brusqueness borne out of an under-resourced service. After a few minutes, the door opened and one of the officers that had restrained Mr Blessed opened the door.

"Yes sir?"

"I talked to one of your colleagues this morning about the gentleman you have in there and I feel responsible for what's happening" explained Russell.

"We appreciate your concern sir but it's Police business now and you need to leave it to us sir. We are pretty busy right now".

Seeing in Russell's eyes that this was not an adequate response, he added "We can see he's vulnerable, sir, and we're just contacting Social Services"

"Ahh, good" replied Russell.

"YOU!!" bellowed out of the trailer . . .

"You gave me that sign yesterday, you did!" Mr Blessed shouted, still crying.

"You said it was *good* to meet me, you did . . . *good to meet me*!" he moaned, hunched over the table sobbing. "The shop doesn't mind . . . they say they don't mind . . . "

"Look sir, we have your details, I'll get someone to call you later. He's in good hands" assured the officer.

"OK. Thanks". The door shut and Russell felt he had done all that he could, but he still felt very uncomfortable about the whole situation.

Mr Blessed was well known to Social Services, his story, like so many others, was one of difficulty and sadness. His mother died in childbirth, his father had left him at three . . . a succession of foster parents, sectioned in his teens, treated for schizophrenia . . . His life had not been easy, although in later years he had enjoyed working part-time for the council, helping keep the town centre clean.

He was well-known in the supermarket, something of a local character . . . He had never been any trouble, never hurt anyone, but sometimes he did have to be moved on.

The Police interviewed Mr Blessed and he said he hadn't seen anything, having left the square at five o'clock, as confirmed by Russell. So he was released under the proviso that he needed to stay local for the next few days as he may need to be talked to again.

"You're lucky none of our officers were hurt" pointed out the detective.

"I'm sorry" said a contrite Mr Blessed.

Late that night, Mr Blessed and young John, the shop assistant met in the unit they had been renting for the last few months. The cash machine sat in the middle of the concrete floor. It had taken some planning but £400,000 wasn't bad for a few months work!

"Here he is!" said John to Mr Blessed as he heard the roller door of the unit open . . .

Russell strolled in with a huge smile on his face.

"You played a blinder, Russ!" said Mr Blessed excitedly high-fiving him.

"Hah, hah, hah, hah, hah, hah, hah".

The Key

It was a terrible day for a walk. Half an hour ago, the weather looked quite kind to Mark, even glimpses of autumn sunshine but, as he walked down the lane, clouds gathered, the wind picked up and things took a turn for the dramatic. Dark clouds were churned by swirling winds and heavy rain bounced off the stubble in the fields as Mark looked across the haze of the valley. It was normally picturesque, but today the weather and the stark emptiness of the fields had conspired to produce a sepia-tinted autumn scene.

Mark had heard it said that "there's no such thing as bad weather, just inappropriate clothing" and Mark's top half was appropriately dressed in a hooded rain jacket. Unfortunately the bottom half was less appropriate, the rain pouring off his jacket to soak his jeans, shoes, underpants, everything. He'd reached a point in the walk where he was so wet that turning back was pointless, he couldn't get wetter, so he soldiered on, the dramatic weather almost adding to the walk. He enjoyed a good storm.

Through the gloom, Mark could see a lone figure. On the side of the valley, in the middle of a large field was the black silhouette of a person. He stood alone and motionless. "Scarecrow?" was Mark's first thought . . . crows *were* circling in the area, adding to the bleakness. "If it is, it's not working" Mark thought . . . Then the scarecrow moved! A slow, shuffling walk . . . It was alive! Although Mr Scarecrow was a fair distance away from Mark, the only feature in the empty stubble field, it appeared he wasn't wearing a coat . . . certainly no umbrella, just a dark jumper and jeans. "Very inappropriately dressed!" thought Mark.

Earlier on his walk Mark had noticed an old silver car parked at the edge of the field that wasn't usually there. "Maybe it was his? What was he doing? . . . in *this* weather!"

Distracted by the almost horizontal rain, Mark continued his walk on a circular path that rose up the other side of the valley. His view of Mr

Scarecrow was obscured for a while by a hedgerow but eventually his route bought him back to the area where the car was parked. By now, Mr Scarecrow had returned to the car. Mark watched as he drove quickly across the muddy edge of the field, wheels spinning, eventually turning onto the tarmac lane and disappearing out of view through the rain.

Sitting in the porch of his cottage, invigorated by the walk, Mark started to remove his sodden clothes. Fresh clothes, a warm fire and a cup of coffee restored a feeling of comfort and contentment. He was so lucky to have such scenery on his doorstep and really enjoyed his walks. A welcome contrast to the hours of financial planning meetings that occupied most of his week in the City.

Over the coming days, Mark's thoughts increasingly turned to the lone jumpered person in the field and later that week, while he was driving back from the station across the valley, he saw him again! "It must be him . . . " Mark thought, "on his own, same jumper, car parked at the edge of the field . . . mmmm" he thought. Now he was curious. Partial to a Friday night drink at the village pub, he asked some of the locals if *they* had seen him, or knew anything about him.

"Yeah, seen him a few times this year I have" said the local builder.

"Metal detecting, that's what he's doing. Out in all weathers too. I'm told he lives on his own in one of the villages out Sarndon way. Found a few things too apparently . . . "

"He's keen isn't he" Mark commented. "Must be worth his while I suppose . . . can't have found anything valuable or he'd have bought himself a coat!". They laughed and carried on drinking. Others had noticed him too, same description, jumper and jeans, but no-one knew who he was or much about him at all.

Gradually life's regular pattern overtook Mark's thoughts and the dilemma of the jumpered man faded into the background. Until he saw him again on another walk, this time a rather pleasant day. With time on his hands, Mark couldn't resist having a word with him, so he walked across the raised grass verge and over the crunchy stubble towards him. As he got closer, Mark could see he was a large man, not fat but broad-shouldered, middle-aged, dark long hair and short beard with flecks of grey, still wearing the black baggy, probably home-knit jumper and jeans.

"Hello" Mark said in as friendly a fashion as he could, not wishing to cause the man any concern.

"It's all OK I've got permission from the landowner" the man replied defensively in a broad West Country accent.

"Oh no, that's fine . . . just wanted to say hello as I've seen you a few times out walking. Just wondered what you were doing, that's all" Mark replied, trying to allay any fears.

"Looking for a key" said the jumpered man, still sweeping his metal detector back and forth. "I dropped a key here a long time ago and I've been looking for it for a while now"

"Oh, can't you get another one made? What's it for" asked Mark.

"Thing is, it's quite big. You'd have thought it'd be easier to find than this" said the man, still sweeping.

"Sorry, I'm Mark" he said extending his hand for a shake.

"Ah, yes, I'm Bernard, pleased to meet you". Bernard's large hand had a firm friendly grip.

"What's the key for?" enquired Mark.

"Nothing in particular sir, just a nice old key and I'd like to find it" Bernard replied.

"Have you found much stuff while you've been out here?" Bernard's detector looked better than your average toy-shop model.

"Oh yes, plenty. I can show you if you like?"

Taken aback slightly, Mark said "That would be good sometime"

"I'm just finishing here for the day, so I can drive you to my place to see them if you like. I'll bring you back of course."

"That's very kind but I really don't want to impose" said Mark, torn between really wanting to see the items and accepting a lift from a human scarecrow.

"It's up to you sir, of course, but I'd be happy to do it, honestly. Don't get to speak to many people these days"

"Do you live far away? asked Mark. Bernard seemed a good sort.

" 'bout fifteen minutes drive, that's all" said Bernard.

"Why not, I've nothing planned today. Yes, I'd like to" said Mark and with that, they made their way across the field to Bernard's well-worn silver car.

"Ah, it's an old Sierra 4x4. Bit of a classic these days" said Mark, thinking it had seen better days.

"Been good to me the old girl has" replied Bernard.

The journey was about fifteen minutes but to any other driver, it would have been at least double that . . . Bernard set off at a blistering pace and said nothing on the journey, his whole attention needed to negotiate the lanes like a professional rally driver. Mark also said nothing on the journey, his body fully braced, his breathing short and rapid, his eyes shut half the time.

Their arrival on Bernard's impressive drive was dramatic . . . a handbrake turn into a perfectly parked position to the left of his front door!

"Thank you" said Mark, really aiming his thanks to God for their safe arrival rather than Bernard for the lift.

"I *really* like driving" said Bernard with a huge grin on his face.

"I can see that" replied Mark, shaken "you should try it professionally!"

"Had years of it, sir. Absolutely loved it, but couldn't get my head back together after we lost Brian".

"Oh . . . " said Mark

"Yeah, my co-driver. Rolled into a ditch, we did. Wasn't even going that fast" said Bernard distantly . . . "couldn't get him out of the fire . . . "

"I'm sorry to hear that" said Mark

"Long time ago sir" Bernard said. "I do miss him though. We were like brothers"

"Listen to me!" said Bernard snapping back into real time, "you didn't come 'ere to listen to me ramble on! Come in and I'll put the kettle on!"

Bernard's home was a picture-postcard cottage: sloped tiled roof with recessed wooden windows and red roses rambling over the wooden arbour that surrounded the heavy oak front door.

"Lovely place you have here" commented Mark, walking into the well-used tiled porch.

"Thank you. I like it sir".

Bernard led Mark through a dark hall into a sparsely furnished front room . . . just a small chandelier and four large oak tables strewn with small metal objects.

"Wow . . . so this is the display room is it!" said Mark.

"I s'pose so but it's only you apart from me that's seen 'em! I'll just put that kettle on. Feel free to have a rummage if you like".

"OK, thanks, I will" replied Mark.

It was a very impressive collection. The condition of most of the objects was quite poor . . . a lot of rusty items . . . but some beautiful things too.

He had saved *everything* he'd found, even rusty old cans, bits of random iron work, old hinges, even bits of colourful pottery that had a metallic content to the paint. Old paint pots, bits of wiring, all manner of rusty detritus . . . but some objects stood out . . . a few coins, some new, some old, some gold and silver jewellery, the gold still beautifully bright. Some items bore the scars of being ploughed up but a lot seemed to have escaped unscathed.

"Better pickings after the fields have been ploughed, of course" said Bernard returning with the teas.

"It's quite a collection you have here" said Mark "why do you keep it all?"

"I don't know really. Interesting though, isn't it . . . even the stuff people throw away" replied Bernard.

"What do you do, then?" said Mark sipping his tea, hoping he wasn't being too intrusive.

"I told you, I'm looking for a key".

"What, all the time!?" pushed Mark.

"When I'm not resting or eating. Been looking for three years now".

"Wow, that explains the collection then. This key you lost . . . what's it for?"

"I dropped it while I was out for a walk! Didn't notice till I'd got back 'ere. The size of it though sir! You'd think it would be easier to find!"

"Yes, but what's it *for*" Mark persisted politely.

"It's hard to tell you more sir..I'd rather not say if you don't mind . . . would sound silly. I just want to get the damned thing back!"

Mark respected this, although he was keen to know the purpose of this unusually large key. He enjoyed his tea, and chatted easily to Bernard for a few more minutes about the hundreds of items he had found.

"Best be getting you back before dark sir" suggested Bernard.

"Of course, thank you so much for showing me your stuff" said Mark.

The ride home was terrifying, the twilight adding to the feeling of imminent death.

"I'll see you soon hopefully sir. Thanks for the company" said Bernard.

"Likewise" replied Mark "I'll see you out on my walks, I'm sure . . . and good luck".

"Oh thank you sir . . . it's out there somewhere, just a matter of time. If you happen to see it, of course, I'd be grateful if you could drop it in?"

"Of course I will" said Mark.

On every walk in future, Mark looked out for Bernard. He wasn't there every time, maybe once in every three or four, but he always gave him a wave. A couple of times he approached him for a chat, even pushed him a little more to find more out about the key . . . but Bernard always politely evaded the issue. Mark even once invited him back to his place for a cup of tea, but Bernard politely declined.

With work in the City very demanding of late, time had slipped by quickly for Mark. He'd intended to call at Bernard's house . . . he was sure he wouldn't mind him popping in . . . but he somehow just never got round to it. Eventually, it struck Mark that some months had passed by and he hadn't seen Bernard out on the fields. He asked at the pub and no-one else had seen him lately either. He resolved to call at his cottage at the weekend, first thing Saturday morning.

Driving at legal speeds it seemed a lot longer journey to Bernard's cottage, a good twenty-five minutes. Pulling up on the drive, little seemed to have changed. The silver car was parked in the drive but the garden hadn't seen attention for a while. Brushing a wayward rose branch away from his face, he knocked on the front door . . . no sound from inside . . . he knocked louder . . . still nothing at all. Tentatively, he tried the door and it was unlocked . . .

"Hello . . . hello, Bernard, are you there?" shouted Mark. No reply.

"Hello!" he shouted louder "It's Mark here". Still no reply. He went through the porch into the small hall and entered the room with the artefact collection. It was much as he had left it several months ago, except for a metal detector laying across one of the tables on top of the objects. He climbed the steep stairs to the first floor and looked into the small bathroom . . . empty . . . opened the door to a small front bedroom . . . and there was Bernard. Lying on his back, facing the ceiling . . . pale, motionless . . . obviously dead.

"Jesus!" Mark recoiled in shock. He had never seen a dead person before, let alone someone he knew. His heart raced and pounded in his ears. He was having trouble taking in what was in front of him. Bernard was still in his old jumper and jeans, his beard a little longer than he remembered, his hands crossed over his chest . . . for all the world looking like a stone figure of a knight laying on top of his grave, his face the same grey. He had probably been there for some time and clearly Mark was the first to find him. Bernard didn't get many visitors . . .

"Jesus, The key!" Mark said to himself. Clasped in both hands against Bernard's chest was a large, green tarnished key. Mark steeled himself and opened Bernard's stiff cold fingers to release the old key. Bernard had said it was big and he was right . . . the largest key that Mark had seen, the size of a small envelope . . . it would take both hands to turn it . . .

Bernard opened his eyes. "Hello sir!" he said cheerily. "How the devil are you?"

"Jesus Christ!" shouted Mark, his heart almost stopping. He leapt back across the room pushing over a chair, ending up on the floor with his back up against a small cabinet.

"I'm sorry!" Bernard smiled "I wasn't dead, just not *here* . . . Looks dead though doesn't it!"

Mark's eyes were as wide as they had ever been and shock had frozen him to the spot, his breathing fast and heavy . . . till now, he'd only ever seen the dead come back to life in films . . .

"Try to calm down sir, I really am OK" assured Bernard.

"Jesus Christ!"

"Haven't met him sir!" laughed Bernard.

"Maybe one day! I've just been talking to my parents. Been gone twenty years now . . . they're fine though"

"Had a chat with old Brian too, he's doing OK too. It's great to keep in touch"

Mark had his doubts, but Bernard would soon teach him how to use the key. And he eventually understood why Bernard had gone to so much trouble to find it. As much as he liked his job, Mark never returned to the City . . .

. . . he had much more interesting places to visit.

The Juggle

Mummy, I really love it here, with all my friends". Jemima's heart melted. "That's lovely darling, it is a lovely place isn't it" she said, whisking Jon up in her arms and giving him a huge cuddle before dropping him off at the company creche.

It wasn't easy . . . both working, mortgage, bills . . . the usual juggling act . . . but Jemima and George considered themselves lucky from the start. Their paths had crossed at University and it was love at first semester. "You look fantastic in glasses and a lab coat" George used to say.

In many ways they were similar. Both from affluent families, both had similar aspirations, similar tastes, flying in the face of the "opposites attract" theory. And it was a theory they happily disproved.

"Jemima & George" *sound* like names that should be together" Jemima always said.

Both scientists, Jemima a microbiologist and George a geneticist, they worked for Lyraxus, an international company set up to research the ageing process. The company was successful, most people wanting to be around longer and look better, and was generously funded by a conglomeration of pharmaceutical and beauty product companies.

The Lyraxus site was not as clinical as some might expect. Certainly clean and modern, but really rather beautiful. Located in the countryside next to a small village, the site had a low-lying profile, so as not to interfere with the open views of rolling woodland . . . you wouldn't know the site was there at all from the road. It was futuristic with graceful, wave-shaped buildings, some with turfed roofs, most featuring large expanses of glass . . . the site all curves, one flowing into the other, beautiful paving, tear-drop shaped flower beds flowing to a large mirrored globe sculpture, flowing into another wave-shaped building. Stunning integration, easy on the eye and, like all good modern art, fitting into the older, established landscape in a surprisingly complementary way.

Lyraxus was a good company to work for. Competitive salaries, 36 days holiday a year, a health-care plan, good development opportunities, flexible working, cutting-edge facilities . . . even a generous pension scheme. On paper, it was hard to fault. And scientists were keen to work there. It looked good on the CV.

The other major bonus for Jemima and George was the on-site crèche that the company had built two years ago. Lyraxus recognised that child-care for the professional couple could be a challenge so, for a competitive annual fee, Lyraxus parents could drop off their child just before work, knowing they were never too far away. There were benefits for the company too . . . scientists less stressed, more focussed on their work . . . they could even pop in and see their children at lunch-time. It really couldn't be more convenient. Best of all, the staff were very good and the children loved it.

Jemima had some holiday to use up and had taken the day off shopping, leaving George to pick Jon up from the crèche late in the afternoon.

"How was your day, old boy" said George picking up Jon and spinning him round like a chair-o-plane.

"Ha, ha, ha, ha . . . ." Jon loved a spin and couldn't get his answer out. It was pretty obvious that all had gone well.

"We played trains and played in the sandpit too!" said Jon excitedly.

"I LOOVE THE SAAANDPIT!!" he growled in his best grown-up voice, smiling up at his Daddy.

Jon was two now and had attended the crèche for a year, although it was possible to start at 4 months old, and many did. There was a wide age range and it was very popular, not surprising as the atmosphere was very homely, very jolly. Just what a working parent would want. Modern, clean, full of bright colours, pictures everywhere . . . and lots of smiling and laughter. And, like the best establishments, learning was embedded into the fun activities. Through their laughter, they were learning to read, count, interact socially and respect each-other. It wasn't just a place to leave your kids for the day, it was a really good grounding for school.

George strolled back to the car, Jon holding his hand skipping alongside.

"So what did you get up to today?" George enquired, strapping Jon into his car seat.

"LOTS OF THINGS! We played with numbers, and I can count up to 10!

One, two, three, four, five, six, seven, eight, err nine AND TEN! At two years old, Jon was full-on boisterous.

"Well done Jon, that's really good!" George said encouragingly, genuinely pleased, pulling out of the car park.

"What did *you* do today Daddy?"

"Well I was using numbers too, lots of them actually, in a big experiment that I'm doing".

"We do experiments too!" Jon said excitedly.

"Really? What do you do then?" asked George.

"Well we mix stuff together and it changes colour, and we see what happens when it's put in the fridge, *and* we get to make things with clay!"

"Wow, sounds pretty good old boy" laughed George.

"And there's a *big* experiment downstairs, Daddy"

"What's that then?" said George distracted by negotiating a roundabout . . . and a little confused as the creche was a single story building.

"I think it's a secret!" whispered Jon excitedly.

"Oh, *really*" George smiled, playing along.

"We're not supposed to, but *Jack* showed me!"

"Showed you what?" said George, his curiosity pricked . . .

"All the little babies with tubes in them, downstairs . . . " said Jon

"I like them, they're my friends!"

A Road to Nowhere

"Morning!"

"Morning" replied Iain, through the passenger window of his black cab, half-thinking a "good morning" was unusual . . . people usually get straight to the destination.

"Where to mate?" Iain prompted.

"I don't know" said the passenger smiling, "surprise me."

"Do what?!" Iain wasn't really in the mood for a smart-arse so early in the morning, quite tired from a late night with a friend at the cinema. He could be quite tetchy when he was tired.

"You're probably aware that traditionally us taxi drivers work with a destination . . . "

"Seriously just drive, I don't care where" said the passenger, light heartedly.

"I'm not sure I've got time for this mate, would it surprise you if I asked you to leave the cab?" said an annoyed Iain.

"Look, I'm not trying to be funny here . . . you'll get paid, here's £50 in advance" the passenger said, pushing the note into the opening in the separating window. "Please, just drive anywhere you like."

This put a different complexion on things . . .

"OK mate, you're the boss" and Iain pulled away from the taxi rank into the extremely slow moving traffic leaving Kings Cross station.

Approaching some traffic lights, Iain glanced back to his silent passenger who was looking out of his window.

"Left or right?"

"Oh . . . right, let's go right" the passenger said whimsically.

"Ooh, let's!" thought Iain to himself sarcastically.

"No work today then?" Iain enquired.

"No, not much work at all these days" replied the suited passenger.

With a small, uncharacteristic pang of guilt, Iain replied “Sorry to hear that”, more to fill the silence than anything else. He didn’t much like silence.

“Oh no, please don’t be sorry” said the passenger “I’m not looking for work! Just a little bored really.”

The passenger was not giving the impression that he was on his uppers . . . well-cut suit, expensive looking briefcase, well-groomed, fifties liberally distributed . . .

“So what do you do?” said Iain.

“I worked in derivatives”

“Ahh yes . . . ” said Iain knowingly.

“Have you heard of them?”

“Well, kind of . . . futures, options, all that jazz . . . the values based on the future value of commodities . . . ”

“Well, I didn’t expect that!” exclaimed the passenger.

“Read the Financial Times and have a few shares” Iain replied, well used to being a book judged by its cover.

“Really? You must tell me about them.”

“They’re doing piss poorly, that’s why I’m driving a taxi! Where too now mate?”

“Oh . . . just keep going straight on. If you feel like turning off that’s fine too.”

“Whatever you say” Iain said, relieved that this man could indeed afford to drive around aimlessly.

“Driving a taxi isn’t all bad is it?” said the passenger “I thought you could make a decent living.”

“You can, it suits me” Iain replied curtly, not really wanting to share his life story with a random city hot-shot.

“I’m a great believer in the saying “you make your own luck in this life” . . . it’s what my father said to me and it has proven to be true.”

“Was he in derivatives too?” Iain enquired, half facetiously.

“He was” the passenger replied commandingly “built the family firm up from nothing, and then I took it on.”

Iain continued to drive, heading up the Marylebone Road out towards Shepherd’s Bush, the traffic predictably heavy.

“The old family firm has been pretty good to you, then . . . ” said Iain, filling another silence.

“Not bad at all old boy, not bad at all. Sold it in the end though, got bored with it all”.

"I suppose you're going to tell me 'it's not all about money' now!" Iain replied.

"Well it's not old boy. I have a lot of the stuff and I'm in the back of your taxi passing the time, aren't I?"

Iain well understood it was not all about money. He wasn't rich but he was comfortable. The taxi-driving suited him, bought in enough money, but more importantly, filled a lot of time . . . broke a lot of silences. Ten months earlier he had lost his wife to cancer and his daughter in a road accident . . . in the same week. Wife on the Tuesday, daughter on Friday afternoon . . . crossing a dual carriageway with a friend, coach driver didn't see her. Iain hadn't had a "good day" since then. In fact, it really didn't matter to him whether he was alive or dead. Some said he was still in shock, still in the "grieving stage" but he knew it was worse than that. This was one situation that time wasn't going to heal. And it wasn't that he "couldn't see this because he was in it" . . . he'd seen friends in that situation, where there *was* a light at the end of the tunnel . . . there was hope. For him, he knew there would be no light. His light, and any future light, had been extinguished that week. There was no hope. He *really* didn't care. He had even thought of "ending it all". Most often, when he was in the taxi . . . more than once . . . A deep melancholy . . . a cold, grey day . . . a rude passenger . . . combinations of events that had sometimes almost overwhelmed him. Some people describe an experience of standing at the edge of a cliff and having an overwhelming urge to jump. His was the same feeling . . . an all-consuming urge to bury his foot in the taxi carpet and accelerate into a wall. To "end it all" had a deep appeal on some days. But this wasn't one of those days.

"Here's another £50, old boy" said the passenger passing the two twenties and a ten through the hole in the screen.

"No need for that yet, your only up to thirty" said Iain.

"No, I insist, this makes a nice change. If we can drive a little longer, I would appreciate it?"

"You're the boss."

"I'd have thought you'd have your own car, a*nd* a driver, if business has been that good" said Iain, now pulling into the Acton area.

"I have, but this makes a nice change, as I say" replied the passenger as Iain hesitated at a junction to a quiet residential backstreet.

Iain heard the shot, even though the gun had a silencer fitted. Instantly his face hit the steering wheel and he was disconnected from the world as quickly as losing the channel from a TV . . .

They say the devil makes work for idle hands . . . He certainly had today.

The passenger had often wondered what it would feel like to kill someone. It had become rather an obsession in recent months . . .

His heart pounded with excitement as he replaced the gun in his briefcase and calmly slipped out of the car.

Yes, he had really rather enjoyed it.

There must be an Angel

A nagging headache had kept Alan awake and he just couldn't be bothered to get up and get some tablets. Annoyed, he threw his head across to the other side of the pillow in an attempt to get comfortable, and felt a very light pressure on the tip of his nose . . . "Odd" he thought. His nose had just touched the corner of the wooden bedside cabinet, the lightest pressure indenting its tip . . . another inch forward and he would have broken his nose.

"How lucky was that!" he thought to himself, turning over. His narrow escape took his mind off the headache and he slept quite soundly after that.

Not that he'd dwelt on it much but this wasn't the first time he'd narrowly escaped injury. Falling a long way out of a tree and getting away with a few bruises; watching his brother jump on an old wooden slide and going straight through it, that was nasty one . . . Bob lying on the sofa, his Mum bathing his back and picking out long splinters with tweezers . . . but Alan had jumped onto it only a minute before, probably weakened it being a fairly chubby chap back then. Crossing the road on his bike was another example . . . car approached faster than he'd noticed and clipped his back wheel, spinning the whole bike round and throwing him off . . . only minor cuts and bruises. He'd even managed to put the front wheel of the same bike down a slotted drain cover, jamming the wheel into it and going straight over the handlebars, with only scratches on his palms to show for it. Most people could think of similar narrow escapes, it's just part of growing up, but sometimes he really felt like he had a guardian angel. He certainly considered himself lucky over the years.

The alarm went off for work as usual at 6.45 and it was a struggle to get out of bed after the disturbed night. He tip-toed out of the bedroom, grabbed his clothes that he'd hung off the landing balustrade the evening before, crept across the creaky floor to the bathroom and cleaned his teeth. As usual, he was trying not to disturb his wife, Beth and his daughter Holly, who didn't need to get up for another half an hour . . . thirty minutes that they *both* considered quite precious.

Stark naked, he crept downstairs and got dressed in the hall. It was a chilly morning and the heating hadn't been on long. He had a busy day ahead running a training course for the local council . . . Three-quarters asleep he wandered into the kitchen to grab his usual bowl of muesli . . .

"That was a close one earlier, wasn't it" said a voice behind him.

"Christ on a bike!" shouted Alan involuntarily, nearly jumping out of his skin!

"Ha! That's great—haven't heard that one before! He moves in mysterious ways but I've never seen him on a bike!" Sitting at the kitchen table was a muscularly built middle-aged man looking down at some paperwork. *That* was surprising enough, but there was more . . . he had a pair of large feathered wings hanging over the back of the wooden chair! Alan was wide-eyed in shock . . . there was an angel sat in his kitchen!

"Sorry Alan, didn't mean to startle you old chap". David was very used to being around Alan, but Alan certainly wasn't used to being around David.

"David" said the angel amiably introducing himself, extending a hand of friendship. Alan was almost speechless, but managed "What the hell are you doing in my kitchen!"

"Really? You can't guess? I know you've wondered about me in the past . . . " the angel replied.

"What?" said a shaken Alan. Then a penny dropped . . . "No way!" he whispered under his breath.

"Oh yes, Alan, *way* . . . It's me! Your guardian angel! Sorry to startle you! I'm just sorting out the paperwork for that incident last night. Minor of course . . . "

"Paperwork?" said Alan confused.

"Well, I *could* have done it elsewhere of course but I needed to see you . . . or I needed *you* to see *me* I should say."

Alan shook the hand of his guardian angel, which people don't often get to do. A large hand with a firm shake. There was an air about David that was obviously not human . . . confident and serene . . . although he *was* wearing a T-shirt and jeans. A glow covered his surface. Angels were always painted with a light behind them and this one fitted the bill perfectly.

From his predictably kind face, David looked in his mid-fifties, his skin almost pearlescent . . . "I'm a bit older than that Alan!" said David jovially.

Naturally, the wings attracted Alan's attention.

"*Touch* them, they're real!"

"Bloody hell" said Alan as he passed his hand over the soft feathery surface and looked closely at the area they passed through the T-shirt into his back.

"Not a bad pair eh, if you pardon my French!" said David opening both wings as a swan would open theirs for a stretch and a shake.

"Jesus!" said Alan in wide-eyed amazement.

"No, *David*."

"You *really* are, aren't you" said Alan, slowly coming round to the idea.

"Yes, I *really* am! You might want to keep your voice down with your family upstairs . . . they can't see or hear me but they'll hear you!"

"Oh, OK" said Alan.

"Why paperwork? Angels don't need *paperwork!"* said Alan under his breath, trying to find a reason not to believe.

"You'd be surprised. He runs a tight ship you know" David pointed out.

"Who?" asked Alan,"God?"

"Well sort of—not in the biblical sense" David replied.

"What do you mean—not in the *biblical* sense?" Alan said disbelievingly, still under his breath.

"Well, no robes and beard and stuff. You probably wouldn't recognise him. Look, your family will be up soon and we haven't got much time . . . this sort of thing is a little unorthodox, you know. I'll speak but you just think your replies and I'll hear them."

"Really!" said Alan in a loud whisper.

"Yes, really . . . I'm a bloody angel" said David impatiently.

"OK" thought Alan.

"Right", said David "now you have usually left the house before they get up haven't you . . . so I want you to shout up "goodbye, have a good one, etc", then shut the door as if you've left to walk to work . . . then *I'll* take it from there. Just come back in here after you've shut the door".

"What?" said Alan out loud.

"Think man, think! Please, just do it Alan, I promise you there is a good reason" assured David.

So Alan did as he was asked . . . "Bye chaps, have a good one" he called up the stairs and two muffled, sleepy "bye"s came tumbling back. He opened and closed the front door and then returned to the kitchen.

"Now, this will be a little odd for you now" said David, "we can talk normally now, but your family will neither hear nor see you. We will be here but they will have no indication of us at all. Also, I have taken the liberty of cancelling your work today"

"What!" said Alan, back at normal volume.

"Don't worry, I have said it's an illness and I can assure you that they completely understand and it in no way jeopardises your future work there. In fact, I think you will find that your future work there may grow" said David.

Alan went to say "What?" again but David interjected.

"Don't ask, all of this is a little unorthodox shall we say. Now come over here, take a seat and let's talk . . . "

Alan sat down immediately opposite his guardian angel.

"So you've looked after me all this time! All those times as a kid, on the roads, up the trees . . . "

"Yep, that was me! Since the day you were born. That's what we do!"

"Are there *others*?" enquired Alan.

"Of course! You're special but you're not *that* special! All of you have one of us allotted at birth—you may have noticed that, as a species, you can be quite accident prone! Right, down to business. We have a problem, Alan . . . you're supposed to die today."

"What!"

"Yes, I'm afraid it's true. Now *I* certainly don't want you to die yet, and I'm pretty sure *they* don't want you to either" said David looking towards Holly who was sleepily mooching into the kitchen.

Half awake, she opened the cupboard, took out a breakfast bowl and dragged herself across the kitchen for some cereal. Beth then followed Holly into the room. She hadn't had a great night's sleep but to Alan, she still looked good.

"Do you want ham in your sandwich?" asked Beth. "Sure, could I have a couple of Chunky Kit-Kats too?"

"A couple! What makes you think you've deserved a couple!" said Beth jokingly.

"Aww, come on, it's part of my "Five-a-day"

"What, five crappy chocolate snacks?"

"Yes", said Holly laughing.

"Fair enough" said Beth but this banana is going in as well"

"Nooo! Not the fruit of the devil!!" shouted Holly melodramatically. Beth well knew that Holly hated bananas, commonly known in the house as the "fruit of the devil". She sneaked an apple into the box instead. David was privately amused as he'd heard that the devil *was* actually quite partial to bananas.

Alan loved the family banter, and he knew how lucky he was.

"I don't want to die" he thought.

"We'll do our best to avoid it" replied David

They really can't see us can they!" Alan commented, walking right up to Beth's face . . . he could still smell her, but she didn't register his presence at all.

"Don't worry, it's a temporary thing. Look, I'm going to have to turn the sound down here so we can get on . . . " Beth and Holly's voices gradually faded and they went about their morning business as usual leaving Alan and David free to concentrate on theirs.

"I don't want to die today" said Alan looking directly at David.

"No, *indeed*" replied David "now we *really* need get a move on".

"So I had a day planned for me?" asked Alan.

"Everyone has their day" replied David "but there is a bit of flexibility in the system".

"Thank God!" said Alan.

"Yeah, you probably should. He pushed through the exemption and, it's taken a while to work through the system but I *do* have it!" David waved a small ticket from his pile of paperwork in Alan's direction.

"That's good" said Alan smiling, stating the obvious.

"*Undeniably!*" said David, "good for you, good for your family . . . you get more time! Very few people do, you know. You wouldn't believe the paper-work involved in this!"

"Thank you. Not just for this, but for all those times in the past. I knew someone was looking out for me!" said Alan.

"Not at all" replied Alan's angel "it's my job! . . . and Colin covered for my holidays . . . now he *is* an angel to see! Never lost *anyone* in all his years. You know he's looking after the *Pope* now? Of course you don't ! He's the *best* you know . . . You're lucky to have us, you know, not a bad team!"

Alan was finding it hard to take it all in.

"Look we need to act quickly, there's not much time" said David. "At 10.44 a concrete canopy over a shop doorway is going to collapse and you are supposed to be under it."

"Shit!" said Alan.

"Quite" replied David, "but, don't worry, it's not going to happen. The only thing is this whole thing is going to be easier if we are there *together* . . . you will be drawn to it, you see. Your morning will *arrange* itself so that you *will* be there, so it's better for me to stay with you and get you there just before."

"But why me?" Alan asked, "why do *I* get more time?"

"I don't know the details! It's on a need-to-know basis, this one" said David, "but I *do* know it's come right from the top."

"But there must be a reason" said Alan . . .

"Oh yes, there's a good reason all right. Doesn't happen every day you know! Whatever it is, I'm pleased I can carry on looking after you . . . I get more time too you see!" said David smiling.

"Hold my hand, we need to get going now" said David as he quickly gathered his paperwork and placed it into his small leather satchel.

Alan placed his hand into the glowing hand of his angel and, as they touched, they both appeared on the pavement just across the street from the coffee shop, just down from the council offices . . . the bustling public oblivious to their arrival.

"You were due to walk down the street to grab a cappuccino from "Frappo's on your break from the council office" explained David to Alan . . . "At 10.44, that damaged concrete canopy over the insurance building was due to collapse, killing you instantly"

"At least it would have been quick!" thought Alan.

It was 10.42 and Alan felt an irresistible urge to cross the street to the shops . . .

"Now, that's the pull of destiny you are feeling there! I am going to need to hold you now, Alan" said David. In the middle of a busy pavement, with people walking by them and through them, unseen and unheard, David wrapped his wings around Alan, completely enclosing and softly restraining him.

"Now, there's a few things I am allowed to tell you . . . " said David

Alan was enveloped in a soft, white cocoon. He wanted to leave but a calmness was descending on him.

"Number one: You will live well into your 90's . . . I won't say exactly when, but you'll have all your faculties and die quietly in your sleep. Nice to know I'd imagine . . . and helpful for planning your finances!" said David. "Number two . . . Don't worry, it's not the end"

David wrapped his wings a little tighter around Alan and his calmness was complete, bathed in a bright white light . . .

"And Number three: I'll see you later, my friend and you can meet the whole gang."

The ground shook as the canopy collapsed . . . and David was gone.

Alan looked on as, almost in slow motion, people screamed and ran about through the dust. No-one was hurt at all.

Many years passed and Alan often thought of David. He *had* mentioned it to Beth, but being even less religiously sympathetic than Alan, she had dismissed the whole thing as a dream. She believed it was important to Alan, but she wasn't at all convinced of the reality. She *had* noticed a change in Alan, though. He seemed happier, more calm. Alan was certainly very grateful for the time he had been given.

Nineteen years later, Alan and Beth celebrated their 15th wedding anniversary, with a holiday in Rome. They had a magical week, the weather was great . . . even the new Pope was in town having just returned from a European tour. And this man was causing a stir, really shaking up the status quo. He was pro gay-marriage, pro women priests, promoted use of condoms in Africa . . . he was helping a *lot* of people, doing a *lot* of good . . . restoring the popularity of the Church too.

David's boss knew it was rare for such people to rise to these positions and, over the years, he'd also noticed that, in the unlikely event they do have some influence, we had a disturbing tendency to kill them! So he'd put Colin on the job of looking after the new Pope. He was still the best and so far had done a fine job of taking care of this gentleman during his years in office. But that day, Colin made an uncharacteristic mistake . . . let one slip through the net . . . he let an assassin's shot get through as his Holiness stepped out of his limousine. It wasn't just Colin protecting him either, he was flanked by bodyguards as you'd expect. But this one slipped through. Colin *did* manage to move him slightly, enough for the bullet to miss his head, but it clipped an artery in his neck, and he lost a lot of blood. Inconveniently special blood . . . This Pope had an almost unique blood type, incompatible with many other types. The local hospitals had supplies, of course, but their stock had been spoiled by a freak refrigeration fault. It was a sequence of events that wasn't supposed to happen . . . but it had.

The assassin was easy to catch. He dropped the rifle and walked straight towards the Polizia with his hands up, welcoming the instant worldwide recognition.

There were other people in Italy with the same blood type, but not anyone in Rome that day . . . except Alan . . . who, with David's discreet help, just got to the hospital in time. The newspapers said the Pope's survival was a miracle.

Just as David had assured him, Alan enjoyed a long ,happy life, with Holly and Beth close by. There were a few close shaves along the way but David continued to look after him well. Always looking out for him. Until, one night, quietly in his sleep, Alan died . . .

"Hello again Alan!" David smiled, his wings outstretched "we've been expecting you!" And there was the whole "gang" . . . all the people that David had ever protected, there to welcome him.

Love

"He loves me, he loves me not, he loves me . . . ". Karen had never really been sure. Even so, Bob's "twenty-seven year itch" was unusual. And for him to scratch it with her best friend, unforgiveable. In *this* room, between *their* sheets . . .

The smell reminded her of queuing at the butchers . . . cold and fresh.

Bob had said the white carpet was a mistake. He was right.

Sitting, Bob's head cradled in her lap, his eyes open but unfocussed, she continued with the pliers and his fingernails . . .

"He loves me, he loves me not, he loves me . . . *he loves me not*".

(Note: This story has exactly 100 words)

A Golden Lining

"I've got my wife's breakfast!" said the cheery old gentleman holding up a jar of baby food.

"Ha, Ha . . . " laughed Jill, joining in the joke, one place ahead of him in the supermarket self-checkout queue.

"No, really. She's paralysed—has been for four years now."

Jill was mortified "I'm so sorry" she said, wishing the floor would swallow her up. It was a heart-sinking moment, ranking No.2 after the time when her sister's very young son had asked, again in a supermarket queue, why the lady in front of them looked like a monkey. Her sister had no explanation. Apparently she took it very well, as did this gentleman. Smiling, he dismissed Jill's reaction, "Don't be silly! Tell you what though, I used to joke about house-husbands, staying at home looking after the family . . . you won't hear me doing that now! I don't know how my wife brought up three children. It's hard work isn't it!"

"Sure is!" Jill said smiling.

A self-checkout became available and Jill's attention was diverted keeping things out of the bagging area, and trying to avoid being the 67th person that morning that had made the checkout crash.

"You take care" she said to the gentlemen as she turned to leave.

"I will, you too" he replied, infinitely more chirpy than the assistant at the self-checkout who, it appeared, had actually lost the will to live.

Jill was used to such random incidents. It didn't matter where she was or what she was doing, she attracted a conversation. She wasn't sure why. She was certainly polite and friendly, but not overly so. The supermarket conversation stayed with her for a while, not just because of the embarrassment, it was the poor man's predicament. She didn't know who he was, or anything about him except he was clearly looking after a loved one with some huge difficulties. Although she would almost certainly do the same in his position, she thought that the deal that some people got was a pretty raw one. Not for the first time she thought "We all take so much for granted . . . ".

Over the years, she'd had some experience of people with disabilities: helping out at a special needs school in her teens; helping at a local swimming club for disabled people in her twenties; a wheelchair-bound friend with multiple sclerosis . . . She had some experience, and empathy . . . not sympathy or pity . . . just a respect to treat people as normally as possible.

Four hundred and thirty eight copies of the Echo were piled in Jill's hall. On most days this would be unusual, but not on a Thursday. It was the day of her daughter, Molly's, paper-round, completed reluctantly of late as it had been a very wet winter and, in her words, it was "a lot of work for a tenner." The original idea of the round was to perhaps instil in Molly a character-building work ethic, and to boost her pocket money. However, more often than not, Jill ended up doing some of the round with her to help but, if she was honest, she enjoyed being out and about and, of course, people talked to her. She felt it was fortunate that people *did* talk to her, especially since the unexpected death of her husband from a heart attack two years ago. The shock of that event was still a big part of their lives and she was only just finding a way through the fog she had been in. Financially things were fine and she didn't need to work. Emotionally things were not great, and not working had led to her feeling slightly cut-off from people. She was lucky to have three or four genuinely close friends, more than most, but it was the day-to-day banter that she was missing—like the gentleman in the supermarket. So, in a strange way, the paper round was therapeutic. Molly was more than happy for her to help . . . not just for the extra pair of hands either, but for the company . . . she'd been in a dark place since the loss of her father. In many ways, her and her Dad had been very similar . . . stubborn, silly sense of humour . . . which had caused some fireworks over the years, but she missed him dreadfully.

Thankfully, Molly had her mum. To some people, Jill may not have appeared to be the strongest person but, when the chips were down and people needed help, she was there, quietly doing what was necessary . . . always saying the right thing. A great Mum.

It was drizzling, dark and cold but, between them, Molly and Jill completed the paper round on time, both keen to get it done. Later that evening, after snatching a TV dinner, they were both relaxing in the living room and Jill started to absent-mindedly flick through the Echo. Most of it was quite depressing, a burglary here, a mugging there but, hidden amongst the gloom, were little gems. She particularly liked the personal ads . . .

"Molly, listen to this one" said Jill eagerly.

"Aww Mum, no! It's going to be gross!"

"No, you'll love it . . . "

"Sexy, petite, fun-loving blonde seeks tall, muscular, broad-minded gentleman for fun and occasional dog-walking. Must have own car and teeth. Husband not experimental but happy for me to seek pleasure elsewhere, with the right animal-loving person".

"Animal-loving! Oh my God!" screamed Molly hysterically.

"Yes, apparently she likes goldfish it says here . . . " said Jill unsuccessfully trying to keep a straight face as they both dissolved into a fit of giggling.

After further chuckles at the personals, Jill's eyes fell on a bold title at the bottom of the page:

'Blind woman speaks about abuse since moving into town."

Back to "depressing" with a crash! As she read the article, she was absolutely incensed . . . an Eileen Madeley had recently moved into town from the Norfolk coast and had experienced several incidents of intimidation and abuse from a "group of youths" in the town centre. This included taunting and swearing, as well as attempts to make her walk into lamp-posts. The youths had apparently videoed some incidents and uploaded them onto You Tube . . . "Oh, very big of them!" Jill fumed. A thirty-one year old blonde lady, she had been born partially sighted and sadly lost all her sight at the age of 16. She was quoted as saying "I am quite a calm person at the best of times so I just ask them 'why did you do that?". Her concern was that other disabled people may be intimidated into not leaving their house. She, however, would not be intimidated. Apparently people round here had far less respect for her than those on the Norfolk coast although she was big enough to say that most people were hard-working, helpful and honest with only a minority causing problems . . . "I don't want to get involved in confrontation. I think it is up to others to make a stand . . . if people see these things they could provide evidence to the police."

Jill's anger increased with every word . . . "How could people do this?! How can people not put themselves in her shoes?! Why don't people stop them?! One day of blindness . . . no, one *hour*, would make them think twice about their actions".

Jill had no intention of blinding them, she wasn't that kind of girl, but she *was* a girl who intervened to help. She couldn't stand by and do nothing. And, at that moment, she resolved to help Eileen.

The following morning, she half-expected her annoyance level to have subsided—perhaps to a 6, but it was still a full-on 10. This kind of "picking on the vulnerable" pressed all the wrong buttons and her resolve to help was as strong as ever. She decided that she would somehow contact Eileen and perhaps offer to follow her discreetly when she went to the town centre. Originally she thought she could do this without her knowledge but that seemed a bit sinister . . . she thought *she* might end up getting reported! No, she would somehow contact Eileen and offer to help. She was obviously upset about the whole thing, or why would she have gone to the papers?

Eileen was easy enough to contact. She was on Facebook and Jill managed to message her, with some help from Molly.

It was a tricky message to draft but she thought it read pretty well in the end:

"Dear Eileen,

You don't know me but I read your article in the Echo this week and was very annoyed at your predicament. I cannot believe people would treat you in such a way and I would like to offer my help, if I may. Perhaps we could meet for a coffee somewhere to talk about this. Maybe I could accompany you when you go into town, perhaps at a distance, so that the youths could be properly identified? Whatever you think might be helpful. I certainly don't want to be involved in any trouble of any sort, or possibly direct trouble towards you. I would just really like to help. As you say, I am sure this is a silly minority of people but I think it is important this stops.

I fully understand if you do not reply to this message but, if you would like to meet, and you think I may be able to discreetly help, please let me know.

Best regards,

Jill

PS. I'm honestly not a nutter, I genuinely want to help!"

Jill deleted the "PS" thinking it made her look more like a nutter and pressed "send", fully expecting no reply. For two days, there was nothing and Jill hoped that she hadn't offended Eileen by the message.

Then, on the Sunday evening, Jill received a reply . . .

"Hello Jill,

Many thanks for your recent message and kind offer of help. I have thought about it and have decided to leave it for now. Things seem to have calmed down recently and may have resolved themselves. I can't thank you enough for your message of support which really helped in itself.

I hope you are well and many thanks again.

With best wishes,

Eileen"

"Yep, she thinks I'm a nutter" thought Jill to herself, half regretting sending the message in the first place and half hoping that things had indeed resolved themselves.

'No problem Eileen. Good luck with everything. Best regards, Jill' . . . and with this message, Jill got on with her day, week . . . life.

Despite her unpleasant experiences, Eileen liked going into town. She loved the hustle and bustle of it all. She really did think the trouble was caused by a tiny minority and she wasn't easily scared. Blindness is pretty scary. It's not often you would say blindness was an advantage, but in this town centre it possibly was. A run-down 1950's new town, there was a dilapidated look about it all. What was once "the place to shop" in the 70's was now quite sad and tatty, like an old lady who'd let herself go. But Eileen saw it through different eyes . . . the bustling sound of people, the children playing, the jokes of the stall-holders. Sure, it wasn't the place it had once been but Eileen's audio town wasn't a bad place at all. In fact, most of her visits there cheered her up no end.

There was one new wing to the town, a modern, undercover, mini-mall . . . a pretty brooch on the worn-out coat of the "old lady". Moreton's chocolate shop was the biggest draw for Eileen, but she found the atmosphere in the mall rather sterile. Apparently it looked good but, to her, it attracted more than its fair share of plastic people . . . well-dressed, harmless enough, well-off, but quite dull. No, her best conversations were to be had outside in the main drag of the centre . . . one long pedestrianized high street, the centre open but the entrances to the shops on both sides under cover. People came from far and wide in the 70's to shop here but now the wear and tear was showing. There had been some maintenance over the years but somehow, the local council had a knack for adding to the seediness with their colour schemes. Fortunately, Eileen was spared the tacky combo of turquoise and vomit green that had been selected for the latest half-hearted refurbishment. A committee somewhere must have actually liked this combination as it was all over the town. A more likely explanation may that it was cheap . . . or a friend of a councillor knew someone, who knew someone, who had no taste at all but lots of paint. Perhaps the committee were blind themselves? The refurbishment had actually made things look worse, a rare talent. Fortunately, to Eileen, there wasn't a big difference.

This main drag was quite well kept, with some of the bigger high street names in the prominent positions, but the numerous off-shoots had started to become neglected, with fewer and fewer people bothering to navigate this far. Eileen loved these little tributaries, as they housed some of the more interesting shops. A tattoo parlour, not really Eileen's scene but intriguing . . . a comic shop . . . she really liked the people in there . . . a proper old-fashioned sandwich bar. The main drag had the Starbucks, the off-shoots had a slightly over-weight lady in an apron with a big metal tea-pot that had 15 tea bags in it that was constantly replenished with boiling water from an urn . . . and tasted fantastic! They always gave Sam, her dog something to eat and drink too. Starbucks was full of people who thought they were somebody, this place was full of people who *were* somebody. At least, that's how Eileen saw it.

Sadly though, the remoteness of the back streets sometimes attracted a less welcome element . . .

"Oi, oi! Here she is boys!"

Eileen could feel Sam tensing and quietly growling, intensely protective of her but, no matter how hard he tried, not very threatening. She had wandered into a remote part of town near the car park with very few other people around . . .

"I don't understand how they fucking allow it do you?" said Big Sean as he was known to his two friends, "I mean if she was in the wild, she wouldn't fucking last five minutes!" Sean was indeed big for an eighteen year old and a well-practised bully. Not your run-of-the-mill cowardly bully, who'd crumble if someone faced them off . . . that was his sidekicks who enjoyed basking in Big Sean's shadow. No, unfortunately Sean was one of the dangerous kind, the 1% of properly nasty bullies who actually enjoyed it, incapable of putting themselves in their victim's place . . . and didn't care anyway.

Eileen wasn't easily rattled but there was something in his voice this time that scared her.

"What is your problem?" said Eileen "I'm just walking through."

"Not today luv"

Eileen could hear Sean approaching her determinedly, not a stroll, more a stride . . . until he was so close, Eileen could smell his clean minty breath.

"This is our patch luv and I don't want to see you and your kind here. Is that clear enough for you?".

"I can go anywhere I like in this town" Eileen replied nervously. She wasn't intimidated easily.

" 'Course you can!" said Sean cheerily, who then turned quickly and kicked Sam in the head as hard as he could, knocking the dog unconscious.

"Anywhere you like, luv, just not here . . . UNDERSTAND!".

Sam didn't make a sound as Sean and his accomplices ran off laughing.

"Bastards!" cried Eileen to Sam . . . "You bastards!" she screamed after the boys, pointing out something that Sean already knew, took a pride in even.

Sam wasn't out for long. Rather than a slow, groggy recovery, Sam snapped back into consciousness, jumping straight up on all fours, immediately assuming a defensive position.

"Are you alright boy?" said a relieved Eileen, ruffling the fur under his chin.

She could tell he was OK. They made their way round the corner to the sandwich bar where they sat down at a table for two at the back of the shop . . . then Eileen started to shake. The lady with the urn could see something was wrong.

"Are you alright, Eileen?" she said concerned.

"I'm fine . . . just had a bit of a shock with those bloody kids"

"Those bloody idiots! You sit there, I'll get you a mug of hot, sweet tea on the house luv. Do you want me to phone the Police?" the urn lady said.

"No thanks" replied Eileen "I'll do it later".

More for Sam's sake than hers, she *did* contact the Police but, although they had been helpful in the past, unfortunately not much had actually changed.

Sean was known to the Police and they certainly sympathised with Eileen, but they just didn't have much evidence to go on. Far from unintelligent, Sean had a knack of covering his tracks well.

After this episode, Eileen really felt shaken. "So much *malice* . . . " she thought. Then she remembered Jill's message and, at that moment, she resolved to contact her.

"Dear Jill,

It's Eileen Madeley here, the lady you kindly contacted a while ago with an offer of help. Well, after some recent events, I'd like to take you up on your offer of help, if it was still available? You mentioned perhaps meeting for a coffee? I was wondering if Thursday at 3.00pm suited you—maybe at the Costa in the Old Town and I could explain the situation? I understand if circumstances have changed but I would be grateful if we could at least meet.

Many thanks for your original offer of help again, Jill.

With best wishes,

Eileen"

Jill was really pleased to receive the message. Things were quiet for her and she did genuinely want to help. Eileen sounded like a good person.

So meet at 3 they did. Over two lattes and ridiculously small complementary biscuits, Eileen and Jill got to know each other.

They got on well, as Jill somehow knew they would, and chatted like old friends . . .

"You tell me how you'd like me to help, Eileen and I'll do anything I can" said Jill, thinking that whatever happens, she has found a new friend.

"Thank you so much. I don't want any trouble, just some information that I can hand to the police so they can take some action. I liked what you said in your first message about following me into town . . . maybe at a distance?"

Jill didn't want any trouble either, mainly for Molly's sake but oddly, there was a part of her who didn't mind it, even quite *enjoyed* a little confrontation.

This trait had gone way back with her. In her primary school days she'd had her own gangs. Not marauding, violent hoards, just gangs who weren't afraid of a little confrontation . . . not at all "urban gangster", just a quiet rural village school. Even then, people gravitated towards her.

The first two trips into town with Eileen were uneventful and Eileen's relentlessly positive side again started to think that perhaps it had run its natural course. Jill enjoyed spending time with Eileen but felt disappointed that she hadn't had a chance to help yet. But, on the third trip, that chance came . . .

Sam stopped and growled in a low grumble . . .

"I thought I fucking told you to keep away from here" rang out from behind them as they walked round the corner near the car park. They turned and there was Big Sean and his two sidekicks. Jill quickly looked around assessing the situation . . . not a soul to be seen. Big Sean really was good at picking his moments.

"Who's yer friend then? What's this, safety in numbers, eh! Ha, ha, ha . . . I could fucking cough and she'd fall over!"

"Fuck off arsehole" replied Jill instinctively, if not tremendously wisely.

"Wo! We've got a feisty one here boys! Even more fun! She's a looker isn't she . . . I think we can calm her down. Go on boys, have some fun".

With that "Sidekick 1" ran towards Jill and "Sidekick 2" towards Sam. Sam got another kick in the head and was held tightly by his collar. Jill was grabbed, bear-hug style and dragged around the corner against the wall. She put up a fight and managed to punch Sidekick 1 on the jaw . . . she was aiming at his nose but the wayward punch lacked any force.

At one point, being dragged round the corner, she had feared rape but she soon realised that restraint was the order of the day rather than violent assault.

Sidekick 2 had no problem kicking Sam and was a more worrying apprentice to Big Sean.

"That's a bit fairer now isn't it. Just you and me now" Sean said to Eileen.

"For Christ's sake just leave me *alone!*" Eileen screamed.

Sean moved round behind her and shouted "Booo!"

Eileen jumped and stumbled forwards.

Sean burst out laughing "Maybe you'll listen to us after this luv. You can't say I didn't give you a chance."

"Boo!" he shouted again.

Eileen jumped forwards again, annoyed with herself for the involuntary reaction, and attempted a stumbling run.

"*I'd* be scared if I was you Iuv" taunted Sean.

"Just fuck off will you!" blurted Eileen, some of Jill's directness rubbing off.

This was no random taunting by Sean this time. He had a plan and wanted to make his point final. Five steps in front of Eileen was an excavation in the pavement, a two metre drop into an earth pit containing some pipework.

"Argggh!" shouted Sean to the back of Eileen's head, laughing and raising his hands in his best comic monster style.

"Arrrghhh!" he shouted forcing Eileen closer to the edge of the pit.

"Bye, bye bitch" said Sean calmly to Eileen's face.

Breaking free of Sidekick 2, Sam ran across the square . . . and launched himself, full stretch, into Sean's face.

"Arrrgghhh!" shrieked Sean, falling sideways into the pit. Sam bounced off his head into the void . . . but landed on his feet. Sean's landing was less fortunate . . . he hit his head on some pipework on the floor of the pit, and was knocked unconscious.

Sidekick 2 had run after Sam and Sidekick 1 let go of Jill to follow him. Laying motionless at the bottom of the pit, Big Sean didn't look so big anymore. Panicking, they both ran off.

"Jesus Eileen, are you all right?!" said Jill hugging her and leading her back a safe distance from the edge.

"I'm OK" replied Eileen, shaken "What happened?"

"You're fine now. He's fallen into a hole here . . . he was bloody trying to make *you* fall!"

"Sam! Sam!" shouted Eileen panicking.

Sam quickly scrabbled out of the excavation and was soon jumping excitedly at Eileen's side, sensing that all was well. Eileen started to cry, "Hello Sam, hello" she said ruffling his fur affectionately, hugging him to her, Sam licking her face.

Big Sean lay motionless in the pit. Of course, Jill called the ambulance and Police . . . Big Sean was alive. But his head injury was serious and would leave him with some lasting effects . . . Firstly, his impressive repartee was slowed somewhat, the edge taken off his character, his speech and thoughts slightly laboured. This visibly frustrated Sean. Secondly, he had lost a little movement in his right arm and, over the years, this got worse, losing most of the movement. Over the years, it turned out Big Sean couldn't cope with disability quite so well as Eileen . . .

The Sidekicks were never seen in town again. Sidekick 2 was destined to lead an inconsequential life, generally irritating the majority of people he met, latching onto other dominant characters in his limited work and social activities. However, Sidekick 1 (The Restrainer) had a moment of epiphany . . . he changed. They say every cloud has a silver lining and this one was Shane. From the moment he saw Big Sean laying in that pit, Shane looked on life, and how he treated people, differently.

This particular cloud also had an additional adornment . . . a *golden* lining. Jill and Eileen had met. Eileen's gracious defiance of her disability, Jill's honesty and compassion, and both their senses of humour, combined to ensure a loving friendship.

This was, perhaps, Big Sean's greatest achievement . . . to bring these people together. Even in Sean's determination for destruction, he had created something good.

Jill liked to think he would find that annoying.

Tangerine Dream

Joe Ryan's father could easily be mistaken for Harold's dad in "Steptoe & Son". Old, skeletally thin, with a well-weathered face that had a resting position of a scowl. Unfair, as Alex was one of life's good guys. He just happened to have developed an uninviting face, a small grey goatee providing the only light relief.

It was 5.15pm and, as usual on a workday, Alex was parked in the lay-by in front of the airbase waiting for Joe to come out of work. His silver Citroen was beyond tatty, every panel marked, never washed, purely a mode of transport. Luckily, it was remarkably reliable and seemed to thrive on the neglect.

"Hello Dad" said Joe chirpily.

"All right, son? How was your day?"

"Ah you know, another day, another dollar . . . "

Joe was necessarily sketchy about the content of his days . . . Official Secrets Act, military contracts, very technical . . . "probably have to kill you if I told you Dad" Joe would say jokingly. He *was* joking. Even if he had to, he wouldn't . . . he loved his Dad.

Not many 53 year olds are picked up by their father after work but Joe liked it, and it made sense with them living together seven miles away in Colchester. Alex didn't work and enjoyed living with his son, keeping the house and tending the garden. At 85 he was remarkably fit, still driving, still enjoying life. "Sharp as a sausage!" Joe would often say.

Joe was popular at work, especially with the ladies. He was a charming man, not caddish, but well-meaning. A properly eccentric mad-scientist, with a wicked sense of humour, like his Dad. He looked nothing like his father, being slightly overweight with black hair receding away from his large glasses. Not classically handsome but attractive, his genuine character and humour shone through.

Joe was a gifted mechanical and electronics engineer. Ever since he could remember, he was building electronic equipment. In his bedroom as a child, he would surround himself with electronics magazines and effortlessly produce radios, telephones, metal detectors, tea-making machines . . . you name it and he made it back then. "Gifted", was a word often used around Joe. He was writing for the magazines he subscribed to by age 13 and he was pretty much instructing his professors at University. His level of natural ability didn't go unnoticed and, in his final year at University, he was approached by the military establishment. Eventually, he was attracted to work at the local air-base with the lure of cutting edge facilities and a budget which, if it had a ceiling, he had yet to find it . . . and he had tried very hard.

His military work was necessarily kept under wraps, even to his father, but Joe, like most people these days, took work home with him. Electronically speaking, he still fiddled in his bedroom, even at 53 . . . always a project on the go, each progressively more elaborate over the years.

"You, my son, need to get out more . . . you really do!" said Alex

"Yeah, yeah, I will. But I'm so close to finishing this"

"Yeah, but I can't tell when one project stops and another starts! The girls at the base won't hang around for ever you know!"

"You're sounding more like Mum everyday" said Joe distracted, continuing to work.

"God rest her soul. I suppose she'd be happy if you're happy . . . "

"I *am!* Very happy. I could just do without the distraction!"

"Even you need a break son, it's not healthy" said Alex.

"Do I look unhealthy?!" said Joe standing up and smiling.

"What you mean apart from being overweight and pasty?" Alex jibed.

Joe threw a cloth at his Dad, as he ducked out of the way giggling. It was more college pals than father and son.

The lights in Joe and Alex's flat rarely went out at night. For years they had been meaning to move from their small flat in a high-rise block.

They had the money. Joe was well paid and Alex had a good pension . . . they just never seemed to get round to it. Very often, their light was the last to go out in the block. When Joe was "in the zone" he was difficult to distract, even with sleep. Fortunately he could function very well with very little.

The flat was small but crammed with tools, storage shelves, workbenches and half-finished constructions. Less a home and much more of a workshop.

Since Margaret had passed away seven years ago, the boys had taken over and there was little of her decorative influence left . . . photographs of course, her old chair . . . Not that they had forgotten her . . . they missed her terribly . . . they had just outgrown the space.

The latest project had become an obsession. Joe had been working solidly on it for three years. Every evening, weekend, holiday . . . Alex could see he was over-doing it but Joe loved every minute.

"Dad! Dad!"

Alex rushed through the hallway into Joe's bedroom workshop, fearing he had hurt himself.

"Are you OK?" he said as he opened the door.

"Dad, I've done it!" said Joe in hushed tones, staring at the tangerine that was floating in the centre of the room, like a planet orbiting the central light bulb sun.

"Jesus, I've done it!"

Joe had indeed "done it". The tangerine was floating in mid-air with a small belt attached to it. The belt had been easy to fashion . . . however, the microchip inside it had taken three years to develop. Complex in the extreme but, in essence, the chip made anything it was attached to weightless. The tangerine still had mass, but for that particular object, the effects of the earth's gravitational pull were cancelled.

Joe's bedroom ceiling was spotted with orange stains, evidence of numerous earlier anti-gravity fruit failures, from a time when he had limited control over these forces. The real breakthrough now was that he *could* control it, and control it well. With a handset that resembled a model plane's radio controls, Joe guided the tangerine quite precisely . . . and promptly chased his Dad down the hall with it.

"Get off you bugger!" Alex howled.

As entertaining as a radio-controlled tangerine was, Joe had the vision to see beyond revolutionising the transportation of fruit. He realised the enormity of what he had just done . . . a*ny* object lifted effortlessly, cranes a thing of the past, construction projects speeded up, air transport revolutionised, huge fuel savings, satellite launches, rocket launches revolutionised, leisure opportunities . . . people could fly! "This could move *anything!*"

"What are you going to *do* with it son?!" Alex beamed, full of pride in his son's achievement.

Joe noticed a small red dot on his father's temple . . . then a bullet from a silenced pistol ripped through that same spot. His father was thrown to the floor . . . he was still smiling, it happened so quick . . . Joe saw a figure by the door . . . before Joe too was hit and killed instantly.

It seemed the air-base disapproved of Joe's "homework" . . .

The light in the flat was on all that night as usual, but no tangerines circulated magically around it. No life was left . . . all the fun had gone. By morning, all signs of Joe's project had been removed, reported as a particularly violent robbery . . . terrible thing. Neighbours were amazed . . . "it was a good block, very little trouble . . . people looked out for each other".

***

"What the fuck was that!" said Joe.

"Buggered if I know" replied his father staring at Joe, both standing in a clean white room.

"Bastards eh" said a white-suited man at the desk in the corner, without looking up from his paperwork.

"Who?" said Joe bemused.

"Those soldiers that shot you and cleared out your flat!" the man said looking up from his desk.

"Unbelievable" said the man shaking his head "and all for the money! It's *always* about the money back there, isn't it!"

"No matter . . . " the man said gathering his thoughts, "right, let's get your balances done"

"What?" said a bemused Alex.

"Over here please, gentlemen . . . if you could take a seat" said the man gesturing towards the chairs. Joe and Alex shuffled across the small, empty room and sat down on two of the three chairs that faced the desk.

"OK, let's start with you Alex . . . do you mind me calling you Alex? asked the man.

"No, that's fine" replied, Alex bemused.

"Excellent, excellent . . . "

Concentrating on his computer screen, the man scrolled through pages of information, interspersing his deliberations with the odd "Mmm . . . "

Joe had questions . . . "Can I ask . . . "

"Ah, ah, ah . . . no, no! Not just now!" said the man, holding up a finger preventing Joe's query from distracting him from his task.

"Mmm . . . " he continued.

"Well I have to say, Alex" said the man looking up "that it's all quite good . . . . *very* good in fact. Very little on the negative side . . . and I can see a *substantial* amount on the positive. You've led a good life sir!"

"Thank you" replied Alex, at a loss for anything else to say.

"Now, Joe . . . you don't mind me calling you Joe?" said the man.

"No, of course not"

"Excellent, excellent . . . well let's have a look at your figures, Joe . . . " he said, his eyes returning to the screen.

"Mmm . . . "

"Mmm . . . " deliberated the man, eventually making a note on his small desk pad. This was taking a little longer than Alex's balance . . .

"Is it all OK?" said Joe, beginning to worry.

"Ah, ah, ah! One moment, please sir . . . " said the man holding up the finger once more. After what seemed to be a long time, the man said

"Not so straightforward, this one . . . not so *cut and dried* as we say . . . "

"Oh?" said Joe, now properly concerned.

"Lots of positives, really very good in fact but, you see, we have these negatives here . . . most of them, of little concern to us but . . . what *were* you thinking of with the military thing?" he said looking Joe straight in the eyes, "Did you not *think* that your actions might have . . . *consequences*?"

Mildly panicking now, Joe replied "Er, well,er . . . I didn't think about it too much, I was just doing my work! They had all the equipment I needed . . . "

"Of course they did" said the man "but you've contributed to some really rather negative things, Joe . . . a little *selfish* maybe, a little *self-indulgent* I would say."

"But, I . . . " stuttered Joe.

"Look, we believe your intentions were good, and I think I can smooth some of these things over with my superiors".

"*Really?*" said Joe, daring a note of hope in his voice.

"Pretty sure of it. That tangerine thing of yours was a cracking idea! Nasty business just *now* of course but, after a few people have made their money, it's going to do a *lot* of good, you know . . . medical stuff, no more wheelchairs . . . more good than you think." he said smiling.

"We *will* be back in touch but, for now, you're both good to go."

Alex and Joe looked at each other.

A young man appeared at the back of room, looking around, disorientated.

"If you could take a seat sir, I'll be with you in one moment" said the man to the new arrival.

"Busy day today! If I could move you along?.." said the man to Joe and his father, beckoning them to the corridor behind the desk.

"Go on through, and turn *first* left . . . " he said smiling "*first* left, mind!"

"I think you'll like it."

Above the Line

A glint of yellow caught Alan's eye. "A flower maybe" he thought, peeking through the cracks in the pavement? He bent down for a closer look.

"Looks like a pill . . . " he thought. He picked it up and, yes, it was a small pill, it's surface a glossy hi-vis yellow, with a bright red line across the middle.

"Unusual . . . " he thought, dusting it down on his jacket and popping it into his pocket. Why he didn't throw it back onto the pavement, he didn't know.

He was in no rush that day, having taken a day off work, fancying a hair-cut and a stroll through the town. He turned into a coffee shop, set his latte on the table with a slice of walnut cake and took the little pill out of his pocket.

He had certainly never seen one like it, not that he had a lot of pill experience . . . never very ill, never tempted to experiment . . . Looking closer he could see, in tiny black print near the edge, "Exp.34."

Why he swallowed the pill was a mystery to him. One of those things that people, do on the spur of the moment, without thinking. When he was a child his mother had baked a cake, perfectly iced. He simply couldn't help running his finger through it for a taste. He knew his mother would hit the roof but he couldn't resist it. This was the same impulsive feeling. With a sip of latte and without thinking, he swallowed the little yellow and red pill.

"Perhaps not my best idea" he reflected, sipping the latte, looking around the shop . . .

The time for this pill to take effect varied from person to person . . . bodyweight, circulation, temperature, level of activity . . . lots of variables. For Alan, it was ten minutes. A bright yellow flash completely filled his field of vision causing him to jump and knock the table loudly with his leg, spilling what was left of his latte. A small collective cheer rose up from the customers in the shop and quickly died down. The bright yellow persisted for around five seconds, like he was caught in a yellow blizzard . . . then a clear, horizontal red line descended slowly through the yellow snow, settling at the half-way point, dividing his field of vision into two. Slowly the blizzard subsided and images began to reform . . . the table, the spilt latte . . . it all came back into view in the lower half but the *upper* half . . . the upper half was something else! Above the red line he saw a magnificent, tranquil mountain top . . . but not just the view, he was *on* the mountain top! If he looked down, he was in the coffee shop. But if he focussed above the line, he was on the mountain, breathing in the cool alpine air, feeling the sun on his face, hearing the birds . . . the beautiful stillness . . . he was there!

"Jesus Christ!" he said to himself under his breath.

"Sorry" said the waitress pointedly, thinking it was a comment on her intrusion to clear up the spill.

"No, no, not you, I'm sorry . . . "

"Are you OK" the waitress said, Alan's behaviour now registering as slightly odd.

"Er yes, yes. I'm all right. Could you do me a favour please and help me to the door. I'm not feeling so good"

"Yes, of course" she replied, and she lead him by the arm to the door, opening it for him. He could see the girl, the coffee shop, the floor, everything as usual, looking below the line . . .

"Are you sure you're going to be OK? Did you want me to call someone?"

"No I'll be fine in a second" Alan said, not entirely convinced, "you've been very kind".

Concentrating on the lower half, Alan made his way across the street to the nearest bench to be alone. He felt fine, extremely well in fact. Sitting down, and trying not to draw attention to himself, he focussed above the line. It was an easy technique, just like looking up into the sky . . . He was near a large rock now . . . the cool air on the mountain was much cleaner than that on the high street . . . and it was still a beautiful sunny day up there . . . odd, as it was overcast and windy in town.

It appeared that, in walking across the street, he had also changed position on the mountain top . . . this was incredible!

"Jesus Christ" said Alan. He focused his attention below the line to check he was still actually in the street, and he was . . . the normal quiet hustle and bustle of an overcast Tuesday lunchtime. He wanted to get away from people so, he made his way round the corner and through to a recreational area . . . very few people there and plenty of space. He walked to the centre of the mown grass field and then re-focussed above the line . . . He was now very close to the edge of the mountain top . . . not a sheer drop, but a grassed, domed mountain top that Julie Andrews from "The Sound of Music" would have looked at home in . . . gently sloping away, progressively steeper . . . leading to snow-capped peaks in the distance. Light mist hung horizontal in the still alpine air, everything calm and lit by ice-clear sunshine.

"Good morning . . . could I ask you to mind the lines please"

Alan turned to see a young man in his twenties, just finishing laying out the lines of his parascending equipment.

"Oh, sorry" said Alan.

"No worries!" said the surf-styled young man, "Didn't see you in the cable car . . . did you walk?"

"Yes, just walking" said Alan hesitantly, not believing the man could see him, "here on a trip".

"You've picked a good time. You'll never see it better than this."

"It really is beautiful" Alan said slowly, looking into the distance.

"Jesus Christ" Alan thought, "I can move around and talk to people!"

Alan watched as the young man connected his harness.

"Good to meet you!" he shouted to Alan and waved.

"And you". And with that, in the complete stillness and silence of the mountain-top, he ran down the shallow grassed slope . . . his chute fluttered, filled and rose up behind him and, shortly after, his feet left the ground. Alan stood watching in awe as, like a sea-gull soaring, he gently entered the scene in front of them, hanging majestically in the silence, slowly exploring the sky, until he became quite small.

"Do you mind mister, you're right in the middle of our pitch!"

Alan looked down to see two boys and a football . . .

"Sorry" and he moved away towards the edge of the playing field. As he walked, the red line across his sight rose slowly upwards and the yellow blizzard returned. Standing still, all he could see was a bright yellow . . . When the football hit him, he was completely back in the playing field . . . no red line and no other world above it.

"Sorry mister!" one of the boys shouted. They honestly hadn't meant to hit him.

"Don't worry" Alan replied, not caring, still trying to make sense of his unplanned excursion.

"Every time you say goodbye, I cry a little,
Every time you say goodbye, I wonder why a little . . . "

Ella Fitzgerald sang. Jean Paul worked better with music. It helped him concentrate . . . but it had to be jazz. Having just returned to his home in Brugges, Belgium, it was time for a stock-take. London, Paris, Munich, Copenhagen . . . his latest tour had been very successful, the limited number of people he had allowed to sample his products having received them very enthusiastically.

Opening his large flat leather case on his oak dining table, he laid the laminated product list out beside it. Inside the case were many vertical columns of tablets stacked in clear tubes, the tubes secured in the case by loops of brown leather. Each tablet was carefully separated from the next by a small piece of cotton wool to avoid damage in transit. Each column a different colour, creating a rainbow effect as you looked across the case . . . and at the head of each column a label . . . Exp.1, Exp.2, Exp.3, etc. 1-25 on the left hand-side and 26-50 on the right. Jean Paul was looking at his life's work. The case represented the culmination of all he had worked for and, at last, he had started to make some money . . . big money. His home/laboratory in medieval Bruge was far from cheap, his car far from economical. Like Alan on the mountain-top, Jean Paul existed in a rarified atmosphere . . . the top end of the drugs market you could say . . . and, at this altitude, there were people who were prepared to pay a lot of money for his "experiences." One day, their manufacture may be cheaper and perhaps they could be made available more widely but, for now, it was a product for the very few . . . an international club almost. Part of Jean Paul wanted to keep it that way too. The money was a bonus but not his prime motivation. He wanted to create a beautiful, high quality collection. Fifty chemically-induced "experiences", controlled so finely that your senses told you that you were actually there.

". . . so strange the change from major to minor, every time you say goodbye."

As Ella sang, Jean-Paul counted his stock. There should be nine in each column . . .

Experience 1. Love

Experience 2. Sex A

Experience 3. Sex B

Experience 4. Sex C

Experience 5. Sky Dive

Experience 6. Vampire

Experience 7. Moon

Experience 8. Eagle

Experience 9. Murder

Experience 10. Whales

Experience 11. Family

Experience 12. Space walk

Experience 13. Princess

Experience 14. Heist

Experience 15. Guerrilla

Experience 16. Formula 1 . . .

Jean Paul was rightly proud of the range he could offer, carefully selected after extensive market research. His particular clientele had an eclectic range of indulgences . . .

On his last tour, he had "tested" each experience once, leaving nine tablets each . . .

"Experience 33. Roman Orgy"—nine tablets.

"Experience 34. Mountain Air"—only eight . . . he counted again . . . still eight.

"Damn it" he said to himself out loud. He looked carefully around the case, in every nook and cranny, but it wasn't there. Each tablet represented a considerable amount of laboratory time and a very considerable amount of money. *"Every time you say goodbye, I die a little . . . "*

"Damn it" Jean Paul was furious with himself. The top of the tube had worked off and it must have dropped to the bottom of the case, where he found a small hole in the stitching. He quickly checked the caps on the other tubes . . .

"Shit!" he said out loud . . . finding the cap had also worked off Experiment 49.

Again, only eight tablets. He checked all through the case, but found nothing.

Eventually his anger at himself subsided, calmed by a chilled champagne. He had learned an expensive lesson and it wouldn't happen again.

It is true to say that Alan had started *his* hallucinogenic adventures at the high end . . . like learning to drive in a Bugatti Veyron . . . and he had loved it. His mind was, as they say, blown. Feeling extremely well after Experiment 34, he ran past the children playing football out of the playing field, round the corner, passed the coffee shop, back to where he had found that pill . . .

"Could be more . . . have to look . . . before someone else finds them . . . "

Trying not to attract too much attention, he searched the area carefully for signs of any more. The last one had stood out to him so he scanned the area, hoping his eyes would pick out any bright anomalies . . . Fifteen minutes passed with nothing but brightly coloured litter, so he widened his search area slightly.

"It's a long shot . . . be lucky to find one . . . forget it Alan" he started to think. Then a small purple object caught his eye lying at the foot of a brick wall. It looked like a sweet that a child had dropped but, to Alan's amazement, on closer inspection, it was no sweet . . . Deep, velvet purple with the same red line across the centre! He looked closer and, yes, in white print it read Exp.49. He couldn't believe it! This time he took it home with him . . . and sat looking at it on the kitchen table with half a glass of water.

This time there was no hesitation from Alan. He swallowed the tablet eagerly, washing it back with water and sat in quiet anticipation at the table. In around ten minutes, a bright purple flash, followed by a purple blizzard . . . and the red line descended . . .

Alan was found four days later by a friend, still seated at the kitchen table.

Jean Paul hadn't got round to health warnings and Alan was unaware that he had the heart weakness.

It had been quite an experience . . .

"Experience 49. Horror"

Part Four

First Impressions

"Tsh, tsh, tsh . . . " tutted the young Asian woman as five packs of honey-smoked ham inadvertently tumbled into her basket. Amanda was wholly responsible for this. In an attempt to reach the cheese slices, her sleeve had clipped an unstable row of sliced ham causing them to "domino" off the shelf straight into the young woman's shopping basket. There was a funny side to this but the lady had certainly failed to see it. It was one of the most disapproving "tut tuts" that Amanda had ever witnessed . . . a bit of an over-reaction in her opinion. "It's not like I've dropped my trousers and shaken my bottom at her!" she thought. What's more, the tutting was accompanied by a shaking of her head, as if the woman actually *despaired* of her behaviour . . . like she had *regularly* been the victim of people tipping packs of ham into her basket, week after week, and it wasn't funny anymore. Except now it was starting to be . . .

"I'm sorry" Amanda apologised, half-smiling, but the woman shook her head and turned away. A giggle rose up in Amanda's cheeks and had to be forcibly restrained at her nose. She was almost successful too, only a small snort relieving the huge pressure of amusement.

Amanda continued her shop, entering the ready-meals aisle where a young shelf-stacker was unloading a cage of quiches, creating a "traffic-calming" restriction. Thoughtfully, Amanda held back with her trolley and beckoned a pensioner couple through with a smile. They smiled back, pushed their trolley through and, as they passed, Amanda heard "Tsh, tsh, tsh, tsh . . . "

"What!?" said a confused Amanda turning round. But the pensioners were quickly on their way.

"Odd" she thought "perhaps it was *their* conversation, not aimed at me . . . maybe I was a bit touchy there"

Shortly after she reached the checkout queue, Amanda noticed the previously quite loud conversations had subsided into small groups murmuring . . . some looking in her direction, and yes, some of those tutting!

"*Really?!*" she said out loud, backing her trolley up, parking it at the end of an aisle. Amanda marched straight the nearby toilets to check herself out properly.

She looked in the mirror and could see nothing wrong. Smartly dressed . . . she took a pride in her appearance . . . recently washed, nothing offensive perfume-wise, quite expensive in fact . . .

"Maybe it's my hair?" She normally wore a hat but was too busy this morning . . . "It's not that bad!" she thought.

Amanda smartened her clothes and returned to the checkouts. People were still looking . . . so she hurriedly put her few items through the quieter self-checkout at the end, and drove home.

Pleased to get home, Amanda put her bags down in the hall and hung up the jacket of her Nazi uniform on the peg.

Then it occurred to her . . .

"*Surely* not . . . that was *years* ago!"

An Artist's Impression

The day started badly for Jean. There are few things worse in life than dreaming the alarm has gone off forty-five minutes before it actually had! She'd even dreamt that she'd woken up and pressed the button too . . . all very confusing. Things didn't look like they were going to get any better at school either. Two days of Art exams, one of her preferred subjects but the teacher, Ms. Bow, was a challenge. Jean's mother was a keen artist and found it hard to understand how Ms. Bow could make art uninteresting . . . the infinite styles, the myriad materials, the cornucopia of colours, themes . . . how could it be boring? But Ms. Bow had achieved this. Jean wasn't looking forward to it. For three months she had been drawing and painting two animal bones . . . a short leg bone and a sheep's skull. She had nothing against bones . . . she rather liked them . . . but *two* bones for *three* months! There was a limit to Jean's bone fascination and it had long been reached. To add to the tedium, each exam she faced was a yawning five hours long, and she figured she only needed an hour, tops.

Jean often drew for pleasure at home, listening to music on her headphones, losing herself in the art and the songs. Her music of choice was currently a heavy "screamo" style, the "singer" literally screaming through the "song", loosely in tune. Her parents found it difficult to understand how she found this relaxing but what parent understands their 15 year-old's taste in music? It worked for her and so she had asked Ms. Bow if she could listen to her music during quiet work in art lessons and maybe during the long exams? Stork-like in her stance and instinctively unhelpful, Ms Bow snapped "Certainly not!"

"I'll just be sitting quietly and I'll keep it low so it won't annoy anyone . . . " Jean said hopefully.

"Are you deaf child?! Absolutely not! No headphones in exams, those are the rules"

"OK Miss"

"She's not kidding anyone with *Ms.* Bow" Jean thought, "no-one would marry her!".

That evening, Jean mentioned the debacle to her Mum, who was incensed. "Where's the harm? Who are you bothering? Leave it with me and I'll have a word with the old witch!" She felt a pang of guilt for describing Jean's teacher like that in front of her, but she was only being accurate.

The meeting went quite well, Jean's Mum deciding that staying calm might be more productive than a verbal fist-fight. She explained that the music helped Jean with her dyslexia, explained that she understood the headphone ban in other subjects, but in Art? What help could it be? And it worked . . . reluctantly the old bat agreed! "I will allow it for this examination, if she finds it helps, *providing* no-one else in the class can hear it at all."

"Thank you Ms.Bow" said Jean's mum, thinking "perhaps she's not so bad . . . "

"No, she *is*" she concluded.

Jean was delighted. It really did help. The next day she settled down for her five hour chore. The subject this time was another still life . . . a twisted tree branch with three apples imaginatively placed to lift the tedium. They weren't working . . . But, with the music in the background she started to get into a rhythm with the drawing.

Shortly into her favourite song of the album, the volume slowly faded out. "Must have moved the volume slider . . . " she thought . . . no, it was fine . . . "Damn, must be out of charge then . . . "

"Hello Jean" said a clear Scottish voice through her headphones.

"What?" Jean said under her breath . . .

"It's important you just listen" the voice said calmly "you know what the old witch is like."

This made Jean smile. The voice was older, male . . .

"Who *are* you?" Jean whispered.

"No matter now, I'm here to help you" said the voice, "and there's no need to talk, just think.."

"OK" thought Jean. And help her he did . . .

"Try smudging that line to blend it" he suggested

"You need to work on the light on the top of the apples"

"That's amazing" thought Jean as the apples popped out of the paper.

"Draw what you see Jean, draw what you see" he advised.

The minutes flew by . . . hours flew by, Jean completely absorbed.

"This is going well. I think we can do a good job of this!" said the voice reassuringly. "We work well together, don't you think?"

With an hour and a half to go, the picture was finished . . . and it was beautiful. They *did* work well together.

"OK, what shall we do now?" said the voice.

"I don't know" thought Jean, intrigued what the voice would come up with next. It was a lot more fun than art normally was.

"I've got an idea, Jean" said the voice "Look at her up there . . . smug as you like. Why did she become a teacher? Just to mess with people?!"

"Beats me!" thought Jean.

"Ok Jean . . . " said the voice "did you want to hurt her, or did you want to help her?"

"What!" thought Jean.

"I wondered if you wanted to *hurt* her, or *help* her?" repeated the voice, "I can organise both . . . "

"I'm not sure" thought Jean uneasily, concerned things had turned odd.

"Don't worry, I won't do anything serious to her!" the voice laughed.

"Err, OK . . . don't *hurt* her" Jean thought instinctively. "*Although* . . . " a very small part of her was tempted . . .

"No, *help* her" Jean said emphatically, "*Help* her"

"Och, I was hoping you'd say hurt! She's terrible! OK, I'll help her but we'll have a bit of fun first shall we?"

"Er . . . " she hesitated, but before Jean could answer, Ms. Bow released perhaps the loudest and longest fart that any human being had produced. Clearly audible by everyone in the room, it was a great leveller! The whole room dissolved into laughter, even the second invigilator was in hysterics!

Ms. Bow left the room, to return a few minutes later. A ripple went round the room as she entered but gradually things calmed down.

"I enjoyed that!" said the voice.

"Oh, you've made my day!" smiled Jean, her face still wet with tears.

"OK, you said you wanted to help her . . . " said the voice. "Any ideas?"

"No! You said *you* could organise it!" Jean thought.

"I mean *how* do you want me to help her? Financially? Spiritually? Socially?.."

"I don't know . . . how about *socially*" thought Jean "I don't want her to be a rich witch! She could be a *real* one if we went down the spiritual route!"

"Aye!" he said laughing gently "OK, I can do that. Leave it with me"

And with that, her music faded back in.

As Ms. Bow walked back to the staff room she bumped into an Ofsted inspector, dropping her files. Gathering them up she went to snap at him, but . . . his suit . . . his clipboard . . . it was a case of love at first sight! Ms. Bow couldn't believe it. Things like this didn't happen to her! He couldn't believe it . . . things like this didn't happen to him! But it *had* happened to both of them. The Scottish gentleman had certainly helped Ms. Bow . . . changed her life very much for the better. And, after a while, it really took some rough edges off her. She was still a stickler but, over time, *Mrs.* Bow was to be a lot easier on the children.

Jean got an A, her first in any subject. The examiners would have given her an A+ but her work was so reminiscent of the style of the late Ken McLeish, they thought it a little derivative . . . thought perhaps she'd memorised it or practised beforehand. Either way, it was very good.

From that moment, Jean's love for art really blossomed and her work eventually started to get noticed. Ken would talk to her many times in the future, always through her headphones . . . guiding and advising her.

Jean had also started to do very well selling McLeish reproductions.

She was always very honest about it being *her* work . . .

. . . but even the experts couldn't tell the difference.

The Mistake

"You're making a mistake. When you realise you *have* made a mistake, get back to me and we'll see what we can do" said the business man on his mobile.

That's all Les heard as they briefly shared the shop doorway, business man leaving, Les entering. At least he *looked* like a business man . . . eccentrically trousered in tweed, sporting a blue blazer and bow tie. His almost comical look slightly undermined the serious tone of his message. "What mistake?" thought Les as the shop door closed behind him, "Was it *that* bad?.."

Largely empty except for a couple of desks and dusty artificial plants in tall vases, the shop had a retro 70's feel about it. In reality, the shop hadn't actually changed since the 70's . . . the same orange carpet tiles, the same aluminium framed suspended ceiling with some tiles missing . . . as if time had stood still. In the centre of the room a large old railway station clock hung from the ceiling from two chains, with a red sticker across the face "Not in Use" . . . "Time really *has* stood still" thought Les, amusing himself.

It was the three clocks in the shop window that had made Les curious enough to call in . . . Three black and white, plain clocks hung in a line facing outwards, like you see on a stock exchange floor . . . except these had no "London, Tokyo, New York" labels, just three different times . . . 3:50, 2:50, and 7:35. Three clocks in a largely empty, nameless shop. "Intriguing!" he thought.

"Morning sir" said the T-shirted young man behind the counter.

"Morning. I hope you don't mind me asking, but I was just wondering what those clocks are for in your window?" asked Les, gesturing towards them.

"That will be a pound please sir."

"Sorry?" said Les, confused.

"A pound, please sir" said the shopkeeper, pointing to the sign above the counter.

All clock enquiries £1

"We used to say "If we had a pound for every time a person asked that . . . . . . then we thought we would actually charge it!" smiled the shopkeeper.

"Ah ha, very good!" said a semi-amused Les, reaching into his pocket "well look, you've got me so here's my pound" he said sliding it across the old counter. "What are they for then?"

"Telling the time sir"

"Well, *yes* but for what purpose . . . the three times?" replied Les, thinking this geek had the potential to be really quite annoying.

"Sorry sir, couldn't resist . . . no, we've got three people out at the moment and those are the times they're due back."

Les noticed that the clocks displayed the same times inside the shop as they did outside.

"Back from where?" asked Les.

"Let's see . . . " said the geek sliding over a dusty red book and opening it to the page marked with a ribbon.

"Denise is in Rome, Brian is in Australia and Lee is in Sussex"

"So, you're a travel agency?" Les suggested tentatively.

"I suppose we are, sir . . . of a kind. Yes, a travel agency"

"But why the clocks? Why do you need to know when they're back?" said Les thinking this was the scruffiest, most brochure-free travel agents he had ever seen.

"Oh it's important sir, our trips can't be late. It really is quite critical" replied the geek.

"Really, there must be flights to Rome every hour?" said Les.

"Not *Ancient* Rome sir"

"Pardon?" said Les.

"Ancient Rome, aboriginal Australia and the Battle of Britain at Biggin Hill . . . they're a bit trickier sir. Timings have to be exact" said the geek.

"Ah, OK" said Les, now concerned the conversation had taken a definite turn for the bizarre.

Before he could back politely out of the shop, the young man suggested "Want to try it?"

"What?" Les said smiling.

"A trip sir"

"Ah . . . well, I'm a bit busy . . . " said Les almost backing away.

"Try it *now*, if you like sir, we're quite quiet at the moment. I can see you have your reservations, sir, but don't worry, it's perfectly safe"

"Now?" said Les, still intrigued by the whole affair.

"Take a seat" said the shopkeeper smiling, gesturing towards a completely unremarkable, lightly padded wooden chair.

"Just need you to wear this, sir" said the shopkeeper with an air of routine, passing him a baseball cap with a lead dangling from it.

Les thought this was hilarious—his girlfriend wasn't going to believe this!

"Are you serious?" said Les incredulously.

"Were you expecting some grand HG Wells Time Machine contraption, sir!? Bit more basic here I'm afraid."

"When you're ready sir, just plug the lead into the USB port on the chair"

Les couldn't believe what was happening to him . . . "Ha, ha, go on then!" And he slotted the connector into the port.

Immediately, he was back outside the shop:

"You're making a mistake. When you realise you *have* made a mistake, get back to me and we'll see what we can do" said the business man on his mobile as Les brushed passed him to enter the shop . . .

"Morning sir" said the geek . . . and the whole conversation they had had so far was replayed, right up to the point that Les plugged into the chair . . .

As Les did, the geek said "Welcome back sir, you're back on real time now"

"What the hell!" said a shocked Les.

"It's quite something isn't it sir"

"What is it, some kind of hypnosis?!" asked Les

"Oh no, nothing like that. Quite simple really" replied the geek.

"It was amazing!"

"Glad you enjoyed the free taster session, sir and if you are interested, please call again. We are always open".

In a daze, Les thanked the geek and left the shop, not really taking notice of anything around him until he reached his house.

He was right . . . Hannah his girlfriend, didn't believe it. She wasn't convinced at all. In truth, she was a little concerned about him but she was already late for a night out with the girls.

"You're bonkers! Tell me more in the morning" she said, hurrying out.

Les found himself on his own for the evening. Not for the first time. Hannah was a nice girl but she was more often out than in. The "girlfriend" arrangement was loose and irregular, her choice not Les'. He knew it wasn't going to last. He could have done with the distraction of Hannah's company as he found it difficult to think of anything else but the shop . . . There was no question about it, he *was* going back. It was incredible! But he still had his doubts . . . "Maybe some kind of David Blane character . . . " he thought to himself, spooning down a hastily prepared Pot Noodle, "some kind of hypnotic state . . . " He was *definitely* going back . . . and he knew exactly where he wanted to go.

By 7.30, he was standing across the street from the shop. It looked very unassuming, a bakery shop to the right and a roller shutter door to the left. And the three clocks were still in the window, all of them now reading 12 o'clock.

"Good evening sir" said the business man from behind the desk.

"Ah, hello" replied Les, recognising him by the blazer and tweed.

"We thought you may be back today. It's quite something isn't it!"

"So, how do you do it" said Les bluntly "is it a trick?"

"A trick sir? No, not a trick as in a deception sir, more a manipulation . . . *a manipulation of the laws of physics!"* the business man announced rather extravagantly, with the air of a circus ringmaster.

"Did you want another go sir?" he said smiling, looking directly at Les.

"Yes" said Les getting straight to the point. He couldn't wait.

"You understand that this time there will be a cost?"

"Ah yes, I imagined there must be. Can you give me a rough idea?" asked Les.

"Well that rather depends on where and when you want to go" replied the business man, "do you have any ideas?"

"Where might you suggest?" said Les, wondering what the possibilities were.

"Well there's a lot of past to choose from sir . . . you may like to look through this" he said handing Les a glossy brochure.

It was quite a brochure too. Very glossy, obviously expensive, beautifully photographed . . . "nice brochure" said Les, for no apparent reason.

""It *is* a good advert for us isn't it sir—there's the web-site too of course . . . we try to keep up with the times but still pride ourselves on a good old-fashioned personal service".

Les sat down and flicked through, glancing at random titles . . .

Planning your trip . . .
Ancient Cultures
Key Political Events

Wars
The Rich & Famous
Sporting Achievements
Scientific Landmarks
The Dinosaurs
Key Geological Events
A World Before Man, etc . . .

Quite a selection! It wasn't that he wasn't interested in these . . . he really was . . . but he knew where he wanted to go . . . or rather *when.*

"Actually, I don't need to travel very far from here or go back in time very far at all" said Les, passing back the brochure.

"Are you sure? You could go anywhere you like sir" said a surprised business man.

"Quite sure" replied Les " . . . and it's probably all I can afford!"

Twenty-two years ago, when Les was seven, his father hadn't come home. He'd been to work that day . . . they knew that . . . but he just didn't come home.

"Missing person" is a difficult thing to come to terms with over the years, especially when it's your Dad. Broke his mother's heart too. And Les, being the only child, had a constant reminder of that awful day for years. He was sure it took its toll on his mum who he had lost the previous year.

Weds 17th April 1981—a date he would never forget . . . the day his father didn't come home. That's where he wanted to go . . . at 5.15pm.

"And the place sir?" asked the business man, "where do you want to be on that date?"

"Doncaster railway station"

"Really sir, we are *in* Doncaster!" the business man pointed out.

"Shouldn't be too expensive then!" hoped Les.

"I'll sort the price out now for you sir" said the business man tapping on his calculator.

"Four hundred and thirty four pounds sir"

"Not *that* cheap then" replied Len.

"We'll call it four hundred sir. We do take all the major cards."

"That's fine" said Les, passing his VISA card over.

"Out of interest, how much is Ancient Rome then?!"

"If you have to ask sir . . . "

"*Really,* that much . . . Just as well mine's a local trip!"

“Indeed sir” said the business man smiling “but, you have to agree, we provide a fairly unique service.”

“I’m hoping you *do* . . . ” said Les starting to realise the enormity of what he was attempting. To see his Dad . . . catch him as he left the station where he worked . . . and follow him, to find out what happened.

“OK . . . Re-living or observer sir?”

“Pardon” said Les.

“Re-living or observer sir . . . You can re-live the time or be a passive observer of it”

“Oh, observer . . . yes, definitely observer”

“Splendid sir, although I need to mention that you will not be able to interact at all with anyone. You will be there, but you will not be seen, or indeed have any physical effect on anyone. It’s best not to try either sir.”

“No, that’s fine, I just need to see” said Les.

“As you wish sir. If you could place this cap on your head as before and take a seat on the chair over here” said the business man gesturing to a similarly plain wooden chair behind a screen next to his desk.

Joining Les behind the screen, the business man said “Just plug in when you’re ready sir” and bending before him he looked into his eyes and said “I hope you find what you are looking for Les”. With that he got up and turned back to his desk.

Les plugged in without hesitation. The machine was incredible . . . as soon as the plug pushed home, he was outside Doncaster station. He really felt like he was there, standing outside on the pavement . . . He could smell the cool spring breeze, hear the noise of people bustling around, the laughter of the guards as they shared a joke. He *was* there!

“Time . . . what time is it?” Les thought.

He knew his Dad finished work at 5.30 . . . He quickly walked round the corner into the station and a large hanging clock said 5.22. He hoped he hadn’t missed him. “Maybe he’s finished early?” He hoped not.

He knew he’d use that exit . . . had to . . . it was the only way to the car park . . .

“There he is! I think it’s him . . . looks like him . . . ”

“It *is* him!” Strolling out of the station heading for the path to the car park! Les ran down the gentle slope towards him. It was definitely him!

“Dad it’s me!” shouted Les alongside him, without thinking. “It’s *me!* It’s Les Dad!”

Of course his Dad couldn’t hear him.

"*Dad!*" shouted Les as he tried to grab his arm.

No response . . . like trying to grab smoke. His Dad seemed to scratch an itch on that arm. Walking briskly alongside his father, he pulled on the same arm again . . . no itch this time.

Transfixed, he followed his Dad to the car. He watched as his father opened the passenger door and put his satchel on the seat . . . Les slipping onto the seat with the bag before the door was closed. It was like a dream.

His father flicked the radio on and started humming along to T-Rex, "Ride a White Swan" . . . and he drove towards the town, completely unaware that his son, now two years older than him, was sitting beside him.

Les couldn't take his eyes of him. They say we all turn into our parents eventually . . . apart from his father's long hair, it was like looking in a mirror. It was fantastic being with his Dad, Les still looking through the wide eyes of a child.

His father parked up in the main street and went to the newsagents for some cigarettes, Les following him the whole time.

In the shop queue, Les shouted again "Dad, it's me, *Les*, I'm here!", again trying to grab his arm. His father scratched his arm again, as if to relieve an irritation as he turned from the counter and left the shop.

Les watched him light a cigarette and casually wander up the street, unwinding for a moment, slowly exhaling the smoke up into the air . . . Eventually, his father stopped outside a shop window. A shop window that was familiar to Les . . . on one side a roller shutter door, on the other a bakery and in the window, a single, large railway clock hung from chains facing the street, reading 6:40.

Les watched his Dad staring at the clock, smoking his cigarette. His father glanced at his watch and then, after throwing his cigarette stub on the floor and treading on it, he went in.

Les couldn't believe it. The shop looked exactly the same, right down to the artificial plants . . . and the business man stood behind the counter! Same blazer, same tweed trousers . . . and the same age, not younger!

"Good evening sir" he said in his familiar voice.

"Hello" replied his father "couldn't help wondering what that clock in the window is for"

"Ah yes sir, people do wonder . . . It's to tell us when people are due back" said the business man.

"Back from where?" Les' father enquired.

"Wherever we have sent them sir"

Les could see his Dad was intrigued. "Do you mind if I smoke?" he said

"Not at all sir, make yourself at home" invited the business man.

"Actually, if you have time sir, take a seat . . . "

As his father took a seat in the basic wooden chair, Les suddenly re-joined the businessman in real-time.

"That's it sir, you're back with me now" said the business man.

"I hope you found it useful?"

"He tried it didn't he!..You know where he is, don't you! You know where my Dad *is*!" cried Les.

A haunted looked crossed the business man's face and his eyes fell on the old railway clock hanging from chains with the red sticker "Not in Use" . . . "I'm afraid the process wasn't quite as reliable back then sir . . . I really am truly sorry."

"Send me to him! It's in the book isn't it, in that red book!" shouted Les pointing towards the large red book on the cupboard behind the counter.

The business man reached for the book and, opening its dusty pages on the counter, he looked straight into Les' eyes and said "I understand why you want to sir, and I *will* do this for you . . .

. . . but you're making a mistake. When you realise you *have* made a mistake, get back to me and we'll see what we can do."

Rainbow's End

"Raaaainbooww!" "RAAAAINBOOWW!" screamed Davy.

"Raaaainbooww!" he screamed wide-eyed for the eighth time. He was surrounded by children, most of them laughing, as if he'd been dared to shout "rainbow" at the top of his voice, as many times as possible.

But he didn't have the look of a child playing a prank. Children doing it for devilment don't break down in tears, shaking and exhausted . . .

The laughter gradually subsided to an uncomfortable silence as Davy sobbed, curled into a foetal position on the school field.

"Raainbow" Davy groaned, exhausted.

Some closer friends went over to help him. The less empathetic drifted off in search of other events in the playground to hold their short attention spans.

"OK lads, break it up now! . . . What's all this then" shouted Mr Wenham, breaking into a jog. "Davy? Are you all right son?"

Davy didn't reply, still shaking.

"What happened?" he said, turning to his friend Owen.

"He just started shouting sir and got himself into a right state"

"OK, let's get you inside young man" said Mr Wenham, slowly helping him to his feet, brushing the grass off his jacket.

"Can you come with us please Owen"

"Raainbow" Davy murmured faintly as Mr Wenham and Owen helped him across the field to see the school nurse.

The previous day had been glorious. A perfect summer day of the sort that happens about three times a year in the UK. Blue skies, hot, sticky . . . a little oppressive . . . but it was a small price to pay. All summery dresses, T shirts, and lifted spirits . . . *And* it was a teacher training day! Perfect timing! Davy and Owen had been inseparable since they started school together. From day one, they had gravitated towards each other, laughing and having fun, and today was no exception. They had almost finished a ramshackle tree-house in the woods a bike ride away, and that's where they were headed. Their "treehouse" was really only some old planks nailed to the trunk of an old willow tree, wigwam-style to provide some shelter for no more than two. The arching fronds of the old willow provided a wonderful natural domed space over the wigwam, its walls a leafy green, the floor carpeted with dappled light and dead leaves. Quite spacious. They had upturned plastic crates to sit on and brought drinks and snacks for sustenance. It was a perfect base to explore from, the woods spreading extensively in all directions, eventually emptying into open, idyllic fields of haystacks and hedges. In the summer they could often be found there. Not easily though. As far as their parents knew, they were out on their bikes . . . the wood was private and, strictly speaking, they shouldn't have been there. With only one wide entrance, they decided to set up camp a long way into the wood, so no-one would notice. And they had never seen a soul . . . until that day.

The day had got steadily more oppressive, no breeze, just still air heating up like an oven. Big clouds bubbled up. The birds had stopped singing as a grumble of thunder rolled across the sky, like an ogre clearing its throat. Owen and Davy looked at each other.

"We're fine in here Davy" said Owen chirpily "no lightning's gonna get us in here"

"S'no problem" Davy agreed "I don't think it'll leak". Neither of them were worried. They wouldn't have been in the depths of a private wood if they were. They were having a ball and the storm just added to their adventure.

The grumbling continued until the ogre tore the sky with a rip of lightning. The boys jumped but they still didn't worry, grins over their faces.

"Bloody hell!" said Davy excitedly laughing.

After more grumbling, an almighty crack announced a torrent of rain. No wind, just the heaviest rain, hitting the broad leaves of the wood, filling the air with a static hiss . . .

Davy was right. Only a few drips penetrated the leaf dome of the willow. It was a good shelter. They sat there, dry, looking at each other, enjoying the spectacle, looking around in awe as the rain continued to fall.

"Argh!" shouted the man as he burst through the draped branches of their shelter.

The boys scrambled back to the side, his entrance causing them to jump much more than the lightning.

"Jesus" he said putting his broken shotgun down and shaking his head like a dog to clear the water from his long hair and beard. "Ahhh!"

This tall, broad, Hagrid-like intruder made the shelter feel suddenly small, with his big leather coat steaming above moleskin trousers and boots.

"We don't mean any harm, mister!" blurted out Owen.

"Jesus H Christ!" said Hagrid as he turned to face them.

"We're just playing mister, don't mean any harm!" repeated Owen quickly, properly frightened.

"What the devil are you doing 'ere?! It's private you know!"

"Just playin', that's all" said Davy, shoulder to shoulder with his friend.

"My God, you gave me a fright!" said Hagrid laughing "Just wasn't expecting anyone . . . " He turned to pick up his shotgun and looked down the barrels. The boys had felt safe in their shelter. They didn't feel very safe now . . . so frightened they couldn't move.

"Oh sorry lads, didn't mean to frighten you . . . just trying to get out of that rain!"

"Sorry, the gun . . . don't worry I'll put it down!" And he did.

"I'm the woodsman round here. It's for pigeons, rabbits, you know . . . "

Some colour returned to Davy and Owen's cheeks and they started to breathe.

"Don't worry lads, you can stay 'ere, just gave me a fright that's all" Hagrid laughed.

"I won't tell anyone, don't worry. Won't tell Mr.Searle, I won't. You carry on playing"

"OK" Owen said wide-eyed, "thanks mister"

"Sorry to frighten you lads, I'll leave you to it . . . rain's easing off now"

"You carry on playing" Hagrid said laughing "you're not young for long you know!"

"Thanks mister!" said Owen and Davy in unison, full of relief. What an adventure the day had been so far!

The rain eased off. Some brightness returned and the birds started to sing again. The boys played a little more in the shelter, amazed at how dry it had kept them. They laughed and they played and they ran through the woods, the occasional string of bramble catching their bare ankles . . .

"Douuuffff!" They heard a loud bang echo through the woods . . .

"Was that a shot?!" said Davy.

"Could be lightning, or one of those bird scarer things?" replied Owen, looking around as the sky murmured, the ogre moving on to the next village.

"Reckon Hagrid's got another pigeon!" joked Davy.

As they walked, the woods thinned into a large pea-green field with tall haystacks in the corner.

"No-one's going to believe we've actually met Hagrid!" laughed Owen.

And they played on the giant hay steps, leaping and climbing and covering themselves in hay.

After a while, they lay exhausted at the foot of the haystack, looking up at the almost cloudless blue sky, the warm day flowing over them like treacle. What a glorious day it was now! The ogre had definitely moved on.

Well, one certainly had . . . but "Hagrid" wasn't quite the same as the amiable character in the film. He liked children, certainly. And he was friendly . . . to start with. His grooming was a gradual process. He didn't earn a child's trust overnight . . . it was a waiting game. The trick for Hagrid was to have more than one on the go . . . then there was always one at the right stage. For years, that had been the case.

The boys got up and looked across the field down the valley . . . a beautiful rainbow as clear as you would ever see! And it looked so close!

"Wow!" said, Davy, transfixed.

"Look it's coming down at the edge of the woods over there! Let's go and find the end of the rainbow!" shouted Davy.

"What, for the pot of gold?!" laughed Owen.

"Yeah, the pot of gold!"

"I really need to get back now, I said I'd be back an hour ago" said Owen reluctantly.

"Aww c'mon Owen!"

"No seriously, I need to get going . . . I'll see you at school tomorrow" he said, turning to run back for his bike.

"Bring some of that gold in for me!" he shouted back to Davy.

Davy ran down the valley towards the edge of the wood. The sun had gone in and the rainbow had faded but he knew the spot . . . Exhausted, he started to jog at the edge of the field, walking the last few steps . . . and, there, in the long grass that lined the path, lay Hagrid . . . on his side, curled up in a foetal position. A thick dark puddle of blood had pooled on the mud path by his leg. Hagrid normally carried his shotgun broken . . . but not today. It had slipped from his wet hand and blown most of his left hip away. He'd moved a little across the grass, but not far. It hadn't taken long. Davy knew he was dead. No movement at all . . . too still. No breath from that friendly beard.

He couldn't scream.

He ran all the way back to his bike . . . "must get home".

He couldn't cry.

He bowled into his house, mumbling and headed straight to his room.

"Davy, your tea's here!" . . . no reply.

His Dad put it down to being 11 . . . "I'll leave it outside your room" he called.

Davy took it in but he didn't eat a bite.

The night closed in and Davy told no-one.

And in the morning, he walked to school.

Strange Brew

One bottle of Radox "Stress Relief" shampoo, one individually wrapped exfoliating sponge, a roll of cling-film, a box of firelighters and two unusually large bottles of cheap sparkling white wine. It was an interesting selection on the supermarket conveyor and, for Dan, it was the same shopping list every week.

"Hello Dan" said the friendly checkout lady.

"Hello love" replied Dan warmly.

"Getting the usuals in then I see . . . " she smiled, slightly bemused.

"Oh yes"

"Don't tell me . . . " she smiled "you're having a bath in the wine, next to a nice roaring fire?"

She tried to guess every week, never successfully.

"If I told you, I'd have to kill you!" he said jokingly, as he did every week.

The checkout lady smiled "Do you need a car park token, luv?"

"No thanks, I've got my trolley" replied Dan.

"'course you have. Well, have a nice one. Weather's supposed to be good they say"

"The weather can do what it likes" replied Dan "I'm gonna be inside! Bye."

"Bye, Dan, see you next week luv"

"He's a lovely chap" she said to the next customer.

"Yes, he seems it" the customer agreed, not entirely convinced.

It wasn't just Dan's purchases that were unusual—he had quite an unusual look . . . Short, stout with tight grey trousers and a bright blue cardigan. His grey hair was thinly scraped across his bald head, only a light wind needed to lift it away to reveal the impressive length required to traverse his head. His teeth were yellow and randomly arranged but this didn't detract from a genuine, friendly smile. He was a good guy. A little eccentric, but his heart was in the right place.

His council house was modest and he'd lived alone for some time. And Dan had the air of a man who had lived alone for some time . . . He liked people and enjoyed his weekly shop, but Dan was equally happy at home with his own company.

"Did you see the fight last night, Dan?" shouted over his new neighbour.

"No, who won?" he said politely.

"Bailey in the 12th with a knockout, you should have seen it!"

"Sounds good but I haven't got a TV!"

"Really! I don't blame you, there's not much on!"

"Good. I'm not missing much then!" smiled Dan.

He wasn't missing much at all . . . cooking, gardening, celebrity plate spinning or whatever the latest must-see programme was. It didn't interest him much.

He laid out the shampoo, the sponge, cling film, firelighters and the two bottles of wine on the kitchen table.

He did this every week. Each time, the same ritual.

He poured himself a glass of wine. It was cheap but he liked it. He poured the rest into a metal bucket, gently stirred in the shampoo and placed the bucket on the stove over a gentle heat. Once simmering, he melted the whole pack of firelighters into the solution. It was a strange brew . . . the airways-clearing pungency of the firelighters competing with the stress-relieving bouquet of the shampoo . . . and winning.

He had tried many shampoos, many firelighters, many, many wines, before coming up with this formula. The firelighters didn't seem critical, but the shampoo had to be Radox "Stress Relief" and the wine, a sparkling Lambrini. It had been a process of trial and error.

"Mmm, looking good" Dan thought, stirring the concoction with a wooden spoon. The simmering time seemed to make a difference—25 minutes the optimum. The mixture was then left to cool, still quite liquid . . . around the consistency of runny honey.

He had tried eating it but it was quite disgusting. After much experimentation he had found it best to apply the mixture to his legs, gradually absorbing the active ingredients through the skin. Once the legs were evenly covered, he then wrapped his legs in cling film to seal it in, quickly pulling on the tight grey trousers . . . ladies trousers that had zips all the way up either leg. Ideal for this purpose, he had found.

To most it would seem a strange ritual but to Dan it was a process that he had been trying to perfect over several years. And he felt he was close . . .

After this careful preparation, he would usually settle himself in his favourite chair, and wait. He figured that this time, applying the mixture with the exfoliating sponge would speed up the absorption process . . .

Dan tried to clear his mind in preparation for what he knew one day *would* come . . . what he had worked all these years to achieve . . . a state of complete spiritual contentment. Not a crude chemical high, but a transcendental enlightenment, way beyond mere Radox stress relief . . . and he felt sure he was close to a breakthrough . . .

And then, it happened . . .

the mixture leaked out of the cling film onto the carpet. Not quite the breakthrough he was hoping for . . .

"Back to the drawing board!" he thought, already planning next week's modifications.

Dan really *did* need a television.

The Prune

"Looking good!" said Paul, admiring his new neighbour's neatly pruned wisteria. It perfectly framed the front window of his cottage, just enough draping lilac to look "picture-postcard".

"You can come and do mine when you've finished!" Paul continued, inwardly wincing at the unoriginality of his neighbourly small-talk.

"Of course, just say when!" his neighbour replied as he descended his step ladder.

"New pair of secateurs" his neighbour proudly announced, "*really* sharp!" he said, flexing the jaws.

"Here, look . . . " and he grabbed Paul's hand, as if to shake it . . . quickly, he slipped his hand down to hold Paul's index finger and jokingly placed it between the blades . . . Paul snapped his hand away instinctively. He knew it was a joke . . . of course he did . . . but he was quite shocked and, momentarily, it made him feel quite ill.

"Ha, ha, I'm Thomas" laughed his neighbour, extending his hand for a more conventional shake.

"Paul" he replied, reluctant to go in for the second shake.

"How are you settling in?" Paul asked, to move on from the awkwardness.

"Good thanks, we can't believe our luck with this place"

It *was* a pretty cottage, white walls, climbers, red door . . . The village didn't have a postcard but, if it did, the cottage would be in one of the small squares, the others being the church, the war memorial and the village green in summer, speckled with white cricketers.

"We've been trying to buy in the village for years, and here we are!" smiled Thomas.

"Well, welcome" replied Paul, now more composed "I'm sure you'll enjoy it, everybody's pretty friendly. If you need anything I'm down the road at number 44".

"Cup of sugar, anything" Paul thought sarcastically.

"Thank you Paul, much appreciated. Now, do you happen to know of any village clubs and such?"

"Oh yes, there's plenty. Bowls, badminton, tennis, Women's Institute . . . " said Paul.

"Ah, Pat may be interested in that. We want to get involved in village life you know"

"Well you're in the right place for all that, I'll drop in a copy of the Parish Magazine if you like. All the contacts are in there."

Just then, two young boys bowled out of the front door onto the gravel drive chasing each other, giggling. As they saw their father, they stopped so quickly they left skid marks in the gravel. Frozen-still, sitting on the drive, they looked at Thomas as if they'd seen a ghost.

"This is Paul, boys . . . from down the road. Say hello" Thomas blustered, much in the manner of Toad of Toad Hall.

"Hello" said the boys in sheepish unison, as they backed away into the house.

"If you could drop that book in, that would be excellent" Thomas said.

"Will do. I'd better let you get on" Paul replied, completing his small-talk collection.

"See you soon".

"I met the new neighbours yesterday" said Paul's wife Karen as she made them a sandwich.

"Me too, what did you think?" replied Paul

"Seemed nice people to me . . . very quiet" said Karen.

"Really?!" said Paul surprised,"What, Mr Toad!"

"Who?"

"Toad of Toad Hall! All he needed was the tweed suit and open top car!" laughed Paul.

"Ah, no I only saw Pat and the kids" said Karen "Did you notice the older one's hand?" she added.

"What?"

"Max, yes, Max I think it was . . . had a little finger missing" she said.

"Oh, poor kid" replied Paul.

"Yeah, born that way apparently"

"How do you know that?" Paul asked, impressed by her comprehensive knowledge of the new family.

"She told me . . . think she saw that I'd noticed. I felt a bit bad—it's no big deal! Apparently from his grandfather. Skipped a generation."

"Poor chap" said Paul with genuine sympathy "I suppose at that age you learn to live with it pretty quickly . . . or without it I should say!"

"Stop it!" said Karen smirking. She'd married him for his sense of humour but it could wear thin.

The glorious summer seemed to have no end and it continued into the following day when Paul dropped the magazine through Thomas' door as promised. There were plenty of opportunities to socialize in the village.

"Good for him" Paul thought to himself "he's making an effort".

Paul wasn't a person inclined to join things and occasionally thought he could have made more of an effort.

As he turned to leave, a bright red open top sports car swung into the drive.

"How do you like Jenny?!" shouted Mr Toad.

"Please be wearing tweed trousers, pleeease . . . " thought Paul.

"She's a beauty isn't she" Paul replied.

"Isn't she!" Thomas agreed " '67 Sunbeam Tiger, kids love it, don't you?"

Max looked directly at Paul. Dark hair, he was older and much taller than his borther, Finn . . . about eleven Paul thought. The look on his face caught Paul off-guard. Completely expressionless, not a flicker of a smile as he slowly turned to get out of the car. His blonde-haired little brother managed a small grin.

"Just dropped the magazine off, Tom"

"Thank you. It's *Thomas* though, *Thomas*" he said getting out of the car.

"Oh, OK" said Paul awkwardly, disappointed to see he was wearing denim jeans.

"How are you settling in?" called Karen to Pat across the playground.

"Not bad thank you" replied Pat "if you need any cardboard boxes, just let me know!"

"It's a nightmare, isn't it!" agreed Karen. "We've still got unpacked boxes in the garage and it's been two years!"

Karen liked Pat. They could be friends.

"Say hello, Molly . . . " Karen encouraged her daughter.

"Hello!" Molly beamed to Pat's youngest son, Finn.

"Hello" he sheepishly replied.

"That was cruel of me" Karen whispered to Pat as the two children headed into school together, "they're not keen on girls at this age are they"

"He's quite shy" mouthed Pat "prefers his books".

"*Finn! Your bag*!" Pat called across to Finn. He ran back and grabbed the strap.

It was then that Karen noticed . . . no little finger on his left hand.

"Oh, that . . . " Pat said, noticing her reaction.

"Got Thomas's side of the family to thank for that! At least it's not his writing hand like Max's!" Pat laughed.

It struck Karen as an odd thing to find amusing, but it was probably the best way to cope with it.

"He's only got a red sports car!" said Paul to his wife over a TV dinner that evening.

Karen smiled with a full mouth of food.

"He's an odd one" Paul continued, "I got told off for calling him Tom yesterday! It's *Thomas* apparently . . . he seems OK though" Paul quite liked odd.

"I *like* Pat" said Karen "saw her at the school this morning"

"What did you think of the kids?" said Paul

"What do you mean?"

"I saw them and they seemed a bit . . . odd"

"Harsh!" said Karen.

"Yeah" he said "maybe just shy".

"Pat said Finn *was* shy. He's got the finger thing too" said Karen through a mouthful of noodles.

"What?" said Paul

"Little finger missing again . . . other hand though. Same family thing . . . "

"Bloody hell" Paul said.

"Would it bother you *that* much not having a little finger?" Paul pondered, opening and closing his hand.

"I suppose you'd just have to get a grip and move on!" joked Karen, trying to keep a straight face.

"Oh ho!!" cheered Paul appreciatively. She had been with him too long.

* * *

"Happy Birthday dear Karen, Happy Birthday to you!" her friends sung in unison, almost in tune. Thirty-one. Karen didn't feel thirty-one, but she was. As tradition dictated, her friends had taken her out for a meal, ending up with an evening drink in Jackie's hot tub. All girls, all gossip.

To be neighbourly, they had invited Pat, not really expecting her to accept, but she did. Party lights twinkled on the eaves of the large bungalow, blurred by the rising steam from the tub, and conversation flowed around the circle of multi-coloured swimsuits and champagne . . .

"Did you hear about Brenda at the WI last week . . . going out with a chap from the town half her age!"

"Apparently he's a plumber"

"He can sort out my plumbing anytime, he's gorgeous" blurted a tipsy Louise.

Karen laughed out loud. Louise really didn't care.

"And how are you settling in Pat?" asked Louise.

"Oh very well thanks" she replied, feeling a little out of place amongst the close-knit group.

"Well it's good to see you" Louise said "anything we can do, just let us know".

And she meant it. She was loud but her heart was in the right place.

"Thank you, that's very kind" replied Pat.

"These tubs are lovely aren't they" said Pat visibly relaxing, lowering her shoulders under the hot water.

"You'll have to have a word with Tom!" said Louise.

"Oh no" said Pat adamantly "I don't think Thomas would like it".

"He's got his sports car hasn't he! You should have your tub!" said Louise, defending her.

"Yes, I suppose so"

"No suppose so, about it, I'll have a word with him!" Louise joked.

"No, don't do that! Please!" Pat said, quite shocked "*I'll* talk to him. I'll have to pick my time"

As she felt more comfortable in their company, Pat absent-mindedly raised her foot luxuriously out of the water . . .

"Good God—what happened to your toes!" blurted out Louise.

"Louise!!" chastised Karen.

"*Sorry*, but I couldn't help noticing! Sorry Pat, I didn't mean anything . . . "

"It's fine" Pat said smiling "it was an accident"

"Oh dear" Louise said, genuinely regretting her outburst.

"It was years ago when I was a child. Playing on a building site, would you believe! A wall collapsed and crushed the toes badly . . . had to be amputated in the end"

"You poor thing!" sympathised Karen.

"Don't even think about it now" Pat said matter-of-factly. "Lucky really, apparently a big toe is worse, messes up your balance they say"

Karen was home late that night, Paul already asleep as he had a five-thirty train to catch for a meeting in Manchester. She woke up earlier than usual that morning and turned over to reach for her phone . . .

"You're not going to believe this" she texted Paul, "Pat is missing two toes!!" Paul *couldn't* believe it, almost choking on his coffee on the train. "That's two fingers and two toes between them!!" he texted back. It *was* semi-amusing but he felt uneasy . . . what were the chances of that happening? Fair enough, there could be some congenital problem but *her* toes too? It just didn't stack up. Then he remembered the time Thomas placed his finger jokingly between the blades of the secateurs . . .

"No way!" he thought.

"No, there's no way . . . " he smiled to himself, dismissing the possibility.

Thomas was in his cottage, asleep on his bedroom chair. He hadn't quite made it to bed. His head rested back on the plush leather, his arm rested on the cushion, and his hand was held by Max, his eldest son. Pat slept soundly across the room in their bed. She should have been at work by now but she hadn't woken up. She wouldn't for another couple of hours . . . Max had crushed sleeping tablets into her late bedtime drink. Same with Finn . . . he was fast asleep, late for school. Max wanted to be especially sure with his Dad, so he crushed some tablets into his bedside water too. And he'd waited awake for hours, for all his family to fall asleep.

He had some ether too . . . "tablets might not be enough" he thought. He'd read about it on the internet . . . and stole some from the school lab. He soaked a cloth, the spirit vapour stinging his nose and the back of his throat . . . and he held the cloth over his father's face, letting him inhale a few times . . .

Max picked up his father's new secateurs. Without hesitating, he cut his father's little finger clean off at the root. Thomas didn't flinch . . . not a flicker . . . Max expected the blood . . . he knew he had to do this quickly. Snip, another finger fell, snip . . . they *were* good secateurs . . . snip, snip, until all the fingers from both hands lay on the floor . . . the thumbs, he left . . . his father couldn't do much with those. Crying in shock, he wrapped dressings tightly over the stumps to stem the flow of blood.

"No more . . . " he sobbed quietly, shaking his head as he tied off the dressings . . .

"No more, Dad."

Money for Nothing

"Charlie! Char . . . "

The train had gone through a tunnel and he'd lost reception.

It was hot, it was stuffy and this was the third time a tunnel had thwarted his conversation. He was annoyed, chewing gum almost violently.

"Charlie?! Charlie? Are you there? Char . . . "

The fourth tunnel really stretched his already taught patience.

"Fuck!" he shouted out loud in the carriage to the world in general, and slammed his mobile down on the newspaper on his lap.

Mark sat directly across the aisle and inwardly sniggered . . . it *is* funny when someone loses it so publicly.

Just then the crowded train wobbled over a suspect piece of track, tipping Mark off his seat, falling across the aisle. Instinctively, he grabbed the thigh of the annoyed stranger to save his fall.

"Sorry!" said Mark, mortified.

"No probs" said the man curtly.

Oddly, the stranger's leg was incredibly soft to the touch, almost marshmallow-like, Mark's hand sinking in unusually deep. He thought there must be a bone in there somewhere but he certainly didn't reach it.

"Maybe he *is* actually made of marshmallow" he contemplated.

"Maybe I'll tear a piece off for a snack!" . . . but he didn't think this would go down very well in his present mood.

After a short period of uneventful travel, Marshmallow Man leaned across the aisle to Mark and asked "Would you like five hundred pounds?"

"Ahh, no you're fine thanks" replied Mark, thinking he had unluckily picked the seat next to the train nutter. The question was awkward . . . so "out-there" that suspicions are aroused.

"Honestly, I would like to give you some money. You seem a good sort"

"No, no . . . you keep it for yourself, but thank you" said Mark, wishing the two remaining stops on his journey were much closer.

"Sorry about earlier. I'm just on a bit of a short fuse today and these bloody mobiles drive me nuts. Last chance . . . do you want five hundred pounds? I'll give it to someone else in the carriage if not!" It sounded almost like a threat.

"No, honestly, you're fine" replied Mark, grateful for the offer but looking around for Marshmallow Man's care assistant.

"OK, if you're sure . . . "

Marshmallow Man put his newspaper down, stood up, steadied his portly frame by holding the handle on the back of the seat and announced to the carriage "I know this sounds a little odd, but would anyone like five hundred pounds cash now? I want to give it away."

Most passengers were shocked. Someone had spoken out loud in the carriage . . . don't they know the rules? How un-British! You're supposed to read your newspaper and ignore people!

Quite a few people laughed. Some looked away awkwardly and joined Mark in the care assistant search. One or two shouted "Yes please!" laughed and carried on reading their paper.

"No strings! I just want to give it away" said Marshmallow Man "five hundred pounds".

There was a slightly more awkward pause from the carriage.

"Anybody interested?" pressed Marshmallow Man.

"Come on!" piped up an older gentleman "Five hundred quid! No strings? . . . Do me a favour!"

"I would like to sir, but it appears I can't give it away" and with that he produced a full envelope.

"Look, I can walk off the train with this or I can give it away" he said waving the envelope.

"Is it stolen?" the older gentleman piped up slightly concerned.

"Certainly not! My family and I have worked hard for this!" he said indignantly

"I've just got enough of the damned stuff! If you think you need it more than me, take it, with my best wishes"

"No thanks, I'm not touching it" the older man replied smiling and shaking his head.

The train pulled into Silverton village station, the last stop before Mark's journey's end, fifteen minutes away. Only four people left the carriage, three of them choosing the exit furthest from Marshmallow Man, despite the longer walk. The last person, a lady, smiled politely at the envelope-wielding stranger, walked past him and disembarked.

Only two new passengers chose this carriage to get on the train.

"Charlie!" shouted Marshmallow man "I thought you were in York!"

"Do I look like I'm in York?!" replied Charlie smiling, extending his hand.

"I've been trying to contact you" said Marshmallow Man, shaking it.

"I know, I know, I thought this would be easier. Thought I might catch you"

"Excellent, it's good to see you my friend. Hard work without you!" beamed Marshmallow Man.

The other new passenger was a young, slim, well-dressed business woman.

As the train pulled out of Silverton station, Marshmallow Man continued:

"You know what, I was going to move up the train but I'm going to persevere with you!"

"Perhaps our new passenger would like the five hundred pounds?" he asked directly to the twenty-something in smart jacket and black pencil skirt. She smiled and politely ignored him, logging onto her iPad.

"Welcome to the madhouse, luv" said the older gentleman.

"Perhaps not" Marshmallow man said disappointed "someone must want it! Look it's all here!" he fanned out the twenty pound notes displaying them for all to see.

"Tickets please, tickets from Silverton please"

"Could I interest *you* in five hundred pounds sir?" he asked the guard.

"Ooo, thanks very much don't mind if I do!" he said jokingly going to take the money.

"He means it!" said the older gentleman.

"He's trying to give it away" said Mark, by now open-mouthed at the spectacle.

"And it's proving quite difficult!" interjected Marshmallow Man.

"OK. Thank you, but I can't accept it sir" said the guard "I don't think my employers would like it!"

"Blow your employer's man!" said the Marshmallow Man starting to lose his patience "if you want it, take it with my blessing!"

"Sorry sir, couldn't possibly . . . now if you could sit down sir" said the guard professionally.

"It's hard enough to give away five hundred pounds standing up . . . it's downright impossible sitting down!" shouted the Marshamallow Man.

"Please sir, you are causing a disturbance"

"A disturbance, you say! Well bloody arrest me then! I'm trying to give away five hundred pounds!"

"Don't take it, its stolen!" shouted the older gentleman.

"It's not bloody stolen!" shouted back Marshmallow Man.

"Please sir, just calm down or we'll have you ejected from the train"

"Ejected from the train he said Charlie! EJECTED from the train, well hush my mouth for trying to make people's lives a little bit better!"

"Might be an idea to sit down" interrupted Mark, trying to calm the situation.

"Hmmph" grunted the soft-legged stranger "Maybe so . . . maybe you're right"

"Yeah sit down, we not getting anywhere with this" said Charlie, "we'll get off at the next stop."

"Hmmph". Marshmallow man was unconvinced.

"Tickets please, tickets from Silverton" the guard continued down the carriage and walked through the sliding door to the next.

"Right!" said Marshmallow man standing "where were we?"

"Let's make it a straight thousand pounds then" he said pulling another envelope out. "A thousand pounds cash . . . can I interest anybody in this gift of one thousand pounds? You have my word it is not stolen, it is not marked, there will be no comeback, I just want to give it away"

"Bullshit" piped up the older gentleman.

"*Really*? Is it *really*" said Marshmallow Man "Charlie, hand me some money"

"How much?" replied Charlie, suitably smaller as befits an assistant.

"Two thousand pounds"

Charlie handed over two more envelopes and Marshmallow Man fanned out the twenties.

"Two grand in twenties that I don't want . . . there it goes" and he gradually fed the notes out of the little drop-down ventilation window in the carriage to a collective gasp from the passengers.

"I don't need it, I don't want it!" and with that the Marshmallow Man sat down.

There was five minutes to the next stop.

"Why would you do that?" said the older gentleman.

"I don't know, frustration I suppose!" said Marshmallow Man, sarcastic and annoyed.

"You try to do some good Charlie, you try, but people don't make it easy, they really don't. Give me the gun Charlie".

"Just leave it" encouraged Charlie "just leave the money on the seat"

"No, someone is going to fucking take it now!" he shouted manically.

"OK, if that's how you want to do it . . . " Charlie said reluctantly, and he pulled out a pistol that looked convincingly real. Marshmallow Man checked the pistol over, in a way that suggested he had handled one before and pointed it across the faces of the passengers.

"Now which one of you is going to take the money? Eh?"

This *did* attract everybody's attention. People ducked down behind their seats. Some people screamed. The girl looked up from her iPad. The older gentleman was remarkably quiet. One person managed to leave the carriage with a swish of the sliding door . . .

"Ah, ah, ah . . . " said Marshmallow Man disapproving, pointing the gun at another passenger who had thoughts of leaving.

"Nobody leaves".

"I'll take it" said Mark, trying to diffuse the situation.

"What?" said Marshmallow Man caught off-guard.

"I'll take it" said Mark, "Give the money to me."

"At last, a grateful recipient! About bloody time! If you don't mind me asking, what's your name?"

"Mark" he replied calmly.

"Well here's a thousand pounds, Mark. I hope you enjoy it" Marshmallow Man said warmly.

"Thank you very much" Mark replied, controlling his nerves well, thankful the tension had eased. Marshmallow Man sat calmly back down. He passed the gun back to Charlie, checked the time on his watch and folded his newspaper.

Mark tucked the money into the inside pocket of his jacket.

As the Marshmallow Man rose from his seat, he announced "It's been fun, ladies and gentleman but now we must bid you adieu" and with that he and Charlie made their way through the carriage.

Of course, a passenger had already alerted the guard and, being a professional sort, he'd phoned through to the next stop. The Police were homing in on Marshmallow Man and Charlie . . . giving away money wasn't illegal, but brandishing a gun in a train *was*. The train had made good time and arrived a little early . . . and unfortunately the Police officers missed them by two minutes. But they collected plenty of good descriptions from passengers, even found images on CCTV . . . but to no avail. They were on the run . . . fugitives from justice! Marshmallow Man and Charlie, like Bonnie and Clyde, redistributing wealth at gun point. Money for nothing . . . or else!

Marshmallow Man was a good judge of character and Mark *was* a good sort. But nobody had mentioned the thousand pounds he'd been given and Mark, although honest, hadn't felt the need to mention it either . . .

It had been a long time since Mark had enjoyed a holiday and he and his girlfriend certainly enjoyed their unexpected trip to Norway that spring . . .

As the sun went down on the decking of their lodge, the last of its honey light dancing across the fjord, two tall hot chocolate drinks arrived . . .

"Marshmallows on top sir?" asked the waiter.

"Oh, yes please" smiled Mark.

The Show Must Go On

"We've made it!" shouted Adam.

"So it *does* exist!" smiled his wife Felicity, open-mouthed at the scene of picturesque grandeur opening up around them as they drove into the city centre. They'd tried to visit the medieval centre of Brugges a few years before as they were driving back from Denmark, but somehow missed it, despite numerous signs. Since then, its existence had fallen into folklore. If friends ever gushed about its beauty, they would be rebuffed with comments such as "Oh yeah? *Historic centre* of Brugges you say?! I suppose there's a Father Christmas too!"

But here it was! Everywhere they looked, every corner they turned in their wanderings through the city that day, presented scenes of such large-scale architectural quaintness that photographers would soon run out of memory space and an artist run out of paint. By the end of the first day, the onslaught of twinkling canals, weeping trees and Belgian chocolate shops was such that Adam was starting to feel jaded.

"I can see why they built the new town now! The odd tower block or MacDonalds would break it up a bit!" he said, half tongue-in-cheek.

"You can keep those" Felicity said, already under the city's spell. "It's like we're actually *in* the scene on the chocolate box lid!"

"Yeah . . . or the charity shop jigsaw!" Adam replied, the spell wearing thin. He was *trying* to enjoy the weekend break, but it didn't help that he was missing the European Cup final. All his mates around the big screen . . . except him.

Adam's Arsenal shirt looked out of place and Felicity was annoyed he'd packed it. "Do you have to wear that thing *all* the time?" she commented.

Dismissing her comment, Adam's eye was caught by a man who looked like he'd just walked straight out of the past . . .

"Hold on a second" he said, stopping his wife from crossing the street "Let's have a look at this . . . "

"Oh how lovely" smiled Felicity, surprised at Adam's interest in something other than sport.

At least 70, the Music Man appeared out of nowhere, wheeling his antique wooden wind-up barrel organ, the iron rims of its cart wheels rattling across the cobbles. Adam was fascinated with his gypsy-like appearance . . . short grey hair, neat moustache, red neckerchief, moleskin waistcoat, light blue trousers and wooden clogs . . . any jigsaw lid of Brugges would have been incomplete without him. It was as if he was *made* for the city.

"And you don't see many of those in Basingstoke!" Adam smiled, nodding towards the ornate instrument.

"You're right there!" Felicity replied in a rare moment of agreement "thank god he's not got a monkey!"

Adam oddly saw some beauty in this old instrument . . . this delicately carved, shoulder-high wooden organ decorated with a painted floral front panel and, rising above this, a wave of cylindrical wooden flutes supporting the carved name of the maker.

They settled at the back of the small group that had gathered since the Music Man's arrival, Felicity for the romance of it, Adam out of pure curiosity. Odd as it wasn't his bag at all. And he was missing the football.

They watched the Music Man position his instrument in the corner of the small cobbled square, smiling at the curious crowd, a joyous smile that rarely left his face. He then lightly stepped behind the organ and started cranking the handle to play. A wonderful sound rose up, a breathy flute-like sound of fairgrounds and merry-go-rounds . . . a sunny sound that lifted spirits and reminded Adam of happier, simpler times. Young or old, it was very hard not to smile. And the song seemed to be perfectly in keeping with the surroundings . . . "The Cuckoo Waltz"! The wooden flutes faithfully reproducing each cuckoo! The cadences of the tune rose and fell and bounced around the square . . . new to the young, familiar to the old . . . a magnet that drew people in, to sway and bob their heads as one.

Adam saw the Music Man silently beckon over a small boy, eager to try his hand at turning the wheel. Delighted, he ushered the boy to the back and placed his hand on the crank handle. Then up rose the sound . . . but this wasn't quite as polished a performance as the Music Man's! Impromptu waltzers had to work hard to keep up with the boy's erratic pace . . . starting briskly, then gradually winding down, the crowd willing the pace to pick up, which it did . . . to gold medal Olympic waltzing speed, then winding down, almost to a halt . . . like a record player with a slipping belt. But it seemed of no concern to the Music Man. He was smiling, delighted that the child was enjoying himself playing a tune so old. The audience were amused too, but more at the slow, slow, quick, quick, slow than the child's enjoyment.

"Jesus how hard can it be!" laughed Adam, too loudly for Felicity's comfort.

"What!" she winced.

"It's just turning a bloody handle!"

"He's a *child*, Adam!"

"Even *so*!" Adam mocked.

In that moment she was thankful they hadn't had children "One child called Adam was enough!" she thought.

And he *always* had to have the last word! Which annoyed her almost as much as the Arsenal shirt.

"Can I have a go" asked another child politely to her mother. "Go on then, ask the man" she replied. He silently beckoned her over and settled her on the crank. Fortunately, her time-keeping was marginally better, the waltzers much more settled.

"He doesn't say much does he" observed Adam curiously.

"Doesn't need to . . . " dismissed a swaying Felicity, "let's his music do the talking". The Music Man swayed too, swinging his arms in huge arcs, helping the girl to keep time, conducting the crowd. And always a beaming smile.

"It's odd that he doesn't speak" said Adam almost to himself, completely engrossed.

Felicity turned to see Adam's preoccupation and sensed an opportunity for devilment.

"Why don't *you* have a go!" she said

"What?"

"If you think it's so easy, *you* should have a go!"

"I don't think so!" he chuffed.

"Ahh, *not* so easy then". She knew what buttons to press to get under his skin. And for some reason she couldn't resist pressing them.

"*Go on . . .* " Felicity pouted falsely.

"For me?" she said half sarcastically, half wishing he would do it, for *her.*

Adam *really* didn't want to . . . Felicity had a talent for setting him up for such things "but if it keeps her quiet" he thought, "I suppose it is *her* weekend . . . "

Felicity was surprised when he actually made a move towards the organ.

He very rarely did things she asked him to do. And she didn't feel she was unreasonably dictatorial. Never a dance at a party, never a trip to the cinema, hardly ever a meal out . . . the little things that would have meant a lot. For the twelve years they had been together it had been all football, mates or television with Adam. She felt she was never put first, not even third lately. The weekend was Felicity's idea, an attempt to recapture something from a long time ago . . . something Adam seemed to have long forgotten and she had almost lost hope in. His immaturity had become too much. At first she found it endearing but, in recent years it had become wearing. In Felicity's eyes, this was a last chance for him.

Adam jogged up to the Music Man, acknowledging the crowd with a raised hand as if walking onto the pitch to take a crucial penalty. His false enthusiasm masked a fear of making a fool of himself.

"Be careful mate!" said the father of a small boy that Adam nudged aside.

But Adam was single-minded.

Smiling, the Music Man led Adam behind the organ and placed his hand on the crank, as he would for a child. The handle fell easily to hand for Adam . . . felt very comfortable. Like it belonged there somehow. The Music Man got him started and the music rose again. Briskly, the correct speed was reached, but not just reached . . . it was beautifully sustained! The tempo was perfect and people began instinctively to dance! Felicity smiled . . . a flicker of the past returning. Adam was never backward in coming forward, and she liked that. She almost felt this dance was for them.

No-one was still, the whole crowd swayed to the swing of the Music Man's arms and dancers glided across the cobbled square as if on air. The Music Man stood back and perused the scene Adam had created. Smiling, he raised his arms to the air and then placed them on his hips, shaking his head. He was absolutely delighted.

Adam smiled along with him, a beaming smile as he turned the crank, eventually slowing to a graceful end, finishing note perfect. The dancers curtsied, the crowd applauded . . . and so did the Music Man, with genuine enthusiasm.

"Have you got another tune?" Adam asked child-like, partly confused by his zeal. The Music Man raised his hands and face to the sky in celebration. "Could this be *him*!" he thought.

Nodding, he stepped over to the organ and selected another Viennese waltz from an extensive bound collection on top. He fed the card into the machine and beckoned Adam to play. Again, it was music to his ears . . . a perfect rendition, the people under the spell of the waltz. Even the Music Man danced through the crowd, beaming, moving from partner to partner.

"When will it be *my* turn?" asked the little boy that Adam had nudged.

"Soon" his mother said "be patient. I'll ask after this man".

The tune eventually came to a natural end, dancers parting to curtsey, but Adam played on . . . straight through from the beginning without drawing breath, the tempo metronomically steady, the smile fixed on his face.

Sensing a shift in the mood of his audience, the Music Man gently held Adam's shoulders, encouraging him that perhaps it *was* time to move on and let the children have a turn. Adam grunted and shrugged him off, turning that crank, keeping that tempo steady. Sweat beaded on his brow in the heat of the square, patches of sweat appeared under the arms of his Arsenal shirt . . . it was now more a work-out than a musical performance. He was a man on a mission and no-one was going to stop him.

"It's not fair!" shouted the boy to his mother and he started the cry of a young boy who was not used to waiting so long for what he wanted.

Felicity was horrified . . . "What is he doing?! He's spoiling it all!" she thought, moving towards the front.

"Come on, let someone else try it now!" shouted the boy's father above the relentless waltz. Adam looked him square in the eyes, still smiling but the message was clear, "Back off!"

Another father stepped forward in support, entering the performance area. "I think that's enough now, don't you?!" he shouted, giving Adam a look that equally clearly said "Stop it *now*!"

Smiling, the Music Man hopped round to them and silently placated the two men, gesturing them to calm down. He then reached to the side of the organ and discreetly pressed a button. Adam's hand leapt off the crank and he jumped back, as if receiving an electric shock. As the last echoes of the waltz subsided, the tension of the crowd was eased. No-one was dancing now . . . the previously happy fairground atmosphere irrevocably tarnished. Adam held his cranking hand as a drop of blood trickled down his wrist . . . he thought he had caught his hand on something sharp and, in a sense, he had. A tiny needle had protruded through the handle and retracted quickly. Adam had been chosen.

"What the hell do you think you were doing!" Felicity screamed at him, crying.

"You've spoiled everything! One weekend, *one weekend* is all I asked and you had to screw *that* up!"

Adam was still smiling, holding his hand.

"What is your *problem* Adam?! Talk to me, *please*. What have you got to say for yourself?!"

But Adam just stood there smiling. Felicity had reached her limit. She hadn't realised how close it was until now. Looking him directly in the eye, a calm came over her.

"I swear if you don't answer me Adam, you'll never see me again"

She meant it, but Adam had nothing to say. He tried to say something, but he couldn't . . . he couldn't speak anymore. He just smiled . . . which was not the best reaction for that moment. Felicity stormed off crying. This time, her dance with Adam was really over . . . a 12 year dance with a child that had lost all direction, and lost all feeling.

The Music Man moved on and the crowd gradually lost interest, slowly dissolving into the jigsaw box cover. But Adam was still smiling. He felt good and started to make his way slowly back to the hotel. For the first time he could really see, really *feel* where he was . . . the architecture, the weeping trees, the twinkling canals . . . more than he could remember, he felt at home. He was in no hurry to get back.

When he finally got to the hotel, he could only smile at the concerned receptionist.

"You missed her half an hour ago sir . . . left in an awful hurry. I hope everything is alright?" she said concerned but eager for more detail to tell her next shift.

Adam just smiled, raised his hands and shook his head.

"Oh, and this was left for you earlier sir. An old chap handed it in, didn't say anything. Nice man though. Lovely smile"

Adam nodded to the receptionist in thanks, took the parcel up to his room and laid it on his bed. "Room 217" was all that was written on the brown paper wrapping. He carefully unwrapped it . . . In front of him lay a neatly pressed and folded stack of clothes. A red neckerchief, a moleskin waistcoat, a white shirt, light blue trousers . . . and a pair of wooden clogs.

The phone in his room rang. It was reception again.

"There's another delivery for you sir, you'd better come down"

As he rounded the corner into the foyer, the receptionist called over

"It was the same man. I'm sorry but you can't keep it here for long, we haven't got the room!"

The barrel organ stood on its wheels at the end of the desk.

Brugges had *always* had a Music Man . . . and always would. And the baton had been passed.

The Leg

"Certainly not!" replied Miss Grenfell in answer to Tommy's request to keep the artificial leg that he had found.

"Why not!" said Tommy, crestfallen. "Donald said mine was the *best!* He only found a water bottle!"

Each year, Miss Grenfell gave her 3rd years a project to see what they could find washed up on the shore by the school. It was fun but this year had taken a turn for the bizarre . . .

"I've got *this* too" he said holding up a used syringe.

"I'll take that young man" Miss Grenfell said in her calm Scottish lilt, trying to mask her horror.

But she could see tears welling up in Tommy's eyes . . .

"They *are* good finds Tommy" she said trying to placate him "probably the best today like Donald said . . . but think of the *poor man* trying to get around without his leg!"

Tommy snorted, grinning and crying in the same snotty moment.

"He's probably hopping about looking for it right now!"

Tommy let out a little giggle.

"How do you think he lost it?" she asked, in an effort to properly distract him.

Wiping his eyes, Tommy said with conviction "Maybe he lost it swimming!"

"Oh yes, he *could* have" she said encouragingly "must have been difficult to swim without it . . . going round and round in circles . . . "

Tommy laughed out loud but Miss Grenfell was conscious of not encouraging her children to laugh at the disadvantaged. Tommy interrupted her concern.

"Maybe a shark *bit* his leg off!"

"Oh my *yes* . . . think how *disappointed* the poor shark must have been! He was expecting a square meal and all he got was a lump of plastic!"

Tommy really liked that, giggling away all signs of the tears.

"I can't see any bite marks though, can you?" Miss Grenfell said, encouraging Tommy to join her to look.

As they inspected the leg closely together, Tommy looked up at his teacher and said "I *like* you Miss"

People hadn't said that much to Miss Grenfell.

And *her* tears welled up.

The Man with Goats

"What do you *do* here all day?" asked the American.

"I look after my goats" replied the tanned, lined Greek farmer sitting on the stone wall where he liked to sit, in the sun.

"Do you read books to pass the time?" the American persisted, miming opening a book.

"No" replied the farmer.

The American had stopped his car in a beautiful open glade, cradled in the mountains. It was a prized piece of flat land on an otherwise steep volcanic island, cultivated for centuries by the farmer's family, many of them in the small walled graveyard on the slope nearby.

"What about the Innernet, do ya get it?"

"What is this?" asked the farmer straight-faced.

"The Innernet! The *World Wide Web*! the American fanfared, "Do ya get it?"

"No" replied the farmer casting his eyes over his herd . . . about sixty of them, grazing next to the vineyard, amongst the olive grove.

The American was struggling to make conversation. To fill the silence he said "Beautiful spot, don't ya think?"

"Yes sir, I think . . . " replied the farmer "and I look after my goats".

Part Five

The Chair

"Why is that chair under the tree" asked Susan from the back of the car.

"I don't know" replied her father, "maybe the farmer needs to stand on it to pick the olives".

"Maybe" pondered Susan "but it has a cushion on it"

A floral cushion sat on the mahogany dining chair, looking far too formal for the parched verge that it sat on, under the old olive tree.

"You're right" agreed her father, "maybe the farmer sits down with his wine at the end of the day and looks over the bay. I'd have a chair there with a view like that!"

The road traversed a steep hillside, so high that the whole channel could be seen, twinkling dark blue over to the islands in the distance.

"It *is* lovely" agreed Susan as she watched the wind play on the water's sunny surface.

"Perhaps it's where Zeus sits!" remembering her mythology from school.

"Oh I think that chair would be a bit grander, don't you? A throne . . . bit bigger too!" said her father, concentrating on the meandering road as they left the chair behind.

Half an hour later, just as the sun hit the chair, a wild cat curled up on his cushion. He had many homes but this was his favourite place, a touch of luxury in an otherwise austere life.

The farmer was making his way down the hillside and, as he passed the chair, the cat mewed a loud "Hello".

"Hello Zeus" the farmer smiled, "you're early today . . . "

A Chip on the Shoulder

"It's amazing what they can do now isn't it!" said Norma sipping her coffee.

"It *is*" agreed Val, "but I'm not so sure". They always got together for a coffee on a Wednesday, after Norma dropped Christopher off to school, and today was no exception.

"It's no different to the ones for pets, you know. Bertie's had one for years" said Norma. Bertie the Pomeranian did look very happy despite being fitted with a tracking chip under his skin, although he was easily located today, curled up on his bed in the kitchen.

"Yes, I know but that's for *pets!* It's a bit different for children!"

"It just slips under their skin, just the same. They don't even know its there" countered Norma.

"I'm sure it's very safe, it's just the principle of tracking your kids!" said Val.

"I wouldn't have done it straight away" said Norma, "but now they've been out a few years, it's a no-brainer! They've really come down in price too"

"I don't know . . . " said Val, still unconvinced.

Trackers chips *had* been out for years, and they *were* a lot cheaper than they used to be. Thousands of parents had chipped their children and there had been no cases of reactions or rejections. Like Norma said, they'd been fitted in pets for years. In the earlier versions, the tracking/location service was provided by a company but now, improved, cheaper technology meant you could have the tracking unit in the home. Now, as well as knowing where your pet is, you could also know the location of your child. If a child wandered off from their parents or was somehow lost, their whereabouts could be tracked.

"Why wouldn't you?" was Norma's argument.

"Well, I've decided" said Norma, "Christopher is having one fitted. He frightened the life out of me the other day in town when he wandered off"

"I know what you mean, Norm, but he *was* only in the comic shop" said Val

"Thank God" said Norma, "but he's only ten! What if he'd been abducted!"

"But he wasn't" pointed out Val.

"Yes, but what if he was! You know what it's like in town! I'd rather know where he is thank you!"

"I know, but don't you think we're just frightened of everything these days?" said Val.

"So you think they're just making money out of us being frightened?"

"Yes" said Val, looking Norma straight in the eye.

"I know, but what if it's *your* child"

"I haven't got one" said Val.

"You're lucky! They're a bloody worry!" laughed Norma. Norma and Frank's flat wasn't in the best part of London which added to her level of concern.

"Seriously Val, you might think differently if you had them"

"Maybe" said Val. She didn't really think so.

Val had even heard a radio interview a few days before saying that a paedophile ring had modified equipment to detect the trackers and locate the position of children. Apparently the more modern versions were coded and more secure, but early versions were having to be updated. But none of this deterred Norma and she had booked Christopher into the clinic for fitting.

It all went very smoothly. It really couldn't have been easier, involving no more pain or time than having an ear pierced and, apart from a small lump on the shoulder blade, you'd never know it was there. "It's amazing what they can do now" thought Norma, not for the first time.

The following Wednesday, Val was round for coffee as usual.

"So that's it, is it?" said Val, looking at the tracking station.

"Yes, marvellous isn't it!" said Norma proudly.

"It's smaller than I thought. I was expecting some James Bond type thing with a desk that flips over!" laughed Val. It was disappointingly small, more like a large sat nav.

"It's incredible! Look, that's Christopher there!" Norma said, pointing at the flashing red dot on the screen, reassuringly within the school's boundary.

"It's better than Jeremy Kyle!" laughed Val.

"Anything is better then Jeremy Kyle!" agreed Norma.

"Look, you can even unclip the screen from the charger and take it to work with you!"

"Amazing" said Norma "Busy at work is it?" she said sarcastically.

"It's only like checking your phone" replied Norma, "takes no time at all."

Norma did carry it with her like a phone, frequently checking the location of her son, as someone would check on phone messages. It worked very well, tracking Christopher from where he was dropped off to catch the school bus, all the way to school and back again to the bus stop. Knowing his whereabouts gave Norma great peace of mind, not just for school days but visits to friends house's or to the park. Frank, her husband, wasn't quite so convinced . . . "All you do these days is stare at that bloody screen! Where is he now?"

"Round Max's" replied Norma, half reading her magazine, half looking at the screen.

"You do surprise me!" said Frank "where you left him then!"

"I like to know where he his!" rounded Norma.

"I do too love, but not every 5 minutes!" replied Frank.

"It's no different to you and your games" said Norma.

"That's different. Its relaxation"

"Well *I'm* more relaxed when I know where he is!"

Frank knew he wasn't going to win. It wasn't that he was against the device. It made sense with the area around the town not being that great and lots of people had them. He was just concerned that his wife was becoming obsessive about it.

One day, the red flashing dot just went off the screen . . . one moment it was there, the next not. "Oh my God!" Norma was beside herself and checked to see if there was some fault . . . but it seemed to be working fine. She dashed across the house, grabbed her coat and flew to the school in her car. As she pulled into the school's road, she saw a long line of children walking along the pavement, all holding hands, teachers guiding them on their way towards the park. Norma slowed to a stop, her eye caught by the silver foil wrap coats the children were wearing to keep them warm, like a giant chrome caterpillar. To Norma's huge relief, she noticed Christopher towards the back of the caterpillar.

"Thank God". Norma left her car and ran over to check he was OK.

"Hello Mum" said a confused Christopher.

"Are you OK?!" she said checking him over.

"Yes, I'm fine" he replied, not wanting her to draw attention to him.

"Is everything OK, Mrs Birch?" asked one of the teachers.

"Oh yes, I'm sorry to disturb you. Everything's fine now. I'd just lost Christopher on my tracker. He just disappeared!"

"Oh, OK" said the teacher "I wonder if it's these foil coats? It's the first time we've used them. Don't worry, I'll have a chat with the teachers later about it"

"OK" said Norma.

"If you prefer, Christopher can take his off . . . we were just trying them out and he's got his coat underneath"

"That would be great" said Norma.

"Mum! Stop fussing!" protested Christopher.

Sniggers went up the line of children, as Norma helped him remove his foil jacket.

"Do you mind if I just check the screen in the car?" asked Norma.

"No, that's fine" replied the teacher.

The red spot was blinking on the screen in the car and normal service had been resumed. The metal foil of the jacket had somehow blocked the transmission of the chip. Norma trotted back to the teacher.

"Thank you. That's great now!" Norma smiled, giving Christopher a peck on the cheek before she left, inducing more sniggers from the caterpillar.

"Mum, don't!" Christopher's cheeks flushed with embarrassment at the fuss.

Norma continued to closely monitor her son's movements, her husband and Val concerned that this device that was supposed to be providing peace of mind was rapidly becoming a source of stress.

Then, three months later, it happened. The little red dot didn't take its normal route home . . . it headed into town.

Panicking, Norma grabbed the tracker screen and jumped into her car. The red dot was heading towards the top of the hill . . . not the best area.

"Come on, *come on*" said Norma to herself as she gained on the red dot. It wasn't moving very quickly, "must be on foot" she thought. She sped across the large roundabout and made her way up the foot of the hill, snaking through parked cars as fast as she dared. "*Come on!*" Norma willed her car through the green traffic light at the top of the hill and pulled into the car park at the back of the town. It wasn't somewhere anyone would choose to spend time anymore but she was right on top of the red dot.

Norma parked up. She had the pick of the spaces. She grabbed the tracker screen and jumped out of the car, scanning the car park . . . no sign of her son . . . just a black dog skulking around. But still the red dot blinked, and she was right on top of it.

"Where are you?!" Norma said to herself "Christopher" she shouted "*Christopher!*"

Christopher was at school, where he *should* be at 2.15pm. Kids can be cruel and, after the foil coat incident, word had got around that Christopher had a chip. Nothing new in that as lots of children had them, but it created the "have's" and the "have-nots", and some of the "have-nots" didn't like it. They didn't like the fact their parents couldn't afford it, or worse, didn't care enough about their whereabouts. They wanted to be the "haves".

So an hour earlier, in the corner of the playing field, they had waited for Christopher. He didn't have a chance. Before he could do anything, four boys had him pinned down. They ripped up his shirt, felt for the lump on his shoulder and cut out the chip with a blade . . .

and fed it to the stray dog that liked to hang around the school.

It wasn't just Christopher that had a chip on his shoulder.

Live & Let Die

"Don't you think it's about time you buried the hatchet?" pleaded Bobby.

"Why should I?" replied Jed, consumed with hate.

"Because it's *time* Jed, you should have done it ages ago"

"He didn't sleep with *your* wife *did* he!" Jed pointed out to his friend.

As far as Bobby knew, he hadn't.

"I know it's not easy, but he's your *brother* man!"

"Fuck him!" said Jed.

"So you want to be *ill do you*?!" Bobby shouted "you can't carry on like this! You need to *deal* with it!"

"Look, you live *your* life and I'll worry about mine!" Jed spat back.

"OK, but the longer you leave it, the more difficult it'll be" said Bobby.

"Fuck him" shouted Jed.

Bobby paused . . .

"Just *talk* to him, Jed . . . and see how you feel"

Shaking his head, Jed stood up and walked to the next room where his brother had laid face down on the floor for the last four days.

"Fuck you!" he said to his brother.

He put one foot on his back and pulled out the hatchet.

"OK" he called to Bobby, " . . . you dig the hole and I'll bury it."

Arnie

"What's your secret, Arnie? asked Gerry, "You always look so happy!"

Arnie looked directly at Gerry. He'd been in the psychiatric home for three years, about the same time as Gerry, and they often spent time together.

"Of course, I'm not *always* unhappy" said Gerry, "I feel *good* today"

It was a sunny day and Gerry had spent the morning in the garden. "It's warm out there today, Arnie . . . I'll take you out there one day, what do you think?"

Arnie had never been in the garden. He looked back at Gerry. He didn't say much but he was a good listener . . .

"Yes, I'll take *you* in the garden, that would be really funny!" laughed Gerry.

Gerry liked it at the home and the staff were very kind . . . all friends really. He felt lucky and, most days, he felt happy.

"It's nice here isn't it Arnie? I like it here". Gerry smiled and looked around, "I don't think I *ever* want to leave . . . "

He'd been in homes all his life. He used to have visitors but not for a few years now, not since his parents died. All his friends were *here* now.

Arnie looked back at Gerry. He couldn't speak, so conversation was limited, but Gerry enjoyed his company.

"Time for Arnie's meal now" said the nurse. "Do *you* want to feed him, Gerry?"

"If Arnie doesn't mind" said Gerry excited.

"I'm sure he'd like it!" the nurse smiled.

Arnie didn't look like he'd object . . .

She opened the top of the fish tank and Gerry sprinkled some fish flakes onto the surface. Straight away, Arnie was up to feed.

"There you go . . . " smiled the nurse "Arnie *likes* you feeding him!"

"He does!" beamed Gerry . . . happy in his home, as Arnie was in his.

Omid's List

"They've got cheese & onion, plain or beef . . . " Jake shouted back to Omid from the bar, thinking it was a poor crisp selection.

"Beef please mate" replied Omid "and some dry roasted peanuts if they've got them?" Jake returned to his friend and arranged the beer and snacks on the table.

"Now that is *definitely* on my bucket list!" said Omid, pointing to Jaipur on the Travel Channel on the pub's big screen.

"It *does* look good" agreed Jake, "so colourful . . . I'd like to see it one day"

"So, what else is on this list then?" asked Jake.

"Oh, skydiving, swimming with dolphins, driving a Ferrari . . . " replied Omid sipping his third pint.

"The usual suspects then!" laughed Jake.

Jake liked to think he was pretty adventurous, and he liked travelling, but he couldn't understand bucket lists.

"Sounds great, but why the list?" asked Jake.

"You know, a list of things to do before you kick the bucket! You're a long time dead!" warned Omid.

"Maybe . . . " said Jake, expecting Omid to bite . . . he didn't disappoint.

"Ah, so you think there's something *after*. I didn't have you down as the religious sort!"

"I'm not! I just don't think things end with death" said Jake, matter-of-factly, crunching a beef crisp.

"Sounds pretty final to me!" laughed Omid "I reckon when you're dead, you're dead, and that's it"

"You could be right" laughed Jake "I just don't think so . . . but why the rush to cram in all the experiences?"

"You've got to live life to the full, man! You only live once!"

"Maybe!" said Jake.

"Look, this *life after death* thing sounds a bit religious to me!" teased Omid.

Jake laughed "Definitely not! Now, let me get this straight . . . you think, when you're dead, you're dead"

"Yep, that's it" Omid replied, reaching for the crisps.

"So, you won't be reflecting on what a full and rich life you've had will you! You won't exist anymore! Nothing, no consciousness at all. You could have stayed your whole life in a trunk, you're not going to realise it in the end!"

"What do you mean?" asked Omid, the alcohol starting to hinder his reasoning.

Jake sipped his beer . . . "You won't exist, you'll just stop *being* . . . no memory . . . there'll be no looking back and saying: Wow, I'm pleased I saw Jaipur or, that Ferrari was fabulous"

Omid paused for thought, and then burst into a beer-fuelled Sinatra impression, "Regrets, I had a few, but then again, too few to mention . . . "

"Exactly!" laughed Jake "There'll be no singing My Way!"

Omid looked into his beer. "This is cheery talk, this is!"

"Sorry!" said Jake.

"Still, you've got to go for it haven't you!" said Omid, looking up.

"Definitely!" Jake said "Go for it, by all means! It just won't mean much to you when you die!"

"How do you *know*?" said Omid, raising his voice.

"I don't!" said Jake, matching his volume.

"So maybe it *will* mean something" challenged Omid.

"*Maybe* . . . if you think there might be something after death!" laughed Jake,

"Now pass the nuts!"

Fortune

Tim was blue, lying motionless on the carpet, crumbs across his face.

It had been a bad year and he'd been planning his suicide for a while now. Most people would've just done it, but Tim liked to plan, liked to consider all the options. *Hanging?* Not fair on the person finding you. *Under a train?* Too messy. *Pills?* He'd taken enough of those . . .

Until *this* presented itself . . . it was perfect! Tim couldn't believe his luck! Beside him lay the empty wrapper of the fortune cookie and written in red was his fortune . . .

"You will choke on this and die".

(Note: This story has exactly 100 words)

The University of Life

"I hear you were lucky to get in on those grades!" said Rupert.

"Yes, when I saw that A, I thought that was it!" replied George. He *was* lucky. The University of Life had a long waiting list of students with straight A stars. But George's father knew the Dean, and his donation was very generous.

"So, let me get this straight" said Rupert, "you're joining a team that actually makes new *species* of animals?" Rupert's knowledge of the UoL was restricted to what he'd heard on the news.

"Sort of . . . it's more developing existing species, animals and plants, in the School of Unnatural Selection, working with Professor Bik" said George proudly.

"*The School of Unnatural Selection?!* What happened to poor Darwin!" Rupert was training to be a cabinet maker, but he was familiar with the natural form of selection.

"They're just giving old Charles a helping hand!" laughed George.

"Yeah, and I hear there's plenty of funding for it too" said Rupert.

"Have you seen the building?!" George said excited.

"Of course! I'm alive aren't I!" said Rupert.

Everyone knew what the UoL looked like. Three years old, it had won numerous architectural prizes and its image had been on every newspaper, web-site and TV channel.

"Supposed to be the same shape as DNA isn't it? asked Rupert.

"Yes, the double helix, but wider as it goes up, with the helipad on top!"

"Looks like someone's stuck a giant ice cream cone in the ground to me" said Rupert poking fun.

"If you wanted to have a look round, we could visit the cafe there?" offered George, "after the visits with father over the summer, I've got my own pass now . . . so I can get you in as a visitor. There's a tour I can get you on if you like?".

"That would be great" said Rupert. In truth, he said it mainly to please his friend . . . it wasn't really his thing.

"No camera's though" warned George "or I'll have to kill you!"

George picked up Rupert in his new Mercedes, a gift of encouragement from his father. "You're definitely coming up in the world! I'm surprised you're still mixing with a cabinet maker" Rupert joked. As they pulled into the University drive, the two intertwining spirals of the UoL rose up before them, as tall as a tower block, completely glazed in dark blue.

"It really *does* look like an ice cream cone!" said Rupert. He could see why it had won the prizes. To the right of the entrance in imposing gold script it read: "The University of Life" with the strapline beneath "because sometimes nature needs a helping hand".

"I hate that sign!" said George. Rupert didn't mind the sign but he had doubts about its sentiment. He was pleased for his friend getting in and it was obviously what George wanted . . . he'd already spent a lot of the summer there . . . but Rupert couldn't help thinking that natural selection had done pretty well on its own so far.

For Rupert, walking into the reception lobby was like walking onto the bridge of the Enterprise . . . "Wow!.." he said distantly, trying to take it all in. It was all a long way from his workshop. Clinically clean and colourful, the shapes were very organic . . . a stomach shaped desk, lighting that looped around the space like intestines. All very biologically futuristic.

"Hello Mr. Sindall" said the attractive young receptionist as they approached the desk.

"Ah, part of the furniture already!" joked Rupert. Since his father's donation, George had become quite recognisable around the place.

"Good Morning" replied George "Is Professor Bik still doing his Wednesday tour at three?"

"Actually, he was going to postpone today, but give me one moment . . . " The receptionist tapped on her keyboard to contact Professor Bik. "Yes Kate" came the reply.

"Sorry to disturb you Professor, but George Sindall is here with a friend and he wondered if you were available for the Wednesday tour? I know . . . "

"*Of course*" interrupted the Professor "that's no problem at all. Tell them I'll be down in ten"

"That's fine, Mr Sindall. He'll pick you up in ten minutes from here. There's some refreshments in the cafe if you'd like some?" gestured the receptionist with twinkling eyes "if you take this ticket, you won't have to pay" she smiled.

"Thank you" smiled George, slowly becoming aware of his local fame. He was less aware that the receptionist was making a serious play for him.

"Looks like you're in there!" joked Rupert as they walked towards the cafe.

"Yes, we're really quite lucky, he doesn't always give tours these days"

"I mean the lovely Kate, you idiot!" laughed Rupert.

"Who?" replied George.

"Are you serious! Sometimes I wonder about you scientists!"

Sitting comfortably on their bacterium shaped chairs, they sipped coffee and chatted for a while, until a broad South African voice boomed "George! So good to see you again, how is your father?"

"He's good thank you Professor" George replied shaking his hand "this is Rupert"

"Very good to meet you Rupert" said the Professor, shaking his hand, "a fellow scientist?" he said looking at George.

"Apprentice cabinet maker" said Rupert.

"Well, we all need cabinets don't we" smiled Professor Bik "God knows we have a few here!"

"Does he?" replied Rupert.

"Excuse me?" said the Professor.

"Does *God* know you have a few cabinets here? I'd have thought the *cabinets* here were the least of his worries!" Rupert couldn't resist a quip, often pushing people to the point of irritation. Not intentionally, it was just his way.

"Ha, ha" laughed the Professor, almost hiding his mild irritation.

"You tell *me*" replied the Professor, "I would say *you* were closer to God than us . . . wasn't Joseph a cabinet maker?"

"Carpenter, I believe" said Rupert.

"Quite" said the Professor underlining their crossing of swords.

"You'll have to excuse Rupert, Professor, he's genetically disposed to annoy!" joked George.

“Perhaps a suitable subject for a project?!” quipped the Professor.

Rupert smiled, resisting a retort. He didn’t want to show George up too much.

“Now, if you gentleman would like to follow me . . . ”

Professor Bik held his hand up to the fingerprint reader which allowed him access to the lift from reception. A large painting slid aside to reveal the lift door.

“Oh wow!” said Rupert, genuinely impressed, “that’s real Thunderbirds stuff!”

“Yes, that’s one of my favourites!” smiled George.

The inside of the lift was mirrored to create the effect that you were actually inside the cell of an animal, the cell’s structures appearing to float around you . . . the nucleus . . . the mitochondria . . .

“Quite something isn’t it” said the Professor, used to people’s fascination.

“Incredible” said Rupert “definitely my favourite lift to date!”

The floor numbers appeared illuminated on the lift wall, like the head-up display on a fighter. Professor Bik touched “45”

“I would never have said you had 45 floors, Professor” said Rupert.

“Ah no, this lift only goes *down*, we’re off to floor 45 *below* ground” he replied.

“It’s like an iceberg” said George “a lot more underneath than there is on top.”

The lift arrived at floor 45 and they exited into a much more utilitarian area.

“Let me show you where we are on this plan” said Professor Bik pointing to a 3D holographic image on the wall that ran from floor to ceiling.

“The floors *above* ground were for the architects and the accountants . . . makes a statement doesn’t it?” said the Professor.

“Makes a dent in the *bank* statement!” joked Rupert.

“Quite” laughed the Professor, “the public face of the University is above ground . . . reception, café, conference facilities, marketing . . . but down here, it’s pure research”.

“It’s not quite so flash down here, is it” said Rupert looking around.

“True, but there’s been no expense spared on the equipment and technology down here. In fact, we design and produce a lot of it ourselves on floor 50” said the Professor.

“Now I’d *really* like to take a look in there!” grinned Rupert.

“I’m afraid that won’t be possible today” said the Professor.

“Have a look in here Rupert, you’ll like this” said George.

"Ah, of course, good idea George" agreed the Professor, pushing open a large well-sealed door, "ideal for a man who likes wood!"

The room was enormous. As Rupert entered, it felt like he had just walked outside into a wooded glade . . . the air felt fresh, there was a light breeze . . . it was an indoor forest!

"These oak trees grow three times as fast as their original species" beamed George.

"Impressive" said Rupert "that's a lot of cabinets"

"*And* . . . " joined in the Professor "they produce *six times* as much oxygen through photosynthesis! *Six times*!"

"Bigger, faster, and better" said Rupert.

"Better for the planet!" said George.

"Maybe" said Rupert, "we'll sell a lot more cabinets, that's for sure!"

"Shall we show him the pigs next, Professor" suggested George.

"Certainly" Professor Bik replied and they retraced their steps to the lift. The Professor pressed the button for floor 23 . . . "Going up!".

"Haberdashery, menswear, toys and lingerie" joked Rupert.

As they left the lift, there was a strong smell of vanilla.

"That smells good!" said Rupert.

"We change it every now and then, the smell of the pigs can be very difficult" said the Professor. He led Rupert and George into a viewing gallery that overlooked a large area below . . . an odd mixture of half-farm, half-laboratory.

"Notice anything different?" asked the Professor.

"The pigs have started their own lab on the farm! Now that's what I *call* progress!. Shouldn't they be wearing lab coats?" joked Rupert.

"Very good" smirked the Professor ,"No, about the *pigs* . . . "

"Bigger?" suggested Rupert.

"Yes! This species grows 60% larger!" announced the Professor.

"Faster?" suggested Rupert.

"Why yes, they reach their target weight twice as quickly!"

"So that's . . . *better*!" suggested Rupert.

"Of course!" said the Professor "Think of the yields, think of the hunger problems we'll solve"

"Think of the amount of pig we'll sell!" chimed in Rupert.

"You know, Mr . . . ." said the Professor inviting a surname.

"Rupert" smiled Rupert.

"Quite" said the Professor "*Rupert,* has anyone told you, you can be quite persistent?"

"Yes, *I* have" apologised George, "Rupert, do you mind, the Professor doesn't have to give us this tour you know"

"I'm sorry" he said, "Don't get me wrong, what you've got here is incredible, but I can't help thinking that nature has done a pretty good job on its own so far"

"It *has*" said the Professor "but we're just . . . ."

"I know . . . just giving nature a helping hand" smiled Rupert.

"Absolutely!" said the Professor "it's *good* that you challenge these things. It's something I encourage my students to do"

"Absolutely" said George "but it's not a sin to make some money along the way as well is it?"

"You're sounding more like your father every day" thought Rupert.

Continuing the tour, Professor Bik walked them further down the corridor to show Rupert the production of bacterial-based meat . . . growing artificial meat from bacterial colonies! Rupert was genuinely impressed with this . . . "Grow your own protein! And it only involves the mass slaughter of bacteria! Genius!"

As they headed back towards the lift, Rupert asked "What about humans then? Have you done any work on us yet?"

"Oh no, many other animals, some primates, but not humans. It's still illegal of course!" said the Professor.

"Someone *must* have approached you, *surely*" Rupert said trying to provoke a reaction "champion athletes, perfect soldiers, that sort of thing"

"No, we've got enough to keep us busy here without those complications" smiled the Professor, "I think you've been watching too many films!"

"Ah, at last !" laughed Rupert, "something we can agree on!"

"I'm afraid that just about concludes our tour gentleman" said Professor Bik.

"Thank you very much for your time Professor" said George. "I've got a few things to do here Rupert, so you take the car and I'll grab a taxi later"

"OK, if you're sure, that would be great" replied Rupert "I'm supposed to be meeting Cath at 6"

"Thanks for your time Professor, much appreciated" said Rupert extending his hand.

"The pleasure was all mine Rupert" replied the Professor.

"You're very kind!" laughed Rupert "and apologies if I was a little abrasive earlier"

"Not at all" replied the Professor.

"And I'll catch *you* later" smiled Rupert shaking George's hand.

"You will indeed" replied George.

"So? Did you manage it?" asked the Professor.

"Of course . . . in the coffee, just as you said" replied George.

"Excellent, and the tracker?"

"I'm not that comfortable with the tracker if I'm honest" said George.

"I understand George but you must remember it's for their own good. As his performance improves, it's important we know what's going on"

"That's candidate 56. I must say the café is proving to be a most effective way of administering the therapy"

"You're part of a revolution George, a revolution in evolution! They're going to be fitter, faster, quicker . . . better in *so* many ways, without knowing it!"

"My father sees it as him giving something back, passing on his good fortune, he says" said George.

"Your father is right, George! Look at the improvements we've seen in *him*. He'd be dead now! Look at what we are achieving!"

A loud car horn was attracting some attention in reception . . .

"What's that?" said George.

Rupert's horn was sounding from the parking bay. His head was slumped against the steering wheel. Candidate 56, was the first allergic reaction they'd had. No sign of any problems before, after months of testing on monkeys. But Rupert's heart had failed. Things were not better for poor Rupert. He was now slower, worse . . . dead.

The irony of dying at The University of Life would not have been wasted on Rupert.

Officially, his death was recorded as "natural causes".

Rupert would have had something to say about that.

Wormwood

"Like a Christmas card . . . " Gerry thought as he looked across at the Salvation Army band, frost settling around him in the shop doorway.

"Silent night, holy night, all is calm, all is bright . . . "

Under the glow of a streetlight, the first flakes of snow spiralled down onto a small gathering wrapped in coats and scarves, breath steaming as they sang.

"Round yon virgin mother and child" Gerry mumbled under his breath, "holy infant so tender and mild" Odd that he could remember the words. He hadn't sung that carol since he was at school, when his mother used to take him to church every Sunday.

The doorway was quite spacious. He'd slept there before and it felt safer than the bridge or darker areas of the town. Behind the glass he was leaning on was a chocolate fountain . . . he remembered a Christmas party years ago where he'd seen one. And behind the glass on the opposite side was a smart phone. He preferred to face the chocolate fountain . . . happier memories. His phone had been the start of his downfall. He'd bet on anything—horses, casino, bingo, it was so easy. Too easy.

"Merry Christmas!"

Gerry looked up at the tall smart man who'd just greeted him. He wore a long, black coat over a dark suit and tie, with a burgundy scarf.

"Hello" replied Gerry.

"Merry Christmas to you" repeated the man holding out a small wrapped gift.

"What?" said Gerry confused. People didn't often stop to chat.

"For *you*" said the man bending down and placing the present next to Gerry.

His face was striking. Thin and angular with black lips and what Gerry assumed was eye-liner highlighting ice blue eyes.

"Merry Christmas", smiled the stranger, and he turned and walked away.

Gerry was speechless. It was a long time since he had been given a gift of any sort, let alone one so beautifully wrapped in ribbon.

"Thank you" he said quietly, "Thank you!" He shouted after the dark lean figure. The stranger didn't stop but raised a hand in acknowledgement as he stepped into the back of a large black car.

"Sleep in heavenly peace, sleep in heavenly peace" the choir sang. Gerry had intended to do just that, but he was wide awake now, looking at his gift.

A small box with an old-fashioned holly-pattern wrapping paper, tied with a red ribbon.

"What the hell?" he thought. The most he'd been given in the past was 50p, or the advice to get a job.

It was almost a shame to open it. Almost. Gerry pulled the red ribbon and it fell away. His long nails made short work of the tape and the thick wrapping opened like a clam to reveal a red box, maybe a jewellery box, about the size of his cold hand. He hinged the top of the box back . . .

Sadly, the reality didn't quite live up to his expectation . . . a medical information wrist band!

"And a Merry Christmas to you too!" thought Gerry sarcastically.

On the red silicone wrist band was a red and white label reading:

"Gerry Mann. Severe nut allergy. Carries adrenaline (ANAPEN). Contact 0780 320 6930"

He was fairly certain he was Gerry Mann, but he was unaware of his nut allergy. And he definitely didn't carry adrenaline.

"How does he know my name?" thought Gerry.

Actually, Gerry really liked nuts, although it had been a long time since he'd tasted them. But it really wasn't the present he would have liked. Cider would have been better, numbing the cold, and some of the memories that Christmas was bringing to the surface . . . happier times of family, smiling faces, holidays . . . he even missed his job in IT. It wasn't long after he lost his job that his wife had left him. Gerry didn't blame her, "She was right, it *was* too much".

For no reason at all, Gerry slipped his wrist band on. After all, it was the first present that anyone had given him in years.

The following day passed uneventfully, keeping warm and finding something to eat occupying most of his time. But the blue-eyed, dark-lipped stranger wandered through his thoughts throughout the day. "Who was he? Why the gift? Why me?"

As evening approached, the temperature dropped and he reached into the deep pocket of his coat for his second pair of gloves. As he rummaged, he felt what he thought was a pen. Odd, as he hadn't used a pen or carried one for months. As he held it in front of him, it certainly looked like a pen . . . bright green with the word "ANAPEN" in black along its length. There was some small print along it's base . . . "auto-injector for anaphylactic responses"

"An adrenaline "pen!" he thought. Gerry had seen these before. A friend at school used to carry one, to inject himself in the leg to relieve an allergic reaction.

"How the hell did that get there?" Gerry mumbled to himself.

That night, the shop doorway again provided welcome shelter from the cold wind, curled up in his long, thick coat between the chocolate fountain and the phone. By the time he woke, the weather had calmed and, through the mist of his breath, he could see something next to him on the doorway floor . . . it was another gift, beautifully wrapped, just like the first. Rubbing his hands and breathing into them to warm them, Gerry undid the ribbon. Inside was a similar red box to the one the wrist band was in. He opened it . . . "Nuts!" A bag of nuts! Honey-roasted cashews no less, Gerry's favourite.

"To die for" he smiled, his sense of humour still intact.

"Must have been him . . . " Gerry thought, looking around for the dark stranger but there was no sign of him.

Gerry's stomach rumbled. He'd only found a few scraps yesterday and, although he was going to the soup kitchen later, he was hungry now.

"Honey roast cashews . . . " he thought. And, yes, they were in date too.

"Might have been tampered with . . . " He was poor but he wasn't stupid. He checked . . . "Look fine . . . look very fine" he thought, salivating.

He tore open the corner of the packet and smelled the contents.

"Oh my God!" A warm wave of pleasure run down his back. So rich and spicy! After months of bland scraps and free soup, it was an assault on the senses. Gerry eagerly poured out a handful and tipped his head back to eat them. It was the best Christmas present! Such an indulgence! Gerry forgot all about the cold as he crunched on the nuts, eyes closed, smiling. As the first hit of flavour faded, he poured himself another handful, eager to enjoy it all over again.

It was then that he felt his chest tightening, his breathing suddenly very short and shallow . . . couldn't get enough air . . . a belt tightening around his chest. His heart raced, banging in his ears. Gerry coughed out the nuts and dropped the packet. He whistled in his next breath . . . "can't get enough air". Sweat poured from his hot, red face and he pulled at his scarf and coat collar . . . "must get air . . . the pen!" He reached into his coat pocket and grabbed the adrenaline pen. Biting the cap off with his teeth, he jabbed it into his thigh through his trousers. Some relief, but breathing was still difficult. Fighting for breath and heart pounding, Gerry noticed the tall dark stranger standing in front of the doorway. The stranger bent down and looked into his face . . . the same cold, blue eyes, the black lips. Gerry felt a jab into the thigh of his other leg as the stranger administered another dose of adrenaline.

"Still like a gamble then, I see" smiled the stranger as he stood up.

Gerry felt the belt around his chest drop away and fresh cool air enter his lungs. It was almost as good as the nuts. As he wiped the sweat from his face with his coat sleeve, he saw the door of the stranger's black limousine close and drive away.

"Are you alright mate" said a man on his way into work on the early shift.

"I'm OK" replied Gerry exhausted "thank you"

When he'd composed himself, Gerry picked up the red box and put it in his coat. Why, he didn't know. He had no use for it, let alone two.

"You look like you've seen a ghost!" said Madge. She knew Gerry from his visits to the soup kitchen. "'You alright, luv?"

"I'm OK" said Gerry unconvinced, "bit under the weather"

"There's a lot of weather to be under lately isn't there!" laughed Madge as she filled his bowl with plain vegetable soup.

"You look pale, Gerry. Better get yourself checked out".

"I'm good, honestly. Just had a bit of a turn" he said smiling as he turned to find a bench.

There were a few people in. Most of them Gerry knew. It was a small world.

"What's that?" said Carl sitting across from Gerry pointing to the wristband.

Gerry looked up. "You wouldn't believe me if I told you".

"Try me" said Carl as he blew on his next spoonful of soup.

So Gerry did . . .

"You're right, I don't believe you, you bullshitter!" Carl laughed.

"That's how it happened, I swear!" said Gerry, "Look." he said, reaching into his pocket. "Here's the boxes and the wrapping!" He laid them out on the table.

"Looks like nice stuff" said Carl feeling the paper. He picked up a red box for a closer look. "These are expensive, man! *Somebody* loves you!" joked Carl.

"Yeah, loves me enough to almost kill me" replied Gerry

"What's this *Wormwood* . . . " asked Carl looking at the base of one of the boxes.

"What?" said Gerry looking up.

"*Wormwood* it says on the bottom . . . it's in gold, man"

"Oh yeah . . . " said Gerry inspecting closer, "must be the maker. Strange name, *Wormwood*"

"Doesn't sound very exclusive . . . not Cartier is it!" laughed Carl, "brings to mind worms in a wood!" They laughed.

"It's good to hear some laughter in here gents" interrupted the priest, turning round from the next table.

"Hello Father" said Gerry deferentially, an automatic response from his childhood.

"Did I here you say *Wormwood*?" enquired the priest "I haven't heard that name in years . . . "

"Yeah, it's on this box" replied Carl "he says he was given it by a *tall, dark stranger!* Ooooo! "

"I'm telling you, it happened like I said!" Gerry pressed.

"Oh, yeah . . . icy blue eyes, black lips" laughed Carl waving his fingers like a ghost. "It was the cider!"

"I wasn't drinking!" Gerry insisted.

"Black lips?" enquired the priest, straight-faced.

"Yeah, like he wore make-up . . . around the eyes too" said Gerry

"Ooh!" joked Carl "I quite fancy him!"

"Why do you ask?" said Gerry.

"You say you saw this man?" asked the priest.

"I swear I did. Twice! Why would I dream it twice!"

The priest looked at the base of the red box again.

"*Wormwood*, I haven't heard that name since theological school." said the priest in thought.

"Who the hell is he?" asked Gerry

"A fallen angel" replied the priest.

"A what?" said Carl.

"A fallen angel, who supposedly walked the earth in the shadows" said the priest, "and was said to bring plagues upon the earth"

"Jesus!" said Gerry.

"It's weird" said the priest "because you have pretty much described him!"

"Oh yeah" said Carl, "I bet he drove a bloody limousine in ancient times too!

"What about the reaction, I had! The pen!" said Gerry, reaching into his pocket. There was no pen.

"Wasn't exactly a plague was it!" said Carl.

Gerry lifted the sleeve of his coat showing the wrist band, "What about this!"

"Someone's going to be missing that soon! Lay off the cider, man!" Carl cackled as he rose to leave, shaking Gerry's shoulders.

"I've heard stories, I'll not say I haven't" said the priest "but maybe you *should* watch the drink . . . "

"I know what I saw" said Gerry as he got up, leaving his soup and the boxes on the table.

That night, the Salvation Army band were back. It was Christmas Eve and it was getting colder. Might even be a white Christmas they said. Gerry curled up in the shop doorway and tried to get warm. He'd developed a cough the last day or two and he wasn't shaking it off. It kept him awake for some time.

When Gerry woke up on Christmas morning, it should have been no different to any other. But it was. Standing in front of him, was the dark stranger, his ice blue eyes looking down on Gerry.

"Sleep in heavenly peeeeeace, sleep in heavenly peace . . . .Merry Christmas" the stranger smiled, bending down with another gift.

"Let me guess" said a weary Gerry "another red box?

"Now, don't be like that" said the man.

"Are you Wormwood?" asked Gerry tentatively.

"Ah . . . " smiled Wormwood "I'm flattered you've heard of me"

"You really are?.." said Gerry looking up in awe.

"Yes, I really am" Wormwood replied "now don't be rude and open your gift"

Gerry looked down at the identical looking gift and started to unwrap it . . . he was right, there was a red box . . .

"You could call it a theme, a calling card you might say" said Wormwood "Rather stylish, don't you think?"

Gerry coughed and opened the box. Inside was small scroll of paper.

"Well, read it" said Wormwood "I can't wait!"

Gerry unrolled it and, in gold lettering, it read: "Say it with Pneumonia. Merry Christmas"

"Ha, ha!" laughed Wormwood "Say it with pneumonia! I love it, even though I say so myself!"

"I'm sorry" said Wormwood as his laughter subsided "it's rude of me. Actually it's not so much a gift, more a diagnosis"

Gerry looked up cold and confused.

"You've already got it! Not many symptoms yet, but there will be. Ahh, pneumonia . . . " grinned Wormwood affectionately, "the gift that keeps on giving!"

"Why me" said Gerry.

"Why not! You've brought it on yourself really haven't you"

"I suppose . . . "

"Look" interrupted Wormwood "this is all a little sombre isn't it. Christmas Day, you dying . . . and yes, you *will* die" he smiled, his black lips curling up.

"But, you could exchange this gift if it doesn't suit"

"What?" Gerry was tired now and his patience was wearing thin.

"Swap that gift for this!" said Wormwood displaying an identical gift.

"I don't want to die" said Gerry weakly.

"Of course you don't! Not many people do! It's a struggle sometimes keeping the numbers down! *I* don't want you to die Gerry . . . not yet"

"You don't?" said Gerry doubtfully.

"No. So do you want to exchange your gift?"

"Yes" said Gerry.

"Of course, you do!"

Gerry took the gift from Wormwood's black-nailed hand.

"I'll cure you and give you everything back. Give you your life back!" said Wormwood as Gerry opened the gift. "I will personally guarantee your health, *but*, if you open that red box, you'll work for me. It's up to you . . . take your time. I can understand it's a bit of a gamble"

Gerry looked up at his tall benefactor and opened the red box . . . it was a phone.

"An excellent choice Gerry!" grinned Wormwood "may I call you Gerry?"

"Yes" said Gerry in shock.

"Excellent!" said Wormwood bending down to get closer to Gerry "You, my friend, are going to run the next generation of on-line gambling sites for me. I'll give you everything you need" said Wormwood. "This one is big . . . highly *contagious*, you could say!"

Like fallen angels, plagues can take many forms and Wormwood had moved with the times. He'd gone digital.

"And may I say, Gerry . . . " said Wormwood, helping him to his feet, " . . . how much better you look already."

Preposterous

"Bugger Bognor"

"I'm sorry?" said Brian, settled in his wingback leather chair.

"Bugger Bognor!" repeated Ken from his chair on the other side of their office.

"It's not *that* bad, I used to go there as a boy" Brian defended.

"No" replied Ken looking up from his book "they were supposed to be the last words of George 7th, old boy! Apparently, he was due to visit Bognor in Sussex but he wasn't well enough to make it!"

"Excellent last words!" nodded Brian, cupping his brandy glass.

"Hold on . . . " said Ken "it says here there's doubt about this now and his actual last words were "God damn you" to his nurse when she administered a sedative!"

"Ah, that's disappointing . . . nowhere near as good!"

"Go on then" said Ken, looking across to Brian "what do you think your last words will be?"

"Haven't given it much thought old chap"

"Perhaps we *should*" Ken said playfully.

"Why? Are you going to pull a gun on me!" laughed Brian.

Ken looked directly at Brian with dead gunfighter's eyes and reached inside his jacket, "Oh, I wish I had a toy gun!"

Ken and Brian's working relationship was eccentric. They had known each other for many years, both professors in the Psychology faculty of the University. For as long as they could remember they had shared an office, along with a penchant for tweed suits and a love of good cognac, keeping a ready supply in their cabinet. Brian, with his ginger beard, had an air of Scottish Laird about him and you could be forgiven for thinking Ken, with his shoulder length black hair, had modelled himself on Oscar Wilde.

"*Are you going to pull a gun on me?* would be rather good last words" pondered Ken.

"Yes, but I think we could do better, don't you think" said Brian.

"Indeed. We should agree on what our last words should be and endeavour to make it so!"

"Absolutely! I was always fond of Spike Milligan's *I told you I was ill*" grinned Brian.

"Ha, ha! Yes, excellent! Now, how about making it more specific and saying a last *word*" suggested Ken.

"Yes, I like that, a single word! Is that word to be the same for both of us, or do we choose one each?" enquired Brian.

"Oh, I think the same one for both of us would be more fun, don't you" replied Ken sipping his cognac.

"Quite so!" replied Brian. "To get us started, might I suggest the word *cornucopia*?"

"A delicious suggestion, old boy! A quite lovely word to end one's life on! *Cornucopia!*"

"Should we have a short-list, perhaps?" suggested Brian, refilling his glass, enjoying the eccentricity of their conversation.

"Absolutely!" agreed Ken "I would like to proffer the word, *mysterious*"

"Oh, very good! Again, a beautiful word to end on, with an added air of drama too. A fine choice sir!"

"All right, one more then" said Brian, stroking his chin in thought.

"Mmm . . . how about *preposterous*?"

"Oh, I think you have it sir!" shouted Ken, clapping his knees "*Preposterous!* What a way to end it all!"

"You don't think the suggestion is *preposterous*?" joked Brian, quaffing his cognac.

"Certainly not" laughed Ken "it's *preposterous* to suggest such a thing!"

"*Preposterous*, you say?!" laughed Brian.

"Yes I *do* say it! It's *preposterous*!" wailed Ken, cheeks flushed.

"It is indeed! Utterly *preposterous* to even think it" Brian spluttered, his cognac consumption above average for a Wednesday afternoon.

"Sorry?!" cried Ken "I didn't quite catch what you said!"

"I *said* . . . " belly-laughed Brian, holding his sides in pain "It's *preposterous!*"

Ken quickly withdrew a pistol from the inside pocket of his jacket and shot his colleague directly in the centre of his forehead.

"My, my . . . " Ken said to himself "that was louder than I thought", his ears ringing.

His years as a psychology professor had taken a certain toll on Ken. He had lost a little perspective and allowed eccentricity to develop into something somewhat darker.

Mrs. Butler burst into the room from her office next door and was frozen by the sight of Ken still holding the gun.

"Now I know what this must look like, Mrs Butler" said Ken calmly "but I think I *do* understand *why* this has happened"

Mrs. Butler wasn't easily frightened and, although her heart was beating hard, she fought to remain calm. She certainly wasn't the screaming type.

"Put the gun down, Ken" she said calmly, looking him in the eye.

Ken looked over at Brian, still sitting in his wingback chair, his head resting awkwardly to one side . . . and then looked directly at Mrs. Butler, still holding the gun.

"Please, Ken" she calmly repeated, "put the gun down".

Ken raised the gun and looked at it . . .

"Don't be preposterous!" he said, putting the gun under his chin and pulling the trigger.

Charity Begins at Home

"Bloody waste of time" muttered Julie to herself as she logged out of the Skype meeting. She loved managing the charity shop but didn't appreciate having to report their sales performance to her managers every week.

"If they left me alone to do my job, I'd sell even more stuff!" she said to Maude behind the till.

"Necessary evil these days my dear" replied Maude "in my day the plans would be on the back of a fag packet! Still happened though!"

"Oh, bring back those days Maude!" smiled Julie.

Most of the volunteers in the shop had names that were rarely heard these days . . . Maude, Ethel, even an Ariadne (Julie's favourite). Very few Chelseas or Kylies. Julie got on well with them all and they had gelled into a friendly team. Although, the older volunteers could occasionally be distracted by knitting patterns and Ben Fogle's last TV appearance, Julie loved their old-school thoroughness and customer service.

"How did we do last week then?" asked Maude.

"New record!" beamed Julie.

"That's marvellous!" said Maude "it's definitely been busier since you took over"

It definitely had. One big change was "Retro Corner", an idea that Julie had to showcase higher value antique pieces that had been donated. It could be a piece of china, jewellery, a particularly nice picture or an item of designer clothing. If it was valuable, fashionable or funky, it was highlighted in a display case in the corner of the shop with a realistic price tag, and Julie had become very adept at spotting these pieces. Customers looked forward to seeing what was new in "Retro Corner" and came from far and wide to peruse them. Even some antique dealers were known to call.

"Any discs missing this week?" Julie asked Maude as she straightened the DVDs up on the shelf.

"Only three" replied Maude positively.

"I still can't believe people do it!"

"They steal such bad films too" laughed Maude as the ring of Julie's mobile interrupted their conversation.

"Ah Mr Rennett!" smiled Julie answering, "we speak at last!"

It had been a couple of days since she had left him several messages.

"Hello" said Mr Rennett "I'm sorry, I've been very busy."

"No problem at all" replied Julie, covering her slight annoyance professionally. "I just wanted to mention that some of the items you donated may be quite valuable, and to double-check that you're still happy to donate them?"

Retro-Corner had already attracted some attention and the last thing Julie wanted was a newspaper charity shop scandal "Charity shop sells Picasso . . . shopkeeper buys Ferrari and country estate . . . it hasn't changed me, she says . . . ". There were no Picasso's in the old suitcases Mr Rennett had dropped off but there *was* a framed sketch that, according to initial enquiries, could be a Constable and some seemingly valuable Japanese china.

"They really are quite valuable" stressed Julie.

"Ah yes, mother had a good eye" said Mr Rennett.

"She certainly did!" agreed Julie "but are you aware just *how* good?"

"What the Constable?" he said.

"*And* the china, and some other things too" replied Julie.

"Look, it's good of you to call" said Mr Rennet "but I just want to get rid of them. Get them valued if you like and we'll go from there. Consider them yours though . . . it's just money and it's better with you than with her now"

"Your mother is aware of these donations?" checked Julie, covering her concern.

"Yes, of course! Aware as she is of most things these days, you know how it is as they get older. Comes to us all I suppose!"

"Is it possible to talk to her, Mr Rennett?"

"I'll do better than that, I'll bring her in. She could do with some air"

"It would be lovely to meet her and we look forward to it. We'll put the kettle on for you both. Meanwhile I'll get these items valued and you can make a decision"

"They're yours!" said Mr Rennett insistently "we really do have no use for them now"

"OK Mr Rennett. Look forward to meeting you and your mother".

"What's this going in The Corner for?" asked Maude holding up the Constable.

"Ahh, that one's getting valued. I think it'll be sold separately".

"I like it" said Maude "whoever did it shows promise"

"I think he's already showed it Maude! It's probably a Constable! He's in the National Gallery!"

"Oh my goodness!" said Maude, putting it down carefully.

Julie had sent photographs of the sketch and the china to Christies, who were very interested to have a closer look, so a visit was arranged for the coming Wednesday.

"My, my" said the valuer gazing at the sketch. "It looks genuine . . . of course we'd have to run some tests, but . . . my, my".

"It's OK then is it?" asked Julie.

"OK!?" said the valuer "it's breathtaking! If it's the genuine article it's the first Constable sketch to materialise for 50 years!"

"Damn, he'll want it back!" thought Julie uncharitably.

The valuer reacted similarly to the Japanese china. "My, my! This needs to be protected. Please, please take good care of this. I have never seen such pieces. They belong in a museum not a charity shop!"

"Who donated these?" asked the valuer.

"Oh a local gentleman . . . on behalf of his mother"

"She has a good eye" he said.

"She has indeed!" replied Julie.

"He didn't happen to leave anything else?" enquired the valuer tentatively.

"Only some old costume jewellery. The stones are quite vulgar. Huge!"

"May I see them?" he asked.

"Sure, they're in the back. I'll get them".

The valuer took an eyepiece out of his pocket and examined the stones quietly, taking in the cut, the way the light danced on the facets . . .

"My good lady, these are genuine stones! This sapphire alone is worth around £15,000! Who is this woman?! I might be asking for her hand in marriage" he joked.

"She's calling in with her son on Wednesday if you'd like to meet her?"

"I will make time in my diary!" announced the valuer smiling.

It seemed a long wait to Julie for the following Wednesday to come round. Concerned about the value of the donations, she had decided to take them home with her in a case rather than leave them in the shop. In her flat, half-looking at the TV and half sipping some soup, she looked across at the case. "Enough to pay off my debts right there" she thought. If the valuations were true it was easily enough, but she wouldn't dream of ever "acquiring" a piece for her own ends. That just wasn't Julie.

Wednesdays were usually a quiet time for the shop and the valuer arrived early at quarter to 10.

"He seems keen!" said Maude as they prepared him a coffee.

"I think *I'd* be keen if there was a chance to auction that lot for us!" laughed Julie.

"Thank you" said the valuer accepting his coffee.

"Any news on the Constable yet" enquired Julie.

"We are still in the process of verification but from what we know, we feel there is a very good chance that it *is* genuine"

"That's amazing!" said Julie.

"It really is" agreed the excited valuer "I don't believe I will see another and there are collectors that would *love* to own it"

"What might the value be then?" asked Julie

"It's not a painting of course but, if it's genuine, and all the indicators are that it *is* . . . conservatively, £80,000"

Julie was dumbfounded. She turned to Maude laughing "Well we've definitely reached our targets for this month!"

The ding of the shop door-bell announced the arrival of Mr Rennett, pushing his mother ahead of him asleep in a wheelchair.

"Good morning!" smiled Julie ushering them into the shop "tea or coffee?"

"Thank you, coffee for me please. And mother is fine thank you"

"Are you sure?" checked Julie.

"Oh yes, I'm afraid she's like this a lot of the time now" said Mr Rennett. "But it's good for her to get some fresh air away from that home, as good as they are . . . *.isn't it Mother*"

Mrs Rennett didn't stir as she was wheeled through the shop into the back office, resting against a pillow propped up on her chair.

I hope you don't mind me asking but is she well, Mr Rennett?" enquired the valuer under his breath.

"Reasonably so, for her age" he replied "87 you know. But she gets very tired, and her memory is definitely not what it was"

As the conversation around her continued, Mrs Rennett started to wake and she focussed on the items laid out a small table in the back office.

"Ahh" she smiled "the Constable . . . "

"Ah, yes Mother" said Mr Rennett standing up. "Now *do* try to rest! You know these outings take it out of you." He reached behind her arm to make some adjustments.

"Mrs Rennett" said the valuer deliberately "*can you hear us?*"

"I don't think you'll get much more out of her" said Mr Rennett. "She loved these pieces you know . . . and the rest. Absolutely adored them. But over the years they've just collected dust and its time someone else enjoyed them as much as she has"

"The thing is . . . " explained the valuer, "we need the permission of the owner to sell these items"

"Oh yes, I understand. I have the necessary paperwork here" said Mr Rennett handing over a document "My solicitor has looked over it and believes it to be in order"

The valuer took the documents from Mr. Rennett, his smile hiding a scepticism borne of experience. It wasn't the first time he'd been involved in selling family items whose legal ownership turned out to be less than clear.

"The papers do indeed seem to be in order" replied the valuer, looking up. "Very thorough"

"Splendid! Well do I need to sign something?" asked Mr Rennett

"Are you quite sure these are legitimately for sale, Mr Rennett?" said the valuer, looking him straight in the eye.

"I can assure you they belong to my mother and I have a legal right to sell them on her behalf" he replied. "It was always a financial thing for her . . . buying and selling. She would be pleased to see them go to a new home, and for the charity to benefit of course"

"Very well, if everyone is agreeable we will arrange the sale of the Constable, the china and the jewellery on behalf of the charity" summed up the valuer.

"Thank you so much to you and your family for your generosity!" said Julie. "It's an incredible gesture and you and your mother will be helping countless people, you can be sure of that"

"It is my pleasure. We are very comfortably off and you can only accumulate so much stuff!"

"Please let me know if you are thinking of disposing of any similar *stuff* as you describe it Mr Rennett!" smiled the valuer "your mother's eye for *stuff* is impeccable!"

Mrs Rennett did indeed have a keen eye. She had been collecting for years, buying extremely shrewdly and very rarely selling. It was nothing to do with the money, the family had plenty of that. It was all about the objects . . . her dear, exquisite objects. Her "children", she used to call them.

Mr Rennett pushed his mother up the drive into their Georgian mansion.

She moaned a little as her wheelchair squirmed on the gravel, so he reached down next to her arm and pushed a little more sedative from the syringe into the cannula in her arm. She was rarely awake these days and had lost a lot of weight.

"Home again!" said Mr Rennett cheerfully as he settled her into the stark basement room. It had been used for storage for spare furniture for decades and he saw no point in redecorating it for a woman with failing eyesight.

He had considered professional care for her but decided against it as he saw an opportunity to balance some of the injustices of his childhood.

Although he was an only child, he had never felt like it. He grew up surrounded by his Mother's other children . . . grand pieces of foreboding furniture, paintings, china . . . beautiful to some but not to young George.

Long days with these static, silent, siblings looking down on him . . . taking all of his mother's time, travelling, buying, selling. George never came first.

"Here's some dinner for you mother" said George handing her the bowl and a spoon, which she drowsily picked up.

"Some of your other children left today" said George, smiling.

"What?" said Mrs Rennett looking up from the bowl, tired and confused.

"Yes, the Constable has gone now"

She dropped the spoon onto the floor and started to sob.

George slowly picked up his mother's spoon and without wiping it replaced it into the bowl.

"I wonder who will leave tomorrow?" George whispered into his mother's ear, " . . . we'll see."

www.ingramcontent.com/pod-product-compliance
Lightning Source LLC
Chambersburg PA
CBHW051301210726
48287CB00002B/614

* 9 7 8 1 9 1 0 7 5 7 2 6 0 *